## Praise for the
## by

"A kind of Nick and Nora for the '90s, this couple radiates warmth and charm..."

—*Kirkus Reviews* on *So Dear to Wicked Men*

"This enjoyable book tells a good story while making a powerful social statement."

—*Midwest Book Review* on *Go Close Against the Enemy*

"...the secondary characters are well-developed, and the weaknesses and injustices that drive people to murder and lesser crimes are drawn with genuine sympathy."

—*Kirkus Reviews* on *There Lies a Hidden Scorpion*

"...the lead protagonists make this a one-sitting novel."

—Harriet Klausner on *There Lies a Hidden Scorpion*

## Praise for the Undersheriff Bill Gastner series by Steven F. Havill

"A consistently strong, underappreciated series."

—*Booklist* on *Out of Season*

"Full of bright local color and suffused with a compassionate understanding of human motivation...deserves a wide and appreciative readership."

—*Publishers Weekly* on *Out of Season*

"Quiet yet powerful human drama resting comfortably within the procedural formula."

—*Booklist* on *Dead Weight*

"It is so great knowing when you pick up a book by an author such as Havill, you are going to get drawn in and have a great read."

—*Mystery News* on *Bag Limit*

**Praise for the Cat Austen/Victor Cardenas series by Jane Rubino**

**"A zinger debut..."**

—*Publishers Weekly* on *Death of a DJ*

**"...more than enough story here to satisfy those who like their characters and settings served with some action."**

—*Booklist* on *Fruitcake*

**"...intriguing and thought-provoking."**

—*ForeWord* on *Cheat the Devil*

**"...quickly finds its pace, smoothes out into a captivating story and leads you unsuspectingly into a wallop of a finish..."**

—*The Mystery Reader*

**Praise for the Elderhostel series by Peter Abresch**

**"A good mystery—in every sense of the word!"**

—*Eclectic Book Reviews* on *Bloody Bonsai*

**"...*Bloody Bonsai* is a fun to read who-done-it."**

—*Dorothy L*

**"Mr. Abresch has come up with a winner of an idea..."**

—*Mystery News* on *Killing Thyme*

**"What a great book! The characters are marvelous."**

—*Mysteries Guide*

# DEADLY MORSELS

Takis & Judy Iakovou
Steven F. Havill
Jane Rubino
Peter Abresch

TORONTO • NEW YORK • LONDON
AMSTERDAM • PARIS • SYDNEY • HAMBURG
STOCKHOLM • ATHENS • TOKYO • MILAN
MADRID • WARSAW • BUDAPEST • AUCKLAND

**DEADLY MORSELS**

A Worldwide Mystery/April 2003

ISBN 0-373-26452-6



**Printed in U.S.A.**

CONTENTS

# ANOTHER'S CURSE

by Takis & Judy Iakovou

Yet shall my dying be another's curse,
that he may learn not to exult at my misfortunes;
but when he comes to share the self-same plague with me,
he will take a lesson in wisdom.

—Euripides, *Hippolytus*

# ONE

THE GREEKS HAVE a saying that as the year begins, so it will go. This is probably based upon an old wives' tale called the "first foot," which dictates that the first person to cross the threshold in the new year brings his luck, good or bad, to the house. When Marcia Lowery turned up dead, Nick and I could only hope that the old Greek wives were badly mistaken.

On the morning of January second, Marcia Lowery was, indeed, the first person to cross our threshold at the Oracle Café, our little restaurant in Delphi. I had just finished setting up the back dining room, tables draped in cloths as starched and white as tuxedo shirts, centerpieces and shining cutlery in place. Gleaming chafing dishes awaited a hot breakfast buffet and carafes of hot coffee sat expectantly on every table. Everything was ready when I joined Nick at the front door to greet the Delphi Chamber of Commerce. We were hosting the organization's New Year kickoff breakfast.

"Yo, Mr. Nick," Otis said, coming through the door from the kitchen. He pointed in the direction of the parking lot. "Medusa's here."

Nick turned away from the window with a groan. Behind him our guests, in groups of threes and fours, were drifting toward the front door. Marcia Lowery, Health Inspector, made an end run around them to reach the door first. She'd been nicknamed Medusa by our cook, Spiros—who hasn't a bad word for man nor beast—because of the thick gray-streaked brown ringlets that spiraled out of control all over her head. Or maybe it was because of her personality.

"She was just here two weeks ago. What do you suppose she wants now?"

Before he could answer, she was through the door, clipboard gripped in a white-knuckled fist. She ignored Nick's outstretched hand.

"I'm not here for the breakfast," she said crisply. "Following up on that cooler problem."

The last time she'd been to the Oracle to inspect, she'd caught Nick, Spiros and me in the middle of a minor problem. The cooler wasn't cooling and we were stacking bags of ice inside until Jim Boggs could get there and coax it back into operation. Although the temperature was still well below the maximum, Medusa wasn't happy. In fact, she'd hung around most of the day, periodically rechecking the thermometer and letting in warm air, breathing down Jim's neck and terrorizing Otis. Nick was irritable. Even Spiros was cranky.

"The cooler's working fine, and this is a very bad time—"

Medusa plucked a thermometer from the breast pocket of her black suit jacket. "You're using chafing dishes for the buffet?"

"Well, yes, but you're not planning to—"

"Just go on with what you were doing. I can find my way," she said, and turned toward the private dining room. Nick's stricken gaze followed her back.

"Julia, you'd better—"

"I'm on it," I assured him and hastened after her.

When I reached the back, she was already positioned in front of the buffet, jabbing her thermometer into the water in the first chafing dish. Spiros had begun setting out the buffet, and a pan of steaming sausage links rested on her thermometer. She snatched one out of the pan, smelled it and took a bite, turning to let her gaze drift over the tables. Behind us, the first of the guests were trickling in. Mike Blalock, outgoing president of the Chamber, set a small podium on the head table and sent a concerned frown my way.

"Ms. Lowery," I said quietly, "if this could just wait until we've gotten breakfast up—"

"It can't." She snatched the thermometer out and scrutinized the reading, noting it carefully on the form clamped to her clipboard before plunging it into a pan of grits. She hadn't bothered to lower her voice, and it seemed to rise another ten decibels as she continued.

"The point of health inspection, in case it eludes you, Mrs. Lambros, is to make sure that food is preserved and prepared in a safe manner. It's my job— Look, what's this?" She dipped two scarlet fingernails into the pan and pulled out a silver, coiled hair.

"But that's—"

"You're not suggesting that you can serve this."

"No, of course not." Given her temperament, it didn't seem prudent to point out that the hair belonged to her and matched several others scattered over her shoulders. I pulled the pan and carried it over to the order window with instructions to Spiros to start another batch of grits.

While she moved from one pan to the next, I waited helplessly, turning my attention to the increasing crowd of local businesspeople and moving over to block their view of her. The Buffaloes were all there and had claimed several long tables for themselves, littering the tops with the usual Buffalo droppings—empty sugar packets and creamers. They circulated, coffee cups in hand, using the opportunity to network.

Sonny Weaver claimed he sold at least one insurance policy at every Chamber meeting. He was working on Ed Greer of Piedmont Pride Spring Water at the moment. Ed's taciturn expression suggested that Sonny might have chosen the wrong target this time. At least they weren't looking at us.

Medusa dropped her thermometer into the last pan and rustled through the pages on her clipboard. Neither of us noticed Fran Bonaventure until she appeared at my elbow holding a microphone.

"Julia, we need an exten—" She stopped abruptly, staring past me at Marcia Lowery, who had turned and was glaring back at Fran.

"Well, well..." Medusa said, baring her teeth in a malicious smile. "What is it today, animals? Or husbandry?"

Fran turned back to me, her cheeks so flushed they looked hot to the touch. "We need...um, we need an extension cord. For the sound...um—"

"I'll get one for you, Fran. Go ahead and finish setting up," I said. Fran hurried away as Medusa turned toward the kitchen.

"By all means," she said, "go and help our perky local pet primper. I don't need an escort." With a last, flickering glance at Fran, she marched past me and through the kitchen door.

I found an extension cord in the wait station. Unfortunately, I also found Tammy and Rhonda, bristling at one another. "Look, I don't want your tips. I just want it to go smoothly back there," Rhonda said. "That party's too big for you to handle alone."

I should have used common sense and put Rhonda on the party in the first place, but Tammy had sniveled and begged until she'd worn me down. She was looking for big tips from this group. We've never been able to convince Tammy that there is an analogous relationship between service and tips.

"Let her help you get the fruit plates on, Tammy. Then you can take over. It should just be coffee refills and clearing buffet plates after that." I'd tip Rhonda out later myself. It was easier than haggling with Tammy over the gratuity. Rhonda took Fran the extension cord, while I got a couple more pots of decaf started for those who didn't want regular coffee, even at breakfast.

In the kitchen, biscuits and muffins waited in the warming cabinet. Plated wedges of honeydew and cantaloupe sat in a bed of ice as Spiros sprinkled the tops with sliced strawberries and grapes, and a dab of whipped cream, before sending them out to the dining room. *"I gorgóna eine exo, Zulia,"* he grumbled, pointing his chin toward the back of the kitchen.

Behind us, a door slammed, followed by the jackhammer rattle of heels on the tile floor. I met her in front of dry storage.

"Now—"

"Rats."

"Excuse me?"

She turned over the page on her clipboard and snapped the clip into place. "Your Dumpster has rats. They're a clear hazard to the health and safety of—"

*Rats!* The word screamed at me, and I felt my knees buckle. Give me spiders, give me snakes. But rats tapped into my worst fear. My imagination went crazy—gray furry creatures swarming over the Dumpster, through the back door, up my legs.... For a minute, the kitchen seemed to spin around me. I grabbed the ice machine to hold myself up. "No—we couldn't have...we've never had—"

"Well, you do now."

We'd never had vermin in the Oracle. Never a roach, never a mouse. And never, ever a rat. But though my heart and gut protested, my brain thought what she said might be true. The woods behind the café were being cleared for a new apartment complex, and the clearing might well be driving all kinds of undesirables out of the kudzu patches. Thankfully nothing had gotten into the building. At least not yet.

"I'm giving you a week to get rid of them."

"Don't worry, we'll take care of it."

A crash from the wait station brought both our heads around. Medusa seemed amused when I excused myself to see what had happened. Strawberries, melon slices and fragments of broken white crockery were scattered everywhere, and Tammy standing over them all, a pot of decaf in her hand and her mouth agape. Beside her foot, a large tray rested upside down against the wall. "I was just going to—"

"You tried to balance that tray in one hand? Tammy..." At a loss for words, I reached into the kitchen to grab a broom. When I turned back, she was gone and Nick was standing in her place.

"Start plating more," he said with a sigh, taking the broom from my hand. "I'll take care of this."

I should have recognized then that Marcia Lowery's luck had just paid a call. But I didn't, of course. I was so preoccupied with getting the remainder of the fruit plates out that I completely forgot about her until everyone had been served, and Spiros had started sending pans of spinach omelettes out to the buffet.

I discovered her in the cooler, standing over a case of lettuce, a clear plastic bottle in her hand. "What is this?" she said.

"I don't know. Water?"

"There's no label. You know perfectly well that you can't store anything for personal use in this cooler, and you can't have anything that isn't from an approved food source," she said, twisting the cap off.

"I don't even know what that is, let alone where it came from."

She sniffed the top of the bottle, then poured a drop of clear liquid into the palm of her hand and licked it, her tongue darting out and back like a snake.

"Look Ms. Lowery, if it's just water—"

She fixed me with a hard stare, cutting me off in midsentence, spun the cap back onto the bottle, and brushed past me. Bewildered, I followed her back out into the kitchen and found her, still gripping the bottle in one hand, while viciously stabbing at the keypad of a cell phone with her other thumb.

"Is there a problem, Ms. Lowery?"

She didn't answer me, but cocked an eyebrow, as if to suggest that I already knew the answer. I suppose I did. Something was definitely wrong. I headed for the back dining room to get Nick.

"While you're all finishing your fruit, I'd like to start introducing our new officers." Mike Blalock stood at the podium. To either side of him sat incoming officers: Fran Bonaventure of The Perfect Pet, Alex Childress of Childress Commercial Realty, car dealer Frank Longman and president-elect Pam Walton, manager of local radio station WDEL. Nick stood at the back of the room watching as Rhonda, and a disgruntled Tammy, collected fruit plates and stacked them on large trays. I grabbed his arm.

"We've got a problem," I said.

Nick put a finger to his lips and pulled me into the wait station. "What now?"

"That's just it. I don't know. I mean, I do know one—"

"For crine out loud, Julia, I don't have time for games."

"It's 'crying,' not 'crine,' and I'm not playing—"

And then, from the back, we heard the voice of the gorgon. "Ladies and gentlemen, I'm sorry to interrupt your breakfast but—"

Medusa had commandeered the microphone. Nick and I exchanged a look of horror before he bolted out of the wait station. I arrived in the dining room right on his heels.

Our guests were a tableau—arched eyebrows and heads tilted toward one another, their mouths fixed round in surprise. Mike Blalock had half risen from his seat and Pam Walton gazed at the mike that had been snatched from her hand. The guests all stared at the woman in the black suit.

"I'm afraid breakfast will not be served today. By order of the Health Department, I'm closing down the Oracle Café until further notice."

# TWO

OVER THE YEARS, we've had all kinds of health inspectors, good, bad, picky, tolerant and every shade in between. Most of the time they're fair and considerate. They know how hard the restaurant business is. They don't inspect at mealtimes, when chaos reigns in the kitchen, and they don't ask the impossible. Nick and I know they have a job to do, and we respect the fact that they protect the public.

Marcia Lowery was far and away the worst inspector we'd ever had to deal with, taking delight in breaking all the tacit rules of consideration. She'd begun her reign of terror over the restaurants in our region about eighteen months earlier. Several other local restaurateurs were at the breakfast and stayed for a few minutes, after the other guests had left, to commiserate with us before hurrying off to make sure their own houses were in perfect condition. Medusa was on a rampage, and no one was safe.

"Why," Nick said, his head in his hands, "do these things keep happening to us?"

I thought about that for a moment. It was true that we'd had more than our share of problems, beginning with a dead man on A deck. "I don't know. Maybe we just have bad restaurant karma."

Nick made no response, but Spiros stroked his chin thoughtfully. "Bad karma, *neh.* Ve-ree bad."

We sat at the family table in the front dining room, waiting while Sheriff Sam Lawless and a couple of his deputies searched the kitchen. He hadn't wanted to do it, but Medusa had insisted, and even now was in the kitchen nipping at their heels like a Jack Russell terrier.

"She called ATF," Sam explained sheepishly when he first arrived. "They're in Atlanta, so it'll taken 'em a couple of hours to get here. They called me. Wanted to be sure you were locked down before you could get rid of the stuff."

"Who's ATF?"

Sam dropped into a seat at the table. "Bureau of Alcohol, Tobacco and Firearms, Julia. The Feds."

Well, that made as much sense as anything else had that morning. The bottle, Marcia Lowery had informed everyone at the breakfast, contained moonshine. Her announcement was greeted with chuckles from the audience, which only made matters worse. Nick had tried to reason with her, explaining that we had no idea where it had come from. She said she'd found it in a lettuce crate.

When Sam arrived, she'd argued with him at some length about whether a full search of the restaurant was necessary. "Miz Lowery," Sam drawled. "My wife works for these people. If there was moonshine on the premises, Rhonda'd know about it."

"All the more reason for you to be scrupulous in your search, Sheriff. You wouldn't want anyone accusing you of favoritism."

Sam blushed, a red tide creeping up his face to the roots of his strawberry-blond hair. His voice was low, and his drawl deepened. "Are you threatenin' me, Miz Lowery?"

Medusa was shaking all over, as though a high voltage current coursed through her body. She seemed out of control, so overcome with rage that she had to curb some violent impulse. She had a key on a ring with a leather fob in her hand, and jabbed at the air with it, bringing it perilously close to Sam's chest. "I am only requiring you to do your job, Sheriff. And if you can't do that, then the public will have the right to ask why not."

"Go ahead, Sam," Nick intervened. "I'm not hiding anything."

Meanwhile, Nick and I stayed busy trying to explain to arriving lunch customers that we weren't open for business. A minor emergency in the kitchen. No, we couldn't make take-out orders; yes, we thought we'd be open tomorrow. Be sure to check back with us then.

Sam's men finished their search some time after lunch. His deputies hadn't found anything but another plastic bottle—this one empty—in the trash. It was like the one Medusa had found, an ordinary two-liter clear plastic bottle impressed with a few ridges in the middle. They were taking it in for analysis. Sam duly reported their findings to the Atlanta ATF office and set the phone back in its cradle.

"I've got to seal the place until ATF comes. They're tellin' me now that they won't have anyone out here till tomorrow." He turned to Marcia Lowery. "They'll want you to come in tomorrow morning and make your statement."

"Aren't you going to make an arrest, Sheriff?"

Sam was polite, but I could see it was an effort. "I don't think the evidence warrants an arrest just yet, ma'am."

"But they might flee."

Sam sighed deeply and turned to Nick. "You gonna run away, Nick? You gonna leave a business you been buildin' for nigh onto ten years and make a break for it over a little bottle of shine?"

"No, but—" Nick dug down into his pocket and brought out his wallet "—you can hold onto my green card and my driver's license if you want, Sam."

"I don't believe that'll be necessary." Sam waved a hand over the empty dining room. "Might as well send everybody home, though."

Rhonda had set herself up with her books on B deck. She only worked for us part-time, now. After marrying Sam, she'd enrolled at Parnassus University and started working on a degree in psychology. She'd stayed on at the Oracle, not because she needed the money, but because she knew how much we depended on her.

"Come on darlin'," Sam called to her. "I'll take you on

home. I'll come back after I drop her off and seal the doors," he said, turning to us. "That'll give y'all time to shut everything off and lock the place up." I think he just didn't want us to be there when he put crime scene tape over the doors. Sam has a kind heart.

I found Tammy in the back dining room among the ruins of the breakfast, her feet propped on a table while she filed her nails. The tables were just as the Chamber of Commerce had left them, cluttered with crumpled napkins, plates of half-eaten fruit and cups of cold coffee. Medusa had insisted that Sam not allow us to clean up until Alcohol, Tobacco and Firearms had been there. "Preserving the crime scene," she'd explained. Oh, please.

Tammy was pouting. "I didn't make any tips, Julia. I wanted to get my hair colored, but I won't be able to now."

"I'm so sorry," I snapped. "When you go back to your locker, tell Otis he can go."

"He already left." Tammy pocketed her emery board and stood up. "Right after that woman called Sam. He just went out the back door."

Come to think of it, I hadn't seen Otis since...when? When Medusa left the cooler and stopped to make her phone call, he'd been rinsing pots at the dish machine.

"Spiros," I said, returning to the family table. "When did Otis leave?"

"Otees?" He shot a wary glance around the room, as if Medusa might be hanging from the eaves, and lowered his voice. "*O, Otees,* he go when Medusa goes to party. Shh. Ve-ree quiet. Back door."

Nick had walked Marcia Lowery to her car. I could see them standing in the parking lot next to a shiny red sports car. Nick was gesturing as he spoke, not big, broad gestures, but a gentle turn of his hand this way and that. He looked perfectly calm, but his fingers were rigid and splayed, and I knew what that meant. He leaned against the car; she said something. He straightened up and checked the car for a handprint. It was an MG TD circa 1953—a model I recognized only because my uncle had driven one for years. The kind of car Nick would love to own and probably never will. A car completely out of character for the woman who drove it.

Marcia Lowery was a study in contradictions as sharply contrasting as her black suit and white blouse. The graying curls that framed her face might have been appropriate—though not actually stylish—on a young woman with a soft, round face. Medusa was square of jaw and the long lines that pulled down her mouth had taken at least forty-odd years to develop. She had an uneven complexion, mottled with dark, dry patches beneath her eyes that made her look permanently exhausted. Her suit hung as loosely on her square frame as it would have on a wire hanger. She was shorter than me, maybe five-two or -three, and stood with her feet apart as though braced against some great force that threatened to knock her down. Even from a distance, I could see that she was still shaking, before she got into the MG and slammed the door in Nick's face.

"Nick, did you tell Otis he could go?" I asked as he came through the door.

"No, why?"

"Spiros said he slipped out the back after—" We stared at each other then, both of us wondering how we'd missed the obvious.

"Let me lock up," Nick said.

"I'll get my coat."

MANY IS THE TIME, while scraping plates of hardened egg yolk and bacon grease, I've wondered why we continue to employ Otis. Shiftless and unreliable, Otis averages only about half the normal workweek, calling upon a vast collection of wildly improbable stories to account for his absence. He is not your ideal employee.

I think we keep him on because he fascinates us. He drifts through life, skimming its surface, never putting down roots or, for that matter, bottoming out. I used to think he was completely unflappable, but then Spiros came along. Otis is scared to death of Spiros, which is why we took our cook along when we went looking for our dishwasher.

Actually, Spiros took us. He's far too big to seat comfortably, or even safely, in our Honda, so we set out in his archaic Pontiac, bobbing down Broadway, through town and out toward College Road and Otis's last known address. We turned in at the Apollo Court Mobile Home Park and followed a winding gravel road to trailer number 36.

For a moment we all just sat and stared at the small trailer in front of us—white, dented and striped with long streaks of rust, with a feeble wooden staircase leading to an aluminum door. I'd never thought of Otis as actually living anywhere. He just didn't seem that concrete, more like a shadow that blends into his surroundings and evaporates into the dark of night. But this was Otis's home. I recognized the orange T-shirt printed, inexplicably, with the words Hokey Pokey Dance-a-thon, slung over a makeshift clothesline to the side of the trailer. Although the day was cloudy, and the grounds shaded by thick pines and oaks, there was no light on inside.

"*Ella, pame,*" Nick said, and we all got out of the car. I followed Nick to the door, leaving Spiros to circle to the back. There was no sign of our dishwasher, no answer at the door, no quiet movement inside.

"He's probably hiding in there. Now what?" I said.

"We go in." Nick rattled the doorknob, but it was locked, of course. There was no dead bolt, but then I couldn't imagine Otis having anything a self-respecting burglar would want.

"*Signome,*" Spiros said, brushing past us. He took hold of the knob and turned it, wrenching it with such force that the lock popped like a champagne cork. He stepped back and held the door open, waving us inside ahead of him. I hesitated long enough to point out that we were breaking and entering.

"You think he's going to press charges, Julia?" Nick

turned away, calling out, "Otis? I want to talk to you. You'd better come out here, or I'm calling the sheriff right now."

The silence told all. Had he been there, Otis would have appeared, armed with a story so fantastic as to almost make us forget why we were looking for him. Spiros's heavy footsteps thundered through the trailer while Nick and I stood in the little living room trying to take it in.

There was nothing unusual about the decor, a fifties modern sofa with wooden legs and shabby blue upholstery and a low coffee table covered in blond Formica; two chrome-and-red plastic kitchen chairs from roughly the same era; a cheap three-light pole lamp, missing one of its teardrop shades, and a small TV sitting on an old typing table. But I couldn't put Otis on that sofa, couldn't imagine him lounging as he watched the Super Bowl on television, or napping on a warm afternoon. He was a phantom, a specter, incapable of leaving dents in the cushions or footprints on the vinyl floor.

Nick reached up and touched the bare bulb on the lamp. "He's been here. It's still warm."

Spiros returned from the bedroom, reporting that there was no sign of Otis anywhere. He crossed the living room and began slamming cabinet doors in the kitchen. Nick soon joined him and they made a quick but thorough search of the place. If Otis had been storing moonshine in his trailer, he'd gotten it all out.

"Now what?" We stood on the steps peering out over the wooded trailer park, waiting while Spiros jammed the doorknob back into place. Music blared from a neighboring trailer, a heavy metal sound with a thumping base.

"Let's ask around and see if anyone's seen him or knows where he might have gone."

"Nick, do you really think any of these people even know Otis?" My gaze moved over the trailer park, full of sport utility vehicles plastered with Parnassus stickers and fraternity and sorority logos. Only a quarter mile from the campus, it was an ideal location for students. What was Otis doing, living there?

Nick shrugged. ''Probably not, but let's try anyway.''

There was no one home at the first two trailers we tried. The third one—much larger than Otis's—was where the music was coming from. An old bathtub covered with chicken wire fencing sat smoking in the yard. A makeshift grill, I surmised. The door to the trailer was propped open with an Eskimo cooler, and the living area crammed with students sitting on the floor, on the furniture, leaning against the walls. Several plates of Jell-O shooters were making the rounds. One girl, in a corner, was trying to balance a bright red cube on the end of her nose. A young guy in jeans and a torn sweatshirt answered our knock.

''Hey! Watcha need?''

Nick told him, but without much hope of getting any information. Most of the group looked as if they'd have trouble focusing on the question. Apparently the cocktail hour at Apollo Corners began earlier than in the rest of the civilized world.

''Shadow Man? Sure I know him.'' He looked past us and up the road toward Otis's dark trailer. ''Thought he was coming down for the party.''

''Coming here?'' I said. Well, why not? Shadow Man, as he'd called Otis, probably would fit in here about as well as he fit in anywhere else.

''I'm Vince,'' the student said, thrusting out his hand. ''Why don't you come on in to wait for him? Any friend of the Shade's is welcome.''

But we declined. Nick was fairly sure Otis wouldn't be back any time soon. Spiros, however, had other ideas.

''Veence,'' he said. ''Veence, no?'' Vince nodded happily. Spiros gestured up the road to his Pontiac. ''I go. Come back later, yes?''

''Sure, man. Whatever. You see Shadow Man, you bring him on down here. We're all waiting on him.''

Hmmm.

# THREE

"WELL, THAT WAS a surreal experience," I said to Nick as we pulled into our driveway. "I don't understand why Spiros is going back there."

"Because he figures Otis will try to sneak back in some time in the night. Spiros is going to be waiting for him."

"At Vince's party."

"Probably, at least for a while."

As we got out of the car and went in the house, I pondered Spiros doing Jell-O shooters against a background of Metallica. Spiros playing "Never Have I Ever."

Jack was waiting for us, sitting in front of the door with his leash clamped in his square little jaws. It was obedience school night, Nick's bonding time with Jack. Not that Jack knew what night it was. He always meets us holding his leash.

"Not tonight, Jack," I said, taking the leash from him.

"No, it's okay. I'd rather be working with him than sitting around worrying about what's going to happen tomorrow."

I agreed that it was probably a good idea after all. Besides, Jack needed all the obedience training we could get him. Scottish terriers are very inner-directed, and Jack's inner voices are too often in conflict with ours. He'd already failed the course once, although Fran Bonaventure had assured us that he'd catch on eventually. I wanted to believe her.

In all the chaos of the day, I'd forgotten to mention to Nick Medusa's other find, the rats. Or maybe I'd just repressed it. But it couldn't be ignored. In fact, being closed might just work in our favor, since there would be no customers there to observe an exterminator's truck in the parking lot. I told Nick about the problem while I fixed dinner.

"She told me," he said. "And she's right. I went out and looked."

"I don't want to hear about this, Nick," I said. "You know how I feel about them. What if...what if they actually get in?"

"They can't get in. The doors are all tight, the building is brick on a slab. There's no way for them to come in. Anyway, why would they come in when they're happy out at the Dumpster?"

"I suppose you're right," I said. But down deep I knew that I would never be able to feel quite comfortable in the restaurant as long as there was any possibility that a rat could find a way in. I think it's a full-blown phobia, actually. When we have problems or I'm under pressure, I dream about rats. I don't know why, or how I developed it, and I never probe my subconscious too deeply to find out. I'm afraid it's something deep and dark in my past. Something better off staying there.

I fixed a quiche and a salad, but neither of us was very hungry. In fact, the sight and smell of eggs only reminded us both of the mess we'd left in the back dining room, and the mess we were in with the Feds. I could hardly wait to get my hands on Otis.

After dinner we set off for the high school gym. Basketball practice was just ending when we arrived. Fran sat in the bleachers with Dale Moffit, watching the practice wind down. Their conversation stopped abruptly at our appearance. They'd both been at the breakfast that morning. What else would they be talking about? Nick hesitated a beat before leading me in their direction. Jack yipped and danced at the end of his lead, eager to join the players on the court, but Fran pacified him with a chew toy from her tote bag.

"I'm talking about breaking bad chewing habits tonight," she explained. Most of the dogs in the class were not yet a year old. Jack, as the oldest living obedience class graduate—or prospective graduate—had long passed the chewing stage. Still, he was enjoying the Nylabone she'd given him.

I took my place on the bleachers next to Dale Moffit. He was a tall, slender man with silver-rimmed glasses and a marked resemblance to a cartoon stork. Dale managed The Corner Bakery plant, a mass production bread company on the outskirts of town. "Tough break, Nick," he said, leaning past me to shake Nick's hand. "How'd you draw the inspector from Hell?"

"Sometimes you're just dealt a bad hand," Nick said.

"Come on, Jim. Mom's waiting dinner on us," Dale called to his son on the court. He turned back to us. "Knew her when she was with the FDA. She used to inspect the plant. I heard she took early retirement. She couldn't get along with anybody in the office, including her boss."

"Well, the agents from Alcohol, Tobacco and Firearms will be there tomorrow," Nick said. "So I hope we can get it all straightened out and set a new breakfast date."

Dale waved at his son, a broad come-on kind of wave. "Did you say ATF? How typical of her, blowing it all out of proportion." He stood up as a lanky boy slung a backpack over his shoulder and headed in our direction. "Ready."

Dale clapped him on the shoulder and eased him toward the door. "My advice," he said, turning back to Nick, "is to complain to her superior. Didn't work with the FDA, but it's always hard to get rid of a federal employee. The county's not all tied up in political knots, though. The more complaints they get, the sooner they'll get rid of her." It wouldn't be soon enough for us.

We watched in silence as Larry, his son in tow, stopped to talk to the coach on the floor. It was an uncomfortable silence, as the sight of Fran reminded me of Marcia Lowery's odd remark. *Animals? Or husbandry?* she'd said. Her meaning was fairly obvious. At length, Fran cleared her throat nervously.

"I suppose you're wondering about…about what happened today.'' Before I could make any hollow protests, she went on. ''She was talking about David, her ex, or at least he will be in a couple of days. I've been seeing him for a while.''

''Fran, this isn't any of my business.''

''No, maybe not. It's just that I have a feeling she took it out on you, seeing me there. I should have insisted she leave.''

''I doubt if that would have done any good. She's not the type to knuckle under out of courtesy.''

Fran studied her hands, her unpolished nails trimmed to a square, neat edge. They had the immaculately clean look of someone who has her hands in soap all the time, as she probably does, being a pet groomer. ''No, but I could have forced her. I have a restraining order against her.''

''Against Medusa? Um...that's what we call her, just sometimes, you know, because she can be—''

''You don't have to explain her to me. I know all about how she can be. She never gives David a minute's peace, calls him night and day. One time she even showed up at his Intro to Geology class. A two-hundred-person lecture class and in she marches, straight up to the podium. Can you believe the gall?''

''So he had to take out a restraining order against her?''

''Not David. Me. She was calling me, coming out to my place, threatening me. The woman's nuts. He's still trying to reason with her. He's agreed to give her everything, their house, their savings. Even his car, and he loved that car, just to get her off his back. And she still finds reasons to call him. You wouldn't believe it, Julia. When she's talking to David, she's so sweet. And she acts helpless. If she can't get him with sugar, she turns into a... Well, it would be insulting to my dogs to call her a bitch. A witch, anyway.

''David lived with it for eighteen years. I met him a year ago when he came looking for a puppy for her. He thought it would be good company for her when he left. He didn't buy one, but he moved out anyway, three weeks later, and she's been trying to get him back ever since.''

''Jack, get out of there!'' I tugged on his leash, but he persisted, sticking his nose deep into Fran's tote bag to come out with a multicolored, twisted rope. I made a grab for it, but he romped out of reach, shaking his head so hard and fast that I could hear his jowls vibrate. ''He always does that,'' I said. ''I wonder if something's wrong with him.''

''It's instinct. He's breaking his quarry's neck. Scotties are small game hunters,'' she said. ''That's how they kill their catch.''

''Small game, like...rats?''

''Rats, squirrels, possum.''

Rats. They caught rats. Not that I'd want Jack confronting one, but surely he'd smell it if there was one at the Oracle. I put the question to Fran.

''Well, yes,'' she said. ''But I don't think it's a good idea to test him. He could get badly hurt if he tangled with one. Why?''

Reluctantly, after extracting her promise to keep it to herself, I told her about the problem we were having. It wasn't the kind of thing we wanted broadcast about the Oracle, even if they were just in the Dumpster.

''I know how you feel. I had a problem with them in my barn. They kept getting into the feed. David mixed me up something that took them right out. Why don't I ask him to make you some?'' She stroked the base of Jack's ears and gently took the rope out of his mouth. ''It's much safer than sending Jack after them. I'll bring you some tomorrow.''

''We're not opening in the morning. We have to wait for ATF, and then Med—uh, Marcia has to sign us off. But we'll be there waiting for them if you want to come by.''

Fran stood. The court was clear, the basketball players long gone, and a motley collection of dogs and owners were assembling on the floor. ''I'm really sorry, Julia. If she hadn't seen me at your place, she might not have overreacted. She's a walking powder keg and I'm afraid I was the spark that set her off.''

"If it hadn't been you, it would have been somebody else, Fran. That woman probably has a lot of enemies.''

"Sometime when you've got a couple of hours, I'll give you a list,'' Fran said, before turning away to start the class.

I could have started a list myself, with at least ten local restaurant owners and managers at the top. And according to Larry, she wasn't too popular with her former co-workers, not to mention all the plant managers she'd driven crazy.

So Marcia Lowery had been with the FDA. A Fed herself, I suppose it made some kind of sense that she'd called the ATF instead of Sam. She was just the type to go over heads to get to the top, figuring she knew better than anyone else how to take care of a problem. A minor bureaucratic dictator who left a trail of enemies everywhere she went.

I turned this over in my mind as I watched the obedience class in progress on the floor. They were working on some kind of signals. When the owner jerked the leash, attached to a chain collar, the pet was supposed to promptly sit at his master's heel. Most of the other dogs had grasped the idea. Jack, on the other hand, seemed annoyed by it. Each time Nick tugged the leash, Jack wheeled sharply, as if to say "What?'' His diploma, I suspected, would be a long time coming.

Sam was already at the Oracle when we arrived the next morning. He'd taken down the crime scene tape, used Rhonda's key to get in, started a pot of coffee and shown two ATF agents through the place. They were going over the kitchen an inch at a time while Sam lounged at the family table, reading *The Delphi Sun.*

"They've made it clear that it's their operation,'' he said with a shrug.

"*Operation* is kind of a strong word for one bottle of moonshine, isn't it, Sam?'' I said. Not a Southerner myself, I'd always had the idea that the subject of stills and white lightning usually elicited a wink and a nudge from local law enforcement. But, of course, this wasn't local law enforcement. This was the Bureau of Alcohol, Tobacco and Firearms, and the two agents standing before us didn't look like they did a lot of winking and nudging.

"Agent Charlie Holler and Agent Steve Vine," Sam said, by way of introduction. Both nodded solemnly and shook our hands. I bit back the question that sprang to my lips.

Holler was a handsome man, tall, with broad shoulders and smooth, brown skin. Agent Vine was younger than Holler. He had thick, black hair and heavy features that seemed to fit his olive complexion. They were both dressed in suits and ties, very businesslike. Very federal.

"Mr. Lambros," Holler said, "the Sheriff has convinced us to take Ms. Lowery's statement and wait for the analysis on the bottles before taking any action." Nick started to thank him, but Holler held up one hand, clearly not finished. "But I suggest you start getting your business records together. And I'm warning you not to leave the area until this matter is cleared up."

I SOMETIMES THINK that one circle of Hell must be a vast waiting room. Everyone in it is waiting for something—something urgent—and everything else is suspended until the wait is over. Agent Holler had said that we could reopen as soon as a health inspector signed us off on another inspection but, of course, we had to wait.

"It's County Health's turf," he explained. "We don't want to step on any toes."

Sam had promised that he'd ask Medusa to come out to the Oracle as soon as she'd given the agents her statement. Nick followed up with a call to the health department. Ms. Lowery would have to do the reopening inspection, they explained, since she'd been the one to shut us down. Medusa hadn't come in yet, but they'd give her a message.

After Sam and the agents left, Nick and I got busy cleaning up the back dining room. Greek omelettes of spinach and feta cheese adhered to the bottom of the hotel pans in the chafing dishes. Biscuits and muffins, bacon, sausage and thick slices of ham, crispy hash browns and thick buttery grits, all bound for the trash. What a waste of good food and time, and all because of one little bottle of moonshine. Standing over the dish machine, I thought again about our dishwasher-non-grata. If he'd stepped through the door at just that moment, I'd have hanged him from the pot rack by his thumbs.

Spiros rolled in around eleven-thirty. He sat at the family table, holding his head in both hands and drinking coffee through a straw. "Too old," he explained. "Too old for parties."

Spiros had spent most of the night at Vince's party. He was unable to tell us the particulars, which was probably just as well. He had gone back to the trailer around 3:00 a.m. Otis, he said, had not reappeared. He explained to Nick, in halting whispers, that he'd placed an inch of cellophane tape across the top corner of the outside of the door and it was still undisturbed when he got back. Spiros has been watching *Magnum, P.I.* reruns. Nevertheless, he was sure that Otis had not returned. Somewhere out there, Otis was lurking under a rock, waiting for things to cool down.

Fran arrived while Nick was still nursing Spiros. She handed me a small glass jar filled with peanut butter. "Just make sure you don't get it confused with food," she said. "David mixed it up this morning. He says to spread it on paper plates and put it out around the bottom of the Dumpster. They should die right away."

She looked tired, the skin under her eyes thin and darkly stained. Her voice was breathy, as if she just couldn't put much energy into speaking. "Sit down, Fran, and I'll get you a cup of coffee."

I was back in a minute and joined her at a table on A deck. She took a long sip and closed her eyes, as if she were waiting for the caffeine to kick in.

"Are you all right?"

She tapped her fingernails on the top of the creamer cup

I'd brought with her coffee. "Just tired. I was up fairly late. Marcia making trouble again."

"Doesn't that woman have anything else to do? Sounds like she needs to start pulling herself together and getting on with her life," I said. "And if we're lucky, maybe she'll decide to do it somewhere else."

Fran snorted. "Not much hope of that, Julia. She's determined to get David back.

"She cries, she wheedles, she flatters and flirts. When none of those works, she bullies. She tried claiming to be sick, but David told her to go to the doctor and leave him alone. So now her latest ploy is threatening phone calls."

"What's she threatening?"

"No, she's not doing the threatening. She's the one getting the calls, or so she claims. Someone's trying to kill her, she says. She called David last night and tried to lure him over to the house because she was afraid. They had a huge fight about it. I can't take any more of it."

Fran gazed out toward the parking lot. The noon sunlight reflected in the tears that pooled around her eyelashes. "Poor David. I told him I thought we should stop seeing each other, at least until he's signed the papers and she's completely out of his life. I think he's afraid that will never happen." She swiped the heels of her hands across her eyes and turned back to me. "To tell you the truth, I don't think it will either."

NICK WAS DETERMINED that when Medusa arrived the place would be in perfect condition, so after Fran had gone, we started on the kitchen. Nick drained and cleaned the fryers, while I wiped down every surface with bleach. Spiros cleaned out the cooler. I could hear him moan from time to time. Too much vodka, he'd explained to Nick.

At three o'clock we sat facing one another around the family table. Marcia Lowery had still not checked in, her office said. "Maybe it's just taking a long time to give her statement," I offered. Spiros suggested she might have stopped to get her claws sharpened. We were still speculating on the possibilities when Sam's car pulled in. Nick met him at the door.

"How did it go?"

Sam followed Nick into the dining room without answering. The radio on his shoulder buzzed with static, broken up by an occasional transmission. I couldn't understand most of it, just a word here and there, mostly in numeric code. At length, he reached up and turned it off.

"Nick," he said, "I just don't know how to tell you this. I'm afraid I have some real bad news."

# FOUR

"SHE DIDN'T SHOW UP to give her statement, and those ATF fellas wanted to head back to Atlanta. She wasn't in her office, so we went on over to her place." Sam shook his head solemnly. "We were too late. She's dead."

"Dead? How?"

"We're working on that now," Sam said.

He took his customary seat, but when I tried to pour him a cup of coffee, he waved it away. "You got anything stronger than that around here?"

Nick disappeared through the kitchen and into his office, returning with a bottle of Metaxa Seven Star and a tray of wineglasses. Sam watched as he poured a shot of the cognac into each one, then picked up his and tossed back half of it in a gulp.

"You're supposed to drink that slowly," Nick said, taking a measured sip and rolling it over his tongue.

"Good stuff." Sam picked up the bottle and examined it, holding it up for the sun to shine through and spill deep golden light onto the table. He was stalling. At length, he topped off his glass, screwed the cork back into the bottle and set it down with a thud.

"Her car was there but she wasn't answerin' the door. Tried calling her from the car, but no luck there. Holler and Vine were wantin' to leave for Atlanta so I knocked one more time and tried the door. It wasn't locked. I went in, callin' out to her."

Sam rolled his glass between his palms, watching the cognac coat the sides of the glass. ''Smelled bad in there. Real bad. I called in Holler and Vine and we started goin' through the house, lookin' for her. Found her on the bathroom floor.''

I couldn't stand it another minute. ''What happened to her, Sam?''

''Don't know yet. Holler called in the GBI. Crime scene's out there now. Pete Redmond—he's an old friend of mine—he's runnin' the show. Gawd a'mighty you couldn't pay me enough to do that job, especially with the mess he's got out there. Anyway, he's calling it a 'toxic episode.'''

''Toxic? Like poisoning?''

Sam nodded slowly. The pained expression on his face made the roots of my hair tingle unpleasantly. ''I'm thinking it might be food poisoning.''

''If either one of you know anythin' about this moonshine business, now is the time to tell me.'' Sam set his glass down firmly and looked from Nick to me.

The ME, he had said, would not know anything definite about the cause of Marcia Lowery's death until he'd autopsied her, and that might not be for a day or two. Sam's suspicion of food poisoning was based on the condition of the bathroom and the body, but he mercifully spared us the details.

''Holler and Vine wanted me outta there. They're pressuring GBI. Red's between a rock and a hard place.''

''Why don't they want you around?''

Sam shrugged. ''Just bein' careful. The Feds don't think much of country cops.''

I laid my hand on Sam's forearm. ''Wait a minute. I don't understand what any of this has to do with that bottle of moonshine.''

Sam looked away, out the window, then back at the cognac bottle. Nick poured him another small shot.

''I'm not sayin' it is, mind you, but it could be. It's just a precaution, just in case her death wasn't accidental.''

It took a minute for that to sink in. Marcia Lowery had eaten a sausage at the Oracle yesterday morning. And she'd tasted the moonshine. If something was wrong with them, it was going to look very bad for us.

"You withholdin' any information's gonna make it worse, for me, that is, and maybe for you, too."

Nick and I exchanged glances. He gave a short nod in Sam's direction. I took a deep breath. "Well, there is one thing."

I confided our suspicions about Otis to Sam. He wasn't happy. "Why didn't you tell me this before?"

I answered the question, because it was my fault. I had convinced Nick not to say anything about Otis until we'd gotten his side of the story. The Oracle was already closed, and ATF were on their way. Marcia Lowery wasn't likely to let us reopen just because we claimed that Otis had been responsible for the moonshine. Another inspector might, but not Medusa.

Otis was many things, lazy, unreliable and slightly devious. But Otis was no hardened felon. Not that he lived by any solid moral code. It's just that serious criminal activity requires too much work. "It just doesn't seem right not to hear his side of the story first," I'd said to Nick. "Maybe he didn't know what was in the bottle. He might have thought it was water."

Nick had greeted that with an astonished stare, but my secondary argument carried the day. "Besides," I said. "You and I both know what it's like to be accused of something we didn't do."

Nick had agreed to wait until Otis had a chance to acquit himself. At the time, I was sure Spiros would find Otis and bring him in, dragging him by the scruff of the neck like a naughty child. At the time, one little bottle of moonshine hadn't seemed like such a big deal, and although the incident had been embarrassing, and the closing costly and inconvenient, there was nothing we could do about it. But then, at the time, no one had died.

"WELL, THAT'S IT." Nick dropped the phone back in the cradle and stared out at the parking lot. Fortunately it was cloaked in a thick January fog, since there were pitifully few cars in the parking lot. He turned to me. "He's not going to sign us off until he talks to Sam and the ATF officers. He doesn't think he'll get another inspector out here today. They have us under a barrel."

"Over. It's 'over a barrel,'" I said, although when I thought about it, it did feel more like under, but under a steamroller. Marcia Lowery's supervisor was just as intimidated by the ATF agents as everyone else, including me. Just the presence of a Fed in a suit was enough to curdle the cream in my coffee.

I glanced up at A deck, where the Buffaloes waited expectantly for their coffee. We'd stopped giving them menus, since they never ordered anything to eat. At least we'd put a stop to the free coffee refills without a food order. Now the single average purchase was $1.20 per morning, which was just about enough to cover the labor of cleaning up after them. Half the time they forgot to pay, anyway. "Are you sure we should have let them in here?"

"No, I'm not sure of anything. I think we're all right, as long as they don't have to pay for their coffee." He followed me into the wait station and began mechanically setting out lemon slices for tea and butter for toast—not that we'd need them.

"No, we wouldn't want to do that. It might set a nasty precedent," I said, refilling the brew basket in the coffeemaker. "So now what do we do?" I pinched Nick playfully and waggled my eyebrows. "Want to go home and go back to bed?"

He pondered a lemon, turning it over carefully in his hand. "You know, she found the bottle in a lettuce crate. Maybe it belongs to the produce guy."

"Ronnie? If it does, he's not going to admit it with a bunch of Federal agents hanging around, Nick. Besides, why would he hide it in a lettuce crate? Why not just stick it under the car seat, where he could get to it?"

"Maybe because he was delivering it."

"To...?" I looked at Nick, and our thoughts connected. "Otis," we agreed in unison. "Where do you think he's gone?" I said.

"I have no idea, but if we're right, maybe Ronnie's delivering it to other people, too. I've got a produce order in for this morning. Maybe we can find out."

Although this was the second day we were closed, Nick had put in a produce order, hoping that we'd be allowed to reopen right away. We should have had plenty of lettuce and tomatoes for salads, but when the Feds went through the cooler they did a pretty thorough job of tearing things up. We'd had to throw away sixty percent of the produce that had just been delivered. I suppose it's the price we pay for being dangerous criminals and a threat to society.

Without the usual breakfast rush and daily prep, there was little to do but wait—for Marcia Lowery's supervisor to send out a new inspector, for Ronnie to arrive with the produce order, for Nick to win the lottery and take us away from the insanity of the restaurant business. Meanwhile, we joined the Buffaloes up on A deck. Nick ushered me into a chair next to Sonny Weaver and took the seat across from us.

"So, you're in trouble again, eh, Nick?"

Sonny is not the most sensitive of men. An infamous gossip, he's also our insurance agent. I try not to wonder if he's out and about Delphi telling everyone our affairs. On the other hand, too often our affairs have appeared on the police blotter of *The Delphi Sun,* so I don't suppose it matters much anyway.

"That's what comes from letting foreigners into the country, Sonny," Nick said, trying unsuccessfully to mimic a Southern drawl.

"Aw, now, Nick..." Sonny's voice trailed away, as if his feelings were hurt.

"So what do you know about Marcia Lowery, Sonny?" I asked.

He shook his head ruefully. "Not much. I don't have

the account. I know her boss, though, and I know she doesn't…didn't get on too well with him or anybody else in that office. He'd had a lot of complaints about her from other restaurants in the area. Didn't you know her, Mac?'' Sonny asked, leaning toward the end of the table.

Mac McKay swished a last swallow of coffee around in his mouth, stood and, digging into the pocket of his jeans, found and tossed a dollar on the table. ''Yup. Knew her when she was workin' for the gov'ment. Gawd a'mighty, that woman'd scare off a junkyard dog.''

Mac McKay was one of Sonny's finds. The ranks of the Buffaloes had been depleted by a local scandal a few years earlier, and Sonny was making it his mission to restore them to their former glory. It didn't hurt that they were all his clients, and all made a comfortable living.

Mac's fortunes were on the upswing. His vast apple and peach orchards had earned him a modest living until his wife, Lillian, noticed how many flavored vinegars were popping up on grocery store shelves and suggested they market her mother's family recipe for a subtly spiced cider vinegar. McKay's Apple Cinnegar was the new darling of the gourmet catalogues, and their premier line of chutneys would hit the stores next month.

''She just about lived at our place when we were getting our operation set up,'' he said. ''Made us pull out all the existing plumbing in the barn and completely renovate. Delayed our start-up three months. I thought Lillian was going to take a shotgun to her. You remember, Cobb? Hey, didn't you just do a job for her?''

Cobb Wilson, a local builder, pulled a pencil from behind his ear and tapped it nervously on the table. ''Started it, more like. Got the slabs poured and a new well dug, then two days ago she calls me wantin' to pull out. Glad you mentioned that, actually,'' he said, snapping a cell phone off his belt.

''What kind of a job?'' Nick said.

Cobb set the phone on the table and resumed his drumming. ''Guest houses, cabins, really. She had great plans for starting up a bed-and-breakfast arrangement. Gonna put in a stocked pond and a swimming pool. Can you imagine spending your vacation with her? No way. Not me."

This echoed my sentiments exactly. "So why did she change her mind?" I said.

Cobb shrugged, picked up his phone. "Said her plans had changed. She didn't think she could run the place alone. I told her we had a contract. I won't tell you what she told me to do with it. And now this is gonna be a helluva mess, trying to collect my money." He punched a series of numbers into his phone.

"Think I'll leave it to my lawyer to figure it out."

THE BUFFALOES HAD JUST cleared out when Spiros appeared, staggering in just as he had the previous day. "Shhh," he whispered, a finger to his lips. He pointed to his head. "Hurt. *Poli.*"

"Did you party again last night?" I said, placing a mug of coffee in front of him. A slow nod was his only response. "At Vince's?" Another nod.

"This Jell-O," he whispered, after consuming his coffee in a couple of swallows. "Den-ger-ous."

"What about Otis?"

"No Otis. No one knows. No Heather, no Todd, no Chad, no Lauren. No Megan, no Alex, no—"

"I have the picture, Spiros. I think you'd better move home before they invite you to pledge Sigma Chi."

Nick joined us bearing a bottle of aspirin and, after watching Spiros consume a handful, began questioning him in Greek. The story was the same. No one had seen Otis. Spiros had discovered one thing, though. The infamous Jell-O shooters were not made with vodka, but with another clear, high-content alcohol. White lightning, of course.

"Does Vince have a still?"

Spiros didn't know. He hadn't seen one, and he'd managed, one way and another, to inspect Vince's entire trailer.

"But he'd have it out in the woods somewhere, Nick.

That's how they used to do it. Build a fire, put on a big kettle of sour mash..." No. Somehow I just couldn't see Vince tending his still by moonlight, and neither could Nick. But that didn't mean that Heather, Todd, Chad, Lauren, Megan or Alex didn't have one in their trailers. Spiros was checking them out one at a time, but so far he hadn't found a thing.

We were still commiserating with Spiros when Ronnie arrived with the produce delivery. Nick met him at the back door.

"I'll help you with that," he said. "Which of these crates goes to me?"

Ronnie scratched his head and looked down at his clipboard. "Says here you got two crates of lettuce, one tomato..." He rattled off the produce list for Nick.

"Yeah, that's my order," Nick said. "But which ones should I take?"

"Any of them," Ronnie said, scooping a lettuce crate onto his dolly. "Doesn't matter."

And that was the key point. If it didn't matter which crates Nick selected, there probably wasn't any moonshine hidden in the produce for covert delivery. Nevertheless, when Ronnie pulled out of the parking lot, Nick wanted to follow him.

"He's going to The Venetian next," he explained. "We can pick him up there."

"What's the point, Nick? If we know he's not carrying any moonshine—"

"We don't know that. We only know that the crates near the doors don't have any in them."

"We're grasping at straws here," I said.

Nick sighed. "I know. But I can't just sit here and watch traffic go by."

I agreed. At least it would make us feel as if we were helping ourselves. We left Spiros slumped over the table, his head cradled in his arms, waiting for Marcia Lowery's boss to inspect us and piled into our Honda.

WE PICKED RONNIE UP at The Venetian, a small Italian place downtown. He was just climbing back into his van as we cruised past the driveway. Nick pulled over to the side of the street and waited for Ronnie's van to pass us.

"I feel silly."

Nick pulled out behind the van, leaving several car lengths between us. "Not me. I'm just worried," he said, his accent thickening, as it does under pressure.

We followed Ronnie on a twisted route through downtown Delphi, dropping off bok choy and bean sprouts at The Forbidden City, cabbage and onions at The Bavarian Hideaway. We stopped at several of the houses on fraternity row and caught a glimpse of Vince chatting with a deliveryman at one of them.

"He looks a lot better than Spiros," I commented.

"He should. He's thirty years younger. I don't think we should ask Spiros to go on staying out there, Julia. It's not good for him." I had to agree.

A curtain of fog enveloped us as we made the rounds of fast food, slow food and haute cuisine, if the term even applies to any restaurant in Delphi. We even dropped off lemons and limes at several local bars, a hopeful possibility that yielded no other fruit. By noon, we were finished with downtown and moving out into rural Calloway County.

"There aren't any restaurants out here, Nick," I pointed out.

"Maybe he's on his way to a still."

Ronnie was well ahead of us, though still in sight, on Industry Road. We passed Nickerson's Dairy and the D-Luxe Flea Market before entering the redolent air of The Corner Bakery plant. Nick pulled into a parking lot across the street to watch, but we lost the van amid a lot full of bakery delivery trucks, eighteen wheelers and smaller vendors.

"What's he delivering here, anyway? What kind of produce would they need?"

Nick shrugged. "Probably nuts. Maybe some dried fruit."

At The Corner Bakery, deliverymen swarmed in the parking lot like wasps, dollying out trays of breads and muffins to delivery trucks and wheeling racks of baked goods to semis. The water deliveryman toted recycling crates to his truck, while the Calloway Canteen man hauled cases of candy bars and chips in to the vending machines. We lost Ronnie in all the activity, picking him back up just in time to see him slam the back doors of the van. Whatever he'd delivered, we hadn't been able to see it.

We picked him up again just as he was turning onto Route 73, a rural road that took us slightly northeast. Route 73 is not well traveled. Ronnie's van was a hundred or so feet ahead of us, with nothing in between. "I'm feeling a little exposed."

"It's still foggy. He probably hasn't noticed us anyway," Nick said, but he let up on his speed, causing us to drop back a few more car lengths. The road ascended the mountains, twisting and turning on switchbacks that kept us out of view. After a couple of miles, Nick slowed down, pointing to a gravel driveway on the left.

"Look at that."

Several orange cones had been set up across the drive and were bound together with a yellow ribbon that looked painfully familiar. "Do you think that's where…where she lived?"

Nick took his foot off the gas and let the speedometer ease down, pulling onto the shoulder of the road. "Sam said she lived out in the country."

We gazed at the site from the roadside, but nothing was visible except the receding gravel drive that curled back into the woods. "I'm surprised Sam doesn't at least have a car stationed out here," I said.

"It is odd," Nick agreed.

It was a lovely area, with piney thickets trimming the road on both sides. I studied the woods, the tops of barren trees disappearing into woolly whitecaps of fog and thought that maybe Marcia Lowery's idea for a bed-and-breakfast might not be too bad. I expressed the thought to Nick. "Maybe we should do it when we retire. One house, just a few bedrooms…"

His gaze met mine and we both shook our heads. If the restaurant business was tough on a marriage, how much worse it must be to have guests in and out of your home day and night. Never a moment of privacy. No wandering around in torn nightshirts; no cold pizza or tuna sandwiches for breakfast. Beds to change; phones to answer.

And that was when the question first occurred to me. Why hadn't she called for help?

# FIVE

WE TRIED TO CATCH UP with Ronnie when we left the Lowery property, but he'd disappeared off Route 73, down any one of a dozen gravel driveways that intersected the road for the next few miles. We could have tried to find him, but it would have been difficult to explain why we were rumbling in and out of private driveways in search of the produce van. Instead, we gave up and returned to the Oracle, hungry and dispirited.

To our surprise, Medusa's boss had inspected the Oracle while we were gone. By the time we got back, Spiros had hamburgers on the grill and was dropping fries as fast as the fryers would take them. Rhonda was hustling tables while Sam leaned back in his chair at the family table, a clean plate in front of him and a toothpick dangling from his lips.

"You know as much as I do. They're keepin' me out of the loop, Nick," Sam was saying when I joined the men at the table. "'Cause of Rhonda workin' here."

"I'm the best-looking liability you've got," she said, chucking him under the chin as she hurried by.

"Sam, was the phone working out there?"

He watched Rhonda disappear into the wait station before turning back to us. "Far as I know. I called it in on my radio. Red's real tetchy about messin' up a scene."

"But she didn't call for help?"

"Nope. No record of a call from her place. I checked. But you know how that is. You start throwing up, you think it's gonna stop pretty soon. She passes out before she can get to the phone.''

It made sense. Another blind alley.

''I've been doing a little thinking, though,'' he continued. ''Why would ATF come all the way out here from Atlanta for one little bottle of moonshine?''

''And...?'' I said.

Sam rocked forward, bringing his chair to the floor with a thunk. ''I'm thinking they're lookin' for something much bigger, Julia. Coupla three years ago, they busted thirty people in North Carolina and Virginia during something called Operation Lightning Strike. I don't remember all the details, but seems to me it may have been the biggest moonshinin' ring since the end of Prohibition. Keepin' millions of tax dollars out of government hands.''

''Lightning Strike, huh? Cute name. What are they calling us, Flash in the Pan?'' I thought it was funny. They didn't.

''Seriously,'' I said, ''why would she call a federal agency in the first place?''

''Well, I'm just guessin' here, Julia, but she was a former FDA inspector. ATF probably put the word out that they were lookin' for a big operation, figurin' that FDA inspectors might be in a position to notice if somethin' was funny.''

''So what else can you find out about it?'' Nick asked.

Sam waggled the toothpick up and down in his mouth. ''Not much. I gotta be careful. They don't want me to know, or they'd tell me. Red's my friend, but I don't want to make things awkward for him, so I'm out in the cold.'' He plucked the toothpick out of his mouth, snapped it in half and dropped it into the ashtray.

''Sides, I've got work of my own to do. If they want to go chasin' around in the woods like a couple of revenuers in Dogpatch, fine with me. At least it'll keep 'em out of my hair.'' He stood and stretched, just as the radio on his shoulder squawked. I couldn't make out what was said, but Sam listened attentively, sighed and pushed in his chair.

''Guess I'd better go fight crime.'' He tossed Rhonda an

air kiss as she went by with a couple of Philly steak sandwiches. "I'll be back, darlin'," he said and lumbered out the door, passing Fran Bonaventure on her way in.

"I'm so glad to see you're open again," she said. "I'd like to reschedule the Chamber event as soon as possible."

That was our preference, too. The sooner we could wipe out memories of the disastrous breakfast, the happier we'd be. We settled on a luncheon this time, and set it for the end of the week.

"I'm also meeting David for lunch," Fran said, glancing over the full dining room.

"How's he doing?"

"Well, he spent the morning talking to the GBI, so I don't know, really. He was pretty depressed when he left."

I grabbed a couple of menus and led her up to A deck, where she could watch for him out the windows overlooking the parking lot.

"He wanted to come by and say how sorry he is for all the trouble Marcia's caused you," she continued, after she was seated.

"Fran, it's not his fault."

She unrolled her silverware and carefully spread the napkin in her lap. "No, I know it isn't. And so does he, but there's no one else to makes apologies for her now. I guess he feels it's his responsibility, in spite of all the hell she put him through."

Rhonda appeared at my elbow then, with a glass of ice water and her order pad. Nick had gone into the kitchen, and there was no one at the register to answer the phone when it rang. I excused myself, leaving Fran to study the menu while Rhonda went to get the drinks Fran had ordered for herself and David. Miss Alma's soft drawl greeted me as soon as I answered.

"Julia, have you seen Spiros? I haven't heard from him in several days," she said. I could hear an edge of worry under her casual tone.

I never stopped marveling at the change Spiros's friendship had wrought in Miss Alma. When we first met her, she was a frightened old lady, leaning on a walker and spending her days alone. Then Spiros moved in next door to her house in Markettown, and subsequently into her life. He, a former cook for the Greek merchant marine, and she, a retired teacher forty years his senior, had formed a friendship unlike any I had ever witnessed. He admired and respected her intelligence and wisdom; she enjoyed his enthusiasm for life and his kind attention. She could call upon him for help; he called upon her for advice. Theirs, it seemed to me, was the perfect friendship.

"Oh, he's all right, Miss Alma," I said. It took some time to catch her up on the events of the past forty-eight hours, finishing with Sam's story about Operation Lightning Strike. She asked the probing questions of a retired history teacher. I just didn't have any answers to them. At length, I called Spiros to the phone.

While I was on the phone, David Lowery pulled into the parking lot in the MG I'd seen Marcia driving only a few days before. When he joined Fran at the table, she waved me over to introduce us.

"I'm sorry we have to meet under these circumstances," he said. "Fran told me about the way Marcia behaved at the breakfast. I wish I had a reasonable explanation for it, but I'm afraid I don't. My...wife had a mercurial temperament."

To say the least. I felt sorry for David Lowery, having to deal with her all those years. He didn't look like a man who smiled much. He was tall and extremely thin, the bone structure in his face so prominent that he reminded me of an icon. There were two deep furrows between his eyebrows, like permanent worry scars.

"I'm sorry about her death," I said. "It must have been a shock to you."

David squeezed a lemon wedge over his glass of tea, wringing it for every drop of juice. "It was. And it wasn't." He pulled out a chair and nodded me into it.

"I think you deserve an explanation, given the problems

she caused you.'' I couldn't argue with him there. He emptied a packet of artificial sweetener into his tea, tasted it and tore open a second packet.

''I just finished meeting with the GBI. Marcia claimed she was getting threatening phone calls. I'm sorry to say I didn't really believe her, although I should have realized that it was a possibility. No one could feel neutral about Marcia. But I didn't think anyone would really threaten her life.''

''Did you ever hear any of the calls?''

''No. I haven't been living at home. I was trying to make a clean break from her, but there was no such thing as a clean break from Marcia. She was always trying to get me to come back, using every ruse in the book.'' David took a sip of his tea and carefully blotted the ring of sweat the glass had left on the tablecloth.

''Anyway, the fact is that I didn't believe her, and I told her as much. I figured it was just another game. Marcia was a master game player. Apparently I was wrong.''

Rhonda interrupted us to set a Greek salad in front of Fran and a gyro with homemade potato chips at David's place. He picked up a potato chip, looked it over and set it back on his plate with a sigh.

''David, are you saying that Marcia's death wasn't accidental?''

''No. I don't know. The GBI is treating it as a suspicious death until the autopsy results come in. But if she was really getting threats… The agent on the case tells me that there were five or six calls on her caller ID that were made from public phone booths. He wanted to know what I knew about them. It sounds like she might have been telling the truth.'' He shook his head slowly. ''If I had just believed her, she might not be dead now.''

Fran placed her hand on top of his, thumbing his knuckles lightly. ''There's no way you could have known, David. She was always crying wolf.''

Fran turned to me. ''She tried everything. She started building on their land. She even said she'd get pregnant if that's what he wanted, although she'd never wanted children before."

David stirred uncomfortably in his chair, as though he wished Fran would let the matter drop, but she didn't seem to notice. "Then she told him she was sick, even sent him a couple of doctor's bills, but they hadn't come up with a diagnosis. Obviously it was just another game to get him to come back. She would have done anything to keep him, so you can understand why he didn't believe her about the threats."

David turned his gaze toward the window. The afternoon light seemed to deepen the creases in his brow and the hollows in his cheeks. He spoke as though he'd forgotten we were there. "A family, and someday, when we retired, a bed-and-breakfast. Marcia never understood that those dreams died years ago. For the last twelve, all I've dreamed about is being out of the marriage. And now, finally, I've got my wish."

He turned back to us and pushed his plate into the center of the table. "Sorry, I just don't have much appetite."

I left them, after assuring David that he had no reason to be apologizing to me. Rhonda and Nick were rolling silverware at the family table and discussing Sam's predicament. She picked up a fork, shined it with a clean bar mop, positioned it on a napkin and picked up a knife.

"He's more worried than he's letting on," she said. "You know sheriff is an elected position. If there's anything, any scandal, or even rumors connected to his name, he may not be reelected." Rhonda carefully folded the napkin up at the bottom corner before rolling it into a neat bundle and setting it on a tray.

"Besides that," she continued, "this GBI business has him upset. He's worked with those guys on cases dozens of times. Now all of a sudden, these hotshots from ATF are telling the GBI that Sam can't be trusted. It isn't right, Nick. No one's more trustworthy than Sam. You know that."

We both knew it and knew that this situation could seriously damage his reputation. All over one little bottle of white lightning.

"We've got to do something," I said to Nick. Out in the parking lot, Fran and David stood together, his hands lightly resting on her shoulders. They had lingered over lunch, quietly talking with their heads together, until almost closing time. Up on A deck, Rhonda was just now bussing their table.

Nick stood at the register, letting it run through its close-out program. It made a rhythmical chi-ching sound as it printed each transaction on the tape. Today its music was especially sweet, knowing how silent it had been the day before.

"We're trying, Julia. I'm sorry about Sam, but don't forget this isn't great for our business, either."

"Julia, catch him!" Rhonda waved toward David in the parking lot. Behind him, Fran was pulling out onto Broadway. "He's left his keys," she said, tossing them over the railing to me.

David had already discovered his mistake and was headed back in the front door. "I'm afraid I—"

"I was just going to try to catch you," I said, holding the keys up by their leather fob. When he reached the register, I dropped them into his open palm.

He thanked me and turned away, then back again. "I think maybe I need to explain something to you," he said. "I know Marcia was a very difficult woman, and she caused you a lot of trouble, but to be fair, her problems weren't entirely her fault. I wouldn't want you to remember her as just a harridan, although I know that's what a lot of people think."

He hooked his middle finger through his key ring and flipped the keys and fob back and forth into his palm, much the way Nick flips his worry beads. Some nervous gestures must be universal. "In the time we were married, Marcia saw five separate therapists."

"Psychologists?"

He nodded. "Three were psychologists, one was a marriage counselor and the last one was a psychiatrist. They all agreed that her background was the major cause of her problems. A father who couldn't hold a job and periodically abandoned his family, a mother who struggled to make ends meet and spent the little leftover money on cheap booze. Marcia had a helpless childhood at the mercy of a feckless father and a drunken mother. It produced an adult obsessed with the need to control everything and everyone around her. We went from one counselor to the next, but as soon as they'd finished unpacking her emotional baggage, she'd want to cut and run."

"But why would she run away from help?"

"Because that's when the real work began. They expected her to work on changing her behavior, and she wasn't willing to do that as long as she could maintain the status quo. I left my wife, Julia, not because she was hard to get along with, but because she refused to help herself. I thought if I left, she'd have no choice."

He looked down at the keys resting in the palm of his hand. "Funny, she must have thought, right up to the end, that I'd come back to her. She even gave me back my house key."

I pointed to a bright brass key that was clearly newly cut. "Looks like she changed the locks before she decided that," I said.

David's brow furrowed as he picked up a worn silver key and held it in the light. "This is the house key. That one is to my lab. I have no idea where it came from." He snapped his palm over all of them and dropped them into his pocket. "Well, that's all I wanted to say. Don't judge Marcia too harshly. She just couldn't help herself."

As I watched him climb into his shiny MG, I thought that Marcia Lowery must have been a very foolish woman, and that Fran Bonaventure was a very lucky one. I was still thinking about them when Miss Alma called.

"Julia, can you and Nick stop by here on your way home? I think I've found some interesting information for you."

# SIX

"IT'S PRINTING NOW," Miss Alma said as she ushered us through the door.

She pointed toward her dining room, where a new computer fed information to a printer which, in turn, spat out pages of print as quickly as it could load them. Spiros had given her a brand-new computer for her birthday. For an eighty-something-year-old woman who had never touched a keyboard before, she had quickly become an accomplished pilot in cyberspace.

Miss Alma was in her element with a computer. She loved the Internet, citing the Library of Congress Web site as her personal favorite. As a former history teacher, it was a natural fit. She patted the top of her monitor lovingly before taking her seat in front of the keyboard. Behind her, Spiros glowed.

"Miss Alma ve-ree smart, *neh?*"

We agreed she was, even smarter than we'd realized when she brought up a search engine covered in Web sites about moonshining. "I suppose I'm going to start getting spammed by some pretty controversial Web sites now. Oh well," she said with a shrug, "I'll just have to delete all my cookies."

"Quit showing off, Miss Alma," I said, and was answered with a girlish giggle.

She took us on a virtual tour, then, of moonshine Web sites—how to make it, songs about it, lawmen busting it. There were sites about how to build a still and others sharing old family recipes for bootleg booze. And several explained how NASCAR racing had its roots in trying to outrun the law. In all, an interesting experience, but I couldn't see where it was going to be much help to us.

"That's where this comes in, my dear," Miss Alma said, tapping the stack of papers that had accumulated in her printer tray. "Didn't you say that Sheriff Lawless mentioned Operation Lightning Strike? Well, I ran a couple of searches on it and came up with quite a few newspaper articles from North Carolina and Virginia. I think you may find them enlightening—if you'll pardon the pun."

JACK WAS IN A SNIT when we got home. He waited at the door, as usual, but when we got inside he turned tail and trotted off to the den, positioning himself with his nose in a corner. We'd stayed for dinner with Miss Alma and Spiros, which Jack seemed to perceive as dereliction of duty.

"Come on, Jack," I said, grabbing a treat from a jar on the counter. I saw his eyes cut around in a sidelong glance, but he didn't budge.

I've heard other Scottie owners complain of this behavior, so I know it's not unique to Jack, but there's a very personal sting in being snubbed by your own dog. Nick grabbed his leash and dragged him outside for a quick trot around the block while I got ready for bed.

By the time they got back, I was piled up on our bed with the papers that Miss Alma had given us. While Nick brushed his teeth, I skimmed through it all. She was right. There was a lot of information to go through, more than fifty pages of articles from newspapers all over three states. Much of it was redundant, but we split it and dutifully plowed through it, one article at the time.

Operation Lightning Strike had been going on for several years prior to the arrests. Suspects lived in several states, each with his own role to play in the scheme. There were suppliers of equipment, distillers, distributors and even receivers, several of whom were bar owners as far away as Philadelphia. Apparently in some quarters, moonshine was highly sought after.

"Must give you a heck of a buzz," I commented to Nick.

"If it doesn't kill you. It says here that people can die from drinking that stuff. Besides problems with contaminated water, if it's not made right it can make you go blind, do nerve damage, give you ulcers. It can even give you lead poisoning."

"Lead poisoning does brain damage. Maybe that's what's wrong with Otis, Nick."

He turned a skeptical eye on me. "What's wrong with Otis is he's a lazy, useless sonofa—"

"Listen to this. 'On the witness stand, agents from the Bureau of Alcohol, Tobacco and Firearms admitted that they had been investigating local moonshine rings for several years. Early indications in the investigation suggested that, unlike previous moonshine businesses, which tended to be small and local in scope, this ring was extensive and well organized, producing about fifteen hundred gallons of liquor a week'—*a week,* can you imagine that?"

"Why would anyone want this stuff? This article says that bugs and rodents get into the…what's it called?" Nick rustled through the papers. "Mash—like rotting fruit. *Mana mou,* they even use hog feed and—"

I swallowed hard and laid a hand on his knee. "I don't think I want to know any more. Rodents was enough for me."

I went back to the article I was reading, but had a hard time concentrating. Spiros had been drinking that stuff, or rather chewing it in Jell-O. And there were those kids, Vince and the others. Somebody needed to warn them about the risks before something tragic happened.

"Nick! Sam said it might be food poisoning, remember? If the stuff's contaminated with hog feed and rodents, heaven knows what you might get from drinking it. I'll bet that's it. I'll bet that's what made her sick. Maybe I should call Sam," I said, reaching for the bedside phone, but Nick pushed my hand away.

"I don't think there's much chance of that. The real danger

in moonshine is methanol and lead. Besides, you need to be very sure you know what you're doing before you get Sam involved, Julia. If we send him off on a duck hunt—''

''Wild-goose chase.''

''Yeah, that. Anyway, if we're wrong, it's going to look like he's trying to...I don't know the word.''

''Distract the Feds. Yeah, I see what you mean. I guess the autopsy will show what she died of anyway, and surely they'll tell Sam that much.''

Nick set his half of the articles aside and slid down in the bed. ''Anything else in there?''

''Yes,'' I said, pushing myself up higher against the headboard. I skimmed ahead to be sure that I was right. This was important. ''You know how they finally tracked them down? They found the supplier, started tracking purchases of jugs and sugar. It turned out to be a local feed store, which was pretty suspicious because why would a feed store need thousands of gallon jugs and tons of sugar? Who would they sell it to? After that, they just put somebody undercover, and he tracked where the supplies were going. Pretty tricky, huh?''

''Smart,'' he said, stroking my thigh with his index finger. ''So that's probably what they're doing here, too.''

I pushed his hand away. ''But they must not have gotten very far, or they wouldn't be obsessing over one little bottle in a restaurant in Delphi.''

''Unless they think we buy enough sugar.''

Well, we do buy sugar, of course. There's *baklava, ravani, rizogalo,* all the homemade sweets we have on our menu. But we didn't buy that much, surely not enough to look suspicious. I slid down next to him, deep in thought.

''Whoever is supplying must have a legitimate reason to buy the stuff or ATF would have discovered them by now. Bottles and sugar,'' I said. ''Bottles and sugar...''

''Ed Greer,'' Nick answered quietly. ''Bottles for water...''

Ed Greer owned Piedmont Pride Spring Water. He was a

new member of the Buffs, brought in by Sonny Weaver. He didn't seem to fit in very well, perhaps because he was so taciturn. Or maybe it was because he lacked the kind of mon-eyed polish of the other men, although he might well have more assets than all the rest of them together. Ed was a local success story, an old-fashioned man who farmed his family's land for twenty-five years until the nationwide craze for bot-tled water turned his fortunes around. Ed now bottled Pied-mont Pride, a brand of spring water issuing from the most mountainous, rockiest and otherwise useless land his family owned. Ed was doing very well.

"But what about the sugar? According to this, it takes a lot of sugar to make white lightning. If the Feds were track-ing purchases, wouldn't they think it's strange that Piedmont Pride is buying tons of sugar?"

Nick shook his head. "They're not. He's probably getting it somewhere else."

"Well, how are we going to find out if we're right?"

"We're not going to find out anything, Julia. We're going to turn the information over to Sam and let him take it from there." He reached over and turned off the light, rolled onto his side and traced a line down my shoulder.

"We can't do that, Nick. We have to find out for our-selves."

The light snapped back on. "Wait a minute—"

"No, you just said it yourself. If we're wrong, it's going to look like Sam is trying to divert attention away from the real culprits. It will only make him look bad to the ATF. For that matter, if they find out the information came from us, it's going to look like we're trying to distract them, too. We have to be sure we're right, first. The problem is, how are we going to get in there to look around without making Ed suspicious?"

Nick sighed. "There's only one way," he said, and threw the covers back. We rolled out of bed and started to dress.

I wouldn't say we were exactly old hands at this kind of thing, but it wasn't our first nighttime reconnaissance mission, either. In fact, the black turtleneck and pants I wore reminded me of another, similar venture—one that almost ended tragically for both of us. This time, we'd be more careful.

I looked up the address of Piedmont Pride in the phone book.

"It's on Route 73," I told Nick. "I don't remember passing it. Did you see a sign?"

He hadn't, and after speculating how, exactly, we were going to find the place in the dark, in the most rural part of Calloway County, I called Miss Alma. Apologizing for the lateness of the hour, I explained what we needed. By the time we got to her house, she'd printed a county plat off the Internet. We left her with a promise we would call, no matter how late, when we got home safely.

We went equipped this time, stopping at an all night Walmart along the way to get black sweatshirts, flashlight batteries and high-speed film for the camera. The latter was Nick's idea, just to give Sam a leg up on the evidence—if there was any to find—and the layout, should he need it. On Route 73, Nick slowed down as we passed Marcia Lowery's driveway. The cones were still in place, and in the dark we could barely make out the yellow ribbons of tape looped from one cone to the next. There was no sign of a sheriff's car anywhere, and no indication of GBI presence.

We drove on, following the road as it climbed higher into the mountains in a series of short, sharp switchbacks. I studied the plat and watched for rural mailboxes. "There," I said, pointing at an oversize box on a post. "That should be it."

He pulled off the road just long enough for me to hop out and shine a light on the mailbox. A small plaque attached to the front said Piedmont Pride Spring Water. I nodded at Nick. He cut the car lights and pulled thirty feet or so past the box, angling the car as deep into the shoulder as he dared. He popped the hood, then propped it open.

"Car trouble," he whispered, as he joined me back at the driveway. He took my hand and led me off to the side of the drive, keeping parallel with it as we moved as quietly as possible toward the Piedmont Pride plant. The year had begun with an unseasonable warming trend, for which I was grateful. We could see our breath in the dark woods, but the activity and a hefty dose of adrenaline were keeping us plenty warm.

We'd only been walking about ten minutes when we ran into a chain-link fence. "There," Nick whispered, nodding toward a large metal building on the other side. "That must be it."

Three large delivery trucks were backed up to a loading dock, but the doors were closed. Light shone through high windows, and we could hear the low hum of equipment running. Ed Greer had thoughtfully left the gate in the fence open for us.

"How are we going to get in?" I whispered to Nick. He put a finger to his lips and led me on a circuit of the building, staying up close to the metal siding where the shadows hid us. There were no lights in the parking lot, just a couple of outside spotlights at the building's corners. Either Ed wasn't concerned about security, or he didn't want to train a spotlight on his operation. Nick carefully tried each door as we passed—one that clearly led into the office, another into the main plant and a third next to the loading dock. They were all locked.

We were going to have to get a look in the windows, Nick indicated, pointing upward. I spread my hands out. How? Through a series of pantomimes, I learned that my husband thought I should stand on his shoulders. Me. His acrophobic wife.

# SEVEN

MY LEGS HAD ALL the strength and substance of overcooked spaghetti. "Stop moving," Nick whispered. He was stuck in a squat while I, on his shoulders, wobbled and swayed, trying to catch my balance. I leaned forward and braced my hands against the cold metal skin of the building.

"Okay."

I walked my hands up the outside as he slowly, with an unflattering grunt, rose to a standing position. As long as I didn't look down, we were probably both all right. When he was finally upright, my nose grazed just above the window frame. I could see in, but not down. All I needed was a couple more inches. I slid my feet carefully back on his shoulders, even as he pushed against my calves with his hands.

"What are you doing?"

"Tiptoes."

He let off the pressure on my legs and I almost went backward, causing an involuntary gasp and a fleeting picture of him scraping me off the asphalt with a spatula. After I swallowed my heart, I grabbed the edge of the window with my fingertips and gently raised up on my toes. The view was only marginally better, but enough for me to see the activity inside.

It was almost entirely mechanized. In fact, I couldn't see a human being anywhere. Below me, some kind of machine jetted air into a plastic ring and pop! The ring was a bottle. Pretty cool. From there, via a series of conveyers, the bottle went to a second machine where it was filled with clear liquid from a pipe. I traced the pipe backward and saw that it branched off a wider conduit that came in from the outside. The conduit sent the water through a filtering mechanism, then back out through one of four identical branches.

The full bottle moved on to a capping machine, then a mechanical labeler and dropped into a slot next to five others. Plastic collars completed the cycle. There were four stations in all, each one blowing, filling, capping and collaring. But they all were fed from a single main conduit. My heart sank.

We had been so sure that we were onto something really big. I felt foolish, embarrassed, and once again conscious of the tenuous stance I had on Nick's shoulders. "Okay," I whispered, and we began the descent, I, walking my hands down as he slowly dropped into a crouch. Back on the ground, my legs felt like I'd been roller-skating. We slipped back out the gate and stopped in the woods.

"There's no one in there," I said. "And what's worse, I think it's definitely water they're bottling."

"It can't be, Julia. I know we're right. It works."

"Well, I just don't see how—"

Off to our left came a distant rumble. Nick grabbed me, pulling me back out of sight as a pair of dim, round lights appeared in the woods. The sound drummed unevenly—a pickup, bouncing over a primitive road—appeared outside the fence, rumbled to a halt and waited as the silhouette of a man jumped out of the passenger's side, strode to the fence and pulled open a loose section of chain-link. The pickup entered the plant compound and puttered around to the loading dock.

In the light, we could see that the truck was at least forty years old, with slightly rounded fenders. Chunks of rust had eaten away the undercarriage. Had I not seen it myself, I wouldn't have believed the thing would run. But the engine purred happily when it hit the pavement. The driver leaped out and moved to the back to drop the tailgate just as the other man joined him. Ed Greer and his son. I glanced at

Nick for confirmation, but he was gazing at the two of them intently, and his hand tightened around my fingers. The door of one of the delivery trucks went up with a metallic grate.

They were dollying something off the pickup. Nick grabbed his camera and I heard the zoom buzz and a sharp intake of breath, before the shutter clicked several times in rapid succession. "Water bottles," he whispered, and passed the camera to me.

The zoom was as almost as good as binoculars. As I watched, Ed pushed a dolly off the pickup onto the loading dock, swung it around and headed up the ramp onto a delivery truck. The building's spotlight caught sharply on the cases on the dolly, just long enough for me to catch a glimpse of round-shouldered plastic bottles before they disappeared inside the darkened truck. Behind Ed, his son brought a second dolly. Nick caught my hand again and pulled me back farther out of sight.

"They're bringing it from somewhere back there," he said, pointing into the woods. "We'll have to follow them."

We waited until the pickup was completely unloaded. They had taken off seven loads on dollies. I did a quick estimate in my head. Six quarts per collar, six collars per flat, five flats per dolly. I figured it would come out somewhere in the neighborhood of three hundred gallons. Just on this load. By then, they were back in the pickup, closing the gap in the fence again, and once more disappearing into the woods.

"Let's say twenty dollars a gallon," I whispered to Nick as we skirted the fence and drew up next to the gap. "That's six thou in moonshine right there. Not bad for a night's work."

"They may not be done yet," he said. He pulled me onto a dirt track covered in dry, leafless kudzu vines. In summer, the track would all but disappear, and with the vine's incredible growth rate, it would probably overgrow itself overnight. A monstrous plant, I thought, and was glad it was wintertime when there were likely to be fewer creatures living under it.

We must have walked several miles. Nick aimed his flashlight at the plat, trying to get some sense of where we were going. He pointed to the back left corner of the lot. "Somewhere back in here."

Miss Alma had told us that at one time the Greers had owned most of the land between one stretch of road and the loop where it turned back on itself. Over the years, they'd sold off plots in ten-acre tracts to people who wanted plenty of privacy and mountain scenery. A lot of Parnassus professors had bought in the area, I'd been told. We followed the track until we heard a tailgate slam, then dived to our right into a thicket where the kudzu vines climbed up into the trees. They provided us with nice cover, but I couldn't help thinking about the creatures that typically inhabited them. Tonight seemed the night to confront all my worst fears.

"Look at that," Nick said, pointing through the trees.

A large rectangle of light spilled out across the dark ground. I couldn't see where it was coming from, but shortly a shadow invaded the light and two hollow thumps were followed by a low rumble. As my eyes grew accustomed to the light and shadow, I saw the truck parked perpendicular to the light source. Ed Greer appeared, pushing a dolly, followed by Ed Jr. with a dolly of his own.

"*Mana mou,* what a setup," Nick whispered.

The dollies were emptied on the truck and the Eds disappeared once again. They made five trips in all. Six quarts, six collars, five cases. No wonder Piedmont Pride was doing so well.

"What about the bins?" Ed Jr. called out.

"Nah, bring 'em on the last run." Ed climbed into the truck cab and waited. The light source was extinguished, but Ed Jr. didn't appear immediately. We could hear some rustling before a circle of light shone over the ground near the truck and Ed Jr. jumped into the tailgate.

Crouched in the vines, we watched them pass before stepping out onto the track and heading swiftly for...for what? The light had disappeared. In front of us was a small clearing bordered by a wall of woods and vines. Nick switched on his flashlight and played it out over the clearing. It was skirted on the far side by a fence, and just inside the fence stood a large concrete box, maybe twenty square feet in all. I could hear the rush of water, and remembered that the map showed a stream that straddled Ed's land and the property behind it. Somewhere in the distance something hummed.

"A generator," Nick said, and arced the light until it caught on a wooden shack with a half moon in the door. A casual glance suggested an old outhouse. When the light caught the concrete box, Nick explained. "That's the spring box. They pipe the water from here to the plant. Both plants."

"Both?" I still didn't have a firm grip on exactly what was going on.

"Where is it?" Nick said to himself. He handed me the flashlight, with instructions to shine it away from the spring box toward the woods, then headed for the densest section of vines.

"What are you doing?"

He patted the vines with both hands, grabbed hold of a section and pulled. A mat of dry kudzu, cut on three sides into a neat rectangle, came loose in his hands revealing, behind it, a ramp and a rusty aluminum door. I moved closer, casting light around the periphery, and gasped.

It reminded me of Sleeping Beauty's castle, albeit not a very grand one, covered from top to bottom in vines. The castle was a huge trailer, a mobile home that appeared to have been vacated a long time ago. Nick ran up the ramp and pulled on the door. It opened without resistance.

He might not be Jack Daniels, but Ed Greer had a sizable operation going. I would have liked to go through the whole place, see how it was really done, but as uninvited guests, our visit had definite time limitations. Nick snapped as many pictures, from as many angles as he could without venturing too far inside the trailer. Beside the door were several empty plastic recycling boxes and four stacks of cases. Six per collar, six collars per case. The numbers were really adding up. He caught them on film before moving into the plant. There, he whistled under his breath. Greenish copper vats sprouted thick, twisting pipes that intersected at other vats and eventually at something that looked like a large radiator. The end of the process was a bottling station identical to the ones I'd seen in the other plant. Greer's operation was so mechanized that he needed little help, and could limit the number of people in on his secret. More money for him, and more security, too. The Feds were going to love this one.

Next to the bottling machine on the floor lay a couple of crumpled labels that looked as if they might have gotten hung in the labeling machine. Nick grabbed and pocketed them for inspection later. "Let's go," he said.

But something else had caught my eye. "Wait a minute." I hurried across the concrete floor to a corner, where bottle recycling bins were stacked neatly against the wall, and flipped up the lid of one of them. "Okay," I said. "We can go now."

We'd no more than gotten out, closed the door and replaced the camouflage when we heard the pickup in the distance and saw the lights moving our way. Nick and I took off running toward the only place we could hide. We wedged ourselves in behind the spring box with our backs to the cold concrete, breathing hard and listening harder, trying to hear their movements over the pumps and generator. They were taking another load, probably the four stacks that were waiting next to the door.

After the light in the trailer, it took a while for my eyes to get accustomed to the dark. At length, I nudged Nick with my elbow and pointed through the fence. He turned to me with a quizzical expression. Ahead of us, the stream ran about five feet from the fence before it angled onto Greer's property. And across the stream, in the distance, I could see pads of concrete, maybe fifty feet long and thirty feet deep. There were four, turned at angles so that each might face the stream before it meandered onto Greer's land. Next to the last one stood a tall, narrow shed that was contributing a share to the mechanical noise around us.

Cobb Wilson had said he'd poured slabs and dug a new well for Marcia Lowery before she decided to pull out of the building project. Why hadn't I realized that her land backed up to Ed Greer's? I grinned inanely at Nick. Finally, things were beginning to fall into place.

WE DIDN'T CALL SAM when we got home, although we woke Miss Alma at two-forty-five to let her know we were back. It had taken us a long time to get back to the car, waiting as we had until we were sure that the Eds had left. The truck they'd loaded still stood waiting at the dock. In the morning, I suspected, the rest of it would be filled with legitimate bottles of water. What better cover could they have for shipping white lightning all over the East Coast than as fresh mountain spring water?

We needed to have the story straight in our own minds before we brought Sam in on it. And the recycling bins had added yet another dimension to it all. I explained it to Nick as we drove past the cones at Marcia Lowery's drive.

"Guess what was in the recycling bin?"

"Sugar."

Well, that was deflating. "And what else?" I challenged him.

He said he didn't know, but he may just have been trying to make me feel better. "Yeast!" I said triumphantly. "He's getting the sugar and yeast from someplace that can buy it legitimately."

"The Corner Bakery."

"Uh...right." I don't know how he knew that. I knew it, because the bag had a tracking label and number on it. The label very clearly said "Corner Bakery."

"But how's Dale hiding it from his company?"

Nick tapped the steering wheel thoughtfully. "He spreads the expense out. He buys a lot of sugar, anyway. Greer pays him for it, so the books aren't too far off."

"But why would Dale do that? What's in it for him?"

"A partnership, Julia. Greer pays him a percentage of his profit or something. Dale's probably got a nice little retirement fund somewhere."

I sat back and sighed contentedly. We'd had a pretty good night, all in all. This should get the Feds off our backs, and make a nice bust for Sam. Rhonda would be happy. And Fran would be happy because, undoubtedly, whatever had happened to Marcia Lowery had something to do with Ed Greer and his homemade mountain dew.

"NOW, THE KIDS ARE getting it at the frat houses," I said to Sam the next morning. I told him about seeing Vince talking to the Piedmont driver. "He was probably making a buy."

I laid the labels Nick had picked up out on the table, then set a bottle of Piedmont Pride water next to them. "You see a difference?"

Sam scrutinized them carefully before tapping the fake label. "Two registered trademarks."

He was right. Instead of one, there were two, one on top of and slightly to the right of the other, as if it were a misprint. The other difference was the type of label. The fakes were a peel-off type that could be created with a computer printer.

"They must peel off the labels when they deliver the stuff, so it can't be traced back to Piedmont," I suggested. "If anyone wonders why they're throwing them away, they just point out the misprint."

Sam agreed. He picked up Nick's pictures and studied them carefully, shaking his head all the while. "You shoulda told me what you suspected. Won't you two ever learn?"

"We just didn't want to make things worse for you, Sam," I said. He snorted, but underneath I think he was pleased.

"It's gonna take twenty-four hours 'fore I can pick 'em up, though," he said. He stacked the pictures and squared their corners neatly.

"Why? You're not going to have any trouble finding the trailer if we found it in the dark," Nick said.

Sam shook his head. "I don't work like that, Nick. I've got to get warrants, and to do that, I gotta have probable cause. That means, I'm gonna have to stake 'em out—probably from the Lowery property—until I see something suspicious. I'll take a few pictures of my own, take 'em to a judge, say I got a tip...."

Nick and I sighed in concert, but Sam didn't seem to notice. He took a long sip of coffee before setting his cup down gently on the table. "I've got to tell you something else," he said quietly. "The ME's determined the Lowery woman's cause of death. She died of arsenic poisoning."

Nick slapped his hand on the table. "Porfect!"

"Per—"

Nick didn't hesitate a beat. "I read about it. Sometimes groundwater is contaminated with arsenic. She got it in the moonshine."

Sam shook his head and mechanically shuffled the pictures between his fingers. "First off, moonshiners don't usually kill. They're just good ol' boys makin' hooch the way their daddies taught 'em. Besides, the arsenic's not from the water, Nick. Yesterday, I didn't know it then, but GBI went all over the house. Her staples, sugar, salt, flour, and some of the food in her refrigerator, all laced with arsenic. And there was some pretty damning evidence in her desk, too."

"Damning?" I said. "Damning to whom?"

"Well, Julia, let me put it this way. Right now, the GBI likes the husband for the crime."

# EIGHT

I DIDN'T KNOW David Lowery well, but still I was stunned when Sam announced that the GBI considered him a serious suspect in his wife's death. After a second, I found my voice.

"Not David, Sam. Surely not. His divorce was almost final. Why would he kill her?"

Sam squirmed a bit in his chair. "Look, Julia, I'm not saying he did. I'm just telling you what I'm hearing, and it ain't much, since I'm being pretty well frozen out on this one. But I know they found some medical bills and a lab report in her desk. Looks like he'd been poisoning her over about six or eight months."

"And she didn't know? Come on, Sam, how could she not know that? If she'd been seeing a doctor..."

He shrugged. "Slow arsenic poisoning is hard to detect, Julia. It causes a lot of general symptoms, nausea, headaches, weight loss, dark spots on the skin, hair loss, organ damage. You name it, arsenic might cause it. But so could a lot of other diseases and conditions, including stress. If a doctor's not looking for arsenic poisoning, he's probably not going to find it. There are dozens, no hundreds, of cases that have only been discovered accidentally."

"But you said..." I gulped, not really wanting to dwell on the crime scene. "The bathroom...I mean, that doesn't sound like a slow poisoning."

"Yeah, well, I guess she just wasn't dyin' fast enough for him. He was down to the wire. Kill her now or lose everything in the divorce."

"What do you mean, 'lose everything?'"

Sam winced, as though he'd said too much. "Awright, I'm gonna tell you this, but you've got to keep it to yourselves, you hear me?"

Nick and I solemnly agreed. Sam continued, "They also found a copy of a letter in her desk. To her attorney, dated the day before she died, tellin' him to change her will to cut the husband out. She didn't have any other family, apparently, so she was leavin' all her property to charity."

"But even so, Sam, David was giving it all up in the divorce anyway, so what difference would that make?"

"The difference," Nick said quietly, "is now he doesn't have to. If she died before the divorce went through, it would all go back to him."

I couldn't believe it, didn't want to believe it, if only for Fran's sake. Still, what was it David had said to me? *For the last twelve years, all I've dreamed about is being out of the marriage. And now, finally, I've got my wish.* It hadn't seemed like such a bad thing to say at the time, but now it chilled my soul.

I couldn't get my mind off David and Marcia Lowery for the rest of the morning. I was making *kotopites* for the rescheduled Chamber of Commerce kickoff due to happen the next day. I browned chicken breasts on the grill and sauteed mushrooms and shallots in butter, cream and white wine, wondering all the while if Fran knew about any of what the sheriff had told us. David had moved out of the house six months ago, and the way he and Fran talked, he hadn't ever gone back to it. He could have salted her staples with arsenic before he left, I reasoned, but that didn't explain the food in the refrigerator.

Who else might have had access to the Lowery house? The Greers, maybe, but my gut feeling was that Sam was right. Ed Greer was just another good ol' boy who'd discovered he could make better moonshine using new technology.

Marcia Lowery had made lots of enemies over the years, but how likely was it that any of them had access to her house? David did. I'd seen the key myself. It struck me, then, that David had been driving the MG the day he'd met Fran at the Oracle for lunch, and that meant that he probably had been back to the house. Had he taken it the night she died, knowing she'd never need it again?

I HAD JUST LAID PHYLLO pastry out on the worktable when Tammy came into the kitchen. "Julia, there's one of those Chamber of Commerce people here wanting to talk to you."

Phyllo pastry doesn't keep well once it's been opened and exposed to the air. I covered it with waxed paper, rinsed my hands and dried them on my apron before going out to the dining room. Fran was standing next to the register, a microphone and some wiring in her hand and the portable podium at her feet. Her complexion was white, except for the deep-blue crescents under her eyes. She rubbed her free hand across her brow and eyes, as though she had a headache.

"I thought I'd better bring these by today," she said. "Just in case…I…just in—" a sob caught in the back of her throat, and her eyelashes grew dark with threatening tears. I set the podium in the wait station and led her back into the kitchen, explaining my phyllo problem and giving her time to pull herself together.

I pulled a stool up to the stainless steel table where I was working and nodded her onto it. "Just in case…what?" I said, painting a layer of phyllo with clarified butter, before laying on another pastry sheet.

"In case David's arrested and I have to go down to the…jail." Her final word was no more than a whisper.

I wasn't sure how much Fran actually knew about the GBI investigation, and I didn't dare tip her off to what Sam had told us. Unwilling to meet her gaze, I concentrated on arranging the chicken, mushroom mixture and feta on the pastry, and acted surprised. "Why would David be arrested?"

Fran dabbed the pastry brush in the butter. I took her hand and guided it to the baking sheet. "Brush a little on that," I said and watched as she carefully coated the baking sheet before I set the folded pastry on it.

"Marcia was murdered," she finally said. "I'm afraid they think David did it. They're asking me all kinds of questions about him and insinuating a lot of ugly things that just aren't true."

"Murdered! Are you sure?"

She slid off the stool and began pacing back and forth in front of the table, five steps left, pivot on her heel, five steps right. "Arsenic."

"She was poisoned? But why would they suspect David?"

"Because, among other things, up until his grant ran out in December, David was working on a method for extracting arsenic, or neutralizing it, in ground water. He's a geologist. It didn't take long for the GBI to figure out that he has access to the stuff."

"But I'm sure other people do, too."

Fran shook her head slowly. The expression in her eyes was beseeching, as though I might be able to come up with a credible scenario wherein another of Marcia's enemies had routine access to arsenic, could have gotten into her house, filled her canisters with poison and disappeared, leaving no trace. But who would have access to the poison? Scientists, chemical manufacturers, maybe exterminators. I groaned inwardly. "The rat poison, he makes it with arsenic, doesn't he?"

Fran nodded miserably. "You see the problem, don't you? The GBI must think they have a strong case. They came around this morning, asking me all kinds of questions about him and us, and his relationship with Marcia."

"What did you tell them?"

Fran hesitated. "I...well—"

"Fran, you have to tell them the truth. Even if you think it will make David look bad, it's going to look worse for both of you if you lie to them and they find out later."

"I haven't lied," she said. "He hasn't seen her since the day he walked out of her house. But don't you think we have a right to a little privacy? Marcia made David's life a living hell for most of their marriage. Doesn't he deserve a little happiness?''

I took a deep breath. ''What are you keeping private, Fran?''

She dropped back onto the stool, briskly stroking her arms, as if she were very cold. Her teeth were chattering, too, as though she were having a major adrenaline rush.

''Wait a minute,'' I said, and grabbed the Metaxa out of Nick's office. Back in the kitchen, I splashed two fingers in a glass and pushed it across the table to her. She took a couple of deep sips before continuing.

''Remember? I told you they had a fight the night she died? She called my place. She wasn't ever supposed to do that because of the restraining order. Anyway, she said she'd decided not to sign the divorce papers. Well, David just hit the ceiling.''

I went back to folding pastry envelopes, trying to ignore the cold knot that was forming in my stomach. ''Fran, did he threaten her?''

She shook her head. ''Not really, no. He told her we had set a date to be married but we'd put it off if we had to and let the courts settle the divorce. He didn't think she'd come out of it as well as what he was willing to give her to keep it out of court.

''I could hear her screaming into the phone, Julia. She was behaving like a mad woman, calling him all kinds of horrible names and accusing him of terrible things.''

''What did he do?''

Fran knocked back the rest of the brandy. ''He was completely calm,'' she said. ''He just explained that it was time she got on with her life. He said that nothing she could do was going to stop our marriage, that one way or another, he and I were going to have a life together.''

I waited, watching her as she toyed with the pastry brush, dabbing drops of butter on the tops of the pastry I'd just prepared, her thoughts clearly somewhere else. At length I prompted her. "Is that all?"

She didn't look up, so I couldn't make out her expression, but her voice had turned bitter. "No. As always, Marcia had to have the last word. Before she hung up the phone, she said, 'She'll never have you.'"

At length I summoned my courage to ask her the question that had been worrying me all day. "Fran, did David go out to the house the night she died?"

She shook her head. "Not to the house, no. But we did go out there. It was so strange, Julia. So unlike her. About an hour later, she called back. We knew it was Marcia from my caller ID. David wouldn't let me answer it, but she left a message on my answering machine. She sounded, well, like anyone else. Her message was very calm and reasonable."

"What did she want?"

Her brows came together in a deep furrow. "She said she knew how much he loved his MG, so she was giving it back to him. She said she'd leave it at the end of the driveway and put the key in the mailbox, but he should pick it up immediately so no one would steal it. I didn't think anyone was going to take it, but I figured she might change her mind, so I took him out there right away."

This information didn't get David off the hook, yet I felt inexplicably relieved to know that there was a legitimate reason he'd been driving the sports car, and that there had been a witness to Marcia's strange turnabout. But there were still so many unanswered questions.

WE STAYED AT THE Oracle a little later than usual that night to set up for the luncheon the next day. As I smoothed out the last tablecloth and carefully set out the silver in the back dining room, I could hear Nick stamping his feet and yelling outside. "What was that all about?" I asked him when he came in.

"Putting out some more poison. Looks like they're finished clearing the land back there," he said. "They've got a couple of temporary spotlights up, and stakes out all over the place. This should take care of the rat problem. I hope," he added doubtfully.

Out in the parking lot, a shadow streaked in front of me just as I got to the car. I scrambled onto the hood of the Honda and let out a squeak, only because the full-bodied scream of terror was stuck somewhere between my vocal chords and my mouth.

"Julia? What's wrong?"

I could only point in mute horror at the creature that raced across the lot toward the Dumpster. Someone had dropped a couple of French fries out of a carryout order and an enterprising rat had claimed them. The spotlight from the clearing behind the restaurant showered light on eight or nine rats vying for position around three paper plates. One glance was too much for me. I was shaking when Nick helped me down off the car and I kept my eyes closed until we'd pulled out of the parking lot.

"We'd better get here early in the morning, Nick. You'll have to clear away the corpses before any of the customers get here." The Buffaloes were a pretty insensitive bunch, but even they might be put off by a pack of dead rats in the parking lot.

# NINE

THE RATS WERE ALL THERE the next morning. Unfortunately, they were still alive. Instead of arriving early, we'd overslept. The Buffaloes would start showing up any minute.

"That's it," Nick said, unlocking the restaurant door. "I'm calling an exterminator right away. I don't know what that stuff was that Fran gave you, but it's no good."

I followed him back into the kitchen as he switched on the lights and turned on the grill, fryers and warmers. "Great, but how are we going to get rid of them in the meantime? Once the noise from that heavy equipment starts, they're not going to go near that building site."

"Bait. Give them a trail to follow, away from us." Nick grabbed a bag of sandwich bread from the grill and headed for the back door. The Pied Piper of Delphi.

He had just gone outside when I turned around to find another rat, although of a different genus and species, coming through the door.

"Morning, Miss Julie," he said as he passed me on his way to his locker. I watched in astonishment as he took out an apron and tied it on, softly singing "Ball in the Jack" under his breath.

"Otis?" I said. "Otis, where the hell have you been?"

I'd like to say I got an answer to that question, an honest answer, that is, but there wasn't time to stick bamboo slivers under his fingernails or administer minor, but painful, electric shocks to the soles of his feet. Besides, I had a feeling that was a job for Spiros. I started the coffee and ran for the phone just as Rhonda followed Sonny Weaver through the door.

"Not today, of all days, Tammy," I said to the voice on the other end of the line. Rhonda stopped in her tracks and waited for me to finish my conversation.

"She's sick. Or so she says," I said, slamming the phone back in the cradle. "Says she twisted her knee bowling last night and can't walk this morning."

"Tammy doesn't bowl. She hates bowling because it breaks her nails," Rhonda said. "She's just punishing you because you wouldn't give her the party. You want me to call her back?"

I thought about it for a minute, but decided as long as Otis was there to help in the kitchen, we'd be all right without Tammy. In fact, we might be better off without her. I certainly wouldn't miss her carping and complaining. I'd have to help Rhonda serve, but that was all right. We were working out a plan when Nick came through the back door, took one look at Otis and exploded in a Greek tirade. I caught him just in time to stop him from firing Otis on the spot.

"*Ohee, Niko mou. Stamata.* We need him today," I said through clenched, smiling teeth. "Tammy's not coming in."

"The other fruit," he muttered. "Rotten, both of them."

Getting breakfast out was no great problem since the Buffaloes never order food. Apparently it interferes with their normal grazing pattern of eating at home before coming to the Oracle to spill coffee and stain the tablecloths. When Spiros arrived, Nick diverted him long enough to explain that we needed Otis at the moment, but he was welcome to exact revenge after lunch. Otis, I noticed, gave Spiros a very wide berth.

So things went along pretty smoothly until almost time for lunch. I was just finishing plating the salads when Fran arrived and peeked in the kitchen door looking for me. I tossed my apron in the linen hamper and followed her to the back dining room. "What's up?" I asked.

"They brought search warrants last night, to David's place

and mine.'' Fran glanced back over her shoulder, where David was calmly chatting with Sonny. He looked relaxed, almost as if he were having a good time. He hadn't come to the aborted breakfast, which was probably a good thing, but I was glad he'd made the effort this time to come see Fran take office in the Chamber of Commerce.

''David looks fine,'' I said. ''What about you?''

Fran rubbed her palms on the soft jersey dress she was wearing. ''As good as you might expect. David keeps telling me we have nothing to worry about. He says so what if they searched everything? We don't have anything to hide. But innocent people are convicted every day, Julia.''

''Well, they must not have found anything or he wouldn't be standing here.''

She shook her head. ''I wish it was that simple. They carried off boxes from my place and David's too, all our medicine bottles, cleaning solutions. Anything they thought looked suspicious, I guess. They even searched David's car and took something out of it.''

''What?''

''I don't know. I couldn't see very well, and they don't tell you anything.''

Most of the guests had arrived and were taking their seats as Mike Blalock stepped up to the podium and tapped a spoon against his glass. ''We'll talk later,'' I whispered, and left Fran to find David and her seat. In the wait station, Nick was nose to nose with Otis.

''The pot with the orange rim is for decaf, Otis. Is that what you made?''

Otis scratched his head and glanced into the trash at crumpled foil packets for both regular and decaf coffee. ''Now, Mr. Nick you gotta be cool about this. They're not gonna know the difference. It all tastes the same.''

Nick took a step closer to Otis. ''They may not know, but I do. Some of those people out there can't have caffeine, Otis. Now dump that and pay attention to what you're doing this time. Make positive you don't switch them, you got that?''

''Make positive. Yes sir, Mr. Nick, I'll make positive,'' Otis replied with a grin. I wanted to peel it off his face, but we were too shorthanded to attack the help. Instead, I followed Rhonda into the kitchen to pick up a tray of entrees. Nick was on my heels and went straight to the warmer for hot rolls. We had the meal on in short order, thus proving that we were better off without Tammy than we were with her. It was a point to remember.

Once everyone was served, Nick and I sat down at the family table in the front dining room to catch our breath while Rhonda took orders from a couple of tables on C deck. We were still sitting there when Sam came in.

''Well, thought you'd want to know we got 'em,'' he said. ''From what the boys at ATF are telling me, Ed Jr. has already rolled over and is telling them everything they want to know and more. Be right back.'' He stepped to the door of the back dining room and glanced in, then came back to the phone at the register and punched in seven numbers.

''He's here,'' was all he said, set the receiver back in its cradle and pulled out a chair.

''Yup, Ed Jr. was makin' the threatening phone calls to the Lowery woman.''

''Why?''

Sam picked up a menu and studied it, his lips moving silently as he reviewed the choices. As frequently as Sam eats at the Oracle, he probably knows the menu better than I do. I stood it as long as I could.

''Sam, why was he threatening her?''

He grabbed an order pad off the register counter and wrote out his selection, tore off the ticket and held it between two fingers for Rhonda to pluck out of his hand as she went by. That done, he turned his attention back to us.

''She'd started building back there, at the back of the lot. If she'd put in guest cabins, they'd have looked right across the brook at the Greer property—''

"And the guests would be suspicious about what they were doing at night," Nick finished for him.

"That's right. Seems like the two of you had it all figured out pretty good, the labeling, distribution. Ed Jr.'s filling in all the gaps. Pretty obliging of him, I'd say."

"What about her murder?" I prompted him.

Sam sighed deeply. "I told you, Julia, GBI's handling that, and they're sure they've got their man. They're heading over here to pick him up. I'll have to detain him if he tries to leave."

My stomach contracted and my mouth felt dry. Poor Fran. She was going to be devastated. And I still just couldn't wrap my mind around the idea of David Lowery, murderer. It didn't fit him at all.

"*Ohee!* No! You can't pick him up here. Haven't we had enough trouble already? None of those people back there—" Nick turned around and pointed vaguely in the direction of the meeting "—none of them will ever come back here. And neither will their friends. You've got to stop them."

"Sam, do they honestly have any evidence, or is he just a convenient scapegoat?"

Sam pulled open a package of crackers and popped one in his mouth. "The GBI don't work like that, Julia. Of course they have evidence, like the jar of arsenic powder they took out of the husband's car, for example." He let that hang in the air while Nick and I tried to absorb it.

"Look," he said, "you got your means, motive and opportunity. What more do you want?"

I had no answer for that. Sam was right, all of those factors were there in abundance. Means: According to him they'd found the arsenic in David's car. Fran had admitted that David used arsenic in his research, and he'd given it to us as a rat poison. Motive: David had every reason to want her out of his life permanently and had as much as said so. Opportunity: He'd gone back to the house that night. Fran might have been lying to protect him when she said Marcia had left the car at the end of the drive. I also knew that David had a house key, because I'd seen it myself. So that completed the trio. But it just didn't feel right.

I was still pondering this puzzle when Rhonda set Sam's plate down in front of him. He stared down in dismay at a leafy green salad and a small chicken breast cooked on the charbroiler. "What's this?"

"You've had your red meat allotment for the week, honey."

"Aw, Rhonda, what makes you think you have the right to switch my order? Isn't anything sacred anymore?" He picked up the salt shaker, but she quickly plucked it out of his hand and dropped it into her pocket.

"You marry a wife and you get a screw—"

"Sam!"

A red tide rose up his neck. "Not that kind of a screw. A jailer, that's what I meant, honey."

"Like that's better," she said, and stomped away.

Sam sprinkled a little pepper over his salad, but I could see his heart wasn't in it. "She sneaks into my office and searches my desk for potato chips and candy bars. You'd think I could keep her out of my office, wouldn't you?"

"Take away her key," Nick suggested, ever ready to help a brother in the fraternity of husbands.

"She doesn't have one, but my secretary's in cahoots with her."

That's when the synapses in my brain finally started firing. "What did you just say?"

"My secretary—"

"No!" I grabbed Nick's arm and squeezed it. "Marcia had a key to David's lab. I saw it. Now think about it, Nick. The rats didn't die."

It only took a beat for him to catch up with me before he turned to Sam. "Were the husband's fingerprints on the bottle in the car?"

Sam shoved a fork full of lettuce in his mouth and dabbed it with his napkin. "Nope, he'd wiped 'em clean. Doesn't matter, though. The DA's gonna figure he's got an airtight case here.'' His gaze volleyed from Nick to me and back to Nick. ''Means, motive—''

''We got that,'' I interrupted. ''But I don't think it's going to be quite as airtight as you think.''

Sam snorted and sliced into his chicken breast. ''Why's that?''

''Because someone else also had means, motive and opportunity.''

''I've worked with these guys on dozens of cases, and I'm telling you they're rarely wrong.''

''Well, *rarely* is not the same as *never.* What could it hurt to check it all out? You have to admit it makes a lot of sense, Sam.''

Sam shook his head. ''Not to me, it doesn't.''

''That's because you never met her,'' Rhonda said.

In the end it was Rhonda who convinced her husband to call the GBI. ''Let me put it this way, honey,'' she said. ''Who figured out the moonshine ring and tipped you off?''

Reluctantly, Sam admitted that we had.

''And who got most of the credit?''

Sam allowed as how he was looking pretty good to the ATF.

''Then don't you think you owe Nick and Julia a favor?'' she said, pushing the phone into his hand. He dialed, spoke to Pete Redmond and explained what he thought, or rather, what we thought.

''No kiddin','' Sam said. ''Well, I'll be damned. Yep, I'll keep him here till you get here.'' Sam handed the phone back to Rhonda and squinted his eyes at us. ''They're on their way over there now. You may be right, but it'd help if we had more evidence.''

''I think I can get that for you,'' I said, hoping that I was right.

In the back dining room, the guests were well into their entrees, and I needed to buy us some time. ''Mike,'' I whispered to the outgoing president, ''I know this is a lot to ask, but can you stall a little on installing the officers and hearing committee reports? We have a minor crisis to deal with.''

He reluctantly agreed. I knew he figured something was wrong in the kitchen, that we'd burned the baklava or something, and I knew that they'd think twice before holding another meeting at the Oracle, but I could only hope that Fran's position on the board would help clear our reputation. I left him and went to Fran and David, explaining what I wanted in a low voice.

''Why?'' Fran whispered.

Why indeed? I didn't want to tell them that Sam was waiting up front and planning to detain David for arrest. I also didn't want to tell them what we thought. In the end, I resorted to an old standby. ''You'll just have to trust me.''

''If you're wrong, Julia, even a bad defense attorney can make me look like Barney Fife—contaminatin' the evidence, involvin' private citizens in a murder investigation. We'll never get into court with it, and the D.A.'s gonna chew me up and spit me out. I might as well start lookin' for a job right now,'' Sam said.

I glanced over at Otis, who was sweeping up shards of a glass he'd just dropped in the wait station. ''Don't worry. We'll have a job for you. How long do you think it will take?''

Sam gingerly wrapped the key ring in the plastic wrap I'd provided for it. ''I'll take it straight into the lab and wait on the results, but you gotta keep him here, no matter how long it takes.''

''You've got his car key, Sam. He's not going anywhere.''

Sam pushed his chair back and stood up, poking a finger in my direction. ''Let me put it this way, Julia. I owe you one, and that's the only reason I'm going along with this. But if he runs, you—'' he turned and pointed an accusing finger at Nick ''—and you had better run with him.''

# TEN

IN THE END, I had to explain to Fran and David why I had needed his keys. Mike Blalock had stalled for a while, but eventually dessert was served, reports were delivered and officers were installed. Sam still wasn't back. By the time he finally got there, Fran had drunk four cups of coffee and was wearing a hole in the dining room tile.

Sam had Pete Redmond in tow. They came through the door looking sober. No one breathed until they had both taken seats at the table with us.

"It's like this," Sam said. "We can't close the case just yet. Red and I can't speak for the D.A., but I doubt that he'll bring charges against you unless some other evidence turns up."

Fran sagged into a chair and took David's hand in hers. "I didn't kill my wife, Sheriff," he said sadly. "I don't know who did, but I didn't."

Sam looked at Redmond, then over at me. "This is Julia's brainchild. Why don't you explain it to him?"

And so I did. Marcia Lowery had been a very sick woman for a very long time. I didn't have to tell David that. He'd lived with it so long, he'd almost forgotten what psychologically healthy people were like until he met Fran. Later, the psychiatric reports that David had released to the D.A. and GBI would confirm what Nick and I suspected. But that day, we could only piece certain things together from the hard evidence.

When David left her, Marcia began hatching plots to bring

him back. Fran said she'd tried just about everything. What none of us considered was that she was desperate enough to make herself sick. Knowing that David wouldn't believe her unless there was hard evidence, Marcia began poisoning herself with arsenic. Her symptoms and complaints were real, and the tests the doctors ordered verified that she was, indeed, quite sick. Not one of them suspected arsenic poisoning because, as Sam had said, the symptoms vary greatly.

"She got it from your lab, David. She knew you had arsenic on hand for your research, so she made a duplicate of your lab key, slipped in and poured it into the bottle the GBI found in the car."

"But the jar was still on the shelf last time I looked."

"That's right," I said. "She replaced the arsenic with something else—"

"The lab's telling us it looks like ordinary kitchen cleanser, Bon Ami, probably, because the color's about right," Redmond put in.

"That's why the rats in the Dumpster didn't die. The poison you made for us had no arsenic in it," Nick added.

"Then she put it in all her staples at home," I said. "It's odorless and tasteless, and she probably wanted to forget about it, so she put it in things she used all the time, sugar, coffee creamer. Anyway, sure enough, she started getting sick. Her doctor ran all kinds of tests on her, all for your benefit. She was losing her hair and getting thinner. She figured that you would have to believe she was seriously ill and wouldn't desert her."

David's expression was stricken, almost as though he really had killed her. "She tried to show me her lab reports, but I wouldn't look at them. She just couldn't believe that I was never coming back to her."

"But of course, eventually she did. The night she died, you told her that you and Fran had set a wedding date. We'll probably never know why, but she must have finally snapped. Do you remember the last thing she said to you on the phone that night?"

It was Fran who answered for him. "She said I would never have you, David. I thought she meant that she was going to get him back," she added, turning to me.

"No. She meant that she was going to see to it that your life together was ruined. If Marcia couldn't have him, she wasn't going to let anyone else have him, either. Obviously, revenge was more important to her than her own life."

David's head came around with a jerk. "Are you saying that—"

"She killed herself, and framed you for her murder," Nick answered. "That's why she didn't call for help. She wanted to die."

Everyone at the table moved uneasily. Fran shuddered. Sam and Red both shook their heads. Despite all their experience, they probably had never seen a case quite like this one. I felt cold all over, and for the first time, I really felt sorry for Marcia Lowery. She had been a terribly sick woman.

"That night, she put together everything she needed to set you up, a letter to her attorney about her will, making it look like you might kill her to prevent losing the property. Lab reports in her desk, very convenient for crime scene techs to find. All the indications would point to arsenic poisoning. Then she hid the arsenic bottle, wiped clean of all fingerprints, in the car. She probably figured you'd find it stuck up under the seat and pick it up. That would put your prints on it for the police to find. Fortunately, they found it before you did."

"And, luckily for you," Red added, "she wasn't so careful in your lab. Her prints are on the arsenic jar."

"Not only that, but she gave you your house key back so the police would be sure you had access to the house to put the poison in her foods. And she gave you the duplicate lab key, so no one would think she'd ever had one."

"Your prints were on the key," Sam put in, "but looks like they got a partial of hers, too. If it goes to trial, you'll want a P.I. to find the locksmith who made the duplicate. He might be able to ID her.''

''But when could she have done all of this?'' David said. ''When did she get into my lab?''

''The day she came to your class and stirred up all the trouble,'' Fran said. ''She went to your lab first, then after she replaced the arsenic she came down to your class. She probably figured that she could tell anyone who saw her around the lab that she was looking for you. But then she'd have to find you, and make sure that everyone remembered why she was in the building, in case anyone said anything to you later. So she created a scene during your lecture.''

''Yes,'' David said sadly. ''They'd all remember it.''

''So you have enough evidence to close the investigation then?'' Fran said, looking from Sam to Redmond.

Sam smiled slowly. ''Well, there's one other little piece of evidence that helps.'' He turned to me. ''You're gonna like this, Julia. And I like it, 'cause you didn't think of it. None of us did. She was careful not to leave any fingerprints on the arsenic bottle in the car. But she left something just as good.''

He reached over and tugged a strand of my hair, pulling it out by the roots. ''Ouch!''

Sam held my hair up in the afternoon sunlight. ''Arsenic causes hair loss,'' he said.

I rubbed my scalp, where he'd plucked the hair. ''Well, she was losing it by the handfuls. She found one in the grits the morning of the breakfast and tried to claim it was mine,'' I said, remembering bitterly her insistence that I was the culprit.

''Yup, she was losing it, all right,'' Sam said. ''When the lab dumped out the arsenic to analyze it, they found a gray hair in the bottle. They've already analyzed it. It belonged to Marcia Lowery,'' he added with a wide grin.

It wasn't proof positive that she'd killed herself. We all knew that David could have contrived to set the whole thing up, from fingerprints on the lab bottle to hair in the arsenic.

But the DA would have to consider one final thing: the psychiatric reports.

Marcia Lowery had been from counselor to counselor, each one confirming what the previous one had said, that she was controlling and manipulative, and needed long-term psychotherapy. She had aroused enmity at the FDA and the Calloway County Health Department, and in every food processing plant and restaurant she'd ever inspected. Yet ironically, in the final analysis, her worst enemy was herself.

After Sam and Red left, Fran and David stayed only long enough to thank us for our help. I watched them walk hand in hand to David's little MG. Before David opened her door, he kissed her and brushed his hand across her cheek tenderly. I wondered if Fran had any lingering doubts, but hoped for both their sakes that she believed in him completely. They pulled out of the parking lot, passing a white Ford on its way in.

"Oh, no," I said, watching as agents Holler and Vine climbed out of their car. Didn't it ever end?

Nick met them at the door and ushered them in. "Mrs. Lambros? Agent Holler, remember?"

"Of course, and Agent Vine," I said, shaking each man's hand in turn.

But Nick had no patience for protocol. "Do you need something from us?"

Agent Vine pulled a small leather notebook out of the breast pocket of his jacket. "We've about wrapped up our case against the Greer family, and by the way, the sheriff says you and your wife were instrumental in breaking it. We appreciate your help."

"No problem," Nick said brusquely.

Agent Holler glanced around the dining room and peeked past me into the wait station. "We need to talk to one of your employees. We don't expect to prosecute him if he cooperates, we just want information on where and how he was obtaining the hootch. Soon as we clear that up, we can remove your names from the suspect list.'' Agent Vine glanced down at his notebook. ''He's your dishwasher?''

''That would be Otis,'' I said, exchanging glances with Nick. We were both going to enjoy this very much.

''I'll call him.'' Nick disappeared through the kitchen door as I ushered the agents to a table. And then, casting prudence to the winds, I asked the question that had hovered on my tongue when I first met them. ''So, where's Wood?''

''Wood?'' Vine said, turning to Holler with a perplexed frown.

''The other agent in your trio, Holler, Wood and Vine?''

Holler chuckled politely and Vine turned a lukewarm smile on Nick, who had reappeared in the wait station door. His fingers were splayed, and his jaw thrust out. He cleared his throat and opened his mouth, then clamped it shut with a snap that would have cracked walnuts. He didn't need to tell me. I already knew.

Otis, aka ''Shadow Man'' and ''The Shade,'' was gone.

# RED OR GREEN?

by Steven F. Havill

Special thanks to David Martinez and Diane Price

# ONE

"HOOOWHUP!" Dale Torrance bellowed, and whatever that language was, the horse under the boy's saddle understood and ducked hard to the left, cutting off a calf's escape. Dale and another of the H-Bar-T hands, Pat Gabaldon, worked the herd counterclockwise around the perimeter of the corral. Every now and then a calf, all gangly and awkward like a teenager, bolted sideways from the flow, figuring who knows what in his little bovine brain.

I stood in the middle of the arena with Herb Torrance, breathing in the sweet tang of red New Mexico dust mixed with manure and horse sweat, feeling the warmth of the late September sun on my shoulders. I'd hit the same count twice with this particular lot—eighty-one heifers, fifty-seven calves, and ten old spinster ladies. The 148 brands were all correct, high on the left flank. I saw no signs of disease—no coughing or diarrhea, no runny or glazed eyes, no hitches in gait, nothing. But then again, I could have inspected any of Herb Torrance's livestock with my eyes closed.

A hundred and fifty years ago, old John Chisum would have shaken his head in wonder at the thought of the government meddling in his ranching affairs, but the West was no longer his West. When Herb Torrance wanted to move his little herd of heifers and their calves to a pasture leased from the Forest Service up on Cat Mesa, the state of New Mexico wanted its cut. And as the state's livestock inspector for the area that included Herb's Posadas County ranch, I made sure that he paid his dues. In this case, the tally included forty cents for each set of four legs, plus a five-dollar service fee, plus a buck a head paid to the New Mexico Beef Council—$212.20 for a permit to move this particular bunch from one little patch of New Mexico to another.

As the herd circled sedately for my inspection, the wind kicked a little—this time just enough to motivate a foam coffee cup lying under one of the pickups parked outside the corral. I saw the flicker of white about the same time Dale Torrance's sorrel gelding did. You wouldn't think that a thousand-pound horse had much to be afraid of, and up until then, he'd been handling the cattle pretty well, oblivious to all those hooves and horns.

Dale had drifted toward the corral side of the herd just as the little foam cup jounced and clattered under the rails. The gelding saw it and promptly came unglued, shying sideways before Dale had time to lift a leg. The animal crashed into one of the fence uprights, crushing Dale's knee against the railroad tie.

A heifer jostled the horse, doubling his panic, and the gelding danced hard to the left, losing Dale in the process. The youngster went down with a crash, a flail of arms and legs. The sorrel planted a hoof on the side of Dale Torrance's right knee and then rocketed off to mix it up with the cattle.

Herb dived into motion a whole lot faster than me as he raced toward his son. Even with his own bad knee turning his sprint into a sort of awkward skipping shuffle, he reached Dale before I could cross through the milling livestock. Pat caught Dale's horse, and the cattle drifted to a confused halt across the way.

By the time I reached him, Dale's face was pasty gray. He'd squirmed under the bottom rail out of the corral, and now lay flat on his back, fists clenched above his head. It didn't take an orthopedic surgeon to see that his right knee was a wreck. His leg was extended, but the lower half pointed off to the west at a bizarre angle. Some of the pain hit him then and he bent at the waist, clawing at his leg with both hands.

"Easy now," his father said. "God damn, that sure as hell's broke, son." He looked up at me as if I had all the answers. I straightened up and glanced around at the options. If they tried to fold Dale into the cab of one of the pickups, he'd have to bend the wreckage of that knee. His mother's old Chrysler was parked in front of the Torrances' house, but as an ambulance, that wouldn't be much better.

"Let's put him in the back of the Blazer," I said. "Keep that leg straight. Find something to use as padding." I didn't give Herb time to discuss it, but set off at my version of a jog. By the time I'd brought the little truck around, they'd found a wealth of saddle blankets and a couple of pillows from Dale's trailer across the yard. With the back seat folded, we had a nice flat spot, and the three of us lifted him in.

"I'll tell the hospital we're on the way," I said. "Herb, you might want to ride in back there with him."

In another minute, we were southbound on the washboards and potholes of County Road 14. For every one I avoided, three others pummeled the Blazer's stiff suspension, prompting a symphony from the back. After seven miles of torture, we thumped across the cattle guard and pulled out on the smooth asphalt of State Highway 56, twenty-three miles southwest of Posadas General Hospital.

"You doing okay back there?" I asked.

"I think he's passed out," Herb said.

"Well, that's probably a good thing, then." By the time I drove by the Broken Spur Saloon, we were creeping up on eighty-five. Traffic was nonexistent, and for another seven miles we had clear sailing. As I rounded the long, sweeping bend around the base of the mesa at Moore, I saw sun flash on paint. By the time I was close enough to see that it was a Sheriff's Department cruiser parked in front of the abandoned mercantile building, the red lights on top had already blossomed.

I picked up the cell phone and punched the auto-dial. When dispatcher Gail Torrez answered, I could hear radio traffic in the background.

"Gail, this is Gastner," I said, and then didn't give her time to respond. "I'm northbound on Fifty-Six. Tell the young hotrod behind me that I've got a kid with a wrecked knee that needs a hospital."

There are some perks that come with being a has-been. When the has-been's life includes thirty-five years as deputy, undersheriff, and finally sheriff of Posadas County, some of those county doors remain open.

"Yes, sir," Gail said, and ten seconds later the red lights flicked off as the white Ford Crown Victoria climbed down off my back bumper.

"Deputy Collins wants to know if you need an escort, sir."

"That's not necessary. But do me a favor. Call the ER and tell 'em we're inbound. ETA about twelve minutes."

"You got it. Who owns the knee?"

"Dale Torrance. His horse stepped on him. It's a mess."

"Yes, sir. Stop in when you've got a minute. Don't be such a stranger."

"If I do that, you'll put me to work." I slowed as we overtook a large RV with Ohio plates. "Talk to you later. And thanks."

I switched off and glanced in the rearview at Herb. His gray eyes were worried, but he looked heavenward when he caught my glance, and the crows-feet at the corners of his eyes deepened. "He's going to end up walkin' just like his old man," he said.

"Maybe not that bad," I said, not believing a word of it. Knees that pointed sideways never returned to as good as new.

Far behind us, Deputy Collins had slowed and U-turned to return to his speed trap. The kid had been my last hire in the final months before Robert Torrez took office. Like most young cops, if he could get three or four years under his belt without making any real bonehead mistakes, he'd probably make a good deputy. But by then, he'd want to move on to some department that paid more than a street person in Albuquerque makes in a good year.

Three miles later, with Dale starting to groan in the back, I glanced in the mirror and saw a kaleidoscope of lights long before my dulled ears heard the wail of the siren.

"Jesus," I said, and flinched to one side as the deputy's car charged by.

"Thought for a minute he was after you again," Herb said.

"Late for his doughnut," I said, and watched as Collins threw the heavy sedan into the sweeping curve just south of the interstate exchange on the south edge of Posadas. "He's not careful, he's going to collect a couple pedestrians."

I slowed for the same turn and found the cell phone again. This time, it rang for half a dozen rings before Gail Torrez answered, as if her long-range intuition told her it was me calling again, and this time just out of an old dog's curiosity.

"Gastner again, Gail. What's the call?"

"Sir, we've got an unattended death over on 1228 Ridgemont."

The address rang a bell. "You have a name yet?"

"Yes, sir. Phil Borman called us. He said his father-in-law had a heart attack."

I damn near drove off Grande Avenue. *His father-in-law* was George Payton, my oldest friend in Posadas County. For years, we joked about who was going to kick off first. The last time I'd been in the hospital for something that turned out to be nothing more serious than a gall stone, George and I had actually made a dollar bet without pausing to worry about how the winner was going to collect. Our string of bad habits was suitably long. At seventy-nine, George was seven years older than me, but we'd each had valve jobs, bypasses, reamed carotids and all those wonderful things that a life of rich food and smoke made possible. George accused me of cheating when I quit smoking—he never drifted too far from a good cigar.

My foot eased off the accelerator as if I'd been charging to help George rather than the busted kid in the back.

"So it's George?" The question came out a little feeble, and I could hear the sympathy in Gail Torrez's voice.

"Yes, sir. Estelle's over there now."

"Thanks," I said. "You called the hospital?"

"That's affirmative, sir. They're expecting you."

"Thanks, sweetheart," I said. I tossed the phone on the seat and glanced in the rearview mirror. "You remember George Payton?"

"Sure I do," Herb said.

"He just died."

A brief moment of silence passed between us. "Well," Herb said, and let it go at that. I slowed for the red light at Bustos and Grande, saw that no one was coming, and slipped through. In another minute, we were backing up to the emergency room door on the lower floor. Dale Torrance had another couple of minutes of torture before a pretty nurse jabbed some sleep into his arm.

By then I was headed toward 1228 Ridgemont. A bet's a bet.

# TWO

I SWUNG ONTO Ridgemont from Sixth Street and saw the cavalcade of vehicles, including an ambulance backed into the driveway. The young deputy who had rocketed past me a few minutes before now stood in the street. He held up a hand when he saw me approaching. I rolled down my window.

"How about right in front of the undersheriff's unit, sir," Deputy Dennis Collins said. "We're getting kind of a snarl here." I glanced around at the congregation of neighbors, emergency med folks and gawkers. Collins patted my Blazer's door sill and pointed ahead toward a vacant spot by the curb.

I saw the undersheriff of Posadas County standing on the front step of George Payton's home, holding the front door with one hand while she talked to someone standing inside, hidden in the shadows. She saw me pull up, nodded, and started down the sidewalk to meet me.

My oldest daughter, Camille, calls Undersheriff Estelle Reyes-Guzman my "fifth kid." Camille is only half joking when she says that, and she says it with as much affection as if it were true. In fact, I've known Estelle since she was sixteen, when she first came to the United States from rural Mexico to finish her high school education. With the typical old man's preoccupation with things in the past, I found myself thinking that Estelle Reyes-Guzman hadn't changed much in the twenty-three years since then. Dark-olive complexion, raven hair cropped a little closer now with an errant strand of steel gray here and there, eyebrows that knit over the bridge of her nose when she was perplexed—her fine features reminded me of the Aztecs.

She caught the door of my Blazer and held it for me as I hauled myself out. "Hey, sir," she said soberly. Sometime decades before, she'd settled on "sir" as the appropriate all-purpose name for me, alternating that with *padrino* when I became godfather to her two urchins. I could count on one hand the number of times she'd called me "Bill," or "Mr. Gastner," or "Sheriff."

"Has Dr. Perrone been here?" I asked.

"Not yet."

I sighed and shook my head. "I'm not ready for this," I said. Estelle slipped her arm through mine with a sympathetic squeeze. "Who found him?" I asked.

"His son-in-law," Estelle said. I knew Phil Borman only casually, enough to greet him by name on the street.

"Maggie knows?"

"She's inside."

I took another deep breath, more to fortify myself for Maggie Payton Borman, George's daughter and only child—and one of those "A" personality types who always made me feel tired. Now in her forties, Maggie hadn't lost any of her spunk. She ran the High Mesa Realty in Posadas with her new husband Phil, managing to make potential home or business buyers believe that the village of Posadas was on the verge of growing like kudzu, rather than the dried-out desert runt that it was.

Linda Real, the Sheriff's Department's civilian photographer, met us at the door. An inch or so shorter than Estelle and tending toward chubby, Linda's passion, besides Deputy Thomas Pasquale with whom she lived, was shooting enough film to keep stock prices up. She greeted me and then lifted one of the cameras that was slung on her shoulder. "I'm finished until the coroner gets here," she whispered to Estelle.

I looked past Linda into the house. George had lived simply, with a fondness for anything related to the firearms industry. His Sportmen's Emporium had been a fixture in Posadas for almost forty years before he'd sold the business when the millennium turned. The young man who'd bought it had streamlined the operation, cleared out a lot of the junk, raised prices to current levels, and lost two-thirds of his customers, closing within the year.

An enormous cartridge collection hung on the living room wall facing the street. Each cartridge, from tiny .22s to things designed to batter elephants, was labeled and mounted on a painted background of Cat Mesa. Poster ads for firearms ringed the room, with paintings reminiscent of Russell or Remington painted on sheet metal—except these were originals, not the mass-produced replicas.

Nothing in the living room reminded me of George Payton's wife Clara, who'd died on daughter Maggie's eighteenth birthday, except the battered upright piano on the east wall. With his wife gone and his daughter headed off to college, George had sold their fancy home behind Pershing Park and pulled into himself, making do in this tiny, eight-hundred-square-foot place. He'd brought the piano with him, even though he didn't know middle C from Adam.

Maggie Payton Borman was standing beside the piano, gazing out the window. She didn't have much of a view, just the neighbor's carport and a tarp-covered boat on a small trailer. I doubt very much if she saw either one. Off to her right, a yellow Sheriff's Department ribbon had been stretched across the kitchen door, a jarring intrusion.

She turned, saw me, and held out both arms. We met in the center of the room and she hugged me for a long time, not saying a word. When she finally realized that I needed to breathe, she relaxed her hold just enough to be able to draw back and look me in the eye. A good-looking woman, tending to be stocky like her father and with the same honest, open face, Maggie was the kind of person who bustled around, taking charge and getting things done. But now she'd been hauled up short, with nothing to do but stay out of the way.

"Maggie, I'm sorry," I said, and the words sounded empty. "I was supposed to have lunch with your dad today, too. A bunch of damn cows got in the way."

She shook her head. "That's the way of it," she said. "Sacred Thursday. Dad would have liked that."

"What happened, do you know?"

Maggie sighed deeply, and I saw her eyes flick toward the yellow ribbon. "As near as we can tell, he sat down to lunch, took a few bites, and then had a seizure." Tears misted her eyes. "I wish I'd been here, but the world turns, you know. I had to show a house, and that dragged on and on. I managed to sneak away just long enough to pick up dad's lunch at the Don Juan, and then another call came in. I had folks waiting for me at the office, and Phil agreed to play delivery boy. I was still with customers when Phil came back over to check on Dad...." Her words trailed off. She wiped her eyes by leaning into me and burying her face on my shoulder.

I patted her back, not knowing what else to do. Estelle moved like a dark shadow across the living room, ducked under the yellow tape and stopped, her back to us and blocking the door to the kitchen. She glanced back at me, sympathy on her face mixed with something more. She waited for me to join her.

"Where's Phil?" I asked, and Maggie snuffled a little and pulled away. She fished for a tissue in the pocket of her stylish skirt and dabbed at her eyes.

"He's outside," she said. "Do you need to talk with him?"

"No, no," I said quickly. She'd said it as if I were still Sheriff of Posadas County. I didn't *need* to talk with anyone, unless George had secreted a herd of cattle somewhere...and that was easily imagined, since he owned little plots of land here and there all over the county. I knew I'd spend a lot of time in the next few days missing George and his garrulous, often profane outlook on life. The world would march on, a little poorer.

"Let me talk with Estelle for a little bit," I said, and Maggie nodded.

"Sure," she said. A hint of a smile touched her handsome face. "She's so thoughtful, isn't she? And thorough."

"Oh, yes," I replied. I always felt better when I was in Estelle Reyes-Guzman's presence. It was only logical that others would feel the same way.

"You go ahead," Maggie said, and turned away.

Estelle didn't move as I approached. I didn't need to be prepared for what was in the kitchen, she had to know that. After twenty years in the military and almost thirty-five in civilian law enforcement, I'd seen enough final moments that I was adequately armored, even if the departed was one of my oldest friends. Just her hesitation put me on edge.

"I'm a little puzzled," she said in that husky whisper that traveled no farther than my ears. She lifted the yellow tape for me and I stepped into the kitchen.

It would have been nice if George Payton had just drifted away in his sleep—at least I *think* it would have been. After seeing altogether too many of them, I still have reservations about final moments.

George was seated on the floor, back against the door that concealed the kitchen sink's innards. His left leg was stretched out straight, right leg flexed at the knee. His right hand lay on the linoleum beside his right thigh. His left hand clutched a brown paper bag to his chest, resting on his ample midriff. His head hung, nestled in his various chins, eyes and mouth open.

The position was one that he might have sagged into had the seizure struck just as he bent over to toss the bag in the under-sink trash.

One chair was pushed away from the table. On the place mat rested a familiar glass serving dish, its plastic snap-on top placed carefully toward the center of the table.

"Thursday," I said, and took a tentative step toward the

table. I knew exactly where the serving dish came from, and knew exactly what savory aroma had wafted up when George pried off the top—a green chile Burrito Grande from the Don Juan de Oñate Restaurant. "And that's not really fair."

"Sir?"

I thrust my hands in my pockets. "He didn't get to finish." Two-thirds of the Burrito Grande remained in the dish.

"Was this a usual thing?"

"What, the burrito?" I turned to glance at her. "Sure. 'Sacred Thursday,' George called it. He's had this same lunch most Thursdays for the past twenty years, give or take."

"That's a fancy takeout, sir."

I nodded. "The restaurant starting packing up George's burrito for him like this a while ago, when George couldn't make it to the restaurant anymore. Fernando couldn't bring himself to mash it all together in one of those plastic boxes. Not for George, anyway. Once in a while, I'd pick it up for him, and we'd have lunch here together. We even talked about doing that today, but I got crossways with work."

I saw the little wrinkles deepen at the corners of Estelle's eyes, but she refrained from making a comment about my eating habits. Unlike George, I rarely let the day of the week stand between me and a Burrito Grande, or the time of day, for that matter. George had had more discipline than me, I guess, saving the treat, always anticipating Thursdays. So much for moderation.

"Does the dish belong to the Don Juan?"

"Sure. Maggie washes it and takes it back when it's convenient. George didn't get out much the past few months."

I saw the fork on the floor, and took another step around the table. A glass had been knocked off the table on the other side, shattering and splashing red wine across the linoleum.

Estelle knelt beside the body, her hands folded. "The bag is from the restaurant," she said. She cocked her head, looking at the crumpled paper. I knew without looking what the inscription on the bag said: From the Don Juan de Oñate: This ain't for no doggy.

I stood quietly by the table, looking across at George. He'd felt the first thunder of the seizure, dropped his fork, spasmed out and knocked over the tumbler of wine. Rearing to his feet, he'd made it around the table. Maybe he'd already spun away into the gray void when his left hand reached out and grabbed, connecting with the bag. In the throes of the final cardiac convulsion, he'd slid down, coming to rest in the tired plumber's position.

"Odd thing to grab," Estelle said.

I sighed. "That's the trick with unattended deaths, sweetheart. They're unattended. Sometimes it's hard to fit the pieces back together."

"I'm surprised he didn't reach out toward the telephone," she said. The small cordless phone rested in its recharging cradle under the first cupboard, beside the toaster.

"No time," I said. "Just boom. He had time to get out of his chair, and that was just about it."

She nodded, rose to her feet, and stepped away from the body. She circled the table, glanced out through the door toward the living room, and when she was standing immediately beside my shoulder, murmured, "I'll be interested to know what caused the heavy discharge of mucous."

I hadn't knelt to scrutinize George Payton's face, but was ready to take her word for it.

"Maybe the Don Juan's chile was a little hotter than usual," I said. I'd sat through more than my share of those dishes, pausing occasionally to mop my forehead or blow my nose as the fumes from the select Hatch green chile blew out the sinuses.

I turned and regarded Estelle, lifting my head a bit so I could bring her into bifocal focus. As usual, I was unable to read past those dark eyes. It was obvious that something was bothering her, though. When a very senior citizen dropped dead of circumstances that all screamed natural causes, we generally didn't string a crime scene tape to close off the room and take a thousand and one careful photographs—unless something tipped us off.

"Let me know what I can do to help," I said. "I'm going to go pay my respects to Phil." She nodded and accompanied me as far as the yellow tape.

Phil Borman was facing the closed garage door, leaning against the front fender of George Payton's old Buick station wagon. He was off somewhere in his musings, and didn't hear me until I was just a step or two behind him. He turned then, left arm across his pin-striped shirt, right arm propped on left, cigarette held a couple inches from his mouth.

I knew that George Payton had thought highly of his son-in-law—that was enough of an endorsement. "Maybe Maggie will smell the goddamn roses once in a while now," George had grumbled to me at the wedding two years before. Maggie and Phil had settled down to carving out their own real estate business in earnest, with satellite offices in both Deming and Lordsburg. So much for the roses.

Phil Borman unfolded his arms and straightened up. "Refresh my memory," he said, extending his hand.

"Bill Gastner," I said. "An old, old friend of George's."

"Ah."

"I'm sorry."

"Well," Phil said, nodding, "So am I, you know? He was getting on, but he still enjoyed life. I'm going to miss him."

"Me, too."

"Hunting is always something I thought I wanted to do, but never had time." He grinned, showing irregular, strong white teeth. "George took it upon himself to perform an attitude adjustment on me. Now I sell real estate when I can find the time away from hunting."

I laughed. "I bet." I watched him grope another cigarette out of his shirt pocket. He held it for a long time before lighting up. "You were the one who found him?"

He nodded slowly. "What a turn. You know, the instant I saw him sitting there, I knew he was gone." He looked over at me. "I called 911, and I don't think it was more than four minutes before the paramedics were here. He'd been dead long enough there wasn't any point in trying resuscitation."

"He was all right before, though? When you dropped by with the food? No signs of anything on the horizon?"

Borman hunched his shoulders helplessly. "I saw him last night, too, and he was just fine. Well...just fine by his standards. And then today, he was chipper as all hell." He grimaced. "But that's the way it happens a lot of times, I guess." He snapped his fingers.

"He'd been living on a third of a heart for a long time, Phil."

"That's what Maggie said."

I turned at the sound of another vehicle and saw Dr. Alan Perrone's dark green BMW glide to a stop.

"I don't understand the procedure, I guess," Phil Borman said.

"What procedure is that?"

"It's got to be so hard on Maggie, her dad just lying in the kitchen like that all this time. I don't know why it's taken them so long to move him."

"The coroner has to earn his salary," I said.

"I suppose so. It's hard, though."

"Any time there's an unattended death like this, things slow down a little bit."

"Even when the cause of death is obvious?"

I shrugged and reached out to pat him on the elbow. Nothing I could say would make him feel any better. Alan Perrone, the assistant State Medical Examiner, hustled up the sidewalk, and I raised a hand in greeting. "Estelle's inside, Doc."

He paused in midhustle and cocked his head. "You suspecting mad cow disease?" George Payton would have chuckled at that, so I did, too. The physician grimaced at his own feeble attempt at humor, and disappeared inside the house.

"What'd he mean by that?" Phil Borman asked.

"Just a very bad joke," I said. "He and George and I go

# THREE

I WENT BACK INSIDE and saw Maggie and Linda Real sitting comfortably together on the old, deep sofa by the front living room window. Maggie beckoned and Linda got up to make room for me. I sank down into the cushions knowing that actually escaping the comfort of the sofa was going to take some determination and planning.

In the kitchen, Estelle Reyes-Guzman and Dr. Alan Perrone were in intense conversation, but their voices were whispers and murmurs—well out of range of my sorry hearing, and apparently Maggie's, too.

"Oh, my," Maggie said wearily. She folded her hands on her knees and looked at me. "So how have you been?" I knew exactly what she meant, as in *Are you next?*

"One day at a time," I said. "I was just out at Torrance's, counting cattle."

"You know, I haven't seen Herb in months," Maggie said.

"That's the way it goes. Time slips by."

She nodded and regarded her hands, deep in thought. "Dad had some land out that way that he was going to sell to Herb." She shrugged, and I could see the tears starting again. She ignored them, letting them course down her cheeks unchecked. She smiled, and the crease in her cheek redirected the running water around the corner of her mouth. "Remember W. C. Fields?"

The question took me off guard. "Ah...he and I weren't close," I said.

She reached over and patted my knee. "No, that's not what

I meant. Remember that when he died they discovered he had all kinds of accounts in various banks around the country? Or at least that was the story? Nobody knows for sure how many. I used to kid Dad about his land deals being like W.C. There must be twenty or thirty parcels that he's picked up over the years. It's going to be a real mess. About half the time, he'd file the deed the way he was supposed to. The rest of the time, it was just jotted down on a scrap of paper or filed away somewhere in his head."

I stretched back against the thick cushions, trying to ease a kink in my back. "He tried to get me to partner with him a time or two," I said. "I'm not much of a speculator, I guess. 'Bill, they ain't makin' any more land,' he'd always say. 'It's a good deal, Bill.'" I chuckled. "Maybe it was. I don't know."

"I never had much success selling you anything, either," Maggie said.

"I have all I need, I guess."

She nodded and picked at a well-fortified fingernail. "He thought a lot of you."

"It was mutual," I said.

Through the open doorway, I saw Estelle stand up and nod in response to something that Alan Perrone said. She ducked under the yellow tape and detoured toward us.

"We're almost finished," she said. "Are you all right?" Maggie had finally dived into the tissue, and was working to restore order to her face.

"We're reminiscing," she said. "Can I help with anything?"

"No, ma'am. Thanks." For a moment she stood there, then turned and left the house with Linda Real in tow.

"What a gorgeous creature," Maggie said.

"Yes, she is," I agreed.

"How's the clinic going for them? What a venture that is."

Estelle's husband, Francis, had opened a medical clinic in partnership with Alan Perrone, building the hi-tech facility on property behind my house on Guadalupe Terrace, south of the interstate. Posadas Health Center included offices for three physicians, a pharmacy, and a soon-to-open dental office.

"They've had their challenges," I said. "Like anything. But it's what they've wanted, and I think it's quite a plus for the community."

"That's for sure. Realtors everywhere burned you in effigy for giving away that land," she said, but a soft smile told me I'd been as forgiven as I was ever going to be.

"Yeah, well," I said. "I didn't need it, they did. It was that simple." I grinned. "I had ulterior motives, Maggie. It gets kinda lonely out there. This way, I wound up with just the neighbors I wanted." She nodded at the logic of that. "Kind of like your dad deciding to give that lot behind the Public Safety Building to the county for the new office wing. He didn't need it, they did...." I shrugged.

Maggie looked heavenward. "And I don't know if dad ever finished with that or not." She shook her head wearily.

Estelle reappeared, lugging the large black suitcase that lived in the trunk of her county car. "May I talk with you for a few minutes, sir?" she asked, pausing on her way to the kitchen.

"Sure. Do I have to get up?"

She smiled. "Yes, sir." She held out a hand. I outweighed her by an embarrassing tonnage, but she was surprisingly strong.

"I'd make some coffee," Maggie said, "but everything's in the kitchen."

"Not to worry," I said. I followed Estelle under the yellow tape, and to my surprise, she closed the door behind us.

"How are you doing?" Perrone asked. He wore thin plastic gloves, and didn't offer to shake hands.

"I'm fine," I said, feeling a little rise of annoyance. "George here owes me a dollar." Perrone looked askance at me, but didn't ask what I'd meant.

Estelle knelt at the suitcase, opened it, and withdrew a selection of plastic evidence bags and a marker.

Perrone leaned against the counter, both hands held in front of him like a freshly scrubbed physician, watching. "What puzzles me," he said, and beckoned me closer. I stepped around the table. "What puzzles me," he repeated in a near whisper, "is the allergic reaction we see here."

"You've lost me."

"Anaphylactic shock is really pretty characteristic," he said, and looked up at me. "Somebody is stung by a wasp or something, and reacts. If the allergy is acute, the whole system can crash." He spread his hands apart again. "In some ways, the symptoms can mimic a massive coronary—and I suppose the end result is the same...the system can't get air, the pulse races, things go from bad to worse."

"You're saying George had an allergic reaction?"

"I would say so."

"He had a bad heart." I remembered that I was talking to George's personal physician, and added, "I mean, you know that better than I."

Perrone nodded slowly. "*Bad* is an understatement, too. An allergic reaction is really dangerous for someone in George's physical condition." He bent down beside George's corpse. "The massive mucous discharge is consistent with an allergic reaction," he said. He had moved the body so it was lying on its back, parallel to the sink counter, and when he pried open George's mouth, I looked away.

"Bronchial spasm makes it impossible to swallow," he said. "The choke reflex is going to trigger all sorts of responses, including that feeling of desperation." He glanced up at me. "All of that happening in someone with George's bad health is as dangerous as a loaded gun with a hair trigger. In this case, his damaged heart couldn't take the strain."

"So you're saying he started to choke, is that it? And that triggered the heart attack."

"Good a guess as any." He resumed his examination of the victim's mouth. "There's still food in the mouth and esophagus. We'll find out about the airway. That's how quick and massive the whole scenario was.'' He leaned back, regarding the corpse for a moment, then pushed himself to his feet. ''Estelle tells me this is a meal that George ate on a regular basis?''

''Sure. Once a week, minimum.''

''Huh. He never mentioned it to me.''

''Some things are best withheld from the family physician,'' I said, and Perrone smiled dutifully.

''Did he have any food allergies that you know about?''

I shrugged helplessly. ''You'd have to ask Maggie. But all the times I ate with him, there was never mention of anything. He loved Mexican food the way Fernando Aragon made it. He loved a big tumbler of red wine with his meals.'' I turned and looked at the table, the remains of the Burrito Grande undisturbed. ''He's been eating this same thing for twenty years, Alan. He stayed clear of red chile because it irritated his gut. The green didn't.''

''Until today,'' he said. ''Then something kicked his system. That's for sure.''

Estelle slipped past me. Hands gloved in thin latex, she slid the glass serving dish into an evidence bag and sealed it. I watched as she labeled it in fine, precise lettering.

''You think there's something in the food that he reacted to, then?'' I said.

''It's possible.''

''Maybe a wasp or something got in the house,'' I said.

''Maybe that, too,'' Perrone said. ''Although to the best of my recollection, George never discussed allergies like that with me. Around here, juniper pollen bothers about ninety percent of the population—George could have stood in the middle of a blooming juniper and not even sneezed. Nah...we'll take a good hard look at that—'' he nodded at the food ''—and at the stomach and esophageal contents. Maybe something will turn up.'' He turned a full circle, scanning the room. ''I'll leave you to it,'' he said. ''You want me to give the go-ahead to the EMTs?''

"Sure," Estelle said.

In another couple of minutes, the silent, white-sheeted figure of George Payton was packed aboard the gurney for his final ride. Estelle held the kitchen door for them, then closed it carefully and went back to work.

The fork George had been using went into a separate bag, and then she cracked open the sealed plastic wrap around a fair-size test tube. She methodically collected more red wine from the floor spill than I would have thought possible, sealed the tube and labeled it. The glass shards went into their own bag. She was filling in that label when she glanced up and saw me watching.

"Everything but the kitchen sink," I said.

"I checked that already, sir," she said. "The garbage can underneath is empty, with a fresh liner."

I stepped to one side and tipped open the small door under the sink. Sure enough, the blue plastic liner wasn't soiled by as much as a coffee ground. I let the door close.

"Do you want to ride with me to Las Cruces, sir?" Estelle asked.

"Maybe. Why?"

She smiled, instantly looking ten years younger. "I was hoping someone at the state lab owed you some favors that you'd never collected." She hefted the plastic-wrapped serving dish containing the Burrito Grande. "As soon as Alan has something for me, I want to run the specimens down to the lab in person."

"That's possible," I said.

"I just hate to have this get all tied up with the weekend," she said. "And that's what will happen without some special delivery."

"Consider it done," I said.

# FOUR

MAGGIE PAYTON BORMAN reached out a hand toward me, and I took it. The yellow ribbon blocking the door was down, the kitchen empty, her father gone. Just like that. Maggie's husband stood in the open front door, smoking, looking down the street after the ambulance. I heard him talking to someone, a neighbor maybe.

"There's something apropos in all this," Maggie said.

"How so?"

She sighed. "Dad wouldn't have wanted to wait around until he didn't have the strength to lift a fork. And he saw that was coming. After that last little stroke in April, and he lost the use of his left hand..." She looked up at me, tears in her eyes.

"Maybe so," I said.

She shook her head and turned in time to see Estelle drop the small evidence bag holding George's fork into her briefcase. For the first time, Maggie saw the serving dish with its plastic lid, now encased in its own plastic cocoon.

"I was going to clean all that up...." she said.

Estelle smiled sympathetically. "That's all right, Mrs. Borman."

"It's routine to run some basic lab tests, Maggie," I said. "We'll all be just a little more comfortable when we know what triggered the episode."

She turned and looked at me, puzzled. "Well, that's certainly all right," she said. "I didn't know what the procedure was. Will you see that the serving dish is returned to the Don Juan?"

"You bet," I said, not surprised that Maggie was concerned. It's trivia that sometimes gets us through tough moments. "And Maggie, if there's anything I can do," I added, resorting to the well-worn exit line, "you let me know."

I helped Estelle lug her equipment out to her car. With no spectacle to watch, most of the neighbors had gone about their business. I stood on the sidewalk, hands thrust in my pockets, probably looking as depressed as I felt.

"Sir," Estelle said, slamming down the trunk of her car, "I'll give you a call as soon as Dr. Perrone has something for me." She glanced at her watch. "I'd like to leave by three at the latest. That way, we'll have everything at the lab in Cruces by a little after four or so."

"Okay. I was going to wander over to the hospital for a few minutes and see how the Torrance kid is doing."

"Bad break?"

"About as bad as a knee can get," I said.

She grimaced. "Wish them well for me," she said, and opened the car door. "See you midafternoon, sir."

I raised a hand in salute, still unmotivated to leave. Estelle Reyes-Guzman was headed right back to work; Deputy Dennis Collins had already left. That's what the young do when someone older dies—pause a minute or two and then get on with life. Us older duffers react a little differently, though. Losing one of my oldest, closest friends had punched out some of my stuffing, and I wasn't ready just yet to draw a line through George Payton's name and say, "Oh, well...life goes on," even though I knew damn well that it did.

I ambled back toward my Blazer, in no hurry to do anything in particular. Despite the lunch hour winding down toward one o'clock, I wasn't hungry. That's how deep the spiral of a blue funk can get. I had intended to drive to the hospital, but I called instead from the cellular phone in my Blazer—and saved myself a trip. Dale Torrance had been transferred to Las Cruces so that an orthopedic surgeon could whack away at his crushed knee. I switched off the phone, relieved. The hospital wasn't good therapy for me just then, anyway. I'd be apt to glance through some door left ajar and see someone else I knew, withered and old, intubated and drugged senseless.

The sun felt good streaming through the window of the truck and I sat for a few minutes, finishing the paperwork for Herb Torrance's livestock transportation permit. It was that sort of mindless attention to bureaucratic detail that allowed my mind to roam free, picking at this and that, remembering this and that. That mixed with old habits—the habits gained from a lot of years spent minding other people's business.

I tossed the clipboard with Herb's permit on the passenger seat. I'd remember to finish dotting the *i*'s and crossing the *t*'s later.

The county building parking lot was its usual empty self. I pulled in and parked in the spot reserved for District Judge Lester Hobart, handy to the back door by the court administrator's office. It wasn't the court that interested me just then. I entered and walked past the first fleet of offices and turned left under the sign for the county assessor.

Why anyone would want Jack Lauerson's job, I didn't know. *Tax* is a four-letter word to most folks, myself included...and the guy who decides how much your house and property is worth so the mill levy can lambaste it accordingly must have skin like a rhino's. I don't imagine that he saw many folks step through the door of his office just to say, "God, Jack...you did such a *great* job assessing my house! Thanks a lot! Can I buy you lunch?"

Lauerson's secretary, a gal who'd gone to school with my youngest son and who still looked like a teenager thirty years later, beamed at me.

"Hi, Sheriff," she chirped. "What's up?"

"Not much," I said, trying to remember her name. The plaque on the desk said Wanda something, but I couldn't read the last name. "Is Jack around and about?"

She swiveled her chair to scan the big, open office, and at the same time I saw Lauerson over by a huge file, one of those things with banks of four-foot-wide drawers for maps.

"Caught him. Can I come around?"

"Of course, you can." She beamed again. I skirted the counter, dodged desks and cabinets and drafting tables, and arrived at Jack Lauerson's elbow without crashing into anything.

Hands deep in the third drawer from the bottom, he looked at me over the tops of his half glasses as I approached.

"Did you bring the doughnuts?" he asked as he extracted a hand from the door and extended it. His grip was firm and brief. His tiny waistline didn't look as if many doughnuts crossed its path. He patted the maps back into place and stood, nudging the drawer closed with his foot.

"What's up?"

"I need some information, if you've got a minute."

He steepled his hands together in front of his chest and bowed slightly. "Absolutely." Then, brightening, he added, "Actually, it's just about time for lunch." He glanced at his watch. "Is this a quick thing, or a long-winded thing, Sheriff?"

"I'm not sheriff anymore, Jack. And it's an I-don't-know kind of thing."

He settled back on the corner of a handy desk, crossed his arms and cocked his head. "So."

"You have a listing of all county taxpayers, I assume."

He smiled indulgently at the stupid question. "Surely."

"If a taxpayer owns more than one piece of property, are they all listed under his name somewhere?"

"Yes. Actually, property is listed, or mapped, in a variety of ways, Bill. But yes, we have a master listing that's always being updated." One eyebrow drifted up. "What was it you were looking for, exactly?"

"Suppose I wanted to inventory George Payton's holdings. How hard is that to do?"

"It's not," Jack said. "A real basic part of our database

is filed by the name of the property owner.'' He stood and crooked a finger. ''Come.''

One of the draftsmen looked up as we passed and grinned at first Jack and then me. ''Don't mind the mess,'' Jack said when we reached the landfill that was his desk. A vast collection of neatly rolled maps and documents flooded the surface. The area immediately around the computer's mouse pad was clear and the assessor sat and pulled himself up to the keyboard. ''How's old George doing these days?'' he asked.

''Not well. He died about two hours ago.''

Jack swiveled around and looked at me as if I were telling a bad joke.

''Apparently a heart attack,'' I added. ''He was eating an early lunch and just keeled over. I just came from there.''

''Well, that's too bad. I'm sorry to hear that.'' He turned back to the computer screen. Life goes on. ''That's going to make for some interesting changes, isn't it?''

''Yes, it is.''

''Here's how they're listed.'' He scrolled down the fine print. ''Get to the *P*'s here. Patterson, Patterson, Patterson...there's a lot of them...Payne, Payton, George. Here we are.''

I bent down, trying to bring the screen into focus through my bifocals. Jack Lauerson scooted back and rose. ''Here, sit.''

The listings were myriad rows of numbers. ''Well, this is mumbo jumbo,'' I said. ''How do I tell what's what?''

''Well, you have to know,'' Lauerson said helpfully. ''What are you looking for in particular?''

''He used to own a chunk of prairie out by Herb Torrance's ranch west of town.'' Jack reached over my shoulder and scrolled the screen a bit, then jotted a number down on a small scratch pad. ''Okay. Actually, he owns three out that way. That's all?''

''Well, I was curious about the lot right behind this building...the one that fronts the alley and wraps around behind

Posadas State Bank.'' Jack scrolled again, jotted again, and straightened up. ''Anything else?''

I twisted around and looked up at him. He waved the little note. ''This tells me what map to look on,'' he said. ''Come.''

Without an instant's hesitation, he walked directly to the map case and pulled open the fifth drawer from the top. Flipping through the corners, he arrived at the one he wanted and hauled out a huge map. He turned to a vacant drafting table and spread out the map.

Before I had a chance even to bring the thing into focus, he thumped a portion with his index finger. ''This is Herb's ranch—actually, let me correct that. This is the portion of his ranch where his house is. See County Road 14 right here?'' I nodded, following the thin blue line down to its intersection with the state highway. Lauerson took out a blue-leaded pencil from his pocket and used it as a pointer. ''This is the property boundary of Herb's ranch. To the south is a block of land owned by George Payton. It runs out to the county road. In fact, if I'm not mistaken, the windmill that Herb uses all the time is right here.''

''On George's land.''

''Right.'' He shrugged.

''How many acres is George's plot?''

He cocked his head, reading the legend under the neatly printed name. ''More or less, 7.215.''

''What's the point of a seven acre parcel out there?''

He shrugged again. ''Who knows. Over the years, these things get chopped up, divided, given away, forgotten, you name it. I can see why Herb would want to buy that piece. It's got some water on it. You know, actually, George bought that land in a deal he did with old Reuben Fuentes, years ago. Back when the Bureau of Land Management was thinking of developing that limestone cave they found over there.''

''They never did, though.''

''Nope. The other two parcels are on the next map north.'' He turned away, rummaged in the drawer, and pulled out another huge sheet of paper. "One parcel is 56.48 acres, the other is—" he hesitated while he found the legend "about 108.22 acres, more or less."

"So, about 160, in that neighborhood."

"Yep. That was part of the exchange deal with the Forest Service ten years or so ago. They wanted some land he had up on Cat Mesa, so he traded for this."

"Okay. And in town? The courthouse lot?"

"Another map," he said good-naturedly. I waited until the third sheet floated down in front of me. "A really irregular-shaped piece. It used to include the old Nolan Pet Shop, remember that? It burned way back when. Back when there were enough people living here that someone could actually think about selling goldfish." He chuckled. "Anyway, it's this narrow little lot that runs down the side of the bank's back parking lot, and then right over to the property boundary with this building."

He waited patiently while I looked at the little blue lines. "What's that assessed at?"

"Just a second." He crossed through the tables again to his desk and scrolled about on the computer. I waited at the maps. In a moment he returned with another scrap of paper and handed it to me.

"This is current?" I said, looking at the figure. "Sixty-two thousand bucks seems on the low side for something right downtown."

Jack grinned. "Not many folks say that to us," he said. "That's the assessed value as of last spring, after the most recent valuation."

"But that's not necessarily its market value, is it?"

He laughed. "God no, not likely. Depends who wants it, of course. The average right now is roughly a hundred fifty to two hundred percent of the valuation. But..."

"But?"

"Well, in this case it's the county itself that wants the property so we can get ourselves some plush new digs, and stop tripping over ourselves. Float a bond issue to build a building, and the land acquisition is what makes it possible.''

''Somewhere around a hundred grand, more or less, then,'' I said.

''Close enough. It's whatever someone wants to pay, Sheriff. Whatever is negotiated.'' He ran his hand along the street front. ''And that's what the established merchants don't want to hear, since valuation is based on recent sales.'' He drew circles in the air with his finger. ''If the county pays George's estate a hundred thousand—or even more—for that lot, then the value of everything else goes up…recent sales set the pace.''

I gazed at the plat for a few minutes, and Jack Lauerson waited for the slow-paced gears to finish turning. Maybe he knew that George Payton had contemplated donating the land to the county, maybe he didn't. Ever discreet, he didn't say anything one way or another. ''How many parcels of property altogether did George own?''

''Looks like twenty-seven.''

''He paid a fair chunk in taxes every year, then.''

''Well, actually, no. Most of that rural range land is nickel-dime stuff. Those 160 acres out north of Torrance's? I could look it up, but my bet is that he doesn't pay more than ten or fifteen bucks a year on that.''

''More on the village properties, though.''

''Sure. That's a different kettle of fish altogether. What else can I find for you?'' It was a gentle prompt by someone adept at his job who wanted to get back at it.

''Actually, you know what I'd like? I know it's a bother….''

''All of them?''

''I really would. It's part curiosity, part just trying to tie up loose ends, I guess.''

He nodded as if he understood, but didn't want to complicate matters with questions. Less than fifteen minutes later, I had a list of all twenty-eight of George Payton's properties—including the home he'd lived in. Along with that I had a neat little stack of plats and legal descriptions, along with the current assessed valuation and the amount of tax the properties generated. Jack tapped the pile into order, ranked by ascending file number, clipped the lot together and slid it into a shiny blue folder with the Posadas County seal on the cover.

"Absolutely wonderful. Will you make enough time so I can buy you lunch?" I asked.

He glanced at the clock again, held up a finger, and walked quickly back to his desk. He shuffled through half a dozen Post-it notes that had accumulated, frowned at one of them, and then nodded. "Never turn down a free meal," he said.

On the way out, I thanked Wanda Something, and earned another of those thousand watt, beaming smiles.

As we walked out to my Blazer, Jack Lauerson squinted against the sun as if he didn't see it very often. "How's the new clinic going?" he asked.

"As near as I can tell, just fine," I said. "Some kinks to work out, but that's natural."

"Wait till you see what *that* place does to property values in the neighborhood," he laughed. "You might want to think about a Kevlar wrap for your house to protect you from angry neighbors."

# FIVE

The Don Juan de Oñate Restaurant in Posadas is one of those sprawling places that grew a little bit at a time. Fernando and Rosie Aragon built the first version in 1959, when he was twenty-one and his bride just turned seventeen. The photo of the original Don Juan that hangs framed in the foyer shows a small, flat-roofed place with big picture windows facing Bustos Avenue.

The name was almost longer than the upper facade of the building could accommodate, the lettering painted sunrise yellow against the brown adobe background. The restaurant snuggled between the Twelfth Street curb and a little adobe house to the west, with parking for about five cars in between.

Over the next forty-four years, the place expanded. The Aragons purchased not only the little adobe house next door, but the next *four* houses. When the interstate was finished and snowbirds could bypass the village, business took a slump for a couple years. In 1967, one year after my own arrival in Posadas, Consolidated Mining opened their open-pit copper mine and Posadas boomed again. The Don Juan followed suit, enlarging the parking lot and diving into an impressive remodeling and expansion.

Undaunted by a nasty kitchen fire five years later followed by the closing of the mine, the Aragons charged on to bigger and better projects. The scorched wreckage of the Don Juan was bulldozed, and the new restaurant sprang from the ashes, complete with banquet facilities, a small bar and enough quiet nooks and corners that patrons could always find privacy.

The number of meals that I'd eaten at the Don Juan during the past thirty-five years was enough to earn me plenty of frequent flyer perks...along with an impressively expanded waistline. The choice seemed simple enough. Did I want to be able to tie my shoes without grunting, or did I want to be able to sigh with something close to ecstasy when I took that first mouthful of steaming green chile, thin-shaved roast pork, generous tortillas made on the premises, all smothered under a blanket of melted sharp cheddar and insulated by a neatly chopped garden of greens...and maybe a little dollop of sour cream on the side to protect the lining of my mouth if the Hatch chile was a bit nuclear for my gringo tongue.

County Assessor Jack Lauerson and I headed toward my customary booth in the back of the restaurant, the one that looked out on the west parking lot and beyond, to the long roll of the San Cristóbal mountains to the southwest. Although she could figure it out for herself after all the years she'd known me, I had left a message for Estelle with the Sheriff's Department dispatch in case she broke away earlier than expected.

JanaLynn Torrez, a waitress who'd practically grown up with the Don Juan, slid two large waters into place without being asked. She was pretty enough that her passing had caused more than one customer to miss his mouth with a loaded fork, but she'd never married...not that at the ripe old age of thirty-one all options had been canceled.

"How are you guys today?" she said.

"Well, things could be better," I said.

"Eewww," JanaLynn said with a grimace. "One of those days, huh? I won't ask."

"Thank you."

She raised a pretty eyebrow at Jack, and I saw a faint tint of red wash up the side of his neck. I didn't know that tax assessors had it in them to blush. "What would you like,

Jack? I already know what the Sheriff wants.'' She leaned against me, nudging me with her hip.

''What's good?'' he asked.

''Well, a menu might help,'' JanaLynn said. She stepped over to one of the server islands, pulled a menu out of the rack, and handed it to Jack. ''I get so used to folks knowing what they want that I forget sometimes.'' She grinned down at me.

Lauerson frowned at the vast selection. He looked skeptical, as if he were skating on very thin ice. ''I'll try a couple of the beef enchiladas, I guess.''

''Red or green?''

The hesitation told me that Lauerson hadn't lived in New Mexico long enough to have memorized our official state question...either that or somehow he'd remained culturally deprived when it came to Mexican food. ''Is your green chile really hot today?''

She shrugged. ''It's not bad. Not like yesterday, when it ate out the bottom of one of the aluminum pans.'' She reached out a quick hand and made contact with Jack's left shoulder, a touch not lost on him. ''I'm kidding. No, it's not too bad.''

''I'll try that, then.''

''Smothered?''

''Sure. Why not?''

''Comin' right up.'' She gathered the menu, slipped it under her arm, and held up both hands as if demonstrating the size of a football. I nodded.

Jack watched her retreating figure. ''You always order the same thing?''

''Of course not. I had the enchiladas once. In the spring of 1972, I think.''

He laughed, still watching as JanaLynn reached up to clip the ticket on the kitchen's Lazy Fernando. I said nothing to interrupt his day dreams. ''Isn't she related to the sheriff?'' he asked after a minute.

"JanaLynn is Robert's cousin. Well...one of many, many, many."

He turned back toward the kitchen, but JanaLynn had disappeared. "She's attractive."

"Oh, indeed she is."

Jack had tried his hand with three or four wives, none of whom stuck. He sighed and leaned back, hooking one arm over the back of the booth. "So how's business?"

"Until this morning, it was just fine," I said. He nodded sympathetically. "Losing old friends is always tough," I added. "Especially when you reach the age that you're no longer buying green bananas. We all sit around wondering who's going next. Not a real healthy outlook."

"How old was George?"

"Seventy-nine. And not a hale-and-hearty seventy-nine, either. Really frail. So it wasn't much of a surprise."

"Maggie's going to have her hands full," he said.

"The properties, you mean?"

He nodded and pulled his arm down. "Of course, that's what she does for a living, so she's used to it. Didn't she just get married or something?"

Lauerson had sort of a sad face that didn't do much of a job hiding his thoughts. "She married Phil Borman a couple of years ago. He's a Realtor, too."

"Yeah, I know he is." He nodded as if to add, *And luckier than me, too.*

He straightened up, pulling away from the table. JanaLynn arrived, carrying two enormous platters. "They're hot," she said. With her hands free, she pointed her right hand pistol-like at me. "You want coffee with way too much cream and sugar. How about you?"

Lauerson looked startled. "Ah...I guess the water's fine."

JanaLynn nodded and turned to leave. "Is Fernando here?" I asked.

She nodded at our plates. "He's actually *working*. Can you believe that? Do you need him?"

"I'll step into the kitchen when we're done here," I said. "You might warn him so he has a chance to run."

"I don't *think* so," she said, and favored us both with one of those radiant Torrez smiles that her sheriff cousin should practice more often.

The county assessor and I dabbed a little small talk between bites of the best Mexican food west of the Pecos. After two minutes, I saw the sweat break out on Lauerson's forehead and a flush creep up his cheeks. His nose started to run, which always makes eating a challenge in polite company. I confess that I paid closer attention than usual to my house special, the Burrito Grande. If anything, the chile was a touch milder than average. The shaved pork was up to standards, no gristle, no chunks, no strands of fat, shaved so thin that it melted in the mouth.

I knew how Fernando's green chile started out in life, coming to him in big burlap bags that he then roasted out behind the restaurant, driving the neighborhood crazy with the distinctive aroma.

"This is *hot,*" Jack said between bites. "God, it's good, though." He gulped water and rolled his eyes. He glanced at my placid face. "Doesn't bother you much?"

"I guess I'm immune by now," I said, cutting another sample. Or maybe preoccupied, I didn't bother to add. In truth, I was thinking about old George Payton, sitting alone in his kitchen, glass of cheap red wine at his left hand, right hand holding a forkful of Burrito Grande just like mine. It's an occupational hazard of being a cop—even a retired one. We always want the answers, with no loose ends. The coroner had guessed that an allergic reaction to something had set off events that led to a collapse of what was left of George's pump.

"Interesting," I said, and cut another forkful.

"How so?" Lauerson asked.

"No...I was just off in my own world."

He smiled and wiped his brow. "I gotta thank you," he

said. "Good stuff. I don't know why I don't eat here more often."

"You're more than welcome. And I don't know, either. It doesn't take much of an excuse to get me over here."

"So I gather."

We worked our way to the end, cleaning the platters as if we'd both been on the run for days. JanaLynn's suggestion of dessert brought groans. "The cheesecake's really pretty light," she said hopefully.

"God," Lauerson muttered. "I'm going back to the office and take a nap."

"That's a good thing," I said.

"You can't, sir," JanaLynn said to me. "There's a young lady back in the kitchen who said to make sure you didn't leave without checking with her first."

I nodded, assuming that she was talking about Rosie Aragon, Fernando's one-and-only bride for forty-four years. I didn't say it out loud, for fear of depressing the oft-wed assessor. Who knew what that would do to our tax rates. "Tell her I'm on my way."

I knew without looking what the bill was within a penny or two, and held up a hand when Lauerson reached for his wallet. "My pleasure," I said. I doubled the amount and slipped the bills under the edge of my coffee mug. "Thanks, doll," I said, and JanaLynn cocked her head, clenched her lips, and punched me lightly on the shoulder.

"Take care of yourself, sir," she said. She nodded at Jack. "Thanks for coming in."

I shook hands with Lauerson and noticed that he took his own sweet time ambling out of the restaurant. I skirted the serving island and opened the polished steel swinging door that led to the kitchen.

Fernando and Rosie Aragon were standing in front of the enormous complex of stoves, Fernando's arms folded across his chest, Rosie holding one hand to her mouth with her face crumpled into tears. Facing them across one of the big wooden cutting tables was Posadas County Undersheriff Estelle Reyes-Guzman.

# SIX

FERNANDO ARAGON looked every one of his sixty-five years. In fact, he looked as if maybe the undersheriff had whacked him between the eyes with the big wooden tenderizer mallet. He saw me and immediately unfolded his arms, reaching out to take my hand in both of his.

"Bill..." he managed to say, then shrugged helplessly. "This young lady tells me that George Payton died today."

I nodded and Fernando looked hurt. "When were you going to tell me?"

"I was working up to it, Fernando." I reached out and rested a paternal hand on Estelle's shoulder by way of greeting. "I'm a little bit cowardly when it comes to breaking bad news to old friends."

*"¡Por Dios!"* he said with a little of his usual flair and humor, "you're in good company. Good company. So now we have to talk." His speech still had the musical cadence of Chihuahua, the state of his birth, a nice rich accent that the years hadn't diluted a bit. "You go ahead and ask all the questions you have," he said to Estelle. "We'll help you any way we can." He looked at me and shook his head. "An allergic reaction. *Hijo.*"

"What I'd like to get from you, Fernando, is a list of ingredients," Estelle said. "George had a take-out..."

"Burrito Grande," Fernando finished for her. "Almost every week, that's what he has." He laid a hand on his own chest. "By *arreglo especial.* That's how I know it's Thursday." He pointed a stubby, parboiled finger at me. "And this one doesn't wait for Thursdays.'' He grinned and showed that he hadn't spent any of the restaurant's profits on dentistry.

Estelle rested a small notepad on the chopping block, pen poised. ''You want each and every thing?'' Fernando said.

*''Todos sin excepcion.''*

''Where do I start a thing like this?'' he muttered.

''Just take one part at a time,'' Rosie said. She'd gotten her tears under control. ''Start with the roast.''

''That's good,'' Fernando agreed. ''I roast the pork, you know. Let me show you.'' He strode to the large walk-in freezer and reappeared in a moment with a wrapped pork roast that must have weighed ten pounds. ''Little ones like this,'' he said. ''So we don't have much waste.''

''May I have the label?'' Estelle asked.

''Of course.'' He peeled off the label and handed it to her. She stuck it neatly on the page of the notebook. ''If you ask me what the pigs ate, I can't tell you.''

Estelle grinned.

''But there's no telling what's in meat these days,'' Fernando said. ''That's getting to be a problem.'' He took the roast back to the freezer. ''I roast that meat, keeping it a bit *¿medio cruda, verdad?* Because it's going to be cooked again, you know.'' He stepped over to the polished, spotless slicer. ''And then I slice, very thin. *Very.* That's one of the secrets. Like paper, eh?'' He jerked his chin at me. ''You know, eh? Best that way.''

''Seasonings?''

''Salt, pepper, maybe a touch of garlic if I'm in the mood. Sometimes some rosemary...but some people don't like that so much. Usually a little bit of sage.''

I'd just finished eating, and already felt my stomach rumble in anticipation of an encore. It was a good thing that it was almost midafternoon. Business was slow, and Fernando and Rosie took us through construction of a Burrito Grande step by step, down to the last dollop of green chile.

''And you know, some people think that the chile is the

heart of Mexican cooking, but it's not,'' Fernando said. ''You can't save bad food with good chile. *That's* what most people forget. The roast, whether it's pork or beef or chicken, must be the best. The tortilla needs to be as only this wonderful woman here can make them...not like some of those things that stick to the roof of your mouth they are so gummy. If you use cheap, bulk cheese, that's what your dish tastes like. If you use the tired, frost-burned lettuce, or tomatoes that are hard and, well, you know...then the chile can't save them. But...'' He shrugged, holding his shoulders up for a long moment.

''If everything is good, and the chile is fresh and good...then you have something worth eating. *¿Verdad?*''

''*Verdad,*'' I said, risking just about the full extent of my knowledge of Spanish.

Estelle rested against the side of the chopping block, eyebrows locked together, examining the list. ''Did you do anything differently yesterday, Fernando?''

''No. Nothing. Maybe a *little* more care than usual. I know...we know...that George is, how do you say it, *delicado?*''

''Frail,'' Estelle translated for my benefit.

''That's it. He's been not so good. That's why the meal comes to him, not him to the meal, you know?''

''Is there any ingredient that came from a fresh batch of something,'' I asked.

''It's always fresh,'' Fernando said, trying not to sound hurt.

''That's not what I meant. Surely you don't open a fresh bag of your frozen chiles every day. Doesn't one last you for a few days, at least?''

''I see what you mean. But I tell you, there was nothing out of the ordinary—nothing unusual. Nothing *new.* Not to cause what you say happened.''

''Did you know that George usually drank a glass of red wine with his meal?''

''Sure. Now there—'' he waved a finger at Rosie as if the

two of them had been arguing that very matter all morning "—there's something to look into. If George could find a bottle of wine for three dollars, why pay four? You see?" He shuddered.

"Tell me again what time you prepared his meal?" Estelle asked.

Fernando crossed his arms again. "He called shortly after ten. That is the usual. By then, he knows if he's going to be feeling well enough to eat, you know. It seems early, I know, but he once told me that he can't sleep late. He's up by four, maybe, every morning. Like us. So by ten he's ready for lunch."

"So it was picked up some time around eleven?"

Fernando nodded. "It seems to me that his daughter picked it up this time. Sometimes it's her husband, but most of the time it's her." He held his hand up to his ear. "She was talking on the phone the whole time."

"And she just paid and took it?"

"Yes. I was a little worried, you know. She was talking to someone and said that she was going back to the office right that minute, that they'd meet right there. That's bad, you know…the food cools off and it's no good. We packed it in one of those little foam chests, but still…" He grimaced, no doubt at the thought of a cold, soggy burrito. I grimaced, too.

I turned to Estelle. "Maggie told me it'd been one of those days. She got a call, and did go back to the office. Phil was there, too, and took the food on over to George."

Estelle nodded absently, as if she were elsewhere.

"I think it's just one of those things, sweetheart," I said. "Maybe he caught a piece of something cross-wise in his throat…not enough to choke, but enough to put strain on his heart. Boom."

"Maybe." She tucked her notepad into her pocket and extended her hand first to Rosie, and then to Fernando. "Thanks for your time," she said.

"You want to take some samples with you?" Fernando

asked. "I'll pack you up anything you want. Chile? Some roast? You name it."

She smiled and held up a hand. "Not just now, thanks." She turned to me. "You just ate, sir?"

"You bet. It was the most fitting tribute I could think of," I said. "And it was wonderful. I also had an interesting chat with the county assessor."

"Ah."

"He survived, too. Barely."

"Will you let us know?" Rosie asked plaintively.

"You can count on it," Estelle said. "Thanks again." We left the Don Juan by way of the back door.

"Still going to Las Cruces?" I asked. "I'm fortified for the trip."

"Yes, sir. By the way, while he was doing some preliminary work, Alan asked the local lab at the hospital to run a whole blood histamine level test."

"Whatever that is."

"It's just a test to determine the level of histamines in the blood. That's an indicator of an allergic reaction. A bee stings us or something, and our system releases histamines."

"Right. The racing heart, the flush, the sweat on the forehead, the constricted bronchials."

"Exactly. The problem is that the test for histamines in the blood is performed so rarely that the local lab couldn't even do it." She consulted a back page in her notebook. "The normal range for histamines in whole blood is somewhere between 140 and almost nine hundred nanamoles per liter."

"That's quite a range," I said.

"The trouble is, the tests are done so infrequently, even the lab techs have to read a cookbook to do it. And the test procedure isn't FDA approved, since no one knows for sure what a baseline level should be."

"But we don't know what George's level was?"

"Not yet. I'm hoping Las Cruces will help us."

"Huh." I walked the rest of the way to her car in silence.

A few minutes later, the rhythmic slap of tar strips across the interstate's concrete sections threatened to work with the sunshine streaming in through the back window. My eyelids grew heavy.

I yawned. "Perrone didn't have any idea what might have caused such a massive allergic reaction, if that's what it was?"

"He has no idea. He's as interested to see some bloodwork as we are."

"Interesting." I glanced across at her. "Don't be surprised if I doze off," I said, and slapped my belly, squirming against the confines of the seat belt.

"Did you ever see the foam chest, sir?"

I opened an eye. "I beg your pardon?"

"Fernando said that they sent the takeout over to George in a foam chest. One of those cheap picnic things. We didn't find it in George's kitchen."

I opened the other eye. "It could be any number of places, sweetheart. In the trunk of Maggie's car...she took the meal to her office. In the trunk of Phil's car...he took the meal to George's. Did you ask either of them?"

She sidestepped my question. "Why would they take the serving dish out of the insulated chest before taking the food into the house, sir?"

"Well, I don't know. People do strange things, sometimes. I'm sure Maggie or Phil can tell you."

"*Es verdad,*" she murmured.

# SEVEN

FORTUNATELY, the undersheriff wasn't the chatty type. She was perfectly capable of lapsing into silences that deepened with every passing mile. I could tell the mental wheels were spinning up to speed. Her fingers would tap out a little rhythm on the steering wheel or on her knee. Every once in a while, she'd hum a little tune, not quite loud enough for me to hear the words.

Because she didn't blab all the way to Las Cruces, my eyelids grew heavier and my neck felt as if the tendons had turned to cooked spaghetti, refusing to hold my head on the straight and level. I finally gave up and leaned my head against the window as we came up on the first exit for Deming. I startled awake some miles later as if Estelle had jabbed me in the ribs.

I glanced over at her, and she was frowning as she watched traffic ahead and in the rearview mirror.

"Shit," I said, and shook my head.

"Good nap, sir?"

"No. I hate doing that." I rubbed my eyes, trying to bring into focus the idea fragment that had jarred what few sharp brain synapses I own. "Pull over when you get the chance."

"Sir?"

"I need you to stop the car."

"There's a truck stop about two miles ahead. Is that soon enough?"

"That'll do fine."

Less than two minutes later, we hit the exit ramp, and

Estelle swung clear of the gas pumps and parked between a Cadillac with Maryland plates and a motorcycle piled high with luggage, the blue-and-white license plate too small for me to read.

"I'll wait here," she said, assuming I was going inside.

"Look," I said, "this is really bizarre, but bear with me. I need to look at the burrito that George was eating when he died."

"Look at it, sir?"

"That's right."

"It's in a sealed evidence bag."

"I know it is. Unseal it. And then you can seal it again. It can't wait."

Her eyes narrowed just a little as she regarded me, trying to assess if I'd finally gone crackers. "All right."

We got out and Estelle opened the truck. The big cooler with PSD painted on the side rode in its own neat floor mount that Bob Torrez had built a number of years ago when he had too much free time. The cage prevented the cooler from sliding about, or tipping over, or springing open in the event of anything short of a catastrophic head-on collision.

Estelle pushed the strap releases, and then opened the cooler. "You don't even need to take it out," I said. The plastic top had been bagged separately, since it had been separate when Estelle found it. I smoothed the top of the glossy plastic evidence bag, and scrunched my head around so I could bring my bifocals to bear on the remains of the Burrito Grande.

"Shit," I said again and straightened up. "You can close it up." I stepped away from the car while Estelle secured first the evidence in the chest, then the chest itself before thudding the trunk lid shut. By that time, I was back in the car.

She got in and never said a word until we were out on the interstate and touching seventy-five again.

"So," she said finally, "were you dreaming?"

"Pardon?"

"You woke up with a start, and had to see the burrito."

I stared hard at the road as it flashed toward us. "This wasn't a food dream sweetheart. Look," I said, and twisted sideways in the seat, my arm over the back. "Fernando Aragon doesn't use chopped green chile."

"I see." Her face remained a sober mask, but I saw the crow's-feet at the corners of her eyes deepen a trace.

"No, I'm serious. I'm an expert at this. Listen."

"I am listening, sir."

"I had a Burrito Grande for lunch. Jack Lauerson and I went to the Don Juan after we finished up in his office. I had the burrito because that's what I *always* have. And today..." I stopped and shook my head. "It was sort of a memorial lunch, if you know what I mean."

"Because of George."

"Sure. And Fernando served his Burrito Grande the way he always does. The same way he's been serving it for twenty years. Just the way he described."

"And so..."

"Fernando takes full-length chile pods and slices them. Kind of diagonally, like French-cut green beans. They're *slices,* Estelle. You look in that burrito you've got in the truck, and what do you see?"

"Some sliced, some chopped," she said.

I looked at her in frank surprise. "Right," I said, the wind rapidly leaving my sails. "Chopped chile. Little squares. Little tiles. The sort of stuff that when people put it on burgers, it all drops out the backside of the roll."

She didn't say anything, guiding us around a row of tankers streaming down the hill into west Las Cruces.

"Do you understand what I'm saying?" I asked needlessly, since Estelle *always* understood.

"Yes."

I waited and saw her right index finger tapping on the steering wheel again.

"You ate just a few minutes ago," she said, glancing at me. "What, about one-thirty or so? Going on two?"

"Right about then. Jack works through the lunch hour so that he's there if that's the only time someone can break away to come in and see him."

"As near as I can tell, Fernando fixed George Payton's take-out burrito around ten-thirty," Estelle said. "Maybe as late as eleven. The call from Phil Borman that he'd found his father-in-law dead was logged at eleven forty-eight."

"What's your point?"

"Well, sir, for one thing, ten-thirty in the morning is a bit early to fix a dinnertime-size burrito plate. It's a possibility that Fernando didn't have any of his famous sliced chile thawed. He used a quick can off the shelf."

"Never happen."

"Please, sir. In a pinch, it could happen."

"Nope," I said stubbornly. "Not for something he was fixing for George. Or me."

She smiled at me. "Serious stuff, this chile," she said.

"Damn right, it's serious stuff."

"The only other alternative doesn't make much sense, sir. If..." She paused, then said it with emphasis. "*If* Fernando prepared his creation the usual way, with finely sliced chile, and if there's *chopped* chile in it now..."

"There is. You saw it."

"I did," she nodded. "Then someone added the chopped stuff later." She held up her index finger. "Fernando didn't have enough cut, so he used some chopped chile that he had on hand..."

"Never happen," I repeated doggedly.

"Or two," she continued patiently, raising another finger, "someone along the route added some chopped chile to the mix."

"And why would anyone do that?" I said.

Estelle looked across at me and raised an eyebrow. "If someone wanted to put something in the burrito that triggered a fatal spasm, sir, there's no better way than just to mix in a little something in the chile sauce."

I ruminated on that for a mile or so as she slowed for the

University Avenue exit. "Mix whatever in with some green chile, and you could add it at any time," I said.

"That's true. Convenient package. I doubt very much that George Payton would take a look, see a piece of chopped green chile, and throw the whole thing in the trash."

"He couldn't see well enough to know chopped from diced from sliced," I said. "He might *taste* the difference, though."

"He might, but I doubt it. And anyway, by then, it could be too late, depending."

My stomach hurt, and not from gas generated by my lunch. "You know what we're talking about here, don't you?"

"Someone murdered George Payton, sir."

"Right." I looked hard at her. "And that's what you've been thinking all along, isn't it? When I first saw the yellow crime tape, I had a little uneasy stir."

"Think of it this way, sir. George is eating his lunch, drinking his wine, all by himself. I don't think he felt a spasm coming on—if he'd been feeling poorly, I can't imagine him wanting to tackle a heavy, hard-on-the-gut lunch."

"They're not so bad."

"Says you. Anyway, I think that George Payton sat down to lunch feeling pretty good. All of a sudden, about what, a dozen bites in from the west end of that burrito? All of a sudden, the seizure hits. It hits hard enough that he drops his fork and knocks over the wineglass. Now there's the possibility that he was *reaching* for the glass, to take a drink. Maybe he feels like he's choking. The wine doesn't help, and he panics. This time, he struggles to his feet, staggers *around* the table toward the sink and, incidentally, toward the telephone, just an arm-stretch away. But he doesn't grab the phone, sir. He grabs the *bag*. The bag from the Don Juan. And then, he manages to turn around, and sinks to the floor, his back against the kitchen cabinets, the bag clutched in a death grip to his chest. He never touched the phone, sir. He never reached for it and knocked it off the base. He grabbed the *bag*."

"And that's what bothers you?"

"Yes, sir. That bothers me."

"Why would he have grabbed the bag, then?"

"Maybe just reflex," she said. "By then, he might have been all but unconscious. His hand swept out, grabbed and clutched. The bag did him no more good than an effort to reach the phone."

"Unless he knew that something in the burrito triggered the spasm, and he wanted us to know."

"I can't imagine him thinking that clearly right at the end, sir. Not in the middle of a coronary spasm, or whatever it was that killed him. But it's a curiosity, just like the missing ice chest."

"If someone put something in the food, then it'll show up," I said. I turned and stared out the window, watching the city scenery flow by.

"That's why I wanted to bring everything down today, sir. And any markers they owe you, maybe it's time to call 'em in."

"You got that right," I said. The notion that someone might have spiked George's burrito made my own three-and-a-half-chambered heart consider a fibrillation of its own. My late lunch felt heavy enough to be two Grande platters.

It was bad enough losing George. It didn't take too much imagination to figure out the chain of people who'd last handled his neatly packaged lunch. Fernando had put it together, with a little help from his wife. Maybe JanaLynn Torrez had helped in the kitchen. At the least, she'd carried the takeout to the front, where Maggie Payton Borman had picked it up. Swinging deals right and left, she'd been cornered by an eager, cash-waving client at the office. You don't make those kind of folks wait a minute. So Phil Borman took up the delivery, running the burrito out to George.

And then George had died.

Who stood to gain from George Payton's death? That narrowed the list considerably, and that made me feel the worst of all.

# EIGHT

ONCE EVIDENCE had been turned over to the state crime lab, there was nothing for us to do but wait. We couldn't peer over the tech's shoulder, prompting her to speed things up. We couldn't offer helpful advice. The lab was a clinical, quantitative world of polished glass, chemicals and measurement. We trusted them to provide us with definitive answers—they trusted us to stay the hell out of their way.

As luck would have it, no one that I knew was working that day—and maybe that was just as well. We couldn't have done better than Whitney Duncannon. She signed in the evidence with rapid efficiency, and at first I thought her hyperdrive was because the time was drifting along toward four-thirty in the afternoon. Not so. The paperwork done, she settled her slender form on the edge of the desk, folded her arms across her white lab coat, and listened intently as Estelle recited the facts as we knew them.

"So let me make sure I understand," she said, and her Kenyan accent broadened all the vowels into soft music. "What would interest you most is if something had been added to the food, is that correct, Sheriff Guzman?"

"Yes."

"Not the analysis of the food itself."

"No."

"Do you have any idea what might have been added? So perhaps we have a direction to start?"

"No." She smiled at Estelle's cryptic responses, a sweet smile that lit up her face and no doubt had melted her husband's Scottish heart. "We think that whatever was added," Estelle said slowly, "caused some kind of massive allergic reaction. The hospital lab in Posadas wasn't able to give us a preliminary blood histamine level, but our guess is that it had to be elevated."

"Significantly so?"

"I would *guess* so. But we have no way of telling, other than by the appearance of the victim."

One elegant eyebrow shifted a millimeter. "An allergic attack," she said. "It would be interesting to establish a histamine level for both the blood and the urine." She pronounced it *yooureen,* with a slightly rolled "r".

Estelle nodded. "Whatever you can do."

"Well, we shall see, won't we?" the young lady said and favored us both with that megawatt smile again. "We shall start in the most logical of places, and go from there, Sheriff Guzman. Where might I reach you?"

"We'll wait here, if that's all right."

"Ah," she said. "Many of the tests have a significant turnaround time, you know. As much as forty-eight hours in the case of blood histamines, for example." She saw my grimace. "But we shall see what indications there might be. Sometimes that can be helpful." She nodded. "We will see what we can do."

She and the cooler of evidence—George Payton's lunch and the preliminary gleanings from Dr. Alan Perrone's hurried preliminary autopsy—disappeared into the depths of the lab, leaving us in the small, sterile inner office.

I settled into the chair behind the desk and found it as neat, efficient and uncomfortable as the rest of the furnishings. Outside in the hallway, I could hear other members of the lab staff making motions to wind up their day.

"What do you think?" I asked.

Estelle had spent a few moments reading the various documents affixed to the cinderblock wall of Whitney Duncannon's office. She shook her head slowly. "I'm trying not to," she said. I saw her heave a deep sigh, and she turned around. "No matter what scenario I come up with, it doesn't make sense."

She crossed the office, head down and hands on her hips. With the toe of her boot she eased one of the smaller chairs out from the wall, but didn't sit immediately. I could see that her mind was wandering far afield.

"You always say to look at the simple things first, sir." She shook her head. "I don't see anything simple. I have visions of some stealthy figure pouring a black vial of cultured wasp venom into George's food."

"Cultured *wasp* venom?"

She shrugged. "Sure. Why not? Or reduced cobra spit." This time, she grinned, but it was an expression of helplessness rather than humor. "Or if he had a secret gluten allergy, maybe they added a ton of powdered wheat germ."

"None of that is thinking simple, sweetheart."

"I know. And I need a simple answer, sir," she said. She rubbed her face with both hands, then rested her elbows on her knees, regarding the immaculate floor tiles.

"I wish I could help. We may be here all night, so something might come to us." I glanced at the large panels of tinted glass that separated office from lab. Mrs. Duncannon and two other lab techs were in a huddle in a far corner. I could see the tops of their polished white plastic hardhats, but that was all. "I've never met the young lady before," I said. "I thought maybe Dave Hewitt would be working today. He'd stay all night to find us some answers, if he had to."

"I think we're in good hands," Estelle said.

"You've met Ms. Duncannon before?"

She nodded. "I like the lack of bureaucratic nonsense," she said. "She never mentioned what else she might be working on that we interrupted."

"I'd like to know what the 'logical place' to start is in her mind," I said.

"*Nos veremos,*" Estelle said. It would have been a dead

accurate imitation of Whitney Duncannon's *We shall see* if the young lab tech had been from Mexico.

We waited just long enough for me to start wondering what restaurant in Las Cruces to trust. I had glanced at my watch and saw 5:17 tick by when the door to the inner sanctum opened partially. Whitney Duncannon was talking to someone concealed behind the wide door frame, and after a brief, confidential-toned conversation, I heard her say, "Most certainly so." She nodded and entered the office.

I couldn't read anything in her expression at first. She walked over to the desk where I saw her carefully place a small, polished clipboard on the corner. "Well, this is most interesting," she said, and this time I detected just a shading of triumph in her tone, an eagerness in those bottomless eyes. She turned and regarded Estelle.

"You are aware of the role of histamines in the body?" she asked.

"Yes."

"That they are a natural compound produced by the body?"

Estelle nodded.

"It is most interesting, then, that we should find histamines in the food sample itself." She glanced down at her clipboard. "In a sample where we would expect to find none whatsoever—" she hesitated "—we find levels that I would characterize as extreme. But..." She hesitated again. "Please remember that these preliminary indications are qualitative only. It is that we are testing for the *presence* of the chemicals only—not how much there might be. Just that they are there. Do you understand?"

We both stared at her. "Histamines in the food," I said.

"Yes, Mr. Gastner. First we establish that histamine was present in the blood. It was so. But not in the urine. It is only logical then to test the food source as well...at the same time."

"I don't understand."

"Well, you see," Whitney Duncannon said in her beautifully modulated English, "histamine diphosphate is a chemical that, while not completely common, is certainly readily available. But we would *never* expect to find it in food. At least I cannot imagine any circumstances when that would be so."

"Histamine diphosphate." I knew I was sounding like a repetitive parrot, but my brain took time to catch up.

"Yes." She nodded. "That is not to say what further testing may reveal. But I thought, in light of what you have told me, that you would want to know those preliminary results. And they are *most* preliminary. Please remember."

I had myriad questions to ask, but none were in Ms. Duncannon's bailiwick. She cocked her head so she could read what Estelle had written in her small notebook. "That is correct," she said. "Histamine diphosphate." She nodded with satisfaction. "By this time tomorrow, we should know so much more. And by Monday, you may have some answers."

Estelle was mentally out the door already, and a few minutes later as we hustled down the long sidewalk toward the parking lot, I nearly had to jog to keep up. I could see by the storm clouds on her face that the part of her keeping me company was running on autopilot. She didn't say a word as we drove out of the city, and once westbound on the interstate she kept the county car in the left lane, blasting by even those folks who thought *they* were going too fast.

Not until the first sign announcing Deming did Estelle finally settle back a little in the seat. She glanced over at me. "Sorry I'm such lousy company," she said. "Are you about ready for dinner?"

"Well, you know I had a pretty good lunch," I said. "But my arm can be twisted."

"It's going to be a long day, sir," she said. If anything, the car picked up a little speed as we shot by a tank truck that was ignoring as many speed limits as we were. "And you were right."

"I'm happy to hear that," I said. "Right about what?"

"You said think simple. I was stuck in a rut thinking that someone put something in George's food that he reacted to, an allergic reaction of some kind. If you have someone who's deathly allergic to aspirin, and you lace their food with a good handful of tablets, then they're going to collapse into anaphylactic shock. Their blood histamines would soar." She didn't take her eyes off the road, for which I was grateful.

"But that's not what happened here," I said. "I'm still trying to wrap my mind around all this. Someone put histamine something..."

"Histamine diphosphate."

"That, too. Someone spiked the food with a dose of that stuff. Where do we go from there?"

"Think about adrenaline, sir. The body produces that, too."

"The old 'fight or flight' response."

"Exactly so," Estelle said. "If you give somebody an *injection* of adrenaline, it accomplishes the same thing. The body reacts. What I'm thinking is that the same thing would happen with a dose of something like histamine. The body generates the stuff as a response to what, foreign proteins like a bee sting? So what happens if you artificially introduce a megadose of that chemical some other way? What is it, an amino acid? A heavy dose would send the system off in loops."

"And if the person had a weak heart, or some other problem, that's all it would take," I said, watching the center line flick by on the right. "*I* have a weak heart," I added. "George Payton's was a total wreck. He couldn't walk across the living room without stopping for breath. On top of that, he had emphysema and diabetes and this and that. You jack his system up with a nuclear burst and that's going to be it."

"Yes, sir."

I settled back, trying to force my spine to relax against

the seat. As if reading my body English, Estelle's lead foot eased up a bit. "Thank you," I said. "What's next?"

"I need to talk with Louis Herrera first," she said. Herrera was the pharmacist at the new health clinic, and Dr. Francis Guzman's best friend in both high school and college. I'd given the bride away at Francis and Estelle's wedding, and Louis had been best man, a natural comedian who kept us laughing during the reception with his roast of the newlyweds. "We need to know something about the drug. Then we'll know what steps to take."

"There are a couple of important questions in the meantime," I said.

"Who and why?"

"That's right. Ms Duncannon said it doesn't occur naturally in food, so someone put it there. That's the *who,* and we've got ourselves a short list."

"Yes, sir, we do." She remained in the left lane, and I'd become accustomed to the periodic flash of metal by my window.

"The *why* is downright depressing," I added. "I told you that I had lunch today with Jack Lauerson. The real reason I did that was to find out the status of some land that George Payton owned out by Herb Torrance's ranch. Herb's got a windmill sitting on some of George's land, and I know that George had talked about giving the land to Herb someday, or selling it to him for a pittance."

Estelle nodded.

"The paperwork from the assessor is back in my truck. George owned twenty-something parcels around Posadas County. In fact, he collected bits of land the way some folks collect postage stamps."

"Of interest to any Realtor," Estelle said, knowing exactly where I was going and leaping ahead.

"Exactly. One in particular. George told me on more than one occasion that he was thinking of giving the village lot between the Public Safety Building and the bank to the county for that new addition they're planning. Jack says that lot's worth a hundred grand or more on the market."

Estelle's eyebrows rose. "*Giving* the lot?"

"Yes. He said he didn't need it, and the county did. And that he didn't need the money."

"That sounds familiar," Estelle said. Her husband's clinic sat on four and a half acres I'd given them for a dollar the year before—my contribution to their risky venture. I'd felt the same as George: I had the land and didn't need it. The Guzmans did. I didn't need the money, they did. It was really pretty simple. My four kids were long grown and gone, with three of the four financially secure and the fourth not caring much about money in the tiny Peruvian village where she lived and worked.

"I'm willing to bet," Estelle said, "that in his will, George didn't provide for disposal of any of his land parcels. If he *had,* there'd be no question."

I held up a cautioning hand. "That's if we're on the right track. Both his daughter and son-in-law are real estate people, and would know the value of that property. And that makes it pretty simple. If George dies *before* he designates where he wants the individual properties to go, then they're just part of his entire estate. As far as I know, Maggie is his only living relative. From what I can see, they were on the best of terms with each other. I'd expect that he would leave his estate to her." I shrugged. "If that's the case, then all the properties pass to her, and when she sells the property at market value, she stands to make a mint."

"Yes, sir."

My stomach churned. Sometimes it doesn't pay to think too much. We finally moved into the right-hand lane and started to slow for the Posadas exit.

"What prompted you to talk to the assessor, sir?"

I looked across at Estelle in surprise. "I had Herb on my mind, I guess," I said. "That property with the water is right next to his. I wanted him to know what the situation was, in case he wanted to jump on it. There's a couple of parcels just on up the road, too. He might want to know about those."

"That's interesting," she said, sounding unconvinced.

"Plus, I'm just plain nosey, sweetheart."

She didn't argue with that.

# NINE

LOUIS HERRERA HELD UP a small, heavily tinted jar about the size of an old-fashioned ink bottle. Like ninety-eight percent of every other drug or chemical in the store, histamine diphosphate was small, white crystals—as unremarkable in appearance to the untrained eye as sugar, salt or even cocaine.

He handed the jar to Estelle and waited. The small room was stuffy, the steel shelving lined with various brews and concoctions.

"Okay," she said, and handed the jar to me. I glanced at the label as if I could read the fine print and handed it back to the pharmacist.

"That's classified as a chemical rather than a drug," Louis said. "We keep it back here in the compounding room."

"It's not something you prescribe?" Estelle asked.

"Not by itself," Herrera said. He hefted the jar thoughtfully. "What's your interest in this stuff?"

"What's it used for?" I asked, ignoring the question.

Louis slid the jar back on the shelf, in its proper space in the alphabet. He smoothed the first signs of a mustache he was trying to grow. "Well, in all honesty, I haven't used it here since we've opened." He shrugged. "Of course, that hasn't been too long. The most common use that's being tried is a mixture of histamine diphosphate with, well, basically caffeine. How's that for a cocktail? That's sometimes prescribed for multiple sclerosis patients. Apparently the histamine-caffeine combination acts as some sort of neural trigger." He laced his fingers together. "It establishes the neural pathway that the MS tries to destroy." He shrugged again. "Nobody really knows how it works. And sometimes it doesn't. But when it *does* work, it's pretty amazing."

"Multiple sclerosis patients," Estelle said.

The pharmacist nodded. "That's the only use *I* know of. Now there may be others. I could do some research on it for you if you like."

"Yes, I would," Estelle said quickly.

The pharmacist looked sideways at us. "I hope this isn't the latest street craze," he said.

"I sincerely hope not," I replied.

"Is this the only form that histamine comes in? Combined with the phosphate?" Estelle asked.

"As far as I know. It's the only thing *we* have, anyway. The two phosphate molecules just act as a binder, so to speak. A carrier. They link with the histamine radical."

"So what are the general characteristics of the drug, anyway?" I asked.

"Well, remember it's not classified as a *drug,* per se," Herrera said. "It's a chemical. It's not something that Doc Francis would write a prescription for. If he was treating an MS patient, he *might* write up an order for the cocktail I was telling you about."

"All right," I said impatiently. "It's a chemical. What's it like...what's it do?"

"For one thing, it's incredibly soluble," Herrera said. He held up the small bottle. "That's five grams, which is a lot. I could dump the whole thing in a few cc's of water, and it would dissolve immediately."

"That's sweet," I muttered. "So it wouldn't be a problem mixing it with food, for example."

"You're not going to tell me you've got someone doing that," Herrera said.

"No," I said. "I'm not, Louis. But we need some answers."

He looked at the bottle skeptically. "*If* someone had some

of this stuff, no, it wouldn't be a problem mixing it with food. You wouldn't want to lick the spoon, though."

I didn't smile, and neither did Estelle.

"Histamine is an amino acid," Herrera added quickly. "Remember high school biology? Amino acids are the building blocks for proteins. Like all amino acids, it's extremely heat sensitive. Heat's the enemy. So if you mixed this in food, and then *cooked* it, it would be destroyed."

I crossed my arms over my belly. "Let me give you a scenario, Louis. Suppose I had a nice big burrito, complete with all the trimmings. Nice green chile sauce, maybe a dab or two of sour cream on top. And then, after everything's cook and dished up, I take a couple of tablespoons of that stuff—" I nodded at the bottle "—and mix it in with the sauce."

He waited to see if I was going to continue, and his right eyebrow drifted upward in anticipation.

"A couple of *tablespoons?*"

"Well, whatever. That's not much of a jar you've got there. Suppose I just dump in half the jar. It dissolves readily, as you say. Then what?"

"Who's the poor soul that's going to sample this concoction?" he asked, but his face grew sober when he saw I wasn't joking. He took a deep breath. "All right. You know what a histamine reaction is...the junipers start squirting their pollen all over the place, and first thing you know, the eyes itch and tear, the nose runs, places in your mouth and throat itch that you can't reach with your tongue...you know the drill, right?"

I nodded.

"And that reaction can be dangerous if you've got serious asthma, right?"

I nodded again, knowing that George Payton's considerable list of ills included the delightful mix of both asthma and emphysema, no doubt soothed by his fondness for a good cigar or a mooched cigarette.

"Well," Herrera said, warming to his lecture, "that's from

a *minute* dose of histamines in your system.'' He leaned against the shelving and crossed his arms over his chest. ''A good lab tech could measure it, I suppose...I don't know what the test is. The results would be measured in nanamoles per liter.''

''Which means what?'' I asked.

''Well, a nana-anything is one *billionth,*'' Herrera said. ''That ain't much. And for some folks, an allergic reaction to something as simple as pollen or cat hair can be dangerous.''

''We're not talking cat hair here,'' I said.

''I'm just trying to be clear,'' the pharmacist said. ''You guys have been around this business long enough to know what anaphylactic shock is—that's the next step up. A little kid who is allergic to bee stings takes a hit, and his system pumps out the histamine until the blood levels skyrocket, but we're still talkin' *tiny* amounts here.'' He held his right thumb and forefinger about a quarter inch apart. ''The body works in tiny bits. That kid could die, conceivably. I've got a customer who's allergic to aspirin. For her, one pill would be as lethal as a bullet from a .45. See, the trouble with a histaminic reaction is that so much of our system is affected.'' He reached up and stroked his throat. ''The salivary glands kick in, the windpipe constricts, the pulse races, the blood vessels dilate. You do that to someone with a weak heart, someone with serious health problems, and it's serious stuff. What would be a little bee sting to most of us turns out to be a visit to the emergency room, and you end up having someone like Francis Guzman work on you. That's if you're lucky.''

''What if I put a couple of tablespoons of this stuff in a burrito,'' I said. ''Hell, go for shaking half the jar in. Why not?''

Louis Herrera laughed without much humor. ''That would be like shooting houseflies with a bazooka,'' he said.

''So tell me what would happen.''

''The bottom line is that the person would die.'' Herrera

shrugged. "Take everything I've said about pollen and bee stings and stuff like that, and magnify it to ridiculous levels." He shook his head. "I'd really like to know where you're going with all this."

"No, you wouldn't," I said. "Trust me on that." I glanced at Estelle, and I knew that she could read the anger in my eyes. She slipped a hand up on my shoulder as if that might keep me from going into orbit. After Louis Herrera's graphic descriptions, she knew as well as I did that George Payton's final moments hadn't been a peaceful passing away.

Estelle surveyed the compounding room for a moment, hand still on my shoulder. "This place looks pretty secure," she said.

"It is," Herrera replied. "You're wondering where someone would get themselves a supply of histamine diphosphate."

"Yes."

"Well, I hate to tell you, but contrary to popular belief, there are a whole lot of pharmacies that aren't particularly secure. I used to work at one in Kansas where everything, chemicals, drugs, all of it, just sat on a shelf out in the open. If the pharmacist happened to be away on break or something, and a clerk wasn't paying attention, there'd be nothing to stop someone from slipping back there and helping themselves. In fact—" he paused for emphasis "—I worked at one place when I was in college where there was a back *door* that opened into the work area. You could walk right in from the alley. And it wasn't locked during the day."

"So it's possible."

"Of course it's possible." He swept a hand to indicate the shelves behind him. "The chemicals are stored alphabetically, with some exceptions. Finding *H* doesn't take a rocket scientist. But we're assuming that the person in this case would *know* about histamine diphosphate, and that narrows the playing field just a whole lot, it seems to me."

"This room is always locked?" I asked.

"Absolutely. Unless I'm in it."

"Is it locked even if you're right out there, at the customer counter?"

He nodded vehemently. "It's locked, period. When I want in here, I card it—just like you saw me do a few minutes ago. When I leave, it closes behind me and locks—just like the doors on ninety percent of all motels."

"And that's all the histamine whatchacallit that you have?"

He looked down at the little jar, and then slid it back on the shelf. "Yes. And that's a lot. And as you noticed—" he smiled tightly "—that particular jar is sealed. It hasn't been opened yet."

For a moment he stood quietly, regarding the little, innocent bottle. His face worked at some inner argument he was having with himself, and finally he turned and looked at Estelle and me. "I don't know what you guys are into, but if it's local, there are only two sources for histamine diphosphate in Posadas—at least I'm guessing that to be the case. I've got some right here, and I'm sure that Guy Trombley has some over at Posadas Pharmacy. You might talk to him. That's kind of an old-style store, and he's an old-fashioned kind of guy." He paused, and I wasn't sure he'd meant the comment as a compliment. "I'd appreciate it if you didn't tell him that I sent you. He doesn't think much of us."

"That's just because you're the new kids on the block," I said. "He's had Posadas County all to himself for thirty-five years."

"And he's had his way of doing things for that long, too," Herrera said diplomatically. He held up both hands helplessly. "I've told you the sum total of what I know about that stuff. Like I said, I'll do some research on it and let you know what I come up with."

"I'd appreciate that," Estelle said. I shook hands with Louis, and as we left, I noticed that the door to the compounding room closed with an authoritative thud and snap of the electric latch.

The drive from the new clinic and pharmacy south of the

interstate—and only a few hundred yards from my home—north to Posadas Pharmacy at the corner of Bustos and Pershing took less than three minutes. I'd been inside Guy Trombley's drug store a thousand times in the past three decades, since chasing various forms of ill health had become one of my major hobbies over the years. I'd never looked at the place as being particularly old-fashioned, any more than I thought of myself as particularly *old* unless I looked in the mirror or started to rise from a low-slung chair.

Until the previous spring, Guy Trombley's drugstore had been the only game in town, and he could second-guess a local physician with unerring accuracy—and didn't hesitate to correct one of their mistakes if the occasion warranted. His prices reflected his monopoly, and I could understand his irritation at having new kids in town undermine his little kingdom.

At 7:23 that evening, Estelle started to swing the county car toward the curb on Pershing. "Let's try something," I said. "Go on around the block and park in the alley behind the store."

"That's a good idea," she said. The alley between Posadas Pharmacy and Glen Dale's auto parts store was narrow, but we found a spot behind a silver Cadillac that was nosed in close to the first of two Dumpsters.

"Guy's caddy," I said.

Estelle glanced at the dash clock. "I'm surprised he's still here. The pharmacy itself closes at five," she said.

"Counting pills," I said. "Or whatever pharmacists do after hours. The rest of the store is open to nine, though. He may be short a clerk or two."

The back of the building was unpainted concrete block, as ugly as the street-facing facade was neat and tidy. A single steel door appeared to be closed tightly. I got out of the car, walked across to the door, and turned the knob.

A steel door, even if it's atom bomb proof, is worthless if it's not locked. This one wasn't. I pulled and felt the resistance, accompanied by the yowl of metal door rubbing away from metal frame. Like some of the rest of us, the old building was starting to sag with age. Estelle and I stepped inside, and immediately had to skirt a welter of cardboard boxes and empty plastic bottles. The storeroom opened to a small hallway with rest rooms on both sides.

"This is nice," I said, and paused. I could have used the rest room, walked five steps and turned right, to find myself behind Guy's customer counter.

A gal who might have been eighteen appeared, perhaps alerted by the groan of the old door.

"Hi," she said as if she meant it. "May I help you?" I knew her last name was Bustamante, but couldn't remember beyond that. Estelle's files were more up-to-date.

"Tiffany," the undersheriff said, "is Guy in?"

Tiffany Bustamante looked sorry, even if she wasn't. "No. He went over to the grocery store for something." She smiled. "He should be back any minute." The front doorbell chimed, and Tiffany turned. Two elderly women had entered, one using an aluminum walker.

"We'll wait a bit," I said, and Tiffany nodded, already turning away.

"So," I said. "This is interesting. You want to trespass, or do you want me to?" I grinned at Estelle. "I don't have a badge, so why not let me? That way, if we get caught, you can arrest me."

I didn't wait for her response, but thrust my hands into my pockets and ambled into Guy Trombley's domain. It looked like any other pharmacy—lots of little jars and boxes with incomprehensible names. Trombley had no separate compounding area, and I'd perused the shelves for some time before I found the spot where I would assume it made sense to store histamine diphosphate.

Unfortunately, Guy's use of the alphabet put the *H* section on a bottom shelf, territory that my bifocals, aging knees and generous belly made difficult. After a few moments, I came to the conclusion that if Guy Trombley's inventory included the drug, it had escaped me. I had been concentrating hard enough that I didn't realize that Estelle was standing just behind me.

"Right there," she said.

"Right where?" I glanced at her in surprise.

She knelt and pointed at the shelf. Guy Trombley's store wasn't new, and perhaps he didn't dust as often as he should. A jar of something had taken up the tiny space between the haloperidol and hydrocortisone powder. Someone had removed it, leaving a nice little dust-free circle about the size of an ink bottle.

There were myriad possibilities, of course. But I was willing to bet that either Guy had a good crop of MS patients and had been so busy brewing that he'd run out of inventory, or someone had lifted his supply of histamine diphosphate.

# TEN

"THE SHELVES aren't labeled," I said. "The bottle that's missing could be almost anything."

"As long as it's between *H-A* and *H-Y,*" Estelle said. "And stored in a small bottle. That narrows the odds. The simplest thing to do is ask Guy Trombley."

She straightened up and her gaze roamed the small room. "It's certainly easy enough to slip in here, either through the back or from the front. It would take only a few seconds." She palmed a small point-and-shoot camera from her jacket pocket. I stepped out of the room so I wouldn't be in her way. I glanced toward the front of the store. Tiffany Bustamante was busy at the cash register, and I ambled up through the aisle of body powders, laxatives and every vitamin known to man until I reached the magazine rack.

Estelle emerged from the back room just as Guy Trombley stepped off the curb across the street. He met the two elderly women at the door and held it open for them.

"He's back," Tiffany called to me unnecessarily.

Every community can claim its institutions, those folks who have no inclination to live anywhere else no matter how many rude jokes they hear—or how many they tell—about their hometown. Guy Trombley had been in Posadas when I arrived fresh out of the Marine Corps, almost forty years earlier. Over the ensuing decades, as first one organ and then another double-crossed me, Guy had sold me enough drugs to stock a fair-size store.

"Howdy, howdy," he said, his West Texas accent still as

thick as the day he graduated from high school. Guy's manner was brisk, as always. He extended his hand, his grip gentle. He patted the back of my hand for emphasis. "Sure sorry to hear about George Payton," he said. "It wasn't a surprise though, I guess." George owned as many bricks in Trombley's pharmacy as I did.

*It sure as hell surprised George,* I almost said. I settled for a sympathetic nod, and Guy released my hand.

"Whatcha need today?"

"Estelle has a question or two for you," I said. "I'm just along as excess baggage."

He smiled, showing the perfect even white of his dentures. He acknowledged Estelle with a little nod as she approached. "Evening, young lady. Come on back. It's been really quiet this week," he said over his shoulder. "How about with you guys?"

"About the same," I said.

"Herb Torrance was in a while ago for a bushel basket of pain meds for the boy. They just got back from Las Cruces. He says you were the hero of the hour, Bill."

"Hardly. I just happened to be there. I drove Dale into the emergency room."

"And I always thought that horses would go out of their way to avoid stepping on humans," Guy said.

"Not when they've been spooked by something as vicious as a foam cup," I said.

Guy laughed, more like a series of deep grunts from the bottom of his little pot belly. He was a tall, thin man, narrow across angular shoulders stooped from years of bending over the prescription counter.

"So, what can I do for you two?" He finally looked directly at Estelle. "How's your husband doing?"

I knew it wasn't Francis the physician to whom Guy Trombley referred. It was to Francis the co-owner of the new drugstore in town, the only competition for Trombley this side of Lordsburg or Deming.

"He's doing fine, sir," Estelle replied. "May I ask you a

question about a specific drug?" I guess I would have understood if Guy had made a caustic remark like, *Why don't you ask your own pharmacist,* but he was too much of a gentleman for that.

"Fire away."

"We're investigating an incident involving histamine diphosphate."

Guy's eyebrows wagged in surprise. "That's a little off the wall," he said.

"I know it, sir. But whatever information you could give us, I'd appreciate."

"You haven't talked to your husband or Louis?" He asked the question with enough tact that it sounded more self-deprecating than anything else.

"Briefly," Estelle said, and didn't elaborate.

"I see." He looked puzzled and frowned with a slight shake of the head. "Well, about the only use we have for histamine diphosphate is in a compound that we make up with caffeine, of all things. Histamine diphosphate isn't a drug, you know." He looked at Estelle with raised eyebrow. "Not per se, anyway. It's a chemical. In compound with caffeine, it's showed some value in the treatment of certain phases of multiple sclerosis."

"It's taken orally?"

He shook his head. "Skin patch."

"So it's easily absorbed through the skin, then."

"Oh, yes. It's pretty squirrelly stuff, folks. Histamine is a natural chemical in the body, as I'm sure you're aware. That's what triggers the body's response mechanisms in allergies, for instance." He turned his head to cough once into his hand.

I leaned against the wall, nudging the step idly with the toe of my boot. "I wouldn't have thought we had many multiple sclerosis cases around here," I said.

"We don't. In fact, the last time I compounded that particular potion would have been sometime this past spring." He didn't elaborate, but looked curiously at Estelle. "What's your interest in this, anyway? Do you need to see the drug, or something? It's never dispensed all by itself…at least *I've* never had occasion to do so. Like I already said, its uses are pretty limited."

"It would be helpful to see some," she said.

"What, some kid's science fair project got away from 'em, or what?"

He slipped past me and turned into the supply room. Before I had time to even turn around, he reappeared, holding a small white bottle. "Here you are." He handed it to Estelle.

"This says haloperidol powder, Mr. Trombley. That's the same thing?"

"Hardly," he said, reaching quickly for the bottle. He squinted at it, looked heavenward, and turned around muttering. "Don't ever, ever get old, either one of you," he said over his shoulder. I knew exactly what he'd done, since I'd done the same thing too many times. The eyes see the target but the hand and the attention drifts a bit, and instead of the intended product, you arrive at home with a truly puzzling selection.

"Too late for me," I said.

"Lest you think the wrong thing," he said from inside the storage room, "I do have a system of checks that would have prevented me from mixing the wrong stuff in a batch for a patient. But…" His voice trailed off. Estelle was watching him from the doorway, so I didn't see the necessity of forcing my bulk into the already crowded room.

"What's haloperidol used for?" I asked.

"Heavy-duty tranquilizer," he said, still looking. "Various psychotic disorders call for it by injection. Sometimes by tablet. Well, damn." I heard the crack of joints and a grunt. "This is where the bottle of histamine diphosphate *should* be," he said. "I don't understand why it's not there." I heard an irritated exhalation, and glanced at Estelle. Her face remained expressionless.

"Okay," Guy Trombley said, appearing in the door. "Excuse me." He slipped by and headed for his computer. "We don't just *run out* of drugs in our inventory,'' he said, rapping keys and waiting with obvious impatience. ''That's supposedly one of the nice things about these damn gadgets here. When I make up a prescription, all the information goes in here, right then and there. When the supply of a given drug, or a given chemical, reaches a certain point, it's automatically added to the Order Now list.'' He glanced over his shoulder at me. ''Just like a hardware store, you know.''

He shifted his half glasses to bring the screen in focus, adopting that characteristic scrunched-up, barred-teeth expression that makes seeing the fine print possible.

''Huh,'' he said. ''The last time I compounded histolatum...that's the particular application that I use with histamine diphosphate and caffeine citrated...'' He scrunched his face up some more, putting a finger on the computer screen to follow a line across. ''The last time was May 10, 2002.'' He stood back. ''In the drug business, that's ancient history.''

''So it's been more than six months ago. Does that stuff have a shelf life?''

''Sure. Probably a couple of years. And the computer knows all about that, too. The reorder would have been automatic. This shows that the supply was virtually new in May.''

''And none since then?''

''No.''

''Would it be a violation of privacy to ask who the patient was?'' I asked.

''Sure, but what the hell?'' He looked at me over his half glasses. ''If I can't trust you, the world might as well stop spinning right now.'' The computer screen dissolved into the saver mode, a parade of exotic fish swimming endlessly across the screen of their cybernetic aquarium. ''You remember Norma Scott? She passed away here a while back. It'd be last spring, sometime. She's the last one I compounded for.''

No,'' I said, ''I don't remember.'' Estelle's eyes narrowed a millimeter, her youthful mind not so quick to draw blanks.

''Phil Borman's sister?'' Guy prompted.

''Well, shit,'' I said, always the master of my automatic responses.

# ELEVEN

ESTELLE REYES-GUZMAN wasn't the sort to snap on red lights and siren when she saw the pathway open in front of her. In fact, I was proud of what the undersheriff did next. She took a page out of my own investigations manual, *How To Plod Your Way to Success,* along with a chapter out of Sheriff Robert Torrez's favorite, *How to Irritate the County Commission.*

Of the twelve officers that made up the Sheriff's Department, nine met with her at 8:15 that evening, along with Jack Adams of the New Mexico State Police and Critter Cop Doug Posey. Posey had chosen a bad time to stop by to see if the coffee was fresh. Conspicuously absent for the evening fun were Sheriff Robert Torrez and Posadas Chief of Police Eddie Mitchell—both in Albuquerque making guest witness appearances before a federal grand jury in an insurance fraud case that had managed to stretch a tendril to Posadas.

On the large whiteboard in the small conference room, Estelle had drawn the simplest of maps for the village, and we all strained to hear her husky voice, barely more than a whisper.

"This represents Trombley's Pharmacy at the corner of Pershing and Bustos," she said, tapping the square in the lower left with her pencil. "There are two Dumpsters behind that store. That's where the drug came from." Her pencil reached westward toward the Don Juan de Oñate Restaurant. "There are three more here, behind the restaurant. The shortest distance between the Don Juan and the High Mesa Realty office is right up Bustos, and there are no Dumpsters on the main street. But on the backside of Pershing Park, behind the post office, the real estate offices, and the auto parts store, there are eight.'' She swept her pencil northward. ''The Bormans' home is on 568 North Third, and you can see that there are a total of five or six Dumpsters along the Third Street alley.'' She took a deep breath. ''This is George Payton's house, folks.'' Her pencil eraser tapped 1228 Ridgemont, the little lane off Sixth Street, and then circled each small red square in the area.

''So basically what you want us to do is dump all the trash cans in town,'' Jack Adams said. As usual, his black-and-silver state police uniform was spotless—just the attire for an evening of Dumpster hopping.

''Almost,'' Estelle said.

''You don't know when the drug was taken, though, right?'' Adams asked.

''No idea. Any time in the past several *months.*''

''Then there's not much possibility of finding anything.''

''Not down by the drugstore. I agree. The drug could have been *taken* any time since May, but it wasn't *used* until recently—and I'm betting *today.* We do know this—the chemical could not have been mixed with the green chile *before* this morning, sometime shortly before 11:00 a.m. Philip Borman discovered Payton's body shortly after eleven.''

''So what exactly are we looking for?'' Deputy Tom Pasquale said, taking the plunge. He was the only county officer who was actually on duty at the moment beyond dispatcher Ernie Wheeler.

''Two things, although obviously the list can change. Number one, a small can of chopped green chile. We don't know what brand.''

''But chopped,'' Adams chuckled. ''As opposed to whole or sliced.''

''Exactly. Chopped. Green. No additives. The second thing is a drug inventory jar about the size of an ink bottle. It'll be dark, opaque brown, with a white label covering most of it. The name histamine diphosphate will appear on the label, along with the distributor's logo, DeMur Pharmaceuticals." She took a deep breath. "That's it. Maybe a plastic spoon. We could be optimistic and think that both had been dumped into a plastic trash bag together."

"So we don't really know if it's been dumped at all," Adams said.

"No. We don't know that. I'm betting that it has been. It's just the logical thing to do. People have trash, they throw it away. The trash pickup is early Friday morning. If that happens, the evidence is gone." She took a deep breath.

"If we don't find anything, then we try something else." She glanced at the wall clock. "There's a time crunch, since the village starts its morning Dumpster runs right around 1:00 a.m. in this part of town."

"They'd be happy not to," I said.

"And we may have to ask that, if push comes to shove," Estelle said.

Sergeant Howard Bishop shook his head wearily. "Fun times," he muttered. "This is when we find all the dead dogs, cats, babies and stuff."

"I don't need to tell you," Estelle said, raising her voice a notch until she had their attention again, "that fingerprints are going to solve this case. The evidence is worth nothing to us otherwise. Be careful." She grinned at them. "I have your Dumpster assignments up here. I'd appreciate it if you didn't use official vehicles. The less attention we attract, the better."

Some of us were better at the Dumpster party than others, of course. I can't say that I dived into the job, since my general physical shape and condition precluded that. But we were stealthy enough.

Estelle, Tom Pasquale and Linda Real had worked over two of the Don Juan's Dumpsters before Fernando Aragon appeared at the restaurant's back door, wiping his hands. He watched silently as Tom Pasquale spun a bulging sack over the rim to Linda. She set it in line with the others that rested on the blue tarp I had donated.

"If you guys can't afford to pay for dinner, just say so," he said.

"We appreciate that," I said.

"What are you looking for?"

"If I knew..." I said.

Fernando couldn't resist the attraction, and stepped over to where I stood. "You're not looking in the bags?"

"We think it's loose," I said. "We might save ourselves a little time by not undoing all your good work."

*"Hijo,"* Fernando muttered under his breath. "You chose a bad day. They hit me on Monday, Wednesday and Friday. Pickup, you know."

"Right. It would have been tossed in sometime today—after Wednesday's, before Friday's."

"So it's going to be on the bottom," Fernando said with resignation. "You want help?"

I glanced at the parking lot behind us, already well filled with customers. "We're fine, Fernando."

He nodded. "Coffee's on whenever you need some," he said. I murmured my thanks, but I didn't think any of us were really eager for any food or drink at the moment.

"Sir," Estelle asked, leaning an elbow against the rim of the Dumpster in which she'd taken up residence. Fernando stopped in his tracks, thinking perhaps his offer of food and drink had a taker. "When you started Wednesday with clean Dumpsters, do you toss stuff in any particular order?" She nodded at the line of Dumpsters behind Pasquale.

"Huh?"

"I mean, do you fill this one first, then that one, working your way down?"

"I guess," Fernando said, glancing at me. "I never think much about it, you know. Most of the time, it's Benito who takes out the garbage, anyway. Who knows how he does it? You want him out here?"

Estelle shook her head. "No. That's not necessary. I was just wondering."

Fernando reached out and patted my arm as he walked past. "She wonders about strange things, you know."

"What can I say?" I replied.

Fernando nodded. "You let me know what I can do," he said, and left us in peace.

For another hour, we waded our way through a day and a half in the life of the Don Juan de Oñate Restaurant. I knew from the determined expression that Estelle had conjured up her own scenario for what had happened that Thursday morning. But when trash is hurled into a Dumpster, it's hard to make it stick to a scenario. Everything else, maybe.

"Yo," Tom Pasquale's voice said from deep inside the steel box. At that moment, Estelle had emerged from Dumpster number one, and had circled two, where the deputy was, to lift out several loose boxes behind him that threatened to bury him. His tone drew us up short.

"Hee-hee," he said with triumph.

He wedged himself between the impending landslide of boxes and a heavy, black bag of table bussings. Nestled in the corner, where I would have expected it to land when tossed into an empty Dumpster, was a small plastic bag, the sort used by grocery stores. He hooked it with a pencil and held it up. "DeMar something?" he asked.

"DeMur Pharmaceuticals," Estelle said, frozen in motion with her hands around a carton of empty number ten jars of mayonnaise.

"I can read it right through the bag," Pasquale said. I moved close, and his grin was the size of the Dumpster lid.

# TWELVE

"YOU DON'T have to go," Estelle said.

"I know I don't," I replied, maybe a little more irritably than I would have liked. She let me stew in silence during the drive over, well aware of the various demons tugging my heartstrings this way and that.

The neighborhood was the deep silence of 10:45 p.m., the good folks either tucked into bed, around each other, or snuggled in front of the television set for a last blast or chuckle before calling it a day. Estelle's unmarked county car whispered to a halt at the curb in front of 568 North Third Street at the same time that Tom Pasquale eased his marked Expedition to a stop across the street.

I heaved a deep sigh and opened the car door, but halted with one boot out on the curb. She watched me chew on my thoughts for a minute without comment. I'd thought the whole thing through six different ways, arriving at the same answer each time. That didn't make me any happier.

Pasquale stepped onto the curb near the front of our car. He'd found time to spruce himself up after his tour of Dumpster duty. He waited patiently for us, hands at ease behind his back, face solemn.

"Okay," I said, and hauled my carcass out of the car.

The Bormans' place was the sort of neatly manicured showpiece that two hard-charging sixteen-hour-a-day working people achieve by having the yard work and home maintenance chores done for them. Estelle and I stood on the tiled front stoop with Tom Pasquale looming behind us. My eyes roamed over the front of the house. Not a paint chip out of place, not a friendly weed trying to muscle in between perfect examples of green things that had never considered the arid southwest until some nursery had forced it on them.

The doorbell was a simple *bing-bong,* and I listened to it echo through the house three times before the front door opened, pulling enough of a suction that it shook the aluminum storm door.

Phil Borman was in his stockinged feet, working to secure the last button on his shirt. "You kinda caught me unprepared here," he said. The time was his first hint this wasn't a social call. Deputy Pasquale's somber presence was the second.

"Phil, good evening," I said, realizing as soon as I'd opened my mouth that this was Estelle's case, not mine, and that it was a long, long way from a good evening. But what the hell. "We need to talk with Maggie."

He gaze swung from me to Estelle to Deputy Pasquale and then back again. I saw one hand slide up along the edge of the door, and his weight shifted ever so slightly, sagging toward the door. Cops don't arrive at your doorstep late at night for social calls.

"She's out in the kitchen, doing some paperwork," he said, and his face brightened a bit. "She just made some fresh coffee, if you'd like some." Being the good salesman that he was, he read the expression on my face correctly. "Something's wrong?"

"Yep," I said. "You mind if we come in?"

He stepped back, still holding the door. "Sure," he said. "Let me get her." He turned as if to yell out her name, but she had already appeared in the kitchen doorway, a cup of coffee in one hand, a cigarette in the other. "It's the folks from the Sheriff's Department," Phil said unnecessarily.

Maggie's neatly tailored pantsuit hadn't seen the rigors of the day. She had that spruced-up look of someone on her way out the door. Our eyes met, and a sad couple of seconds passed between us.

"Mrs. Borman," Estelle said, "I have a warrant for your arrest in connection with the death of your father, George Dwayne Payton, Jr."

Maggie looked wearily at Estelle, ignoring the fit of coughing from her husband, who'd sucked in a surprised breath and gotten his pipes crossed. The expression on his face told me that he'd known nothing of his wife's plans, and now he stared through tearing eyes first at her, and then at Estelle, and then at Tom Pasquale, as if expecting someone to clue him in.

"You didn't waste any time," Maggie said. She regarded Estelle evenly, the way she might look at someone presenting the unwelcome news that her client's property survey was invalid.

"Maggie," I started to say, but she waved a weary hand at me.

"Look, I'm even dressed and ready to go." She brightened a bit. "I heard them at the Dumpsters out behind the house, you know. Earlier this evening. And I thought, 'Well now, is this just a token effort? Or will she...'" Maggie stepped forward and Tom Pasquale moved toward her. She shook her head at him. "Not to worry," she said. "Not to worry." For a long minute, she stood silently, meeting the undersheriff's unflinching gaze. "Then one of my neighbors called to tell me the strangest thing, that cops were pawing through every Dumpster in town."

"Mrs. Borman, before you say anything further, I need to advise you of your rights as provided by the State of New Mexico."

"I need to sign something, don't I?"

"Yes, ma'am."

"Then let's use the kitchen."

"No, ma'am. This will be fine right here."

"Now wait a second," Phil Borman finally squawked. "I don't understand what the hell is going on. Maggie, what are they talking about?"

"They'll make it all be painfully clear, I'm sure," Maggie Borman said.

"Mrs. Borman, I'm going to read the statement to you, and if you understand it, please initial in the place provided," Estelle said. She placed the single rights document on the table near the end of the sofa, and handed Maggie a felt-tipped pen. I watched as Maggie, efficient as ever, skimmed down the page, zapping initials in the little circles. She'd finished long before Estelle's even-cadenced presentation of the Miranda rights was completed.

"Do you have any questions about these rights as I have read them to you?" Estelle said, and accepted the pen back.

"No." Maggie looked hard at me. "I want you to know that Phil had nothing to do with any of this," she said. "Nothing. I watched him care for his sister until she could no longer be home. I watched the money flow into the nursing facility where she spent the last six months of her life, poor thing. None of it made a bit of difference."

"Your father wasn't a bedridden vegetable," I said.

"No. He wasn't. And I guess I couldn't stand to see him become one, either." The hint of a smile touched the corners of her eyes. "This burrito thing he had with the Don Juan was one of his treasures, Bill. Two weeks ago, he ate a portion of one, and you know what he told me when I came by afterward?"

I shook my head.

She dropped her voice a couple of octaves, a fair imitation of her father's. "'Can't even eat goddamn green chile anymore. They're startin' to tear up my gut.'"

"So when he decided to give the burritos one more shot, you saw your chance, is that it?" I asked. "How long ago did you take the histamine diphosphate from Trombley's?"

"A month, maybe two."

"Maggie," Phil said, "you put something in his food?"

"Shush, sweetheart." She waved a hand in dismissal as if he were a child.

''And all this just so that you could sell a few pieces of property that your father had plans to donate,'' I said.

Maggie's eyes went flint hard. ''Is *that* what you think all this is about?''

''Yes, Maggie,'' I said. ''As a matter of fact, I do.'' The room was suddenly way too stuffy, and I turned on my heel and headed for the front door. Behind me I heard the clink of handcuffs.

# CAKE JOB

by Jane Rubino

For Aileen Schumacher

*La fame fa uscire il lupo dal bosco.*
(Hunger lures the wolf from the woods)
—old Italian proverb

# ONE

"SPIES IN ENEMY COUNTRY. Didn't Holmes use that expression somewhere? Well, that's just what I feel like every time I'm in this place." Cat Austen's glance coasted past the glistening green-and-gold tabletops up toward the black orb of the eye-in-the-sky.

Cat's remark nudged Victor's downturned mouth somewhere near a smile. "In *The Red-Headed League*."

"Well, the expo's more like the *Wed*-Headed League. I've never seen so many marriage-minded people since I was one of Rose Cicciolini's bridesmaids. There were twelve of us, not counting the maid of honor, the matron of honor and the two flower girls. Four of them wound up in the ER with broken bones they got lunging for the bouquet."

Cat and Victor—Lieutenant Victor Cardenas—were idling over late-afternoon cappuccino in Café Doux, the coffee lounge tucked away at the corner of the gaming floor in the Sterling Phoenix Hotel and Casino. The unremitting whirr of buzzers and sizzle of falling coins kept the ambience from being quite as intimate as the tinted windows overlooking the Boardwalk, the green velvet valances, the dark glow of high-end imitation parquet sought to impart.

"You and Ellice haven't had to elude Fawn Sterling, have you?"

"Heaven forbid. I heard she's out of town, or I never would have agreed to cover this for *South Jersey*. I can't think of anything more uncomfortable than finding myself sandwiched between Freddy's former fiancée and his current fiancée."

"So this isn't just pre-wedding reconnaissance?"

"Not entirely. Ritchie needed something light and sweet to fill out *South Jersey*'s June issue. And Ellice wants to schedule a consultation with Patty Cake as soon as their next pastry demo's finished, but that hasn't started yet, so I was just treating myself to a cappuccino break. I don't recall *intermezzi* at the Phoenix are a perk of Major Crimes, though."

Victor parried the hint. "Is Patty Cake an entity or an enterprise?"

"Both. It's the name of her pastry shop. But her first name really is Patricia and she went to court to have her last name changed from Torello to Cake. Of course, we could have scheduled the consultation by phone...."

"But...?"

"During the demo, they pass out samples, and I'm afraid I'm one of those incorrigibles Jane Austen was talking about, who can only be kept in tolerable order by more than is good for them."

"More...?"

"*Cake,* Lieutenant."

"Ah. The wedding cake consultation is a new one on me. Doesn't anyone simply phone the local bakery with chocolate-vanilla, number of tiers and so forth?"

"Nothing about a wedding is done simply anymore. You have to have a consultation for *everything.* And if you don't have the time or stamina to consult with the baker and the stationer and the dressmaker and the florist and the caterer and the limo service and the photographer and the hairdresser, you just hire a wedding consultant and they do all the individual consultations, and then you consult with *her.* There are 368 vendors up in the ballroom."

"I had no idea the area accommodated so many merchants of Venus."

"Or merchants of the ingenious. You remember S and M Casting?"

Victor nodded. "Local talent agency. They provided most of the extras for that *CopWatch* segment."

"Well, they'll cast your wedding party."

"I beg your pardon?"

Cat flicked her shoulder length hair away from her face. "Say you want a big wedding party, but you're not a Rose Cicciolini who can enlist a dozen friends and relatives. Or suppose you can, but they 'Do not impart the visual symmetry that will best complement the *tout ensemble*.'"

"Translation?"

"I imagine it means your nearest and dearest aren't quite S and M caliber." Cat's rippling laugh was absorbed by the clamor of buzzers and coins. "So, they're benched and you choose your entourage by height, age, hair color, race. They've got an entire binder with just their identicals. Twins and triplets, mostly children. Enormously popular for flower girls. Which is not as odd as Conjugal Critters."

"Don't tell me. Wedding ceremonies for your pet."

Cat shook her head. "That's Bow Vows. Conjugal Critters will either train your pet to be your attendant or provide a wedding party from their menagerie."

"Well, the anticipation of one's nuptials is said to inspire animal passion."

Cat took out her diagram of the Bridal Expo. "Two of a Kind, they arrange commitment ceremonies for gay couples. Fat Chance. Their motto is 'Romance Takes on a Huge New Dimension.'"

"Self-explanatory. What else?"

"Happily Ever After will transport the bride to the church in an etched-glass carriage in the shape of a pumpkin."

"Drawn by six white horses."

"Well, actually it had only been two horses, but last year, when the trumpeters—"

"Trumpeters?"

"In tights and velvet pantaloons and feathered hats."

"*¡Dios mío!*"

"Let forth with a salute just as the bride got into the carriage and it spooked the horses and they took off at full gallop—''

''The horses?''

''Well, I believe the trumpeters did, too, but the horses had the edge and actually made it halfway across the Ninth Street Bridge. A group of fishermen tried to wave them down, but only got them more worked up, so that they—yes, the horses—ran off the causeway into the marsh, the carriage overturned and the bride wound up in the—''

''Soup.''

''So now it's drawn by a pair of guys in decorated Harleys.''

''In tights and pantaloons and feathered hats?''

''Well, the guys, yes. The Harleys are just draped with ribbons and crepe paper. Here's Looking At You will theme your entire wedding around your favorite classic movie, write the vows, decorate the reception hall, design the menu.''

'''Theme'?''

''Yes. One of the unfortunate consequences of the trade is that *theme* takes its place among *dialogue, conference* and *error* as one more noun that's been unnecessarily verbed.'' She made a face. ''Moving on. Ethcentricity—exclamation point—will *theme* the entire day around your ethnic heritage.''

''Well, a lot of weddings incorporate some sort of tradition, don't they? My grandmother was Mexican, she wouldn't let my sister Milly wear pearls because they signify tears. When my mother and father married, her father carried a plate of coins that represented a dowry.''

''I had to give out these little bags of nylon net, filled with Jordan almonds, because candied almonds signify acceptance of the bitter with the sweet.''

''Milly gave out these lapel pins with ribbons the same shade as the bridesmaids' dresses. The pins were engraved with the names of the bride and groom and the date of the wedding. *Capias,* they're called, or *recordatorios.* The bride greets all of the guests individually, and pins one of them on the guest's lapel or dress."

"What about you? Premarital class? Blessing of the rings? Nuptial Mass?"

"Soup to nuts. And the night before the wedding, my Tio Emilio and several of his SUI friends collected under Marisol's bedroom window and sang until the neighbors called the cops. They only knew one song, *Que Linda Eres,* and after four or five hours, it got a bit wearing."

"'SUI'?"

"Serenading under the influence."

"At my wedding, Carlo and Vinnie got on the stage and sang *La Fuatina.* The Elopement. They meant to sing it a cappella, but my Uncle Condoloro hauled out the *zampogna* he'd managed to get through Customs and accompanied them."

"I'm afraid to ask what that is."

"It's sort of a Sicilian bagpipe."

"*Dios me salve,* that's worse than what I was thinking."

"Well, we have the attitude that the union isn't officially solemnized until you survive the reception." Cat fanned her brochure over her cappuccino, fielded a more direct hint. "I had no idea the subject of weddings was compelling enough for you to leave your office in midafternoon on the off chance that we might dialogue on the subject."

Victor raised an eyebrow. "I phoned your place and when Freddy told me you were here, I rushed right over, hoping to catch you in a conjugal frame of mind."

Cat crossed her arms over her chest.

Victor smiled. "Okay. The fact is, I got called to a meeting on short notice."

"Here?"

"I didn't choose the location."

Cat pursed her lips, glanced around at the prim waitresses dressed in green vests and bow ties over gold satin shirts, the half-dozen patrons plucking at oversize cinnamon rolls and nursing overpriced lattes. "Well, it's not a local cop, because you would have met a cop at Bud 'n' Lou's. And it's not one of the Sterlings, because I read that Blaine Sterling is in Paris and Fawn's in New York, or vice versa. And it's not some employee who wants to *conference* regarding the Sterlings because they would have come to the bureau, so they wouldn't be spied by the eye-in-the-sky. In fact, you would have instructed any civilian or witness to come to your office. So it's someone who gets to dictate the meet, who doesn't mind meeting in public—" She studied Victor's cocked eyebrow. "Who might *ordinarily* mind meeting in public, but is making an exception for some reason, and someone you don't mind meeting in public. Not a cop, not a Phoenix whistleblower, not a witness. Someone with the ability to interrupt a working day. That leaves an informant. A *snitch.*"

Victor ran his thumb along the downward arc of his mustache. "Extraordinary."

"Elementary. Why aren't you meeting in a dark alley or under the Boardwalk? Isn't this awfully public for a get-together with your—what do the boys call it—your CI?"

Victor's cell phone trilled. He pushed aside his coffee.

"You know, I've never met a confidential informant," Cat observed.

"Well, you're not going to start this afternoon." He cupped the phone closely to his ear, pressed a finger against his opposite ear to block the background noise. "Cardenas."

"Lieutenant?" It was Sergeant Stan Rice. "You on your way in?"

"I'm still waiting to hook up with Pavo."

"Maybe he's just jerkin' you around."

"No, he sounded urgent."

"Well, he's gonna have to back-burner it, Raab wants us all to drop what we're doin' ASAP."

"What's up?"

"I don't know, he's on his way over here."

Victor's mouth turned down in a thoughtful scowl. This time Friday, Raab would ordinarily be on his way to synagogue. "Give me twenty minutes." Victor flipped his phone closed, tucked it in his pocket.

Cat studied his frown. "What do you need twenty minutes for?"

Victor cocked an eyebrow.

Six older brothers had immunized Cat against such male impudence. Still, she blushed. "You're shameless, Lieutenant."

"Merely sanguine. This particular twenty minutes is what I'll need to get back to the office."

"And abandon your Baker Street Irregular? If you tell me what *Pavo* looks like, I'll take the meeting for you."

"I suggest you return to the bridal expo and take the cake. You'll be less likely to wind up in a jam."

Cat tossed her head. "Don't be silly, Victor. What kind of jam could I possibly get into picking up brochures and nibbling petits fours?"

"Well, Holmes said danger ceases to be danger if one can define it. And in the nearly six months that I've known you, you've had a bit more of *that* than is good for you."

# TWO

ATLANTIC COUNTY D.A. Kurt Raab, was chatting with the Major Crimes Unit, Sergeant Stan Rice and Detectives Jean Adane and Phil Long when Victor arrived. Victor waited until Adane was seated before he settled behind his desk. Raab sat beside Adane, Rice leaned against the doorframe and Phil Long perched precariously against the makeshift bookcases laden with three-ring binders.

Raab got right down to business. "Okay, long story short. Paulie Forgione, everyone knows the name, right?"

"Hit man. AKA The Apron?" Phil shifted his long legs. "Serving time in Texas."

Victor nodded. He had taken pity on Mrs. Forgione, assisted her in getting some personal items to her husband before his transfer out of state. The reciprocity inherent to The Apron's moral code demanded that Victor receive an equivalent gesture of regard. Forgione passed on the unlisted number of Giacinto, Atlantic City's most exclusive restaurant to Victor; Victor used the coveted information on his first date with Cat.

"Heard he finally agreed to roll on Cholly Mackenzie."

"Where'd you pick that up?" Raab was surprised.

"Street talk. It's true?"

Raab nodded.

Charles Mackenzie was the president of the Southern New Jersey District Food Purveyors, Handlers and Servers Union. He owed this elected position to a bitterly waged "promote the vote" campaign, sweetened with the generous distribution of street money, and to the timely, if unnatural, demise of the two opponents who had the temerity to oppose "Jolly Cholly" for the post. Paulie the Apron had been convicted for the two murders, but the D.A. was not able to persuade a grand jury that the orders had come from Mackenzie, and The Apron wouldn't roll.

"Four months of slow dancing with his attorney, arranging for Paulie's covert transportation back here, get the grand jury primed. He flew in this morning. I'm stowing him for the weekend, Monday at 10:00 a.m., he's supposed to go before the grand jury. So, it's all over the street? That explains it."

"Explains what?" Stan asked.

"I got a call this afternoon from Assistant D.A. Song, who's helping the marshals baby-sit him. Paulie told her he's had a change of heart, he's not gonna take the stand."

"Someone got to his wife, maybe?" Stan asked.

"The wife's not here. She'd moved to Texas to be near him. They got her under guard down in Texas."

Victor could think of only one thing that might stalemate Paulie Forgione. "He has children."

Raab nodded. "A girl in her early twenties, Elizabeth Dana Forgione and a sixteen-year-old-boy, Paul Giovanni Forgione. The girl graduated from college last June. After Paulie's conviction, she rented a condo in Moorestown so that she could act as guardian to her brother. He's gonna be a senior in high school. It's a big deal, him graduating with his class."

"I don't understand why he would want to stay," Jean Adane mused. "It must be difficult for an adolescent boy to have it known at his school that his father has been incarcerated for murder."

"Jeannie, you kiddin' me?" Stan Rice scoffed. "Here in Jersey, that's juice. I'da been ace dog in high school if my Pop'd been sent up."

"And which dog were you instead?" Jean inquired, straight-faced.

Stan let loose a full-moon howl. Phil chuckled.

"Right after I got the call from Song, I get the daughter's number and give her a call. And that's when I find out the phone and the utilities'd been pulled."

"Recently?" Victor had drawn a notepad in front of him, started to take notes, automatically.

"No. At least five months ago. Before the holidays. Next I call the boy's school, I talk to the principal, Mother Annunciata. She starts going on about how young JP is a straight A student, second in his class, she didn't understand why he would want to drop out."

"So you think the kids took off because they knew he was gonna testify?" Long asked.

Raab shrugged. "All I know is, they disappeared. But the past few months, The Apron was going ahead with his plans to take the stand. It was just the past twenty-four hours he pulls back."

Stan ran his fingers through his hair. "Then someone's got his kids in the crosshairs. And let him know it."

Victor propped his elbows on his desk, steepled his fingertips. "You obviously have reason to think the Forgione children are somewhere around here." That wasn't a question.

Raab's nod acknowledged Victor's intuition. "I got a call from Jim Donato, runs that coffee shop across from the Phoenix. He's always given us the credit for helping him out with that eminent domain suit Blaine Sterling tried to use to take over Jim's property. So, something comes his way, Jim'll dime it in. Last night some guy comes in, he's got the look of someone just blew in from out of town."

"Just about everyone within a block of the casinos has got that look," Long commented.

"No, he was a few years from the tour-bus-free-buffet set. The guy looks around, like he's checking something out. Jim says it looks like he decides to come in because the place was empty. He takes the last booth in the back, before he even picks up the menu, he takes out his cell." Raab took a small notebook out of his breast pocket, flipped it open and read from his notes. "The conversation starts out, he asks something about needing some dough, listens a minute and then says, 'Okay, you're my man. It's twenty large up front, another thirty when you take out the rat and the girl.' Then he sees Jim's wipin' down the booth in front of him, and he switches to Spanish. Jim doesn't let on that his street Spanish is pretty good. He said this guy's was pretty generic. Anyway, Jim said the guy goes on to say, 'Just those two. *Pero antes de matar la chica, necesitas que ella diga donde esta el hermano.*'" He looked up and translated, "But before you kill the girl, she has to tell you where her brother is." Then he said, *'Ya no quiero cargar el pan. ¿Como te reconozco?'*"

Victor translated the last remarks. "I don't want to carry the bread—presumably meaning 'money'—around much longer. How do I recognize you?"

"So this man is supposed to pay off someone who has been hired to kill Paulie Forgione's daughter and someone else. Not the brother. It sounds like he doesn't know where the brother is," Adane said, thoughtfully.

"So who's this 'rat'?" Stan questioned. "Forgione?"

Raab shook his head, baffled. "I don't like that word of Forgione's transfer has hit the street, but even if this guy is talking about him, they can't get to Forgione."

"You want us to take over his security?" Stan asked.

"No. He stays where he is. The marshals'll keep an eye. They're provisioned for the weekend. Forgione gave them his grocery list before he got on the plane in Texas. Not even a newspaper gets in there. My priority right now is to try and locate the kids. I've got the whole bottom half of the state checking employment records, school enrollments, rentals, phone records."

"Where did Elizabeth Forgione go to school?" Adane asked.

"Graduated from the culinary academy over ACC. She was working in Philly at Chez Philippe before she dropped out. I've already contacted them and her school, they're both faxing me a list of her co-workers, professors, the name of her advisor. One of them may have a line on who she hung out with, where she might go.'' Raab drew a pair of photographs from the folder on his lap, handed it over his shoulder to Stan. ''These are a couple recent photos of her. I've sent for the boy's high school yearbook.''

The photos were handed to Victor. Victor studied the first picture. He thought he saw a trace of The Apron's clear-eyed determination in the girl's gaze, the line of the heavy, dark brows. Unnaturally brassy hair was pulled into a knot at her crown and the makeup was a bit overdone, but there was a generous upward tilt at the corners of the mouth, and two mischievous depressions that a good laugh would convert to dimples. A silver filigree crucifix on a black ribbon circled the slender neck.

The second photo was of the girl and her mother, in bathing suits posed in front of a beach umbrella. The proportions of the hourglass figures were identical, though better suited to the girl's taller, long-legged physique.

''The girl knows her way around a kitchen. Jim doesn't have her on the books, does he?'' Stan asked.

''Or off the books,'' Long commented. ''Down the shore, a lotta restaurants hire under the table.''

''She's not working at Jim's. There's one more thing we have to go on. One of the waitresses working last night. As soon as this guy goes to the back booth, she goes up to see if he wants coffee. This is just after he pushed one of the buttons on his cell. Like it's a speed dial, maybe. And she heard him say, 'This Al Cocinera?' then he looks up and sees her and tells the guy to hold, waits until she backs off before he continues the conversation.''

''So we got the shooter's name,'' Phil said.

''We have *a* name,'' Raab replied. ''But I've been running it through the system all day, Al, Albert, Alberto, Allan, Alphonse, Aldo, Alvin, variant spellings of 'Cocinera', possible aliases, nothing. I've had Jim in with a sketch artist to see if we can ID the bag man, but..."

"But," Victor concluded, grimly. "Even if he can describe the caller, we don't know where to start looking for him, and we can't intercept him because we don't know where the payoff's taking place. And once the payoff takes place, the hit will go down, and we haven't the least idea how to go about stopping it."

# THREE

AS CAT STEPPED OFF the escalator at the mezzanine level, she realized that she was scanning the mirrored surfaces for a reflection with that telling mix of edginess and guile that might pinpoint a confidential informant out of his element. Nothing.

She headed along the mezzanine's wide, carpeted walkway with an aperture in the center that accommodated a twenty-story atrium. This opening exposed the gaming crowd to those who patronized the mezzanine's chic shops, but only the difference in elevation distinguished one species from the other; in appearance, they were not terribly dissimilar. With all of their pretense at glamour, casino denizens were a pretty pedestrian crowd, and Cat could not look at them without recalling her mother's tales of a more glamorous Atlantic City, where escorted women strolled the Boardwalk in flowered dresses and white gloves.

The atrium also acted as a siphon for the sound that surged upward from the gaming floor. Cat looked around for a pay phone reasonably isolated from the din of the bells and buzzers, colliding conversations and raining coins, so that she could check in with Freddy, who was baby-sitting with Jane and Mats.

She found a pair of phone booths opposite a darkened ballroom, in a tiny alcove between the restrooms. One phone was occupied by a man who gave her a once-over and turned his back to her, blocking the keypad from her view as he punched in seven digits.

The shift in his posture triggered the faintest ripple of indignation. *As if I would bother to eavesdrop.* Still, she could not help but observe, when he turned his back, that there was a cell phone clipped to his belt. *If he's got a cell, why not use it?*

The mind-your-own-business voice suggested that reception might not be all that good in the casino, but its meddlesome foil reminded her that the new cell phones had excellent reception, or so she had heard, not yet having surrendered to this particular inevitability.

Nor could she help observing that his greeting was in Spanish, *"¿Como se llama el centro de los granos de cacao?"*

Cat shored up her rudimentary Spanish as she slipped two quarters into the slot. *What do you call the—the something, she did not know the word* meollo*—of a cocoa bean?* Before she could come up with a translation, the conversation resumed. *"Sí, bueno. Escucheme. Lo vio, el ratón. Cierto. Está aquí. ¿Que quieres que me hago?"*

Cat dialed. *Yes, good. Listen. I saw him, the big rat. I'm sure. He's here. What do you want me to do?*

Freddy picked up on the second ring. "Hello?"

"It's me. Look, Ellice and I may be held up here, go ahead and get something for the kids. Pizza's fine."

*"Yo no sabes que hace aquí. Comida gratis."* (I don't know what he's doing here. Free food.)

"No problem, Mom's coming by to cook. Victor called."

"He stopped by here, I talked to him."

*"No creo que me vio. ¿Quieres que seguirlo o vamos a encontrar?"* (I don't think he saw me. Do you want me to follow him or are we going to meet?)

"How's it going for Nancy?"

"I think she's booked a couple assignments," Cat replied. Their sister-in-law, Nancy Fortunati, was a talented photographer. She had engaged a vendor's booth at the expo.

*"Sí. Entonces, a las diez de la mañana.* (Yes. Then at ten in the morning.) The man hung up and headed toward the

mezzanine. Mirrored wall panels reflected his features, and Cat logged them: late thirties, sandy hair, tinted wire rims, medium height, compact build, agile gait. Dark, nondescript clothing.

"Call me before you leave, so I know when to start worrying," Freddy told her.

"You sound like Victor." Cat said goodbye, hung up and rounded the corner to the broad mezzanine. Several dozen women, taking a break from the bridal expo, cruised past Bon Soie and CapriOH!, eying ectomorphic mannequins garbed in peignoirs of whisper-fine silk, or wedding gowns with boned bodices above frothy chiffon skirts. Here and there, the hapless male, snared by love, or simply snared, trailed his young fiancée with that look of a befuddled captive. Cat knew that Freddy would have been among them, had the expo taken place anywhere but the Phoenix. He had no desire to run into Fawn Caprio Sterling; the memory of their volatile engagement still rankled.

Cat saw the man from the phone booth making his way toward the ballroom. His nondescript facade was so seamless that even the eyes monitoring the eye-in-the-sky would probably glide past him without question, though he had no woman with him, nor did he have the hapless compliance of an imminent groom.

She followed him into the expo and immediately lost him in the maze of pastel-canopied booths, low-hanging garlands of fine nylon net gathered into clusters of pink and silver balloons. Her gaze panned from one side of the room where wedding planners consulted with prospective brides, to the other side where a woman was giving a lecture on "The Language of Flowers" to a sparse audience.

She caught sight of the dark jacket moving toward a gathering at the far end of the room where an amplified voice and the hum of a collective response indicated a demonstration of some sort. The man paused on the perimeter and seemed to slide behind a garland of gauze and Mylar. Cat craned her neck, saw that the crowd had assembled to watch a demonstration by one of Patty Cake's pastry chefs.

Cat caught sight of Ellice and winnowed her way between two clumps of balloons. "Did I miss the food?" She wriggled her hand into her tote bag and drew out a small notebook and pen.

"They haven't passed out samples yet."

Cat stood on tiptoe to survey the long table, spread with trays filled with rectangular slices of cake, serving dishes displaying a variety of buffet foods. In the center of the table was a large frosted cake in the shape of a pumpkin. The frosting was a flawless coating of creamy gold hue, with threads of chocolate marking the vertical indentations. The bowl-shaped base was supported by wire props camouflaged with a delicately constructed network of ivy leaves molded from green-tinted almond paste, a stem that was shaped from chocolate into a small platform for the miniature Cinderella and her prince.

"What are those?" Cat pointed to a silver mesh basket.

"Chocolate glazed corn chips. There's a chocolate, dried cherry salsa to go with it."

"I didn't know they did *food* food."

"Patty Cake said when she hired her—her name's Edie Hannan—they started doing some catering, only for a few clients who want something out of the ordinary. Those are a few of the dishes they created for a couple who wanted their wedding buffet to be all chocolate. Chicken mole crepes, roast duck with orange-chocolate glaze, baked sweet potato cubes with cocoa bean crumb crust, artichokes in chocolate walnut vinaigrette."

Cat looked at the chef, deftly stirring something in a double boiler, smelled the homespun aroma of caramelizing sugar. "What's she making?"

"Something for that wedding cake."

The girl twirled a wire whisk with one hand, gestured toward the trays of cake slices with the other. "Okay, we're going to start passing out some of the cake samples. The cake

I'll be putting a finish on is pumpkin pound cake. All of my cakes are a butter pound cake, but I can do a fat free version, I can do a fruitcake, I can do layers in a flourless meringue. The darkest cake on the tray is a bitter chocolate chestnut cake, which is my favorite. I use a good quality bittersweet chocolate and freshly roasted chestnuts. Then we have mocha-hazelnut, lemon-honey-clove, cappuccino-marble, chocolate chip, raisin, white chocolate-macadamia and a traditional white cake.''

One of the Phoenix food workers began to make her way through the crowd with the cake tray. Cat felt the current shift a balloon bouquet; the balloons generated static that teased the strands of hair along her cheek.

''On each corner of the table, we have samples of a few of our most popular frostings, vanilla bean butter cream, maple butter cream, burnt sugar butter cream, mocha, mocha fudge and dark chocolate, the one Patty's customers refer to as 'oral—'' She flashed a dimpled smile and mouthed, *Sex.* ''I've put plastic spoons out if you'd like to come up and try a sample. Sorry, no finger tasting.''

The crowd chuckled.

As Cat and Ellice inched toward the waiter passing the trays of cake, Cat was jostled by an arm that shot from the cluster of balloons behind her and Ellice; a hand snatched two cake slices from the tray. The arm and the '''scuse me'' were male. Cat caught a brief backward glance at the man, who had already secured a helping of dark frosting; he spread this on one of the cake layers, placed the other over it and consumed this ''sandwich'' in two bites, then caught the eye of the plump chef and gave her a thumbs-up and a flirtatious wink.

As Cat turned back toward the demonstration, she caught a glimpse of the man from the pay phone, still standing on the perimeter of the crowd. His tinted glasses obscured the direction of his gaze, but Cat had the uneasy sensation that he was staring in her direction. *Probably looking at Ellice,* she told herself. *Everyone stares at Ellice.*

Cat turned back to the pastry chef, whose plump fingers spun the wire whisk around the top of a double boiler. She lifted the pot from the burner and boosted herself onto a small stepladder beside the pumpkin cake. Working with astonishing speed, she waved the whisk like a fairy godmother's wand, spinning it in what seemed to be a random pattern above and around the dome-shaped cake, repeatedly dipping the whisk into the pot, and then swirling it in the air. Gradually, a pattern formed around the Cinderella pumpkin, a golden filigree of cooling caramelized sugar in the shape of a barouche.

This feat of culinary sorcery produced a volley of unwieldy applause, as elbows jostled gauze and balloons, hands clutched slices of cake.

Patty Cake, as tiny and fragile as the chef was tall and plump, took up a hand mike. "That's why we call Edie the queen of confection. Please help yourself to the cake and our buffet dishes, and don't forget to pick up a menu and a business card. If there are any questions, or anyone would like to schedule a consultation, Edie and I will be here for the rest of the afternoon."

Cat stared at the crystalline creation. "Where's Nancy's booth? I'd like to see if I can get her over here for a minute with her camera. Ritchie might give me more than a page if I had a picture to go with the copy."

"I'll go get her. I've been standing still for an hour, I need to move around a little."

Ellice disappeared into the festoons and gauze and returned in a few minutes with Nancy at her side. Nancy's dimpled smile was radiant. "I've lined up four assignments, and I'm completely out of business cards!" Her expression turned toward the crystalline barouche. "Wow!"

"There have to be a couple hundred people here." Cat frowned. "But it's directly in front of us. Do you think you can get off a clear shot from here or do you need to get closer?"

When Cat shifted to let Nancy pass in front of her, she

saw that the man from the pay phone still stood on the edge of the crowd, gazing in her direction.

"You see that guy?" Cat asked Ellice.

"Middle aged, medium frame, nondescript clothing, tinted eyeglasses?"

"Yeah. Do you think there's something odd about him?"

Ellice, the scholar, quoted Shakespeare. "'An odd man, lady! Every man is odd.'"

"Seriously."

"Well, he does have that look. Like he was dragged here? Like he wishes he was hugging a six-pack, watching something that takes place in a stadium."

Cat nodded. Someone jostled her and she clutched her notebook to keep from dropping it. A few people wedged in front of her and the gap between her and the table, rather than decreasing, widened and filled with shoving bodies. Cat lost sight of Nancy. "I was hoping we could get a good shot, but it's going to be tough in this crowd. Keeping all the bystanders out of range."

"Off with their heads," Ellice replied, drolly.

Cat did not hear her own aborted laugh, was conscious of the explosion of mayhem before her mind processed the *pop pop pop* that preceded it.

*"Gun!"*

Cat was caught in a riptide of chaos, tumbled into a mass of shoving bodies and scrambling feet. She tried to cry out Ellice's name, but could not hear her own voice over the shrieks and collapsing displays and *pop pop pop.*

Her hair was grasped from behind and she was yanked to her knees. A male voice snarled in her ear, "Move and don't look around, or—" the tip of something sharp slid under her shirt "—I do you right here."

*What's happening?*

"Don't look around, don't try to yell for help."

She was pulled to her feet and shoved into the current that surged toward the exit, navigated by the hand grasping her hair at her nape, prodded with the tip of something sharp and lethal when she faltered.

The pressure of the current eased and then compressed as she was shoved onto the escalator. Cat felt a wave of dizziness as she descended toward the expanse of slot machines on the ground level. Surely the crowd would disperse there, and she could break free, weave through the maze of slot machines and run for one of the exits.

But as soon as she hit the landing, the blade was jabbed upward, its point embedded between her lower ribs. The slot addicts, in their tranced states, were blind to her plight. Their eyes were fixed on the rotating images, they did not see the man with one hand in a woman's hair, another around her waist, steering her toward the Boardwalk exit. Gun, fire, explosion would not have shaken any of them from their torpor, would not have halted the pumping arms or diverted their mesmerized gazes.

And then she was inhaling the chilly salt air of the Boardwalk. She glanced around for help, but police officers were rare on the Boardwalk and the gusty ocean breeze and waning light had thinned the already sparse crowd.

''Straight across the boards to the steps.''

Cat glanced at the swatch of bare arm wedged against her waist, felt the buckle of a belt pressed into her back, several inches above her own waistline, pulled the facts into the beginnings of a profile. White male, tall, perhaps six feet. Young to middle age.

She stumbled down the wooden steps, felt chilly sand seep into her shoes as she was dragged backward into the shadows beneath the Boardwalk. Overhead, she heard the clatter of scurrying feet, people collecting to discover the source of the excitement inside the Phoenix. She heard the distant wail of a siren. Soon the police would be there, perhaps a cruiser would drive onto the Boardwalk above, perhaps she could manage a cry.

Then she was thrown facedown onto the damp, chilly sand. She gasped, inhaling sand into her nose and throat and she began to cough and choke.

*He's going to kill me!*

# FOUR

VICTOR NODDED toward the ringing phone and Jean Adane reached to pick it up. ''Lieutenant Cardenas's office. One moment.'' She put a hand over the mouthpiece. ''Freddy Fortunati?''

Victor ignored the curious attention of the others, took the receiver from Adane. ''Freddy.'' He heard the background whoosh that suggested Freddy was on a cell phone.

''Were you at the Phoenix? You see Cat?''

''Yes, why?''

''I'm on my way over there now—''

Another line flashed on Victor's phone as Raab's cell phone went off.

''—something went down in the ballroom where they were holding that expo. They're saying someone pulled out a gun, fired into the crowd. I'm on my way over there.'' His voice choked up for a second. ''Ellice and Cat are there.''

Victor's gaze connected with Raab's. ''Freddy, does Ellice have a cell phone?'' He knew that Cat didn't.

''No, but Nancy does, she's there, too. I'll call Marco.''

The phone in the day room started to ring.

''I'll be on mine.'' Victor hung up and looked at Raab, who was still talking to someone on his cell. ''There was a disturbance at the Phoenix inside one of the mezzanine ballrooms.''

''What kinda disturbance?'' Stan asked.

''It could be a false alarm. But the initial report is that there were shots fired.'' Victor paused. ''Mrs. Austen was at the Phoenix." His monotone, his grave expression, conveyed no emotion. "She was there covering the event in the ballroom. A sister-in-law and her brother's fiancée were there, too."

Raab started dialing his cell phone. "You head over there. I'll contact CIU and tell them to give you access. They give you a hard time, buzz me. My office has been carrying the state on The Apron business, they owe me a little something."

"You want company?" Stan asked.

"No." Victor pushed himself away from the desk and strode toward the door.

Raab made eye contact with Stan, jerked his head toward the door. "Go. And you do the driving."

"PRETTY SMART OF MAC, using a woman. When'd you start tailing me?"

*Who? What? Stall. Think.* Her mind rewound the past ten minutes, played it back in slow motion. She had been chatting with Ellice, waiting to see if Nancy could get a photo of the pastry chef and her cake. Shots. Someone, a male voice, *his* voice? Crying "Gun!" and everyone scattering.

She raised her head and spat out sand. "Who's Mac?"

"I oughta kill you right here." His knee was in her back, compressing her ribs into the humid sand. Cat felt the moisture seep into the front of her thin shirt. He leaned down to her, close enough for her to feel his chocolate-scented breath on her right cheek. "How did you pick up on us?"

"I don't know what you're—" *Talking about.* Did anyone ever fall for that line?

His expletive was uninspired compared to the scatological ingenuity of her brother Carlo, as was his follow up. "You're a lousy liar."

"Would that be 'lousy' in the sense of unconvincing or 'lousy' in the sense of 'malevolent'?"

It was the deciphering of *malevolent,* she decided, that stalled him long enough for her to brace her right arm, then jerk her elbow upward. Her elbow connected with his cheekbone, sending needles of pain to her fingertips. His grip on her hair loosened and he lurched off balance. Cat rolled onto her side, drew up her knee and kicked out, striking his waist with the flat of her heel.

*Run!*

Late daylight penetrated the slats in the boards, and the streaks of gray illumination revealed a limber figure, a comma of dark hair falling over a pale forehead. Twenty minutes ago he had been sandwiching frosting between cake samples, with the plastic spoon that he had snapped, used as a knife. The sight of that shard of white plastic in his grip detonated a tremor of hysteria in the base of her ribs. Her ribs began quivering with something on the border of laughter.

They heard the sharp *booop, booop, booop* of the patrol car siren as it rumbled up the ramp. Cat could hear the planks rattling overhead and looked up.

She saw a glowing red dot fixed to a rusting bolt on the underside of the boards. She watched, dazed as it slid downward, coasted toward the man huddled, facing her.

She didn't know why; it wouldn't be clear in her mind until later. And later, she would think she had been a fool. But for now, she acted without thinking, pitched into the man, throwing him down on the sand. She heard a faint *plop* and a tiny eruption of sand a foot or two from where they fell.

The man threw her off, charged into the dark, and vanished.

# FIVE

STAN RICE MANEUVERED Victor's Jag toward the black and whites that idled, grille to grille, blocking off Pacific Avenue at New Bedford. Victor jumped out, with the car still coasting, and began jogging toward Oriental. On the corner of Oriental and New Bedford, a single unit idled at the entrance to the Phoenix Self-Park. The waning sun, the glow of the gold bulbs spelling out Phoenix Self-Park, the sputtering pink neon of Jim's Coffee Shoppe on the corner of Oriental and New Bedford, threw a sideshow light on the people who drifted into the street, lured by commotion and crude excitement.

Victor glanced down the long stretch of New Bedford, saw the flashing lights of a patrol car on the Boardwalk. He approached the uniform. "What do you know?"

"Not much. There's some kinda convention on the mezzanine level, someone fired off a few shots and everyone started heading for the exits. No reports of casualties."

"Did Casino Investigation order an evacuation?"

"Not that I heard. You better check with hotel security. Best way would be to cut through the garage and take the elevator or the stairs up to Five."

Victor nodded shortly. He knew where it was. Exactly where Cat had come for help when she had found a body in the garage elevator a few months earlier. The rank, almost metallic smell of ocean air mingled with stagnant fumes. Victor had to duck his head to avoid the low-hanging concrete beams. He opted for the stairwell and trotted up to Five, made his way to the security entrance opposite the executive parking level.

His impatient push on the bell brought a green-jacketed security guard. Victor held up his shield. "The county D.A. has contacted CIU to expect me," he said, when the man opened the door. "I'm going to the mezzanine level first. How would I get to surveillance command from there?"

"I'm not supposed to give out that information."

Victor wondered if he even knew. The central command station was located at a site within the casino that was known only to a fraction of the security staff, to the Casino Investigation Unit and to Blaine Sterling himself.

"I'll find it," he said evenly. "I'll want to view the last hour's worth of tapes from the ballroom, try to narrow it to the source of the alarm. They're time logged, correct?"

"I'm not authorized to divulge information about security procedures."

Victor said nothing, simply kept his gaze leveled on the man. Finally, the man muttered, "Yeah, they're all time logged."

"Ask them to have the tapes queued up."

He strode past the doors of the executive suite to the elevator, pushed the button. Cat. Where was Cat? He remembered some months ago, a body in the Phoenix garage, knowing Cat had been at the Phoenix, the surge of panic. But she had been all right that time. She had to be all right now.

When he exited the elevator, he was struck by the unusual quiet. There were no oases of silence in a casino; bands and vocalists, rattling glassware and intersecting conversations filtered from open lounges, the chronic precipitation of coins, buzzers and exclamations circulated in the gaming areas, incoherent announcements emerged from the PA system, and coherent ones cycled over speakers in the corridors and elevators.

Two green-jacketed security guards and a state police officer stood at the entrance to the ballroom, a third security guard had been posted in front of Clevingers, the jewelry store. *A ruse, to rob the jeweler?* Victor wondered. No, too much commotion was involved, whatever had happened, it wasn't a robbery.

He produced his shield. The state policewoman nodded; obviously Raab had gotten through to the in-house state police unit.

Inside the ballroom, soft, piped-in music contrasted eerily with the toppled booths, their pastel skirts trampled and torn. Garlands that had been suspended from the ceiling lay in shreds. Wilted balloon bouquets, half of the balloons deflated, drifted limply across the brochure-littered floor. Victor heard a sound he could not identify. It resembled the cry of a little child. He followed it through a maze of trampled draperies to a booth, Conjugal Critters. There were half a dozen carriers, four dogs, two cats. The cats were napping but the dogs paced apprehensively.

"Jeez." Stan Rice appeared behind Victor. "People oughta be shot, treat animals like this." Stan's soft heart crossed species. He bent down and wriggled a finger through the grille of one of the cages, and the little cocker spaniel licked his hand. He started to unlatch the cages.

"You'd better leave them where they are," Victor advised.

Stan ignored the order and set the dogs loose. They collected around him. "How much damage can they do, Lieutenant? Look at this place."

Victor nodded. He picked up one of the diagrams from the batch that had been scattered on the floor, traced with his index finger the site of Nancy Fortunati's table. He made his way there, found her brochures, the portfolio of her work on the table. He looked around and turned up a tote bag and her purse tucked underneath the skirt. Whatever happened had happened when she hadn't been at her booth. Or so fast she hadn't had time to grab her purse.

The dogs had trailed Stan to the overturned tables at the Patty Cake display. They took a few steps away from his heels to nose through the spilled food, pick out bits of turkey and duck from the mess. The pumpkin cake had exploded on the floor, shards of the hardened candy sculpture scattered around it.

Victor bent down, picked up a brochure from the floor.

Patty Cake Patisserie
Featuring Cakes and Catering by Edie Hannan

There was a photo of two women, one tall, plump and brunette, the other short, thin and brunette, flanking an eight-tiered wedding cake. Victor shook crumbs from the brochure and pocketed it. "Patty Cake," he murmured.

"Huh?" Stan approached the uppermost portion of the dome, which had dropped to the floor intact. He plucked a small portion and popped it in his mouth.

"You may be eating evidence," Victor told him dryly.

Stan licked his fingers. "Pumpkin." He looked around, lifted a knot of balloon strings from the floor with a ballpoint. The deflated balloons dangled limply. "You thinking what I'm thinking?"

"That a popped balloon may have been mistaken for a gunshot," Victor replied.

"More than one. Just about all of them have burst."

Victor's cell phone trilled and he grabbed it. "Cardenas."

"Victor? It's Marco Fortunati."

The third of the six Fortunati brothers. Nancy's husband. "Where are you?"

"I'm outside on the Boardwalk, just hooked up with Freddy. Nancy and Ellice are with us."

Victor closed his eyes. "Cat?"

"She hasn't turned up yet. They got separated in the commotion. They both said there was something sounded like shots and someone yelled there was a gun and everything went haywire."

"I'm going to check out the security tapes of the incident. If you connect with Cat, call me."

"Will do."

Victor pocketed his cell phone, looked down at Stan who was toying with one of the dogs. He handed him Nancy's purse and bag. ''Rice, have the in-house officer seal this place off and hang around until the crime scene people arrive. Then you join me in security.''

Stan cradled one of the puppies in his arm, let it lick frosting from his index finger. ''Any word on Cat?''

Victor shook his head.

He strode out of the room, closed the door. ''Nobody is to be admitted back in until CUI's swept the room.''

One of the Phoenix security guards spoke up. ''We take our orders from Mr. Sterling.''

''Unless Mr. Sterling's orders come from God, then you take your orders from me for now. If you have a problem with that, register your complaint with the D.A.'s office.''

Victor turned and walked toward the elevator. At the murmur of an expletive, Victor stopped. He didn't turn around, simply halted and said in his characteristic monotone, ''Don't use that language in front of a lady.'' It was probably nothing the female in uniform hadn't heard, but there were canons of chivalry that had been instituted too early and too consistently to have eroded, even a quarter century after his father's murder.

He continued walking. If the expletive was repeated, it was out of his hearing.

# SIX

CAT TRIED TO concentrate on catching her breath. She plucked the thin cotton shirt, soaked through with moisture from the damp sand, away from the spot where he had jabbed the shard of a plastic spoon handle into her sternum.

*Wait a minute, make sure he's gone. Then make your way to the Boardwalk stairs. You'll be safe there. Breathe.*

That took priority, but she gulped in air so desperately that the intake was permeated with sand, and she started to cough in gasping, eye-watering spasms.

"Can I be of some assistance, *señorita?*"

Her head jerked up and she saw a silhouette crouched only a few feet away. *Where did he come from?* She had not even heard his approach.

Cat blinked hard, willing her eyes to adjust to the twilight. She was able to make out dark hair with a single white streak arching upward from the widow's peak, a straight black mustache, dark eyes. For a moment, she thought it was Victor, but it was not Victor's voice and the clinging black nylon T-shirt under a short black leather jacket, tight black denims were not Victor's style.

"Are you all right? Are you hurt?"

Cat shook her head. The movement showered sand toward her eyes and they started to water.

"Can you walk?"

Cat squinted and the face started to take on detail—dark, straight brows, a firm jaw, a perfectly formed mouth, slightly marred by the contraction of the flesh due to a line of scar tissue that ran from the outward corner of his left eyebrow to just below his left cheekbone.

"Can you talk?" The voice was patient, a little amused. *"Parlez-vous français? ¿Habla usted español? Parl' italiano?"*

Irritation splintered her tension. "*Sí, lo capisc'*. But English will do."

The smile seemed to originate with the lopsided scar that hooked the mouth into an uneven smile.

"He went that way," Cat pointed over her shoulder. "If you call it in, maybe someone can intercept him."

"I beg your pardon?"

"Aren't you the police?"

The mouth twisted again in a lopsided smile. "The police? No, *señorita.*"

"*Señora,*" Cat corrected, her voice a bit shaky.

"*Señora.* Intercept whom?"

Cat brushed her hair away from her face. "I don't know. I was attending a trade show and this man just went crazy. He started a riot and then dragged me out at knifepoint—" *Spoonpoint,* she amended, silently. "Forced me down here, and started ranting. The next thing I knew he ran off."

"*Borracho.* Let me help you up." He rose, ducking his head to clear the underside of the Boardwalk, and held out his hand.

Cat ignored the outstretched hand. "No, he wasn't drunk. It wasn't alcohol I smelled, it was...chocolate." She felt a spasm of hysteria vibrate her vocal chords, heard her unsteady laugh.

"It is said that that form of intoxication produces ardor, not aggression."

Cat raised her brows primly. His hand was still extended, and after a brief hesitation, Cat took it and allowed him to pull her to her feet.

"Watch your head."

The ocean breeze had become brazen, making Cat acutely

aware of the transparency of her thin blouse. She crossed her arms over her chest, started to shiver.

He calmly transferred the contents of his jacket pockets to those in his trousers, then slipped off his jacket and threw it over her shoulders. "I insist," he said, before she could protest. *"Por favor."*

*Por favor. Señora. Habla usted español. Borracho.* "You speak Spanish?"

*"Sí."*

"Do you know what the word *meollo* means?"

He did not answer immediately. "Why do you ask?"

She didn't know why she asked, but she was given to hunches and fits of inconvenient intuition. She didn't know why his tone made her retreat a step toward the Boardwalk stair. She glanced upward. Dusk had converted the figures milling on the Boardwalk to silhouettes, only a few of them illuminated by the green-and-gold bulbs outlining the pagodalike towers of The Phoenix.

The rotating lights of the patrol car were switched on, sending a flashing a red strobe over his features. He stepped back from the light, was reduced to a silhouette once more.

She backed up, too, toward the steps, groping behind her for the railing. "I'd better get a hold of a police officer." She backed up a step. "I don't know how to thank you for your help—"

"No matter. I'm not accustomed to being thanked."

He turned and strode down the beach away from her. Cat gazed, baffled at the trail of indistinct footprints, the dark silhouette that was dissolving into the dusk with the swiftness and assurance of a feral cat.

"Wait! What about your jacket?"

She thought she saw the figure raise one hand in parting, then it merged with the night.

# SEVEN

THERE WERE NEARLY one thousand surveillance cameras concealed throughout the Phoenix. Most of them were trained on the gaming floor, a significant number on the exterior and interior of the mezzanine's exclusive boutiques, the hotel floors, elevators, lavatories, employee dressing rooms and cafeterias.

The images from these hidden lenses were transmitted to three dozen monitors inside the surveillance supervision post, commanded by one of the state police officers with the Casino Investigation Unit. Under his direction, a shift of ten scrupulously screened personnel monitored stations with four screens each and performed the taping and cataloguing of the data that streamed nonstop into the site.

Victor noted that the supervision of the parking garage had not improved measurably since he was last there, that the screeners were able to hold and zoom in closely enough to see the face of a single playing card, and that they were more likely to bring up detail of this nature from the gaming tables. Images of people heading for the coffee shop, along the corridor to the parking garage, on the low-end outer perimeter of the slot area flickered by without much scrutiny.

"We got your tape queued, Lieutenant." That from one of the green-jacketed Phoenix security. His attitude was considerably more civil than his co-worker's had been. Victor wondered if they had gotten the word from the state police, or perhaps from one of the Sterlings.

Victor stepped up to a quartet of monitors.

"The disturbance started up inside the trade show. Bridal show. The presenters are from the outside, contracted for the location." Making it clear that they were not Phoenix personnel.

Victor nodded silently. He imagined that a trade show, which did not spell profit or potential loss to the casino, had not been monitored as vigilantly as the blackjack tables. He looked down at the four screens. The overhead shots had shown the room laid out in a maze of booths, bisected by a runway. The perimeters of the room were given over to larger demonstration areas.

Victor watched the images advance in sequence, asked the woman at the post to freeze them on a shot of a woman standing before a large, pumpkin-shaped cake. Victor's gaze panned the screen slowly, isolating individuals. He picked out Ellice. He nodded and the images began flickering again. He saw Ellice moving through the crowd, Ellice with Nancy Fortunati, then he caught the back of Cat's head, her shoulder-length hair, the white shirtwaist blouse.

He felt his pulse accelerate. "Freeze it," he said, and made a mental note of the time log. Almost an hour and a half ago. "Can you zoom in on those two women?" He tapped the center of the screen. The view on the monitor centered on Ellice and Cat. He saw Cat nudge a cluster of balloons aside, lean over to say something to Ellice. Both women looked to their left, looked at something or someone out of the lens's range, then exchanged another comment.

"Pull back." Victor studied the people surrounding Cat, all facing away from the lens, watching the demonstration. He noticed that the person behind her was a man; not many men in the room.

The man seemed to reach up to push away a few balloons that had drifted into his line of vision, and they began to pop, one after the other. Chaos erupted and Cat fell into the mass of motion and Victor lost sight of her.

"Bring up the view of the exit from the mezzanine side, please," he instructed the woman at the console.

Another set of images appeared. Bodies spilled into the broad corridor and scattered toward the shops, the escalators, and the walkways leading to the garage. Victor scanned the image, did not see Cat immediately. He asked the guard to freeze the tape and studied the images again, this time looking for the male figure who had stationed himself behind Cat.

His cell phone trilled. He drew it from his pocket, his eyes on the monitor. "Cardenas."

"Victor?"

The quartet of images blurred and he felt his throat constrict. He cleared his throat. Cat. "Where are you?"

"I'm down on the Boardwalk with Marco, Nancy, Freddy and Ellice. They want to go wait for you at Jim's."

"Yes. What happened?"

"We were watching a pastry demo and Nancy was trying to get a shot of it and then I thought I heard gunshots and somebody yelled 'Gun!' and this man grabbed me and jabbed something that I thought was a knife under my shirt and started shoving me out of the casino. And then after he dragged me under the Boardwalk—shut *up,* Freddy, you can see that I'm all right!"

"Continue."

"He dragged me under the Boardwalk. And then he started acting…I don't know. All I can think of is that he thought I was someone else. He was saying things like how did I know where he was and that I was a liar."

"And you didn't recognize him?"

"I've never seen him before. And I never want to see him again."

"Are you all right?"

"Yes. Victor, I've forgotten a lot of my Spanish vocab. What does the word *meollo* mean?"

"I assume the question is relevant to the matter at hand?"

"You should never assume."

He smiled. "It can mean kernel, or pith. Meat in the sense of substance. Marrow."

"A food term."

"Generally, yes. Not exclusively."

"It doesn't have any kind of, like, slang meaning?"

"No anatomical connotation, you mean?"

"Mind your manners, Lieutenant."

"I'm not aware of any. Why?"

"I just heard someone use it in what seemed like an odd context. But he was speaking Spanish, so I may have been mistaken."

"Who was speaking Spanish? The man who grabbed you?"

"No, the guy on the phone."

"What guy on what phone?"

"That guy, the one I was pointing out to Ellice. Right before all the commotion started. And then the other guy—"

"Meaning the man who took you."

"No, the one who came by to help me."

Victor repressed a patient sigh. "This is developing into quite a cast of characters. Put Freddy on."

He heard her aggravated sigh, but after a moment Freddy took the phone.

"Is she all right?" Victor asked him.

"Yeah. Messed up a little. Someone loaned her a jacket."

"Okay. Look, why don't the four of you go over to Jim's and wait for me there? I'll be about twenty minutes."

"'S long as we don't have to order any food."

He pocketed his cell phone.

The woman at the console spoke up. "Lieutenant, I think I can zoom in a little on this man."

Victor watched the screen. The image of a man stationed behind Cat blossomed. Cat's head blocked a portion of his, but the forehead, nose, angle of the chin were detectable.

*¡Dios mío!*

"Lieutenant? Do you recognize him?"

"Yes."

# EIGHT

"OKAY, start from after we went our separate ways."

Six of them, Cat, Victor, Freddy, Ellice, Marco and Nancy, were wedged into the back booth at Jim's Coffee Shoppe.

Cat looked down at her coffee. An iridescent slick floated on the surface. "I thought we might be running late, so I decided to give Freddy a call. I looked for a phone booth where it wasn't too noisy. That's where I saw this guy."

"Which one? As I recall, there were several."

"The one you pointed out to me in the ballroom?" Ellice asked.

Cat nodded. "There was something about him that struck me as odd."

Victor knew that Cat's instinct for identifying the aberrant or strange was rather acute. "What?"

Cat nodded. "When I came up to the booth, he turned his back to me, as though he didn't want me to see what number he was dialing. And that's when I saw that he had a cell phone."

"So you wondered, why use a pay phone."

Cat pushed a strand of hair behind her ear. "And then he asked this odd question. I mean, you don't often call someone, and before they even get a chance to say hello, ask what you call the meat of a cocoa bean, do you?"

"Come again?"

"That's why I asked what *meollo* meant. The whole conversation was in Spanish. And the first words out of his mouth were, *What do you call the center of a cocoa bean?*"

"Code," Marco grunted. "He doesn't know the guy on the other end, it's how he's IDing him."

Victor nodded. "Odd question, though. What else did he say?"

"He said that he spotted someone he called 'the rat.' 'The big rat.'" Cat saw Victor's jaw set in concentration. "Does that mean something?"

"Continue."

"Why was that significant?"

*"Por favor."*

"He asked if they should still meet or should he follow this rat person, and then he listened for a while and said, 'Okay, *a las diez de la mañana.* Ten o'clock tomorrow morning. Then he hung up and headed right for the ballroom."

"The guy you pointed out to me?" Ellice asked. "The one who was looking in our direction?"

"It seemed so. I assumed he was looking at Ellice."

"What's he looking at Ellice for?"

"Freddy, everyone looks at Ellice."

Ellice patted Freddy's arm affectionately. "It's the skin tone, honey. They think I'm made of chocolate."

"Can you describe this man?" Victor asked.

"Nondescript. Almost deliberately nondescript. Like he was making an effort to blend."

"In a room full of women?" Freddy asked.

"Bridal expos aren't gender exclusive, Freddy. There were caterers, limos, everything."

"But they don't call it a bridal and *groomal* show, do they?"

Cat rolled her eyes.

"So," Victor rolled his coffee cup between his palms. "This man has a phone conversation, then he goes into the expo and he's looking in your direction. And with all due deference to Ellice, it is more likely that this man was watching the man behind you. The man behind you saw that he was being watched, and deliberately started the panic. All it took was popping a few balloons and shouting that someone had a gun.''

''So the guy behind Cat and Ellice, sounds like he's your rat,'' Freddy concluded. ''But what's he grab Cat for?''

''To get away from the man watching him,'' Cat replied.

''Why wouldn't just the diversion have done that?'' Marco muttered. ''All you want is to get away. You don't take excess baggage along.''

''Thanks, so much,'' Cat said.

''What did he say to you?'' Victor asked.

Cat toyed with a strand of her hair. ''He ranted. What did I want, how did I find him. Then I gave him a shot—''

''Which move did you use?'' Marco taught self-defense at the police academy, and also taught women's self-defense courses open to the public.

Cat gestured with her crooked elbow. ''Shot to the cheekbone.'' Her dark eyes clouded.

''What's the matter?'' Victor asked.

''Something else happened. I *think.* I saw this red light and I shoved him aside. It was probably just a reflection of something or, you know, one of those red laser pointers that all the kids were carrying around a few years ago. But...''

''But what?''

''My first instinct was that it was the light on, you know, a scope.''

''Go on,'' Victor said. ''You told me there was another person, someone who came to your aid.''

Cat nodded, one palm running over the weathered hide of the jacket. ''I don't know where he came from. He asked if he could help me out and when he saw that I was all right, he just walked away.''

''What did he look like?'' Victor asked.

''Dark. Latin, maybe. A streak of white in his hair. Mustache.'' She ran her thumb from the corner of a slanted eyebrow downward. ''A scar.''

''Lotta people hanging around the boards,'' Freddy commented. "You're lucky one of them saw you. How you gonna get his jacket back to him?"

"I have no idea."

Victor saw Stan Rice enter. He nodded toward the counter, excused himself and rose.

Stan swung by the table, greeted Freddy and Marco with a handshake, passed Nancy's bags to her and kissed Cat on the cheek. "So you okay?"

"I'm fine, Stanley. What are those?"

"Pix for the lieutenant. 'Scuse me." He walked over to the counter and handed Victor a set of prints. "Surveillance cams picked these up, they printed them off the video."

Victor perched on a stool, studying the pictures. He signaled the waitress who was wiping down the counter, showed her his shield. "Please ask Jim to come out here."

She wiped her hands on the rag, shoved it into an apron pocket. "Jim, it's the health inspectors again!"

Jim barreled out of the kitchen, shoulders first. He was a squat figure with a bulldog face. He eyed Victor. "Hon, he's not the health inspector, he's homicide."

Her look of wary resignation suggested that she believed Victor intended to inspect the stew nonetheless.

"What c'n I do for you, Lieutenant?"

Victor laid the pictures on the counter. "You recognize any of them?"

Jim's gaze swiped the set of photos. He tapped one with a grease-splotched index finger. "He's the guy I told the D.A. about. The guy on the cell phone?"

The man carrying the funds for the hit on Paulie Forgione's kids. "You're certain?"

"You bet. He was in again earlier, 'smatter of fact, but we were crowded. He changed his mind and walked out."

"Did he look like he recognized anyone? Anyone recognized him?"

Jim shook his head. "The crowd, they were my firsta the month reg'lars. This guy's not a local."

"Mail's been slow," the waitress added.

Victor understood the connection. When first of the month assistance checks were slow, Jim was known to provide a hot meal for several dozen people. In cold weather, kids on the way to school knocked on the kitchen door, and left with a foam cup and something wrapped in a napkin passed to them as surreptitiously as if Jim were pushing dope instead of free cocoa and buttered toast.

Victor laid one of his cards on the counter. "If he comes in again, call me."

Jim pocketed the card and headed back to the kitchen.

Victor repeated Cat's story to Stan. "This one—" He tapped the photo. "He was the guy who contacted the shooter yesterday. The one Jim called Raab about. The man he was checking out? It was Pavo. Which means Pavo is this 'rat' they're talking about."

"What's Pavo doin' hanging around the Phoenix?"

"I'm more interested in knowing why he started a riot and dragged Mrs. Austen out of the Phoenix. I'm going to run through the incident with her again. Have Adane put this picture out over the wire, see if we can pull up an ID, something that would link him to Mackenzie. Tell Long to work the street, see if he can turn up Pavo. Leave the pictures with me. Oh, and have the CS team take a sweep under the Boardwalk in the vicinity of the Phoenix."

"You looking for anything in particular?"

"I don't know."

"You could have just asked us to go powder our noses," Cat said, when Victor dismissed Stan and rejoined them.

"Nonsense," Victor replied, evenly. He laid money on the table for their coffee and a tip. "One has to pass through the kitchen to get to the rest rooms, and that's hardly a sight for ladies."

# NINE

VICTOR HEADED DOWN Atlantic Avenue. "The man who grabbed you, can you describe him?"

Cat tilted her head, scrutinized him. "I *already* described him. You're just trying to see if I'm going to remain consistent as to the details."

"Or if you're going to alter them. Sherlock Holmes advised one ought not to trust general impressions, but concentrate on the details."

"Carlo says never trust the details because on the next interview they're likely to change."

Victor reached for the envelope of photos he had tucked under his seat, handed them to Cat. "Recognize anyone?"

She removed the pictures and held them to the light of the open glove compartment. "Yes. This is the man who grabbed me. And this is the one who was on the pay phone."

"Did you see either one speak to anyone else?"

"No."

"Did you see them speak to each other?"

Cat shook her head, tugged at the collar of her shirt. A spattering of damp sand fell into her lap. "I'm getting your car all sandy. You really are a remarkable man, Victor."

"Thanks. How so?"

"If I were shedding sand all over any other guy's car, he would have a fit."

"We'll stop at my place, you can get out of that wet shirt."

Cat lifted her dark brows. "And then maybe you're not so remarkable after all."

"I meant that I'll loan you a sweatshirt. What about the guy who came to help you out? Can you remember anything more about him?"

"I don't know. The Lone Ranger. Here and gone."

"Unusual, just to appear out of nowhere like that," Victor mused.

He made a left onto Delancy and parked along the curb in front of a three-story house. The block was a dead-end street, beach block. The houses were large, older single-family homes, many of them summer homes that lay dormant in the off-season. Only Mrs. DiLorenzo, Victor's landlady, had subdivided her home into apartments. Victor rented the second floor.

Victor opened Cat's door, helped her out of the car. They walked up to the second-story landing, and Victor took his mail from the box. Then he unlocked his front door.

He hung his jacket on the coatrack beside the door, nodded toward the bedroom. "Go find something to put on."

Cat went into the bedroom and closed the door. Victor checked his machine; no messages.

There was a tapping sound, a knuckle against glass. Victor's right hand instinctively reached toward the back of his waistband, drew out his 9 mm. He looked across the living room to the kitchen, saw a face peering through the window above the kitchen sink. Pavo.

He jammed the weapon back into his waistband and unlatched the window, pushed it up. The man scrambled awkwardly from the fire escape onto the counter, hopped to the floor.

"Not the best place for a fire escape, man."

"It's an old house," Victor said evenly. "Next time, try the door." He grabbed a fistful of the man's shirt, rammed him against the counter. "And the next time you try a stunt like the one in the Phoenix? Make sure my woman's not in the room, *me entiendes?*"

"Whadda you talkin' about, *monje?*" the man sputtered.

Victor released him. "Who's trying to kill you, Vincent?" Among cops, the man was known only by his street name, Pavo. But when speaking to him, Victor always used his first name.

"I don't know what you're talking about. Look, you got anything to eat? I'm starved."

Victor opened the refrigerator, took out a small bottle of club soda. He stood blocking the open refrigerator. "Are you going to talk to me, Vincent?"

The man craned his neck to look past Victor. "Look, okay. Just lemme get something to eat."

Victor stepped away from the refrigerator and the man began pulling out the makings of a sandwich.

"Start by telling me why you didn't make our meet."

The man piled sliced ham, cheese, tomatoes, mustard on the counter. "I got hung up. You got any rolls?"

"Whole wheat bread."

"Got any chips?"

"No."

The man reached for a knife and began slicing the tomato into wafers, stopped cold. "Who's in the bedroom?"

"A friend."

The bedroom door opened and Cat came out, wearing a gray sweatshirt with the sleeves bunched up over her elbows, her sodden shirt balled in one hand. "Victor, do you have a plastic bag or something—" She stopped short, the shirt slipping from her fingers. "It's him!"

Pavo's fingers curled around the knife handle. "It's her, man. It's *her.* Do something!"

"Such as what?" Victor inquired.

"Arrest her."

Victor calmly disengaged Pavo's fingers from the knife handle. "For what?"

"She's trying to kill us. Me. She's gonna kill me."

"Kill you!" Cat directed an irate glare toward Victor. "Aren't you going to do anything?"

"I was going to offer to fix you something to eat if Pavo here hasn't cleaned me out."

Cat blinked. "Pavo? *He*'s your *CI?*"

Victor's mouth arced in a scowling smile.

"Wha—you know her? Who the hell is she?"

*"Mi alma,"* Victor replied, imperturbably. "So watch your language. And next time, you watch who you put your hands on. Cat, allow me to introduce Vincent Buonovitti. Vincent, this is Mrs. Austen. She's a reporter."

Pavo's hands tightened over his sandwich. "Who put you on to me?"

"*On* to you? Under the Boardwalk, I think it was quite the other way around!"

"Perhaps we should all sit," Victor suggested. He took a can of Pepsi from the refrigerator, put a few ice cubes in a glass and brought it into the living room, handed it to Cat.

Pavo got back to business, compiled a three-inch-high sandwich and set it on a plate, sliced it in half. He picked up one segment, sank his teeth into it and a blissful torpor settled over his striking features, an expression not unlike the euphoria induced by heroin in the bloodstream.

"Get in here," Victor ordered.

Pavo grabbed a Pepsi and bussed his food into the living room, sat on one of the face-to-face sofas, settled his food on the coffee table.

"So okay. *El monje* here says you're not out to get me, I'll take his word." Pavo took another bite of the sandwich.

"Why would you think Mrs. Austen was trying to kill you?" Victor asked.

"Because I figure next time Mac wouldn't hire someone like me, considering how things turned out. And a woman? Hit woman? Who'd be on the lookout for that?"

"Mac?"

"Cholly Mackedzie," Pavo mumbled with his mouth full.

"You're saying Mackenzie wants to kill you?" Victor asked.

Pavo nodded.

"And that's why you wanted to meet with me today?"

Again, Pavo nodded. He swallowed his mouthful. "And there's this wedding expo, they got a lotta local caterers and bakers, cooking demos every half hour and a ton of free samples, *monje*. The two of them, they're makin' eye contact." He nodded toward Cat.

"The two of whom?" Cat demanded.

"You and Sal. I saw him hangin' out on the side of the room."

"Sal?" Victor inquired.

"Salvatore Mosca. Sally the Fly." Pavo finished off the last of his sandwich, licked his fingers. "I'm gonna make myself another half sandwich. Anyone want anything?" He got up and went back to the kitchen.

Victor perched on the arm of the sofa next to Cat. "You said you wanted to meet a CI, *querida,*" he reminded her in a low voice.

"I thought he'd be a bit more dashing, less..."

"Less what?"

"Famished."

Pavo returned with his food, sat and took a swig of his Pepsi.

"Vincent, let's get on with it."

"Where were we?"

"Salvatore Mosca." He turned to Cat. "The man you overheard on the pay phone."

"I got that," she said.

"Sal's here, he's here because someone made me. They don't send him into the ring until it's time to make the pay-off."

"In other words, this man Mosca is here to pay someone who's been contracted to kill you," Victor interpreted. "Kill you for what?"

"I backed out on a debt."

"I'm not buying that Vincent."

"I did—"

"I believe you did. I'm not buying your story that someone's out to get you because of it.'' Victor paused. ''I'm going to lose my patience, Vincent.''

''Okay, look. I do owe. Back last year, I sort of went living beyond my means, and I borrowed ten grand.''

''Who loaned you the money?''

Pavo took another sip of Pepsi. ''That's not important. Markers're like your mortgage. You sign on with X, Y buys up your loan, six months later, your makin' your checks out to Z.''

''And Z is Charles Mackenzie, correct?''

Pavo nodded. ''You sure you want me goin' into this in fronta the press?''

Victor glanced down at Cat. She sat with her head resting against the back of the couch, perfectly relaxed, but he could see the light in her eye.

''He's never been more sure of anything in his life,'' Cat replied, serenely.

''Go on,'' Victor said.

''So, I get pulled in.''

''You spoke to Mackenzie?''

''No, man. There's two, three layers between Mackenzie and the street. You got any cake?''

''No, but if I knew you were coming...''

Pavo laughed and Cat was struck with how handsome he was. Dark, long-lashed eyes, dimples when he flashed a disarming smile, the lithe build of a track star. He didn't look at all like her image of an unkempt, itinerant CI. He looked like Danny Furina, the high school Lothario who was as handsome as the devil, and as full of wicked charm.

Victor walked up to the counter that separated the kitchen from the living area. He took a wicker fruit bowl and set it down on the coffee table in front of Pavo. ''Keep talking,'' he said.

Pavo checked the fruit, took a banana, began to peel it. ''Okay, so I get the word. Mackenzie's holding my marker, and it's gonna cost me to wipe it out.''

Victor loosened his tie, unbuttoned his top shirt button. "Ten grand's not critical mass."

"Tell it to Mac. He sends a guy to impress on me I pay up one way or another."

"Well, assuming you don't have the ten thousand dollars," Cat inquired. "What's the other way?"

Victor looked down at her.

"Just trying to keep up my end of the conversation."

"The other way is I do a job. Not only does he forgive the ten, but there's another thirty in it for me. Don't do it, and his crew says they're gonna knock my teeth out. I don't mean one to the jaw, I mean, they're gonna take a pair of pliers and yank. Rest of my life, I'm gonna be eatin' out of a blender. Jeezooi. Remember those Rhinebeck murders in Philly a few years back? Nut goes and eats half a dozen people?"

Cat's shudder was a suppressed giggle. The subject had come up on her first date with Victor. Over dinner.

"That's a guy you outta think about yankin' his teeth out."

"Except the Eighth Amendment prohibits cruel and unusual punishment," Victor reminded him.

"Yeah, but he was a cruel and unusual guy, right?"

"Vincent."

"Okay. So it's thirty, like I said. Fifteen once the mark's been located and I'm in position, fifteen the job's done."

"The job being an assassination," Victor concluded.

"Yeah. That's how I met Sal. Because he's one of the layers between Mackenzie and the street. I get a call, the mark's located, Sal and I meet so's he can give me the fifteen grand. I got a week to scope out the mark and take care of business. All that time, I need to communicate, it's through Sal. Always by phone. I do the job, we connect, he tells me where the money's gonna be dropped, I pick up my payoff and lay low. Cake job, that's what they told me."

"So the only time you met with Mosca was when he gave you the down payment."

Pavo fingered the crumbs scattered on his plate, nodded. "Look, *monje.* I'm thinking what's the big deal? It's not like I been a saint. Like I think I can't be bought. Hell, the mark? Her old man's a hired gun. I'm thinking she's no saint herself."

"The mark is Elizabeth Forgione."

Pavo's head shot up. "How'd you know that?"

"You know where she is, Vincent?"

Pavo shook his head.

"Is she still alive?"

Pavo hesitated. "Yeah. Yeah."

"So you took the fifteen grand and skipped out?"

"It's a little more complicated than that, *monje.*" Pavo took a gulp of Pepsi. "They locate her up Moorestown, livin' with her kid brother, he's still in high school."

"Go on."

"So I check out the place, start thinking about how I can get next to her. I meet with Sal and I get my fifteen grand. Now this is last fall, around December, the weather's turned, so I figure, I'll wait for a cold day, kinda cold drives the neighbors indoors, 5:00 p.m., when they're fixin' dinner, 5:00 p.m., people're beat, they worked all day, had a lousy commute, the kids're goin' nuts, the blood sugar's dropped so they're not so sharp, right? You want 'em with their defenses down, you can't beat 5:00 p.m."

"The kid's up in his room with a pair of earphones in his ears. His room's on the second floor in front and she's in the kitchen, first floor in back. I knock, sugar my way in, move her to the kitchen, one to the face, one to the back of the head and I'm out. But the thing is, I go to knock and I can smell it, even in out on the stoop with the door closed."

"Smell what?"

"*Osso buco.* I go around to the kitchen window and she's got a meat broth goin' for the risotto, she's got a gorgonzola sauce goin' for the spinach gnocchi and she's grating lemon—"

"Grating lemon?" Cat interjected. "She wasn't doing a

*gremolada,* was she? That would have been a little overwhelming if she's having *gnocchi verdi* with gorgonzola for a first course."

"That's what I *told* her!" Pavo agreed.

Victor tugged at the downward corners of his mustache, cleared his throat. "When did you tell her this?"

"I go back around front, but the smell of her cookin' is all over me and it's kinda getting' hard to tell myself I'm s'posed to hit her, you know what I'm talkin' about? So I knock on the door and she answers it and I now I get a real good whiff. Plus, she's kinda cute what with the flour from the gnocchi all down her apron and the smell of the lemon zest on her hands and she goes, 'Can I help you?' and me, stupid, I go, 'Don't you think a *gremolada*'s a little bit of overkill if you got gorgonzola in the first course?' And then, so she doesn't slam the door in my face, I go, 'I'm sorry, I wasn't snooping I just wanted to see what smelled so good.' And she smiles, and I mean her smile, it looks like scaloppini picant', you know, tender and sweet and spicy all together?"

Victor cleared his throat.

"And then she goes, 'It's not for gremolada, I'm making a lemon vinaigrette for the salad, just some simmered Swiss chard,' and I go, 'You know, a little grated radish goes good on that.' Then she goes, 'I'm Elizabeth,' and I go, 'I'm Vincent,' and she goes, 'Vincent, I always make too much for just my kid brother and me and osso buco's not like minestrone, you know, that improves the next day. Would you like to come in and have something to eat with us? So, anyway, long story short? No way was I gonna kill a woman can cook like that."

"What did you do?"

"Well, we had dinner and then the kid—he's a great kid, sharp as pecorino—he goes back to his homework and I figure I gotta come clean. I sit her down and I got the fifteen K in my pocket and I plunk it down on the table and she goes, 'What's that for?' and I go, "That's half of what I been paid to hit you and the other half I get when you're dead.'

And before she does anything, I tell her to take the money and get herself and her brother somewhere safe, I'll string them along for a few days. And she says, 'How come you're doing this,' and I go, 'If my mom could cook like that I'd be a better person than I turned out. And that's if I had a mom, which I didn't, at least not one I can remember.'"

"And the girl took off with your fifteen thousand, which means that now you're in to Mackenzie for twenty-five grand, not to mention the fact that you double-crossed him." Victor rose and began to pace. "Where did they go?"

Pavo shrugged. "How would I know that?"

"Because—" it was Cat who responded "—you're obviously in love with her. You wouldn't let her and a lifetime of gourmet cuisine just walk away."

Victor was inclined to agree with Cat, that Pavo wouldn't have let Elizabeth Forgione simply disappear without assuring himself that she was safe. He approached the subject from another angle. "So fast-forward to this afternoon."

"I found out Elizabeth's dad's gonna turn on Mackenzie. One of my hook-ups told me they moved him up from the federal pen. I figure I'd ask if you could get her some protection. Get her somewhere where she'd be safe."

"That must have been some osso buco."

"You don't know the half."

"I suspect that I don't," Victor said, calmly. "What made you think that Mrs. Austen was the person Mosca is here to pay off?"

"Because I heard her tell someone she's angling for a shot, but it was too crowded and how there's too many bystanders—"

"Oh, for heaven's sake!" Cat cried, exasperated. "I wasn't talking about a shot. I was talking about a *shot.*" She raised her hands, clicked an imaginary camera. "A photo. I wanted to see if I could get a shot of the pastry demo to go with a magazine article I'm doing."

"You mean you weren't out to shoot someone?"

"Not then."

"But someone is," Victor said. "If Mosca's in town to make the payoff," Victor said. "You have any idea where the drop-off might be, after the business is concluded?"

Pavo shook his head.

The phone rang.

"I'm going to take this in the bedroom," Victor said. He excused himself and left Cat and Pavo alone.

Pavo looked Cat over. "So you know how to cook, huh? Not everyone knows *gremolada.*"

"My father owned a restaurant. Before the casinos."

Pavo's gaze glowed with respect. "Which one was it?"

"Fortunati's."

"Get out! I heard about that place. Heard you couldn't get a table in the summer to save your life."

Cat thought of her bighearted father with a smile. More than once he had picked up the reservation phone and promised the impossible, squeezed in another table or two, worked another four hours because he couldn't say no to save his life.

"So you and Victor, you really—" Pavo crossed one finger over another.

Cat arched her brows. "Why do you call him *el monje?*" The monk.

"That's what they call him on the street. The ones who don't call him *desconocido.* Because of when he crossed over, you know."

"Worked undercover?"

"Yeah."

"Really? And why do they call you Pavo? Turkey?"

"'Cause I like to gobble. Why d'they call you 'Cat'?"

"Because I have nine lives. Nine lives' worth of questions, too. For instance, that guy, Mosca? Why does he start off a phone conversation by asking someone what you call the inside—the meat—of a cocoa bean? My brother Marco said it was probably some sort of test question. Mosca was making sure the man on the other end of the line was really his contact."

"What's your brother, a cop?"

"Five of them are. I've got six."

"What's the other one, a con?"

Cat shook her head. "A priest."

"Seven kids? That's a lotta mouths to feed."

"We never went hungry."

"Lucky you. Orphanages, foster homes, there's never enough to go around."

Cat nodded, not without sympathy. "Anyway, when my brother said that, I started thinking. If Charlie Mackenzie is behind this—"

"There's no *if*. The Apron turns, there's no more double dipping into the union's pension fund for Jolly Cholly."

"So I guess he's serious this time. About who he would hire," Cat said.

"You mean after he blew it with me?"

"I mean, who wouldn't blow it? Who's the best Mackenzie's union money can buy?"

"The best is Paulie the Apron and he's in custody."

"Second best, then."

His dark eyes widened in slow comprehension. "Bao. Joaquin Bao. That explains that business on the phone."

"What business?"

"Well, they say that aside from the trade? You know, hit man? Aside from that, he's a world-class chef. That's why they call him *El Cocinero*."

# TEN

ON THE DRIVE TO Ocean City, Victor silently reviewed his conversation with Stan.

"No luck locating this Al Cocinera," Stan told him. "Jeannie and Phil are workin' it. You ask Pavo?"

"Not in front of Mrs. Austen. I'm going to take her home. I'd like you to come by here and stay with Pavo. I don't trust him to stay put."

"No prob. Why I called? Your ESP's tracking pretty good. Under the boards? They found one round in the sand under the Boardwalk, near the Phoenix. Rifle shot."

Cat's instinct had been correct again. She had seen the light from a scope. Victor did not want to think about how close it had come to hitting Cat.

Stan arrived in twenty minutes with two whole cheese steaks from the White House, a six-pack of white birch beer, a pound of almond meringues and a quart of Dutch Farm Death by Chocolate ice cream.

Cat broke into his train of thought. "Why didn't they just put the Forgione family in witness protection?"

"Well, you can't draft. The best you can do is get them to enlist. It would be rough on the boy."

"Did you notice that Pavo didn't mention him much? It was 'Can you find *her* a safe place?' and 'Can you protect *her?*' Not 'them.'"

Victor glanced at her. "Very astute, Mrs. Austen."

"Elementary. He's in love with Elizabeth Forgione, that's pretty obvious. You can't know if she's in love with him, but she's been a loving sister to the boy. And when you are protecting someone you love, you do one of two things. You either stick close enough to shield that person, or you draw the danger away."

"Meaning she may be close, but the boy may not be with her."

"Or both may be here, or neither of them may be."

Victor pulled up in front of her beach block home. There were lights in the dining room and both Jennie's red Buick and Freddy's Cherokee were parked in front of the house. "No, she's here," Victor stated, as he turned off the ignition. "I can't see Pavo putting much distance between himself and her haute cuisine."

They found Freddy, Ellice, Jane and Mats sitting at the dining room table. Five-year-old Mats wriggled down from his chair and ran up to his mother.

Cat shrugged off the borrowed leather jacket and picked him up in her arms. "Were you good for your Nonna?"

"Nonna says I'm the bes' boy in the world."

"And what about sister?"

"She's mad at you," Mats whispered.

Jane had wanted to go to the "bride show," and was still miffed at having been excluded.

"Watch this," Cat whispered back.

She took a catalogue she had gotten from Felicity's Formals and dropped it on the table in front of Jane. Fifty pages of bridal wear had an immediate sweetening effect on Jane's disposition.

"Victor." Jennie emerged from the kitchen with a pot of sauce, ladled some over the pasta on Freddy's plate. "You eat yet?"

"Ma, sit down," Freddy said. "I can get that."

"You eat. You're getting married in a month."

"Ma, don't talk like this is my last shot at a good meal," Freddy kidded. "Ellice and I get hungry, there's always take-out."

Jennie gave him a playful smack on the back of the head and went back to the kitchen.

"Good news, bad news," Ellice announced. "Nancy just called, she thinks she got a shot of the cake with her digital. The bad news is that when the commotion broke out, Nancy and I were so frantic looking for you, and then got hustled out of the room, so I didn't get to book a consultation with Edie Hannan. And I've got my heart set on one of their wedding cakes."

"Who notices a wedding cake?" Freddy asked.

For that, he was favored with scathing glances from Cat, Ellice and Jane.

Cat went to the refrigerator and got a Diet Pepsi. "Their shop's right at the end of Thirty-Fourth Street, at the intersection. I'll tell you what, I'll run out there early, pick up some brioche and cinnamon buns and check out her appointment schedule. Maybe she can get you in tomorrow after closing, but you have to be flexible, because they open at seven, and close whenever they run out."

The three hammering knocks were sufficient to identify the person at her door. Victor admitted Carlo Fortunati, the eldest of Cat's brothers. He gave Victor a genial cuff on the shoulder, then proceeded to demand what's this he had heard about a commotion at the Phoenix that afternoon, was it true that chooch Pavo Buonovitti had manhandled he sister and where might he, Carlo, find Pavo and set him straight. The queries were garnished with Carlo's favorite modifiers, intriguing enough to make Jane look up from the pearl-encrusted bodice above the chiffon bouffant waltz-length skirt, to get her fill of her Uncle Carlo's juiciest obscenities.

Carlo was massive, six and a half feet, 250 pounds of bristling indignation. Yet he was reduced to meek submission by his petite mother who said, "You watch your mouth in fronta the kids. What ails you?"

"What the kids doin' up? How come you're not in bed?"

"It's Friday *night,*" Jane reminded him.

Cat had a more effective way of defusing Carlo's irritation. ''Did you have any dinner yet?''

''I could eat something.'' Carlo sank into a chair, reached for a hunk of bread. ''So what's this I hear, the *tacchin'*, he whacks out over the Phoenix?''

''What's a tachine?'' Mats asked his mother.

''Turkey.'' Cat stroked Mat's unruly hair, watched him digest this information, soberly. When his face settled into that earnest concentration, the resemblance to Chris overwhelmed her.

Jennie set a plate of ravioli in front of Carlo. ''Victor, you sit.''

''I'm sorry, Jennie, but I have to get back. I'm not quite off the clock.''

The phone rang and Jennie went into the kitchen to answer it. ''Victor, it's for you.''

Victor took the phone, thanked her. He saw Cat look up, then look away with a calculated concentration that was as obvious as Jane's. ''Cardenas.''

''Lieut, I'm sorry.'' It was Rice.

''Don't tell me.''

''Guy eats all his hoagie, half of mine and downs two birch beers, all the ice cream, you'd figure he'd packed away enough to weight himself down long enough for me to run to the john.''

Victor bit back a curse. ''I'll be right there.''

''Look, I'm sorry.''

''We'll discuss it tomorrow.''

''Tomorrow's Saturday.''

Victor hung up. ''I have to get back, there's a situation.''

Carlo, a retired chief of police, who hadn't quite weaned himself from the streets, said ''What? The *tacchin'* take off?''

''Lemme fix you a sandwich to take,'' Jennie offered.

Victor leaned down and kissed her cheek. ''Not now, Jennie.''

''You don't eat, you know what happens?''

''The sun goes dark, the stars fall into the sea and the earth bursts into flame,'' Victor replied, gravely.

''And that's just for starters,'' she told him.

# ELEVEN

VICTOR'S CELL PHONE trilled as soon as he got out of Ocean City. It was Kurt Raab.

"I called your place, Stan said you were en route. Jimmy Donato came through. Salvatore Mosca dropped in ten minutes ago and I had him picked up. He's on his way here."

"Dropped in to drop the cash?"

"He didn't have more than a couple hundred on him."

Victor frowned. "I'll be there in ten minutes."

The bureau was quiet, the murmur of a few detectives working late, and one custodian pushing a wide mop along the worn linoleum of the second floor.

Raab and a sheepish-looking Stan Rice were in his office.

"I have Long working the streets, he's still got a lot of contacts from back in the day." Long's "day" had been working vice in a wig, satin and fishnets, and the outings had given him a vast and varied acquaintance.

"I got something maybe'll get me a reduced sentence."

"What?"

"Well, the guys pick up Mosca, frisk him. He's not carrying, he's got nothing but the wallet, couple hundred bucks and change, his cell, right? So they turn it over to me when Adane's taking him into the box and I just happened to notice that there were three numbers programmed into his cell. You know, you just hit one button and it dials. That way, you don't gotta remember numbers or write them down. When it dials, the name of the person you're calling comes up on the digital display. 'Member how Jimmy's waitress said it looked like he just pushed one button to connect?"

Raab loosened his tie. "I just came from synagogue. Do I wanna hear this?"

"Look. He didn't object when they took his property, they asked him to empty his pockets and told him he'd be getting it back. He hands it over voluntarily."

Raab looked at Victor.

"So," Stan continued. "You wanna hear whose numbers they are or not?"

"Go ahead," Victor said.

"One is L. Kreipes." He spelled it.

"Lawrence Kreipes reps the union, the one headed by Cholly Mackenzie," Raab said, slowly.

"One is L. Marcus. 'L' as in 'Lorianne.' I traced her, she's sorta for entertainment purposes only."

Victor nodded, "So far, I'm not seeing you getting off with time served."

Stan picked up the small cell phone, punched in a button. "The third *L?* Well, actually it's 'El,' *E, L.* It looks like more of an alias than a person's name."

"I'm waiting," Victor said.

"It reads *El Cocinero.* Isn't that Spanish for *chef* or *cook?* So I guess we can stop looking around for Al Cocinera." Stan grinned.

"Okay. You get a stay. Put this with his other things, and return them after the interview. Don't let him think that you've examined them." He started to hand it back to Stan, then his fingers closed over the instrument. He turned to Raab. "How much latitude do we get?"

"You're skating now."

"I'll try to skirt the thin ice. You know how to reprogram this, Rice?"

"Yeah."

"Okay. Replace the last number with my cell phone number."

"He'll know it's not the guy."

"Maybe. But it's likely he hasn't spoken to this El Cocinero much. On cell phone connections that may not always have been the best. And the conversations—at least some of them—have been in Spanish."

"Victor, where you going with this?" Raab asked.

"We don't have Pavo here to identify Mosca as the guy who paid him off last fall, and we know Mosca wasn't the one who started the panic in the ballroom. We didn't find a suspiciously large amount of cash on him. We don't know if he's made the down payment to this El Cocinero, we don't even know if Pavo and the Forgione girl are alive at this point. Our best option may be to cut Mosca loose and see if he contacts this guy. He ask for a lawyer?"

Stan shook his head.

"Okay. Let's go ahead and question him. Make it look like we pulled him in and decided we didn't have enough to hold him."

"You want me to take care of it?" Stan asked.

"No, Adane can handle him."

"She's never done Q and A," Stan protested.

"It's time she started."

"I don't want him to see you," Raab cautioned.

Victor nodded and walked to the window, knocked. Adane emerged. "Ask him if he knows where Pavo is. Not who he is, assume that and see where it takes you. We have no intention of putting him in a lineup now, but still, ask—"

"Excuse me, lieutenant. Aren't you going to interview him?"

"No, you are. Keep it short. We're going to release him, but I want him to think we're letting him off reluctantly."

Adane hesitated. "Wouldn't you rather that Stan—"

"No."

"Jeez," Stan griped. "You coulda thought about it a few seconds."

"I gave it due consideration, Sergeant."

Adane returned to the room, sat across the table from Mosca. Victor observed that Cat's judgment, that his appearance was calculatedly nondescript was very acute. His neutral-colored hair was short, his build was compact, without being muscular; there were no tattoos, no jewelry. No scars, no birthmarks. Five minutes after he left a room, no one would remember what he looked like, or even if he had been there.

From his angle, Victor could see Adane's clasped hands under the table. "You know why you were picked up, Mr. Mosca?"

"You oughta arrest that *sciocc'* runs that diner. Health department's given him a license to kill."

"It doesn't seem to have deterred you from visiting there daily for the past three days."

"I like the ambiance." *Ambee-yance.*

"Did you like it better than the ambience of the Phoenix ballroom, Mr. Mosca?" She slid the photograph that had been printed from the surveillance video across the table.

He glanced at it, shrugged. "It was open to the public."

"Are you getting married?"

"What's it to you?"

"It would explain your presence there."

"I don't think I gotta explain to you why I was there."

Adane was becoming frustrated, but only Victor saw it expressed in the slight contraction of the mouth. Her serene blue-eyed gaze remained steady, her tone professional.

"How long have you known Vincent Buonovitti?"

"Who?"

"We have witnesses who will put the two of you together. Witnesses who saw you following him into the ballroom at the Phoenix earlier today." She pushed the photo of Pavo across the table. "Don't tell us that you don't know him, because we already know that you do, we know how long you've known him, and why you're following him."

"Prove it."

"We also know," Adane continued, "that Vincent Buonovitti deliberately provoked a disturbance in the Phoenix this afternoon. Since you arranged to be there at a time when he was there, I don't think it would be out of line for the D.A. to suspect you of conspiring with him to cause a disturbance in a public place."

"Prove that."

"All right. Of course, we can detain you while I prove it. After all, Mr. Mosca, you don't have any ties to the community. You're staying in a motel on the Black Horse Pike, driving a rented car. You live three counties away, in an apartment that you rent month to month, and you hold a valid passport. And, it's Friday night."

Now it was Mosca's hands that were clenching. *He hasn't made the drop yet. If the job has been done, or is about to be done, he'll be incommunicado. And scared to death that Mackenzie will think he skipped out with the money, as Pavo had.*

"Would you like to call a lawyer, Mr. Mosca? If it's difficult for you to reach your attorney at this hour, there is the public defender. Friday evening, it takes a while for them to get here, though."

Mosca seemed to consider his options. "Okay, ask me again what you want to know."

He's not calling the lawyer, Victor thought. Which means he's either arrogant or afraid to admit to Mackenzie's mouthpiece that he got picked up.

"The man known as Pavo, Vincent Buonovitti. How well do you know him?"

"I know him from the street. 'What's up? How you doin?' That's it. I was in the casino, I thought I saw him, thought I'd say hi."

"That's why you followed him into the ballroom?"

"Yeah. Yeah. But it was elbow to elbow. And then he flips out, starts poppin' balloons and yellin' someone's got a gun and everyone runs for cover. I don't know where he went."

"Why do you think he acted like that?"

"I don't know. But he's got a rep for weirdness."

Victor saw a little relief seep into the man's impassive

features. *He thinks we're after Pavo now, we just want him for information. He's off the hook. Good.*

"You didn't see him leave?"

"Hell, someone yells 'Gun,' I hit the carpet."

Adane nodded, as if she were buying his story. "Do you have any idea where he might be staying?"

The man ran his palm over his hair. "Don't know."

"Does he have friends, family? A girlfriend, perhaps?"

"Told me once he grew up on the foster circuit. That and orphanages. Like I said, I hadn't seen him around awhile."

"When was the last time you did see him? Before today."

"Maybe, I dunno, back in the fall we ran into one another. He was working some minimum wage. Hustling."

Adane nodded; this time the frustration was more obvious. Victor could see that it was deliberately obvious, for Mosca's benefit. She reached over and switched off the machine. "All right, Mr. Mosca. The D.A. may want to contact you again if we don't locate Mr. Buonovitti, so you'll have to leave your address with Sergeant Rice."

"I can go?"

"For now. As I said, please don't leave the area without checking in with the D.A.'s office."

Victor returned to his office, closed the door and the Venetian blinds. After a moment, Stan and Jean Adane came in. "Jeannie, you did great," Stan told her. He looked over at Victor. "Hope you got your cell phone charged."

"You can go," Victor said. "I'm going to wait here."

"You really think he's gonna call?"

"I know he will. When Adane suggested that he might be detained over the weekend, he got nervous."

"There's a reason he needs to be at liberty tonight," Adane affirmed.

Victor nodded.

Adane's blue eyes clouded.

"What's the matter, Adane?" Victor asked.

"It still doesn't tell us when and if the hit has gone down. The best we can do is surveil Mosca until he makes the drop.

We get him, and the assassin, perhaps, but that may not save Pavo and Miss Forgione.'' She hesitated before adding, ''It's a poor victory in my opinion.''

''Jeannie, considering this was dropped on us just this afternoon, I'll settle for any victory,'' Stan told her.

''Another matter,'' Adane added. ''The conversations that Jim overheard, and that Mrs. Austen overheard. Jim's waitress said Mosca started the conversation by asking the party if he needed some dough. But that doesn't make sense, he's there to deliver the prearranged amount of, well, dough. It was more likely a question about *kneading,* with a *k.* Kneading bread or pastry dough. And Mrs. Austen overheard the remark about the cocoa beans. If you take the call from Mosca, you may have to answer some sort of test question before he'll talk to you.''

''It's covered,'' Victor said. He dismissed them and sat behind his desk and picked up the phone.

# TWELVE

CAT ROSE to a quiet house Saturday morning. Ordinarily, she would throw on some sweats and have an early-morning run on the boardwalk, but she decided to skip it in order to be at Patty Cake's when they opened at 7:00 a.m.

She took a quick shower and pulled her shoulder-length hair into a red elasticized band, blow-dried her bangs and donned a pair of jeans and a loose white sweater. She tiptoed down the hall and peeked in on Jane. She lay with the catalogue on the floor beside her headboard, her expression one of serene contemplation—of her own wedding, heaven forbid. Cat could not envision herself ushering Jane through the exhaustive preparations that had preceded her own wedding.

Mats was fast asleep, his worn plush bunny in a virtual choke hold. Cat's smile was sad. Yesterday, when Cat had explained to him where she was going, assured him she would be home before he went to bed, he had listened to her account soberly and then said, "I'm gonna marry you when I grow up, you know, Mom."

Cat carried her white sneakers in one hand as she padded down the stairs. She decided to start a pot of coffee; it would be brewed by the time she returned with pastries from Patty Cake.

She sat on the bottom step to pull on her sneakers and glanced in the living room, saw her mother stretched out on the couch, fast asleep, the phone on the floor beside her. Victor had called to check on Cat again the night before and after a brief conversation, asked to speak to Jennie. Jennie would not divulge the nature of the conversation that put a conspiratorial smile on her face, but for the remainder of the evening, she would hurry to answer the phone whenever it rang.

Cat bent down beside her mother, shook her shoulder, gently.

"Mmm," Jennie mumbled. "*Pupi di zucchero.*"

Cat called up the expression from the tales Jennie would tell of her childhood. *Sugar dolls?* "Mama?"

Jennie opened her eyes.

"You know what you just said in your sleep? *Pupi di zucchero.* Do I want to know what you were dreaming?" Cat teased.

"Don't talk dirty." Jennie sat up, tugged at the buttoned top of her pajamas, patted her hair. "In Sicily, couple weeks before All Soul's Day? The bake shops have these candy dolls, sugar dolls, *pupi di zucchero.* Soon as they showed up in the shops, every kid'd be good as gold to get one of those sugar dolls. Better than a Christmas present."

"They must have been something if you were dreaming about them."

Jennie gave her daughter a crafty look. "You go pick up the buns, I'll get the coffee on," was all she would say.

VICTOR HAD DOZED OFF in the leather chair behind his desk when his cell phone rang. It jolted him into immediate wakefulness and he grabbed the receiver of his desk phone, hit the speed dial button for Cat's number, checked his watch. After midnight.

The cell phone rang again.

Jennie Fortunati, sounding a bit groggy, answered Cat's phone. "Victor?" she was whispering.

"I owe you, Jennie." He picked up his cell phone and hit the button. "What," his voice was hoarse from sleep; Victor hoped that it would convince Mosca that he was El Cocinero.

"Okay. Kids get a certain kinda candy around All Saints Day in Sic'ly."

Victor closed his eyes. *Gracias.* He knew that it was unlikely this El Cocinero had a broader knowledge of food than Jennie Fortunati, but he didn't expect to be given such a gift. He pressed the cell phone against his thigh and spoke into the desk phone's receiver. "Jennie—in Sicily at All Saint's Day, there's some kind of special candy for children?"

"*Pupi di zucchero.* Sugar dolls. To get ourselves one of those dolls, we were the saints. But we called it *iornu di mort'. Day of the dead, all soul's day.*"

"I love you." He hung up and put the cell phone to his ear. *"Iornu di mort',"* he tried to pronounce it as Jennie had. "Not All Saint's Day. Kids get sugar dolls, *pupi di zucchero.* Let's get on with it."

"It still on for right before 7:00 a.m.?"

Victor exhaled, slowly. Pavo and the Forgione girl, wherever they were, might still be alive. "You tell me."

"You feelin' okay, you don't sound right."

"You got me out of bed."

Mosca hesitated, then switched to Spanish. *"¿Estas bien? No pareces el mismo de ayer."*

*"Estoy el mismo que era ayer, y la semana pasada, y sera la proxima semana. No quiero perder mucho tiempo hablando. ¿Me entiendes?"*

"Gotcha. Okay, the job's still between seven and eight? The cash'll be there by ten."

"No good."

"Whadda you mean, 'no good.' It's what we agreed."

"'We'. Since when is my agreement with you, *amigo?*"

*"Vas a lo que truje."*

Victor imagined Raab, his transcriptionist listening to this. "The point, my friend, is that the drop is out. You think I don't know you were picked up last night? How do I know you didn't turn? How do I know that I won't go to the drop site and find a dozen cops waiting for me?"

"Look, you know better. No one sells out Mackenzie."

"*El pavo* did."

"Pavo's a dead man."

"Not if you're depending on me to do him. You tell Mackenzie that I don't like working with a middle man. I want my payoff to come from him. Not from you, not from Kreipes. Or I'll do what *el pavo* did, take my down payment and hide Pavo and the Forgione girl. Only this time, they won't be found. And that means, *el delante* can go ahead and take the stand Monday morning, *Me entiendes?*

"You know too much to stay alive, Cocinero."

"And yet here I am."

"Mack will never face off with one of his shooters."

"Then we're not talking are we?" Victor hesitated, then clicked the End button.

Raab had been couched out in the day room. At the sound of the phone, he had hurried into the office to listen in on the conversation. "Victor, was that smart?"

"We'll see."

After three long minutes, the phone rang again.

Victor picked up. "Make this the last call."

"Mackenzie's ticked. He says you could have come over and done them both right there at the Phoenix."

Elizabeth Forgione had been at the Phoenix? "What, with a couple hundred security cameras on me? Mack's that stupid, maybe I should cut my losses and walk right now."

"No! No." There was a pause. "You know that old burned-out club on the Longport Boulevard causeway?"

"I know it."

"At 10:00 a.m."

"And he comes alone."

Victor hung up and dropped the cell on his desk, leaned back in his chair. He ran his hands in a slow massaging motion over his forehead and face, felt the roughness of an overnight beard.

Raab looked at him. "You look like a hit man."

"But can I cook like one?"

# THIRTEEN

PATTY CAKE PATISSERIE was situated in a vacated church on the midisland thoroughfare leading out of Ocean City. The road was known as Thirty-Fourth Street, though it remained so only so long as it traveled Ocean City. Once across the bridge that spanned the channel dotted with marshy islets, it became Roosevelt Boulevard.

The wedge of property had been the site of a hundred-year-old church that had neither historical significance nor ample congregation that might warrant its preservation. Patricia Torello had been making cakes from her home—Patty's Cakes—for a year before she decided to open up shop. By the time the little church, sold with the provision that the modest cemetery with two dozen remaining markers would be left intact, was converted, she met up with Edie Hannan, and Patty's Cakes became Patty Cake. And, because she had a sense of humor about the gravestones clearly visible from the rear parking lot, she added the motto, Pastries to Die For beneath the name of her shop.

There were a few parked cars, the drivers sipping take-out coffee, waiting for the Closed sign to be reversed. The aromas of butter, sugar, chocolate, fruit seeped from the closed-up shop, luring gulls in from the marshes, both cars and gulls hovering impatiently.

Cat chafed her upper arms and unfastened her seat belt, pulled the black leather jacket tightly around her. She had run back to the house to grab the first object that would buffer her against the early May chill. She was glad for its insulation, but wondered how she was going to return it to the impulsive giver. Place an ad in the paper, perhaps? Good Samaritan who offered his jacket to a Lady in Distress beneath the Atlantic City Boardwalk, please contact the following number.

One of the cars backed out and drove away. Cat checked her watch. Not quite seven, but often Patty Cake would open a few minutes early if cars began collecting in the lot. Another customer gave up, dumped her coffee onto the asphalt and rolled up her window, drove off, leaving Cat alone in the lot.

She got out of her car. Early May could be as warm as July or as frosty as November. Today it was decidedly frosty, with the chill as dense as the low-lying fog that spread in an irregular pattern over the marshes that flanked the causeway. The concentrated air raised the scent of musk and something else, something a bit pungent from the worn leather, something vaguely familiar.

Cat approached the small structure, with its wooden porch restored and the weathered steeple intact. The stained glass windows had been replaced by simple glass. The shades were still drawn and Cat saw the Closed sign turned face out, though the Hours of Operation plaque clearly stated that they opened at 7:00 a.m.

Cat checked her watch again. The scent of something familiar drifted up from the leather sleeve once more. She bent down and peered in the small space between the drawn shade and the sill. She thought she heard voices in conversation. Perhaps it was a radio. But the scent clearly told her that the baking was well under way. She rapped on the window glass and waited a few minutes. She knocked on the wooden frame of the screen door. The voices fell silent.

Cat walked around the lot to the back of the shop. There was a delivery entrance, a screen door with a wooden door behind it. Vacillating gusts shuttled from one section of marshland to another sent the aroma of salt air, fresh baking and something else, something pungent and burnt past Cat's nostrils. She lifted the sleeve of the leather jacket and inhaled, sneezed and inhaled again. An acridness tickled her nose. Firecrackers?

Cordite.

*Gunpowder?*

Another gust brought a snatch of a conversation, "just leave her," in a voice that sounded familiar.

*Pavo?* Had he somehow sweet-talked Patty Cake or her pastry chef into hiding him out?

And then she heard Pavo's voice saying, "Because I heard her tell someone she's angling for a shot, but it was too crowded and how she's gotta get closer—"

But she and Ellice hadn't been talking about Pavo, they hadn't even been aware of him. He had been standing somewhere behind them. They had been talking about getting a shot of Edie Hannan. The pastry chef. Who was inside with Pavo right now.

Pavo hadn't caused that commotion to protect himself. He had been protecting her. Edie Hannan. Elizabeth Forgione.

Cat reached into her shoulder bag for a credit card. She slipped the card between the screen door's jamb and the door frame, gently knocked the latch hook upward until it released, opened the screen door. She turned the door handle and opened the back door.

Hot air, infused with the scent of fresh baking, overpowered her. She walked between parallel rows of open shelves, laid out with bags of flour, tins of vegetable shortening, bags of white and brown sugar, jars of spices, turned the corner and found herself in the middle of the kitchen.

Behind a rolling rack bearing trays of cinnamon buns, croissants, muffins and brioche were the three of them. Pavo, Edie Hannan, and her Good Samaritan, El Cocinero.

# FOURTEEN

VICTOR CHECKED HIS WATCH. Morning, and he had not gone home, not gone to bed. For the past five hours, he had stationed himself beside a surveillance officer at the Phoenix, requesting her to run, stop, run, zoom the tape of the ballroom, studying each slender, young, blond woman against the photo of Elizabeth Forgione in his hand. Even after more than five hours, he would not loosen his tie, and remained faultlessly patient and polite to the woman.

Kurt Raab was pacing behind him; every once in a while, he would stop, look over the woman's shoulder, continue pacing. "Victor, we could be wrong about this. Pavo being there may not mean anything."

Victor shook his head. "She was there."

"We're almost at the end, again, Lieutenant," the woman told him. "Do you want me to run the tape again?"

Victor looked at the cluster of people, their mesmerized faces watching the pastry demo. The tape did not pick up the filaments of caramelized sugar until enough had consolidated to take on shape.

"Stop the tape!"

The operator was startled by his sudden sharpness.

"Zoom in on her. The baker."

The operator tapped a few buttons on her console, gradually centered the face and enlarged it. Something in the eyes, something he had noticed in the photograph. Concentration on her task caused her to lower her brows in determination, the same expression as in the photo.

"'It is the first quality of a criminal investigator that he should see through a disguise,'" Victor murmured.

The woman looked up.

"Sherlock Holmes," he said. He turned to Raab. "She's stopped coloring her hair and she's put on weight."

"*That*'s the Forgione girl?"

Victor picked up his cell phone, dialed Marco Fortunati's number. Nancy answered, her voice a bit sleepy.

"Nancy, it's Victor Cardenas. I'm sorry if I woke you, but it's important."

"That's okay, Marco's already up having his run. Is Cat all right?"

"It's not about Cat. I need to know if you can do something for me. Ellice said you got a digital photograph of the woman who was doing that pastry demonstration. Did you get a good shot of the face?"

"Yeah, why?"

"Can you print out a copy and fax it to the number I'm going to give you? I can't explain now, but it's urgent."

She was a cop's wife. "Five minutes," she said.

"Do you have an image program?" he asked the security officer.

"Sure. A lot of the card counters, the people who've been banned try to get back in disguised."

"Would you be able to put that woman's image up, so that it can be altered?"

The woman was efficient. In a moment they were looking at the plump, pretty face of Edie Hannan on the screen. "Change the hair color," Victor instructed. "Blond. Brassy."

The girl ran through several colors before she got it right.

"Now narrow the face. Keep the dimples, but take away the plumpness, the fullness of her neck."

It took several steps for the woman to achieve the desired result, but when she did, it resembled the photograph that Raab had given Victor.

The fax machine began to churn out a paper; the image

that Nancy had taken of Edie Hannan. It was a good shot, full face and at reasonably close range. Victor snatched it from the fax machine and handed it to Raab. "This is who we should be looking for. She works at a bakery called Patty Cake."

"I know that place," the woman said. "It's right over the Thirty-Fourth Street bridge. Ocean City. Or maybe it's Upper Township by then."

Victor's cell phone trilled. He grabbed it. "Cardenas."

"It's me, Phil. I got something."

"What?"

"El Cocinero. His name's Joaquin Bao, he's world-class. Sharpshooter and chef. He's got no permanent address that we know of. Moves around a lot. I got a photo, the only one that exists and it's not great. Want me to fax it over?"

"Yes."

"This morning before dawn, a guy fitting his description was seen leaving a condo in Gardiner's Basin. The condo's owned by Mackenzie's union. It's sort of a corporate flat they keep when they wanna put up some hotshot from outta town. Want me to get a warrant?"

"Yes. But don't have a team go over it right away, stake it out first. He may come back."

The surveillance tech handed Victor a fax. He thanked Long and hung up, studied the grim, dark-eyed face in the picture.

Raab looked over his shoulder. "He looks like you."

Then Raab's cell phone began to ring.

# FIFTEEN

CAT LOOKED into his merciless gaze and felt an immobilizing dread consolidate in her stomach. *Jane,* she thought. *Mats.*

"You didn't have to go to all this trouble to return my jacket, *señora.*"

She slipped the jacket off her shoulders, tossed it on a long wooden table. "You'll have to have it cleaned professionally. To get that smell of cordite out."

"I think you should step over here and join your friends."

"I'd think twice," Pavo said. His voice was several notes above normal range, tense. "She's a cop's woman."

"Is that so?" The scar contracted as Bao smiled faintly. "That must be inconvenient, no?"

Cat clenched her fists. "Yes," she replied. "But he's not one to complain."

Absurdly, Cat thought of Ellice's wedding cake. She would have to find someone else to bake it now, and it was going to be hard to get what she wanted with just a month until the wedding. *Of course, if I die,* Cat thought, *they'll postpone the wedding, won't they?*

"Look," Pavo said. He was clutching Edie's hand. She stood in a flour-spattered apron, her dark hair piled under a white head scarf. "She didn't do anything to you. It's me that Mackenzie wants, I screwed up. He sent me to do a job and I skipped out on him. Why don't you just do me and let the women alone."

"Nobility is what got you into this, isn't it?"

"Okay, then how about this. A last request. Do we get a last request?"

"You're wasting my time—"

"You have all the time in the world!" Pavo pleaded. "We're just a job to you, you're as good as they say you are, you can deal with a variation here and there."

"What variation?"

"Marry us."

The "I beg your pardon" was coolly amused, sounded so like Victor, that Cat had to suppress a laugh.

"Look. We got the license—"

"I know. Miss Forgione took it out in her own name." The man turned to her. "That wasn't very bright, was it?"

She looked down, her plump face blushing as though she had been caught eloping with the town Casanova.

"And who is supposed to officiate at this...ceremony?"

"She can."

Cat blinked, had the urge to look around the room. "Me?"

"You said your brother's a priest."

"Yes, but—"

"You've been married, you've been to weddings," Pavo continued. "Just say whatever went down."

"And when were you married, *señora?*"

"Almost sixteen years ago. My husband was murdered," she added.

"There are children?" His voice was indifferent. That reminded her of Victor, too, the quiet monotone that never revealed what he was thinking.

"Two."

"You know the words?"

"You're not serious," she protested. Then she thought, why not? Stall for time, someone surely would get a sugar jones and come pounding on the door. "I don't suppose anyone has a Bible."

"There's an inside pocket in my jacket."

Cat lifted it, prodded the lining. Sure enough, there was a

small inner pocket with a three-by-five leather-bound book. Quite worn, with many of the pages dog-eared.

"Do it."

"Well," Cat cleared her throat. "I guess the first thing to ask would be if you—I need your full name."

"Elizabeth Dana Forgione."

"Vincent John Buonovitti."

Cat flipped through the Bible. There was a passage she remembered hearing at one of the premarital classes she and Chris had attended. Sixteen years ago. Romans?

"Okay, well, then, Elizabeth Dana Forgione, do you take Vincent John Buonovitti for your husband, for better or for worse, in sickness and in health, forsaking all others, for richer or for poorer, in good times and bad—I may be leaving something out, but I think that pretty much covers it."

"I do." She turned to him and squeezed his hand.

"And Vincent John Buonovitti, do you take Elizabeth for your wife, same deal, good and bad, rich, poor, sickness, health, forsaking all others, until—" Cat swallowed.

"Yeah. I do." He turned to her. "Elizabeth, I'm sorry I got you into this mess. I wish your dad'd been anyone else but Paulie the Apron."

"Your father is Paulie Forgione?" the hit man asked.

"Whadda you think Mackenzie wants her whacked for?"

"That's never a concern of mine," he replied, coldly.

"Well, word on the street is that Paulie's gonna turn and Mack wants her hit to send a warning."

"Really?" He looked at Cat. "Let's end it."

Tears started trickling from the girl's eyes. She rummaged in the pocket of her apron, blotted her eyes delicately.

Cat was thumbing through the Bible. "How about something from Psalms? 'Rescue me from my enemies, my God; lift me out of reach of my foes. Deliver me from the evildoers; from the bloodthirsty, save me. They have set an ambush for my life; they powerful conspire against me. For no offense or misdeed of mine, Lord, for no fault they hurry to take up arms—'"

"I think that's enough," Bao said, shortly. But there was a light in his dark gaze that was lighter than before.

"I was going to make a *zu-zuc-cotta* for our wedding cake. I know how much you like it," Elizabeth sobbed.

Cat, desperate to keep the talk going, said the first thing that came to her head. "Do you make your own chocolate sponge? You don't use a prepared pound cake, do you?"

Elizabeth shook her head, timorously. "Neither. I make a macaroon shell instead of a sponge. You spread it in an oven-proof bowl and leave a cavity in the center."

"It's something to see," Pavo added. "She makes the filling first, it's almond-flavored whipped cream mixed with a gelatin custard. You line a bowl with plastic wrap and let it chill till it's set, right? And then when the duomo shell's cool, she coats the inside with a chocolate glaze so the custard filling won't make it soggy and when that cools she inverts the custard filling on the tray, peels off the plastic wrap and sets the meringue cake *over* it. And then you decorate with your cream and chocolate, whatever."

"That's ingenious," Bao said, in genuine admiration.

"It's all she got from Paulie was the food. Everyone always said that Paulie knew more about food than anyone in the mob, and Elizabeth knows twice what he ever knew and then some."

"Face the wall," Joaquin said.

Pavo and Elizabeth turned toward the wall.

"You, too, *señora.*"

"No," Cat said. "If you're going to shoot me, you're going to look at me."

The scar hitched up the smile once more. "What do you put in the custard?"

Elizabeth glanced over her shoulder. "Almond liqueur and toasted almonds. Bittersweet chocolate to line the shell."

"Did you ever try doing a version with sun-dried cherries?" Cat inquired.

"I thought about it," Elizabeth replied over her shoulder.

"But I can't get cherries that are the right texture, they're always a little too tough."

"You could marinate them overnight in cherry liqueur."

"That's a good idea, you know? I'll have to try—" She broke off with a sob.

Bao crossed the room in two strides, grabbed Cat by the wrist and pulled her toward the back door. He kept his gun trained at the pair against the wall, and with his free arm, pulled her close and kissed her.

Cat froze. *Good God.*

He reached around behind him and opened the back door. "Your cop, he treats you right?"

Cat fingered her lips, nodded.

"He'd better." He yanked the door open and backed out, glanced around. "Wait. Do nothing for a few minutes."

"Then?"

"Then go home to your children."

"You—forgot your jacket."

"Keep it. But don't wash off my scent."

FIFTEEN MINUTES LATER, Cat was on the phone with Ellice. She omitted the part about the hit man and so forth, got straight to the point. "I'm not kidding, Ellice, she'll make whatever kind of cake you want *for free!*" she was saying when armed, vested cops burst from every door and window.

El Cocinero was nowhere to be found.

# SIXTEEN

WHEN VICTOR AND Kurt Raab walked into the shop, Cat was sitting at on a wooden stool in the back, calmly answering questions. Raab introduced himself to the assistant D.A. present; since the site was in Cape May County, he had no jurisdiction. In truth, if it had gone down badly—badly, for Raab meant in a manner that would have exposed him to NewsLine90's cameras and mikes—he would prefer that it happen in some other county, that he would see some other D.A. snagged on the six o'clock news.

Pavo would not take his arm from Elizabeth's waist, but when he saw Victor, he opened his mouth to speak.

Victor glared at him, and Pavo shut up. He turned his gaze on the girl. "Where is your brother?"

"He's somewhere safe."

"Safe as in a convent, *¿verdad?*"

The girl's mouth dropped open.

Victor turned to Raab. "As I recall, Mother Anunciata told you she didn't understand why the Forgione boy would *want* to drop out of school. She never said that he did."

Raab shook his head, ruefully. "You all right, Miss Forgione?"

She nodded.

"It's Mrs. Buonovitti," Pavo said.

Victor lifted an eyebrow.

"She—" he pointed to Cat "—married us."

Victor lifted the other eyebrow.

"You come with me," he said to Cat.

"Victor," Raab reminded him. "It's after eight, and we got that thing at ten o'clock."

Victor nodded, and drew Cat outside, closing the door.

"Look," she said, "I was just going to get some pastry and see about making an appointment for Ellice's cake and one thing led to another. Before you know it, we're being held at gunpoint, I'm performing a wedding ceremony and I discovered a totally new way to make zuccotta."

"Just another off-season weekend at the shore." He saw the light waver in her eyes, saw her lips tremble. "What's the matter, *querida?* He didn't hurt you, did he?"

Cat shook her head. "I just...thought of Jane and Mats. It's my fault, you know, when I look for trouble? But I was just picking up pastry. And I don't like to think about how it can happen that fast, while you're just running an errand, or out for a jog...."

*Or escorting a woman in distress to the ER, as Chris Austen had been doing when he was gunned down.* Victor lifted her chin with the crook of his finger, ran his thumb lightly over her lips. "A lot can happen unexpectedly. Your lipstick is smeared."

"Yes, well...he sort of kissed me."

"Really. And did you sort of enjoy it?"

The dark brows lifted. "Enjoyment is a relative state, Lieutenant. I enjoyed it more than going to the dentist. Almost as much as chocolate. And not nearly as much as..." She smiled, slowly, ran her palm over his unshaven cheek. "I would like knowing why you show up here looking like *un asesino* yourself. And why, now that you've found Elizabeth Forgione, you're still on the clock."

"I'm sure your mother will tell you all about it later. Come on, I have to take you home."

"My mother?"

Victor glanced at his watch. "I'm overdue to pick her up. The D.A. is conducting an investigation that requires your mother's particular area of expertise."

He walked back into the shop. Pavo was standing with his

arm around Elizabeth Forgione. "Look," Pavo said. "I know I'm jammed up here, just tell me what I gotta do to make it right. Only keep Elizabeth out of it."

"There is one thing you can do. And I'm going to have to ask Miss Forgione—excuse me, Mrs. Buonovitti—to assist."

WHEN VICTOR PULLED UP to the house, Cat got out without waiting for him to open her car door, pushed through the front door, dropped the boxes of brioche and cinnamon rolls on a chair and called out, "Mama!"

Jennie came from the kitchen, her bright auburn hair combed into neat waves, dressed primly in a dark skirt and hose, a white silk blouse with a rhinestone American flag pinned to the lapel.

"You'd better tell me what's up right now. I'm your blood and don't you forget it!"

Jennie gave her daughter a hug. "I heard Ellice talking on the phone, there was some *confusion* at the bakery. Did you get some nice rolls?"

Victor entered, looked from Cat to Jennie. "Jennie, are you ready to go?"

Ellice came from the kitchen, wearing light drawstring pants and a T-shirt. "I send you out for breakfast, you come back with a free wedding cake. The coffee's ready."

"Let me find a thermos, Cat and Victor can have some to take. I'll put a couple of those buns in a napkin, too. You can't go around with nothing in your stomach."

"Jennie, Cat's not coming," Victor said, quietly.

"Of course she's coming. 'Cause if she doesn't come," Jennie shook her head, regretfully "—I don't know if I can make it." Jennie gave Cat a covert wink. "I look all right for police work? I didn't know what to wear."

"I think you know a lot more than you let on," Victor told her.

"Lieutenant, you're gonna have to take off your shirt, and I'm gonna have to shave a spot for the wire."

VICTOR WAS STANDING with a technician and Raab in the lavatory adjacent to the locker room at Major Crimes. Raab hadn't balked when he saw Cat. "Look, it can't be worse than when the beat reporter hangs out at the station."

"I don't want her anywhere near the scene." Victor unknotted his tie, unbuttoned his shirt. He removed them and laid them over a sink, then shucked off his sleeveless T-shirt.

The technician pumped soap from a dispenser into his palm. "Don't take this personal," he said, and began soaping a small area in the center of Victor's chest, right below his breastbone. He shaved away the hair, leaving a neat circle of bare flesh.

"Don't worry, she won't be. You think I'd let anything happen to Carlo Fortunati's mother and sister? He'd skin me alive," Raab said.

There was a knock and Stan poked his head in. "I got the threads. I hope I got the size right."

Stan pulled some garments out of the bag. He handed Victor a pair of dark, low-rise denims and a short-sleeved pullover. The shirt's fabric was a clingy nylon blend that had black threads woven with gray metallic, so that it came off an iridescent silver.

Victor looked at him.

"So I don't know fashion, but I know what I like."

The technician carefully taped the wire in place.

Victor eased the shirt over the wire, studied the reflection to determine whether or not the device would be visible beneath the clinging fabric of the shirt.

"Okay, let's take off, you can finish changing," the technician said. "I'm gonna go back into the day room and check you for sound."

The three left him alone. Victor changed into the black denims. They were low slung, tight-fitting. *Dios mío.* If his mother saw him wearing such clothes she would think he had gone bad for sure.

He layered his trousers, shirt, tie and jacket over a hanger and hung them on the coatrack in his office.

"Victor," Jennie demanded. "You think your mother wants to see you going around looking like that?"

"No." He signaled for a uniformed officer. "Would you please bring Mrs. Fortunati down to the van?"

Victor waited for Jennie to leave. "Believe me, every sordid simile has already crossed my mind."

Cat looked at him. A slight alteration in the hairline, the small streak of white in the black waves, the scar puckering the flesh on one side of his face and he would be almost identical to Joaquin Bao. "Where did you get that outfit, Victor?"

"Can I borrow that jacket? Unless it's a keepsake that you don't want to entrust to me."

Cat shrugged it off and handed it to him.

"You and your mother are going to be in the surveillance van. And stay where you're told," he said as he slipped on the jacket. "This should all be over within the hour."

There was a rap on the door and Stan poked his head in. "Lieut, lookin' good. Hey, that jacket, you think it's a perfect fit?"

"Almost too perfect," Cat said, quietly.

Victor suspected she wasn't talking only about the jacket.

# SEVENTEEN

JENNIE FORTUNATI was treated like a monarch. She had, after all, given birth to five cops, and first among those five was the legendary "King" Carlo Fortunati. She sat in the passenger seat of the van and Cat sat in back with the technician, Kurt Raab, and a uniformed cop.

The van had a charter boat's logo on the back. It drove the moderate speed limit along Longport Boulevard, past a long-abandoned nightclub planted among the drying foliage and tufts of brown weeds at the triangular convergence of the two roads that headed into Absecon Island. Cat looked out of the van's rear window as they passed and saw Victor's lean dark figure leaning against a black rental car.

Jennie's eyes followed her glance. "Those pants of his are too tight," she pronounced. "You know what happens you go around wearing tight pants all the time?"

The crew, all male, looked at each other.

"Mama..." Cat cautioned.

"I'm just sayin'," Jennie replied placidly. "Your father, he never wore tight pants and I had seven kids."

A rasp of static over Kurt Raab's two-way radio cut the laughter short. Victor's voice was heard saying, "Okay, we're on," with surprising clarity.

The technician handed Jennie a small speaker. "Okay, Mrs. Fortunati, I want you to say something to the lieutenant, count to ten, anything, so we can be sure he's hearing you."

Jennie took the microphone and told Victor that his pants were too tight.

VICTOR'S MOUTH CONTRACTED in the flicker of a smile as he leaned against the impound car. He barely felt the small earpiece inserted into his left ear as he watched, through the reflector lenses of his sun shades, the light changing the color of the rippling marsh grass.

Two roads, Longport Boulevard and the Longport-Ocean City Causeway met at a forty-five degree angle on one of the many marshy islets strewn through the bays and thoroughfares that separated the barrier islands from "offshore." Situating a nightclub on the triangle of land where these two roads met had been someone's good idea at one time. Now the building lay dilapidated, its asphalt lot veined with cracks from which sprouted dying weeds. The land bordering the causeway was overgrown with parched and tangled foliage, littered with discarded trash bags tossed by weekenders on their way back to Philly or Camden County. A billboard with an outdated pronouncement leaned on buckling pillars. Beyond, no more than a dozen feet from where Victor stood, lay the inlet. He could smell it, hear the slap of water against the barrier of underbrush and discarded hunks of concrete that separated the causeway from the water. In high tide, the water would seep through these obstacles to form a tide pool where water fowl and the occasional fox gathered, but it was not high tide now. The quiet lapping of the water did not completely muffle the low hum of an outboard motor.

*Approaching by water,* Victor thought. *Smart.* He wondered if Raab had alerted the marine police.

Victor turned. The foliage shuddered and crackled and a bulky figure emerged. Jolly Cholly Mackenzie was a large man with a red face that expanded from the narrow forehead to bulbous jowls that spilled over his shirt collar. The blue eyes were just a shade too pale to match the disarming smile. The wide, solid frame conveyed either excess muscle or excess fat; he regarded it as fat when he wanted to present himself as a genial man of the people; it was muscle when he needed to take care of business. He looked like the back-slapping, guy next door pushing a lawn mower, manning the outdoor grill.

It was, Victor decided, as good a mask for a back stabber as any. Whatever got you close to the mark.

"So you're him?" Mackenzie approached, held out a plump hand.

"Stay where you are," Victor said, coldly. "I told you to come alone."

"I am alone, *amigo.*" Mackenzie chuckled. "All I got is someone to handle the boat. I gotta tell you, I don't know much about boats. A mortgage, a wife and four kids, that doesn't put you in the yacht club class, you know?"

Ever the working man's friend. "You have it?"

"I don't hear boo on the airwaves."

Victor reached into his back pocket, drew out a black-and-white photograph. Pavo lay faceup, his lids half-closed over lifeless eyes. The girl lay on her stomach, her face turned sideways so that her profile was visible. A black puddle seeped from under Pavo's head, pooled with the stream flowing from the back of the girl's neck. To his credit, Pavo hadn't put up a fight at all when he had to have himself smeared with the only thing they could find, chocolate syrup. In fact, Victor thought he had rather enjoyed it.

Victor jammed it in the breast pocket of the man's plaid flannel shirt. "Okay. My part's done."

"We just got a little thing we gotta go through, first. I gotta know you are who you say you are, right?" Mackenzie asked, amiably.

"Who else would have that picture?"

"Humor me." Mackenzie reached into his back pocket, drew out a sheet of notebook paper. "I hadda have this written down, hope you don't mind. Me, the only end of cooking I know is the eating end."

Light traffic moved along Longport Boulevard. Victor did not see the white van with the marina logo pass behind him. "Let's get on with it."

Mackenzie read off the paper. "You're gonna roast some game, but it's a little dry, whadda you gonna do?"

"To moisten the game, or to give it more flavor?" Victor hoped the microphone picked it up. After a few seconds he heard Jennie's voice in his ear. "You gotta bard it. Bard. Like what they call Shakespeare. You take strips of lard and cover the meat, or you can use a nice bacon. I like a thicker strip, some nice sugar cured bacon—"

"Bard it. Layer strips of lard or bacon over it," Victor told Mackenzie.

"—but it was always hard gettin' the kids to eat anything gamey. My Carlo, he'd do one or two nights in the fall, a game dinner back when we had a restaurant—what? Okay, I was just telling Victor, I'll be quiet."

Victor's mustache twitched, but the dark, mirrored sunglasses kept Mackenzie from seeing the trace of amusement that infiltrated his eye.

"Well, that's real interesting, Coceeneero. Me, I don't go for the gamey stuff, except when I get an invite to the hunt club barbecues once in a while."

Victor checked his watch. "How much longer?"

"Oh, I just got a couple more. I heard you're one hell of a cook, Coceeneero."

"That's right."

"How about this? How can you tell if an egg's still fresh? I mean, aside from when it's really gone bad."

"You mean, how would I test to see if an egg is fresh?"

"That's easy," Jennie replied. "You put it in a bowl of water. Cold. It floats, it's gone bad, it sinks, it's still okay. That's 'cause that little sac at the pointy end of the egg—"

"Put it in a bowl of cold water," Victor said. "It will sink if it's fresh."

"—puffs up with air when it goes rotten—"

"I'll be damned. How about one for the road?"

"I'm getting impatient," Victor said, coldly.

"Okay, look. I need some powdered sugar to put on top of a cake and I'm clean out. What do I do?"

"Go to the market."

"I can't get out."

"You mean what would you substitute for confectioner's sugar?"

"You take a cup of regular sugar," Jennie said. "And you take out one tablespoon and put in a tablespoon of cornstarch. Then you blend it. You can run it through the blender on high, but I found your coffee grinder works better. It's best not to run out."

"A cup minus a tablespoon of granulated sugar," Victor said, calmly. "Add a tablespoon of cornstarch and put it through your coffee grinder on high."

Mackenzie glanced at the paper. "Says food processor here, but I guess you know best." He pocketed the sheet and pulled out a fat manila envelope. "I'm gonna have to try that next time the wife's outta powdered sugar."

"It's best not to run out," Victor said, for Jennie's benefit.

Mackenzie handed the envelope to Victor. Victor opened it and glanced at the bills, thumbed through them. All hundreds. More than he could count.

"This doesn't do it," Mackenzie said. "I may have you do the boy for me. You get the girl to tell you where he is?"

"Yes."

Mackenzie grinned. "But it'll cost me, right? Lemme wait till after Monday, it gets out that Paulie's girl's been whacked. I think he'll get my message, but just in case, I figure they're gonna put some protection on the boy. Not a problem for you, right?"

"Not a problem."

"Only problem's cleaning up your mess. I always gotta get on my kids, clean up your mess. What about Forgione?"

"What about him?"

"You think he's vulnerable?"

"Everyone's vulnerable."

"Even you?" Mackenzie grinned.

"Yes. But you have to get very close to find my sweet spot. You think you want to get that close, Mackenzie?"

"I don't think we're gonna be getting together again."

Mackenzie didn't extend his hand this time. He turned and walked back toward the strand of underbrush and litter that separated the causeway from the bay.

He was walking toward the bushes when the shots echoed across the causeway. Victor spun to his left, let the momentum carry him full circle. He dropped, his weapon already drawn.

"Hands, Mackenzie!" Victor called out. "I want to see them now!"

Mackenzie had one hand halfway behind his waist. He looked at Victor for a few moments, brought it into sight, raised both hands, the genial smile never wavering. "I bet you think you got me, don't you?"

They heard the sirens only a few seconds before the cruisers appeared, pulled onto the cracked concrete. The officers hopped out with weapons drawn.

"He came from that way. Took a boat," Victor told them. One of the officers told Mackenzie to put his hands behind his back, and cuffed him and started to pat him down. "He's not armed."

The other cop moved toward the brush, his weapon high.

Victor felt a burning sensation, no more than a penetrating warmth on his shoulder. He probed the spot and felt a gash in the jacket, slipped it off and saw that the gash had split entirely through the leather and the lining. Victor fingered his shoulder. The shirt wasn't torn. Whatever had ripped the jacket had grazed the fabric without harming him.

The van pulled up and Raab jumped out, hurried up to him. "Where'd the shots come from?"

Victor jerked his chin toward the brush. "Keep the women in the van. Did you get enough?"

"Yes."

"Lieutenant!" An officer stood in the brush, clutching dried branches from something on the ground. Victor and Raab saw the body slumped among the rubble. "He's been shot. Dead.'' He slipped a pen into the barrel of a gun, held it up. ''He had this in his hand, it's been fired.''

''That structure, that was behind me. Have CSU see if they can find a slug. If we can match it up to that guy's gun, we know who fired at you.'' Victor saw the first sign of apprehension infiltrate Mackenzie's counterfeit amiability.

''I didn't have any cops on the water,'' Raab said. ''Who fired at him?''

''Whoever it was,'' Victor fingered the jacket, thoughtfully, ''may well have saved my life.''

''We've got an APB out on this guy, Bao.''

''You won't find him,'' Victor stated.

''I will not!''

Victor turned toward the van, saw one of the uniforms arguing with someone inside. After a moment, Cat jumped down. She took a step toward him and stopped. He saw the look in her eye and knew what it meant. Her husband, a cop, had been gunned down. Now she was with another cop, exposing herself to all the same risks. Danger did not cease to be a danger once it was defined.

A week later, he and Cat stood beside Vincent Buonovitti and Elizabeth Forgione when they were married properly. Victor watched her through the brief ceremony, saw her trace her lip with her fingertip once or twice, as if remembering the sensation of a kiss.

When she caught him watching her, she stopped. But the look in her eye was the wary ambiguity of one who was afraid to risk making the same mistake twice.

# SHEEP IN WOLF'S CLOTHING

by Peter Abresch

# Acknowledgments

For helping me sort out wine and food,
David and Ruth Pursglove.

For helping me sort out vinegars and oils,
John Paul Cook of Austria's Finest, Naturally
P.O. Box 69, Mount Vernon, VA 22121.
http://www.AustrianPumpkinOil.com

I took some literary license in moving some
fictional furniture at Manteo's Tranquil House Inn
http://www.tranquilinn.com
and the 1587 Restaurant. I never had a good meal
there; they were all superb.

For another fine job of freelance editing and
proofing, Dorrie O'Brien.
dorrie@peakpeak.com

In thanks for asking me to be part of this anthology,
Feroze Mohammed.

To ELDERHOSTEL, INC. On all the
ELDERHOSTELs I have attended, I have found
nothing but fun, camaraderie, adventurous spirits
and nary a body…yet.

# ONE

"ISN'T THE VIOLENCE exhilarating?"

Jim Dandy glanced down into Dodee Swisher's smooth face, cornflower eyes crinkled with laugh lines, hair the color of ripened wheat, then stared out at the ocean.

An icy wind cut across the green sea, streaking it with white spindrift and shearing off wave tops as they stumbled over themselves in a rush to shore, only to crash to their death in a rolling thunder against the North Carolina coast.

Great.

Just what he needed.

Walking along on a freeze-your-ass-off morning, chilling the marrow of his sixty-something bones, when he could be back in their room having a snooze.

He licked the sea salt from his lips and nodded. "Oh, yeah."

"You don't say that with any enthusiasm, sweetheart."

And the worst part? They were walking with the wind.

"I'm enthused just being near you, lady."

"Is that coming from your heart or another part of your anatomy?"

Keep your mouth shut. No way to win that one.

Fact was, that might be the real reason he was out here. No, screw it, it *was* the reason.

He put his arm around her, feeling the trim body he knew lurked under the bulky coat from teaching aerobics to senior citizens, and gazed down at her as she took in the assault of sea upon sand. And he realized her artist's mind was seeing things that a semiretired physical therapist from Maryland couldn't. And he loved her for it.

But damn it, couldn't she have seen the same thing from behind the windshield of his Lincoln? With strains of "Scheherazade" coming from the tape deck? And the heater keeping them toasty?

"I said, is that coming from your heart or another part of your anatomy?"

And if they had to face the elements, why not walk up the beach? Against the icy wind? Freezing her lips to her teeth so she couldn't ask dumb questions about where his enthusiasm was coming from. That way, when they headed back, the stiff breeze would have given them a boost.

But no-oo.

She had pointed downwind and shouted, "Look, there's something rolling in the surf. Maybe it's a treasure. Let's go see."

And so they had set off downwind and would now face it in the teeth on the way back.

She poked him the ribs. "You didn't answer the question."

"Didn't I?"

Worse thing was, the floundering treasure had submarined under the foam, so now she'd trek him all the way to the Oregon Inlet before giving up on what was probably only an old log.

"See," he said, "I thought I had answered, but I guess my mind is so frozen that the words never reached my lips, or my lips are so frozen that I didn't realize they weren't working, or my tongue is so frozen—"

"All right, sweetheart," she said, stopping and yanking him about-face, "if you want to turn back, why don't you just say so?"

"Becauthe my tongue ith tho frothen—"

"Bend your head and I'll warm it up for you."

So he did, tasting the sea salt on her lips, and, indeed, her moist mouth did warm his tongue, and everything else for that matter, making the ordeal of trudging through the sand on a freeze-your-ass-off morning all worth it.

Except for one little thing.

Out of the corner of his eye he saw a couple of Frankenstein-monster waves, one piggybacking on top of another, charge up the beach and deposit the missing treasure at the edge of the waterline.

Only it was no treasure, not even an old log…not wearing a shredded green parka and tattered black pants.

# TWO

HE BROKE OFF the kiss as another wave rushed up the beach, fading before reaching the body.

She looked up at him. "What's the matter?"

"Don't turn around."

She turned around. "Oh, God, it's a body, a man."

"I told you not to turn around." He patted his pockets. "You have your cell phone?"

"Back in the car."

"Yeah, so is mine." He scanned the beach to see if they were alone. "Stay away from the body."

But she walked straight up and stared down at it.

He held up his hands and let them flop to his sides.

At least it was facedown, which spared her from seeing his—

"We should roll him over."

"What?"

She turned to him. "Roll him over."

"Are you crazy? A body lolling about in the water for who knows how long isn't a pleasant thing to see, much less smell."

"I don't smell anything."

"Wait. The cold water acted like a refrigerator, but now it's out in the air."

"It's a man, Jim, not a thing."

"One that has been sand-papered in the surf."

"We should roll him over on his back so he can at least face the sky."

"He's dead, Dodee, he doesn't care—"

"All right, I'll do it."

"Okay, okay." He might as well be talking to the gelid wind. "But this is not going to be a pretty sight." He squatted next to it. "You know this is disturbing a crime scene?"

"Crime scene?" She palmed-up a hand. "Who's the perpetrator, the sea? You going to roll him over or not?"

"Okay, okay, but I'm going on record that I'm against it."

"So noted."

He glanced up at the heavens and shook his head—yeah buddy, that would help—then grabbed the cold and clammy shoulder of the green parka, and the tattered black pants at the hip, and heaved the body over. One arm flopped half across the chest, the other half-hidden under the back, and the ankles crossed as they followed.

He stood up as his stomach did a couple of flip-flops.

Yep, it wasn't a pretty sight.

Empty sockets stared up at the blustery sky, sockets that had once been occupied by eyeballs, eaten away now by crabs or gouged out by the abrasive surf that had taken a toll on what had once been a face, now only raw meat with patches of bare skull.

Shredded black pants covered the legs, ripped at the crotch, and a half-open green parka protected the torso, but the thing that caught his eye was the white clerical collar on a black shirt.

"A minister?" Dodee asked.

He shrugged, looked inland for a landmark, and found one in a gray beach house with a widow's walk just over the sand berm that separated beach from road.

"C'mon." He motioned to her. "Let's get back to the car and call the police."

"You go. I'll stay here in case a wave starts to drag him away."

He turned to the foam-streaked sea. "Tide's going out." Already the reach of the crashing surf had receded from the time they had started walking. "Nothing to worry about."

"You go, I'll stay, just in case."

"This is crazy. The body's not going anywhere—"

"I'll stay," she said, turning her back to the wind. "Someone should keep watch with him."

"This is crazy."

"You already said that, sweetheart."

"All right, you go, I'll stay."

"No, you can make the trip faster."

He held out his hands. "This is craz— You'll freeze your rear end off."

She pulled up the collar of her coat. "It's not getting any better with you standing here arguing."

He stared into her big blues for a moment—no give there—then shook his head and lumbered off into the bite of the wind, swinging back to her after ten paces.

"Don't touch anything."

She turned to him. "Go."

"I mean it, Dodee, don't touch anything."

She crossed her eyes.

He let out a sigh and started out again.

At least he had ordered her to leave everything alone.

Oh, yeah, a lot of good that would do.

The wet, gravel-filled sand just above the waterline gave under his feet, making the slog hard going. The Maryland beaches were packed hard, but here in North Carolina it was like marching through chewing gum. And being pelted by salt spray at the same time.

He trudged back to the Lincoln, started the engine, and pushed the heater to high.

Awright, he would live.

And if Dodee insisted on freezing her rear end off, well, he'd be glad to warm it up for her.

He pulled out his cell phone, put in a call to the police, gave them the approximate location and the landmark, then swung the car around and headed south on Old Oregon Inlet Road, passing deserted motels and battened-down beach cottages waiting for the season to start. He found the gray beach house with the widow's walk and turned off onto a side road, pulled up to the sand-berm seawall and got out.

A gray North Carolina State Police car with two troopers pulled up right behind him. A six-foot-three trooper unfolded himself from the front passenger seat, sergeant stripes on his uniform, and tugged a wide-brimmed hat so far down over his brow it gave the appearance his head was deformed. Dark eyes stared out of a suntanned face marred by a white one-inch scar on the jawbone of his right cheek.

"You James P. Dandy?" he asked. A name tag with Atwater on it was fastened above his right pocket.

Jim pointed toward the ocean. "I think it's right out here on the beach."

Sergeant Atwater motioned for the second trooper to follow and they headed up a wooden ramp leading over the sand berm.

"My girlfriend insisted on staying with the body. Didn't want the surf pulling it back in."

"That's fine," Atwater said.

"What do you think? Someone fell off a boat?"

"Or off a bridge. We have a report of a missing person last seen fishing from it. Normally we wouldn't expect the body to turn up, especially here, but with the wind and the currents, you never know."

The second trooper caught up to them as they reached the top of the berm. "Father Pelican?" he asked.

Below them Dodee hunkered down in her coat, sitting cross-legged next to the body, both high and dry now.

"Could be," Atwater answered, leading the way.

"Pelican's a nickname?" Jim asked.

"Real name, as unlikely as that may sound out here on the banks."

Dodee stood and Jim wrapped his arm around her. "This is my girlfriend, Dodee Swisher," he said as she snuggled in close.

"Hello, ma'am," Atwater said, tipping two fingers to his

hat. He continued straight on to the body. "Not a pretty way for a peaceful priest to end up."

"You knew him?" Jim asked.

He nodded. "Just about everyone in the area did. A good guy. My wife thought he could walk on water." He blinked at them. "Didn't mean that to sound disrespectful." He turned to the second trooper. "Leroy, want to check out the pockets?"

One side of Leroy's lips curled as he looked up at his six-foot-three chief, but it really wasn't a question. Leroy knelt and started going through the pockets, pulling out handfuls of sand along with a rosary and a ring of car keys.

Dodee looked up at Atwater. "You said a priest?"

"Yes, ma'am, Father Pelican, although without identification, it's hard to tell from the condition of the body."

She turned in Jim's arms and tilted her face up to him. "How do they know his name?"

"He was last seen fishing from a bridge."

Leroy extracted a black wallet from the back pocket. He brushed the sand off and glanced inside. "Leslie Pelican," he said, handing it up.

Sergeant Atwater studied it a moment, then turned to Jim and Dodee. "What can you tell me? I mean, you just found him here in the sand?"

"We were walking and saw something rolling in the surf," Jim said. "It disappeared by the time we got here, but then a wave brought it in."

"You found it like this?"

Dodee nodded. "Yes."

"Looks like it was rolled over," Leroy said.

Jim squeezed Dodee's arm to keep her mouth shut. "I did that. I wanted to make absolutely sure there was nothing I could do."

Atwater's dark eyes leveled on him. "Are you a doctor?"

Jim shook his head. "I'm an emergency medical technician in Maryland and a semiretired physical therapist."

"Uh-huh. And that's all you did?" Sergeant Atwater

peered down at them from his full six-foot-three height. "Just rolled the body over. Nothing else?"

"No," Dodee said, "nothing else."

Jim studied the corpse for a moment, then stared into the big blues glaring back at him.

"We didn't disturb anything else," she said again.

Which was bullshit.

The arms, which had been in disarray, were now neatly placed on the corpse's belly, and the ankles, which had been twisted, were now side by side.

Atwater ran a finger over the one-inch scar that marred his right jaw line. "You all have a house down here?"

"Just tourists," Dodee said.

The sergeant nodded and pulled out a notebook and pen. "I wonder if I can get your names." He found an empty page and handed it to Dodee. "Names and addresses, please. Where are you staying?"

"Manteo," Jim said, "at the Tranquil House Inn. We're here with a weekend Elderhostel group studying cooking."

"Elderhostel?"

"They're a series of learning adventures held all over the world for those over fifty-five."

Dodee handed back the book with their addresses and the name of the hotel. "A priest, you said? An Anglican priest?"

"He was a Catholic priest, ma'am, Father Leslie Pelican." Atwater studied the book a moment, then put it away. "Thank you for your help. If we have any further questions, how long will you be at Tranquil House?"

"Just the weekend," Jim said. "We leave Monday morning."

He took Dodee's hand and started back to the car.

Did Atwater believe her about not moving the body?

And what about that look on Dodee's face when she asked if he was an Anglican priest? He had seen that look before. It was the look that had gotten him into trouble on past Elderhostels as she meddled into police business.

But not this time.

She turned to him when they were in the car. "I can't believe he said Father Pelican was a Catholic priest."

"Don't go into it, Dodee. It's none of our business." He put the car in reverse, waiting for her to continue in spite of what he said, but she pursed her lips, nodded and turned to the windshield.

Good.

He backed down past the police car and turned around.

Only, she had given up too easily.

He shifted into Drive.

Something not right here.

He put his foot on the brake and draped his arms over the steering wheel. "Okay, why can't you believe what Atwater said— No, forget it. I don't want to know."

He drove down to Old Oregon Inlet Road, checked for traffic, none on this cold, blustery day, then draped his arms on the wheel again.

"Okay, you gonna tell me?"

She smiled with the tips of her lips turned down. "Tell you what, sweetheart?"

"Why you can't believe the sergeant said he was a Catholic priest?"

"But you said you didn't want—"

"Okay, I wanna know. You going to tell me or drag it out? Why can't you believe—"

"Because Catholic priests are celibate men."

He blinked. "You're saying he wasn't celibate?"

"I'm saying he—she wasn't a man."

# THREE

JIM STARED at her for a moment, then turned north on Old Oregon Inlet Road.

"I'm telling you that was a woman's body," she said. "Don't you think I know a woman's body?"

"Why would a woman be dressed— Is that why you re-arranged the clothes?"

"I thought she deserved some dignity, even in death."

"How could you do that? I thought I was going to throw up just looking at it, and I sometimes work with cadavers to keep my therapy license, three Continuing Education units every two years." He swung the blue Lincoln around a hub-cap sitting in the road. "Back to the question. Why would a woman be dressed up as a Catholic priest?"

"Not only that, sweetheart, the priest's identification was planted in the pocket."

"Planted?" He shook his head. "Don't go into this, Do-dee."

"But aren't you at least curious?"

"It's none of our business."

"But what happened to the priest?"

"Leave it to the police."

"Unless the priest did it himself." She pointed to him in her little idiosyncratic way with her thumb and forefinger together. "Suppose the priest wanted to do a disappearing act? Maybe he was milking the collection plate."

He hung a left on a street called South Surfside Drive. "The sergeant said he was last seen fishing from a bridge—"

"But that could have been his cover—"

"His cover?" He shook his head. "You sound like a dime-store detective."

"But think about it. He makes sure he is seen, then he tips the body over the edge, dressed in his clothes and with his identification, and goodbye Father Pelican."

He came to a cul-de-sac on West Side Court. "That doesn't make sense."

"Where are you going?"

"I don't know." He swung around and headed back out. "I thought this went through to the highway. But think about it. If he wanted to skip out and make people think he had drowned, he certainly wouldn't use a woman's body."

"Maybe that was all he could get."

"Oh, yeah, like the local body shop was fresh out of men?"

"Or maybe he figured that by the time the body was found, no one would be able to tell."

"If you're going to think along those lines," he said, turning north on Old Oregon Inlet Drive again, "he only needed a body long enough for someone to see it plunge into the drink. The sergeant said they would never have found the body if it weren't for the strong winds and crazy currents."

She stared at him. "Okay, so why would he want to skip out?"

"You're asking me?"

"It's your idea."

"My idea? When did it become my idea?"

"You said he just needed it to dump in the water."

He shook his head. "I'm not going into it. It's police business. They'll discover it's a woman's body, if they haven't already, and track down the priest."

She turned down her lips, nodded and turned to the windshield.

He took a left on Gulf Stream Street, finally getting over to the highway, Route 12, made the left at Whale Bone Junction and started over the bridge for Manteo. He steadied the

Lincoln against a buffeting crosswind that sent dark clouds scudding overhead and kicked up streaks of spindrift on Roanoke Sound below.

He checked her out of the side of his eye.

Had he convinced her or was something churning around in her head?

He didn't want to get involved in police business. Again. On the last Elderhostel they'd almost ended up in jail. In fact, when had he been with her that something hadn't come up?

Maybe he needed a new girlfriend.

Oh, yeah, like he could give up loving her even if he wanted.

He glanced at her, big blues studying the road, wheaten curls in windblown disarray.

Oh, yeah, and like he was stupid enough to think he could find someone close to her in looks and personality. And, double oh-yeah, like he could find anyone demented enough to love him in return.

So she had a few faults.

Like getting him thrown into jail an odd time or two. He could live with that. Sort of. Maybe. If he could just keep her from getting involved.

The bridge dipped back down to ground level as they passed a marina full of deep-sea charter boats with tall flying bridges for spotting fish.

Her idea was crazy anyway, a priest staging his own death because he dipped into the till. How much could the till be worth in the Outer Banks? Enough to keep the churches afloat?

Except when the season comes in and the population blooms from a handful to a bazillion.

"Wonder what their summer collection brings in?"

She turned to him with a smile that turned down the tips of her lips.

"All right, all right." He held up his hand. "I got carried away. No more. We mind our own business."

He drove down into Manteo, found Queen Elizabeth Avenue in the middle of the historic district, and pulled into the parking lot of the Tranquil House Inn, a long, two-story hotel on the water. The grounds and plants were neatly trimmed. An herb garden lived at the entrance.

"I think we have arrived."

She batted her eyelashes at him. "And you promise not to take advantage of poor little me?"

"Me take advantage of you? Ha. You can't keep your hands off me, lady."

"Oh, really? How would you like to get separate rooms?"

He pulled her close to him. "I'd say that's right up there with the joy of blowing my brains out." He kissed her, warm and lingering, and full of nasty promises. "I love you, lady, I do."

"I love you, too, sweetheart."

He got her sketchbook out of the trunk and had to hang on as a gust of wind tried to sail it like a kite. He passed it to her, picked up their bags and followed her up the wooden steps to the Tranquil House Inn.

The lobby exuded warmth, both in temperature and the appointments of wood and carpet and the smell of herbs from the dining room. A small sign by the front desk on the right said Welcome, Elderhostel. A dark-eyed woman with a bright smile and auburn hair looked up at their presence.

"We're with the Elderhostel," Jim said.

"Yes, if you go into our 1587 Restaurant there's a sign-up table there. Welcome to the Inn."

They followed the lobby around a corner into a small alcove where a well-fed, gray-haired lady sat behind a table near the bar.

"Hi," Jim said, "what's an Elderhostel?"

"Well," she said, "they're learning adventures for those over fifty-five, very reasonably priced, full of fun and camaraderie—"

"Don't let him kid you," Dodee said, "we're signed up for this Elderhostel."

"Oh." She shook her head. "Just when I was going into my big spiel about how they're held all over the world. Are you going to be trouble for me this weekend?"

"I'm Dodee Swisher and this odd man with me is James Dandy. I promise to make him behave."

"I'm Susan Baxter, the coordinator for the weekend." She gave them each a strong handshake and then found their folders and passed them registration cards. "This is our first try at Elderhostel's new weekend format."

Jim passed his card to Dodee.

"You want me to fill it out?"

"You do it so well. You have an artist's hand."

The big blues glared at him, and he gave her a big, phony grin, turned and gazed at the main dining room of the 1587 Restaurant.

White-linen-covered tables, big windows overlooking the water, wooden piers filled with boats from small day-sailors to a couple of large, deep-sea charter vessels. A bridge crossed the cove to an old-time English sailing ship with a high poop, docked on the other side.

"Our professional chef won't be in until tomorrow," Susan Baxter said, "but as an extra this afternoon, a local amateur will be teaching us the intricacies of cooking creatures from the sea."

Jim pointed to the old-time ship. "What's that boat out there?"

"The *Elizabeth II,* a replica of the one that landed the first colonists in North Carolina. It's a big summer attraction." She smiled again. "Welcome to Manteo."

He picked up their bags, recrossed the lobby, and paused at the foot of the stairs to glance at a column of pictures, one above the other, of men standing beside big fish with long bills hanging from a dock weigh-in station. Dodee started up and he followed her.

"If we're lucky," he said, "we'll be on the water side."

And lucky they were; the windows looked down on a large

catamaran swinging on a hook, perhaps stopping over on a trek down the inland waterway.

Dodee pointed to the two blue-water charter boats. "You ever go out deep-sea fishing?"

He shook his head. "Thought about it, but never did. Couldn't afford it when the kids were growing."

"Maybe you should take a day and go."

"In this wind? No thanks. My days of rough-weather fishing are over."

He turned back to the room: king-size bed, dresser with a television opposite it and a private bathroom near the door, all done in earth tones that gave it a warm, pleasant atmosphere.

"So," he said with a yawn, "what do you want to do, lady?"

"I know what you want to do."

"Love in the afternoon, or more accurately, love in the midday?"

"I was thinking you'd want a nap."

"Ah, yes, now that you mention it. It was a long drive down."

She put her arms around his neck and gave him a kiss. "Why don't you lie down and I'll take my sketchbook and see if I can find an interesting subject or two."

He stretched out on the bed while she tested out the bathroom, and waited for her to come out, but as far as he was aware, she never did.

# FOUR

THE OVERCAST DAY had settled into a dreary afternoon by the time the well-fed Elderhostel coordinator, Susan Baxter, conducted a get-acquainted session in the kitchen of the 1587 Restaurant.

"This is our first shot here at the new Elderhostel weekend format," Susan Baxter said at its conclusion. "While we hope we have a great culinary preparation program lined up for you, we will also be learning how to fit this whole thing together."

They circled a stainless-steel table, fifty-five-plussers, although some looked to be in their forties and might be since only one in a room had to be of an Elderhostel age.

Susan Baxter put her hands together as if praying and touched her lips. "Our other problem is that this is a working kitchen where lunch and dinner are prepared daily, so our classes have to work around the restaurant's schedule."

Jim looked at the eager faces. Could he remember any of the names of those he had just met? Thank God for name tags, and for Dodee being at his side—she being one of those who looked to be in their forties.

"Tomorrow, Chef Andrea Davis will be here to lead the professional part of our program, but for this afternoon we have a local chef who has a reputation on the Outer Banks for cooking creatures from the sea. While he is a nonprofessional chef, as opposed to amateur, in his real life he is a deep-sea charter captain. So, with that buildup, let me present our chef for the afternoon, Cornelius Jansen."

A big man, six-two, shoulders to match, and serious brown eyes, stepped up to the counter. His square jaw and crewcut red hair combined to give him the appearance of a cube-headed cartoon character.

"My name is Cornelius," he said in a high-pitched voice that didn't fit his stature, like a clown talking in falsetto, "but everybody calls me Corney and you're welcome to do likewise." He tied a white apron over a polo shirt and faded dungarees which had a sheathed Buck knife hanging from the belt.

"As Susan mentioned," he said, placing a plastic cutting board on the stainless-steel table, "I'm a deep-sea charter boat captain. My boat, the *Commandment,* is docked out here—" he waved a ham-size hand in the direction of the water "—and I give you an open invitation to come by and visit. And, should you get the urge to head out into the Gulf Stream and try your hand at one of the big ones, I can accommodate you with that as well. For a price, of course."

He took the waxed paper covering off one of the pans, lifted out a thirty-inch fish and slapped it down on the plastic cutting board.

"The ingredients for this recipe are one boat, one fishing rod, some bait, some beer, a sandwich or two and a measure of patience."

Grins all around the table.

"Lacking those, buy one fresh from a charter captain," he said in his falsetto voice. "This particular specimen is called a bluefish. It's a voracious feeder, traveling in packs like wolves. One minute you'll be sitting quiet as can be, then the school will move in and suddenly you're pulling fish up hand over fist, then just as suddenly, the blues move on and everything is quiet again."

"The Lord giveth," said a russet-faced man in bib overalls and plaid shirt, Amos Brown on his name tag, "and the Lord taketh."

"That's one way to look at it," Corney Jansen said as he placed a sheathed knife on the table. "Now most of you won't be buying your fish this way. If you're like the majority of Americans, you'll be picking them up at your supermarket's freezer counter. But if you want the best-tasting fish there is, this is how you'll get 'em, fresh off the boat, and you'll eat 'em that very night. The thing is, what do you do with something like this after you buy it?"

Jansen pulled the knife out of the scabbard.

"This is the kind of knife you want to use for slicing flesh from the bone," he said, holding it up in his large right hand so everyone could see the long, narrow blade that widened near the handle. "It's called a fillet knife, as opposed to a Buck knife used to cut line." He unsnapped the sheath on his belt and held that one up in his left hand. "I use a whetstone to keep them both honed. The Buck knife will do the job, but will saw and tear the flesh. The fillet knife will slice the tip of your finger off without you even feeling it, so be careful."

Jansen sheathed the Buck knife and flattened the bluefish on the plastic cutting board. "I've already taken off the scales, but it's a simple matter of using the back of a knife or a scaler and scraping it against the grain of the scales and they'll come right off. Sometimes, on a really large fish, they can be as big as plastic poker chips. First thing we'll do is remove the intestines—" he cut loose the belly of the fish and with the back of his knife scraped it into a plastic bucket beside the table "—then we take off the head behind the gills, because most of us aren't going to eat that."

He severed the head, then skewered it and held it up.

"However, if you were interested in making fish stock, the head is a good candidate for adding to the pot."

He dropped it in the bucket.

"We begin filleting at the tail by slicing through to the backbone. Since all the bones in a fish are in a lateral plane, if we use the backbone as a guide, and keep the blade flat in that plane, we'll cut off the flesh without taking the bones."

He made a slicing motion as he cut the flesh from the backbone and lifted it for everyone to see.

"Most of you will probably buy your fish already cut like this, or in chunks out of the freezer, but I think it's important to know how it's done. Indeed, if you chartered a fishing boat, say the *Commandment*—" he gave them all a big grin "—when you came to shore with a pile of fish, you'll find someone willing to fillet the fish for you at a reasonable price, and they do it so fast and so well it would be silly not to take advantage of it."

He set the fish steak aside and turned the fish over, cut off the second slab and pointed to the remaining skeleton that had hardly any flesh remaining. "And if you were making that fish stock, you'd want to throw these in as well."

"Isn't that an oily fish?" the russet-faced Amos Brown asked, he in the bib overalls and plaid shirt.

Jansen nodded. "Yes, it is, but fish oil is very good for your heart. Some people like to soak this for a few hours in a mixture of baking soda and vinegar to take the fishy taste out of it, but I'm going to show you something better." He laid the two slabs of fish on the board and cut them into bite-size squares. "We're going to batter 'em up and give 'em a quick fry."

He placed a skillet on the stove and poured in two inches of olive oil and turned on the heat. "Normally I'd use peanut oil for myself, but since some people are allergic to peanuts, I'll use olive oil tonight."

"You know, they used to preserve meat in olive oil before they had refrigerators," Dodee said.

"That's right," Jim said. "We learned that on a French cuisine Elderhostel in Baltimore. They'd dunk a pig into a barrel of olive oil, and pull it up to cut off a chunk of meat whenever they wanted."

"Huh." Jansen's brow wrinkled under his crewcut red hair. "Never heard of that." He pulled a stainless-steel mixing bowl from an overhead rack. "I'll have to remember it the next time the electricity goes out and I have a spare barrel of olive oil hanging about."

Grins all around.

Jansen opened a box of Bisquick biscuit mix and dumped some into the bowl, added a couple of eggs, sprinkled in some Old Bay Seasoning, then snapped open three cans of Miller beer. "Almost any kind of beer will do," he said in his clownish voice and smiled, "but since we're in such an upscale place, I figured we better use the champagne of bottled beer. We need two cans here and one we'll hold in reserve."

He poured in a can of beer and started mixing it with a whisk, then added more beer.

"How do you know how much to mix?" asked a woman, Rosario Emalda by name tag, a platinum-blonde in high heels and blue suit that looked like it was designed by Gucci.

"Oh, by hook and quick. I just dump it in until it's a thick soupy consistency."

He dumped the fish squares into the mix, checked the skillet and pulled out some made-up tartar sauce from the fridge. He took another bowl from the rack and combined ketchup, horseradish, some more Old Bay Seasoning, squeezed in a couple of lemon wedges, sprinkled in Worcestershire sauce, then whipped it into a cocktail sauce.

"Okay, we're about ready here."

He dipped a slotted spoon into the beer batter, shook it off into the skillet where the oil bubbled around it, turned down his lips and nodded. Then he spooned in the chunks of fish, filling the air with the sound of the sizzle and the rich aroma of beer and bread.

When the fish were golden brown, he scooped them out with the slotted spoon, three and four at a time, and placed them in a flat bread pan. He picked up one that had cooled, dipped it in the cocktail sauce and popped it in his mouth.

"Mm-mm, now tell me that isn't worth dying for. Try it in the tartar sauce as well."

He passed the plate around and everyone dug in.

Jim had one without the sauce and one with, both getting a welcome response from his taste buds.

Corney Jansen moved on to prepare a few flounder in a light wine sauce, and fresh scallops fried in herb butter.

Dodee hung back when the class ended.

"Can I help you clean up?" she asked Corney.

"Thanks for the offer, but all I have to do is put everything in the sink. The restaurant's dishwasher will take care of it after that."

"You live here long?"

"In the beach area all my life."

"Did you happen to know a Father Pelican?"

Jansen frowned. "Knew about him, yes. His disappearance has been in the local papers lately. How did you hear about him?"

Dodee motioned to Jim. "We went for a walk on the beach this morning—"

"And the police were there," Jim said, cutting her off. "They found the body."

"Really?" The big man pulled his lips down in an inverted U. "Where was this?"

"Down south of here, off Old Oregon Inlet Road."

"Really?" Jansen stared down the length of the kitchen for a moment, then glanced at his watch.

Dodee palmed-up a hand. "They say he was fishing from the bridge and might have fallen off."

"That's what they say?" Jansen glanced at his watch again. "If you'll excuse me, I have to meet a man who wants to charter my boat."

# FIVE

THE ELDERHOSTELERS had dinner that night in the Tranquil House Inn's 1587 Restaurant. Jim and Dodee took a table that looked across the dark cove to the *Elizabeth II* replica lit up by floodlights.

"May I join you?" asked the platinum-blond woman from the class, now dressed in an ankle-length black dress that could be an Armani.

"Yes, of course," Dodee said. "I'm Dodee Swisher and this is Jim—James P. Dandy."

"I'm Rosario Emalda from New Mexico," she said, sitting in the window seat opposite Dodee. "You are from?"

"I'm from Maryland," Jim said, "and Dodee's from Kansas City."

"It was a good class this afternoon, but a little primitive." She rearranged the silverware in front of her. "He was only a filler, I understand from Susan. Susan Baxter, our coordinator. I'm hoping we learn more tomorrow."

Jim looked into the woman's deep brown eyes. "You came all this way from New Mexico to take a cooking Elderhostel?"

"Not just for the class. My daughter has a place down here. She lives in New York. She's coming down Monday and we'll spend a week together. I saw this weekend Elderhostel and thought, why not? I've never been on one before. How about you, Jim?"

He looked at Dodee. "We've been on what, six?"

Rosario's dark eyebrows rose. "So you are here together? It's nice to have someone to travel with."

Dodee's hand slipped over his. "Yes it is, that and more."

"I used to have someone until my husband died a year ago, but—" she looked over her shoulder toward the entrance, then snapped back around "—oh, don't look." She shifted to the aisle seat. "That man has been trying to strike up a conversation with me since I arrived."

Jim looked up to see the man with the plaid shirt and bib overalls that barely reached his ankle-high, laced-up black shoes. The man raised his russet nose, as if he were sniffing the air, then he homed in on the empty window seat, squeezing by Rosario to plop into it.

"Hope you don't mind if I join you, folks. I'm Amos Brown." His bushy eyebrows spiked out in all directions. "Good to see you again, Roseio."

She gave him a smile that would frost a blast furnace. "My name is Rosario."

"Sure it is," he said, a leer turning into a smile as he turned to Jim and Dodee, "but I'm afraid I ain't met this lovely miss here, nor you, sir. I'm Amos Brown."

"James P. Dandy, and this is my girlfriend, Dodee Swisher."

"Well, glad to meet you, I'm sure. Wasn't that a great class this afternoon? And wasn't that great fish with that beer stuff? Just know this is going to be the best Elderhostel I've ever been on."

"How many have you attended?" Dodee asked.

"Well—" he squinted his eyes and pressed his lips together "—actually, this is my first." He turned back to the woman sitting next to him. "How about you, there Roseio, how many you been on?"

She graced him with another icy grin. "Just this one."

"See there." He nudged her with his elbow. "We got something in common."

Jim looked from one to the other. Oh, yeah, this was going to be a fun meal.

They ate a dinner of stuffed pork chops, herb baby potatoes and asparagus with Hollandaise sauce. And for dessert, they had a chocolate mousse that slicked over Jim's tongue like syrup.

Amos Brown rattled his spoon around in his dessert glass, then smacked his lips. "Now that's what I call go-oo-od victuals."

Rosario opened a pill container and took out a white tablet, swallowing it with a glass of water.

Amos grinned at her. "What'cha got there, Roseio, a birth control pill?"

A spot of red appeared on the woman's cheeks as the dark brown eyes glanced toward the heavens. "It's been nice meeting you all. If you'll excuse me—"

"Don't rush off there, Roseio. How about you and me driving over Nags Head and go dancing?" Amos looked across the table. "How about it Jim and Dodee, come along and make it a foursome?"

Dodee shook her head.

"Count us out," Jim said. "It's been a long drive down here and I think we'll make an early night of it."

"Well, Roseio, looks like you and me—"

"Not you and me. And the name is *Rosario.*" A smile belied the pained expression on her face as she turned to Jim. "I am glad to have met you, Jim, and you, Dodee." She stood up. "If you'll excuse me, I'm going up to my room and read."

"Yeah, excuse me there, you two I'm gonna walk Roseio to her room." He hopped up and hurried after the departing woman. "Wait up there, Roseio. Sure you don't wanna go bar hoppin'?"

Jim watched them go. "This could be a long weekend for Rosario."

Dodee pointed to the lighted walkway outside the window. "Want to take a little stroll before we go up?"

He shrugged.

"It will clear our heads," she said, "and when we come in we'll be ready to snuggle."

"Let me get our coats."

They left by a side door to the restaurant and moseyed along the waterfront boardwalk. A car rumbled onto the bridge over the cove and faded away, leaving behind the soft sounds of the night, the rasp of mooring lines as boats shifted in their slips, the gurgle of water as it eased by a piling, a halyard slapping against a mast on the anchored catamaran. The smell of sea salt and marsh grass hung in the gelid air.

"Let's look out here," she said, motioning to the second dock down.

"It's cold here, lady, it'll be freezing out there."

"I just want to take a look at Corney Jansen's boat."

He put his arm around her and she bundled close as they walked out to the end of the pier where the forty-foot fishing boat tugged at her lines. No lights shone onboard and those on the pier were sucked up by black water, but the skeletal shadow of a flying bridge was silhouetted against clouds breaking up overhead. A single word was written large across the boat's dark transom in gold letters: *Commandment.*

"Okay," Jim said, "seen enough?"

"I guess Corney's not on board."

"Or in bed."

She snuggled in under his arm as they turned back. "You go fishing, don't you?"

"Not much. Once a year I go with some old cronies of mine to Chincoteague, where we seem to catch as little fish as possible, drink a few cans of sea water, cuss a lot, tell tall stories, eat like minor potentates and turn into methane factories. Why do you ask?"

"I was wondering if you catch many fish from a bridge."

"Whoa, wait a minute." He spun her around and looked into her eyes, muted to a dull gray in the dim light. "Is this why we came out here? To pump Jansen with questions?"

"No, we came out for a walk, but I thought, since his boat was here—"

"Bullshit, Dodee. You're itching to find out about that body on the beach."

A chill had settled into his bones by the time they entered the lobby, passed the column of charter boat photos and climbed the stairs to their room. He stared out the window while Dodee used the bathroom, listening to the soft whistle of the wind and watching the squiggly reflections of lights on board the *Elizabeth II* on the black-water cove.

He made quick work of it when Dodee came out, brushing his teeth, washing his face and slapping on some PS for Men cologne that Dodee found sexy. He came back out to a bedroom lit only by ambient light from outside.

He crawled under the covers to a spot Dodee had already warmed, and she welcomed him. He kissed her, tasting the residue of her toothpaste, and inhaling her perfume, and they sheltered each other from the stormy night, burrowing down deep, wrapped in each other's skin, and shutting out the world in a series of moans that crescendoed into urgent cries and finally collapsed into quick gasps of breath until the cadence stretched out once more and blended with the darkness.

"Thank you, sweetheart."

"My pleasure, lady."

"Not all." She scooted around until she had her head on his chest.

"Are you quite comfortable?" he asked, wrapping an arm around her.

"Getting there," she said, playing with his belly button. "You never answered my question."

He stared up at the darkened ceiling. "What question?"

"Would you catch many fish from a bridge?"

"Ask that state trooper, Sergeant Atwater. It's his business."

"And you don't have any curiosity about what a woman's body was doing dressed as a priest?"

"I know what it was doing. Nothing. Dead people don't usually—ugh," he grunted from a jab in his side.

"You know what I mean, sweetheart."

"It's not my business. I don't care about it. I am not the least bit curious." He kissed her on her forehead. "Now, go to sleep."

He closed his eyes, felt her scrunch around some more, then settle down.

The worst thing that could have happened to them was finding that body on the beach. Even worse, leaving Dodee behind to find out it belonged to a woman. Even worse for the police to find the wallet of a Catholic priest in the pocket.

There didn't seem to be a ready explanation for that, unless, as Dodee said, the priest was trying to fake his own death.

"But why use a woman's body?"

Only her long, even breathing answered him.

Right, while her questions ran around in his head, she had conked out.

Great. Just absolutely great.

# SIX

SHOWERED AND SHAVED, dressed in fresh jeans and blue sweatshirt, Jim peeked out the window to see that the wind had swept away the clouds of night, leaving only a lingering few to dress up the sunrise. He barefooted it down to the lobby for an early morning coffee, and brought one back for Dodee as she showered and made ready for the day. She dressed in a light chamois cardigan over a blouse of the same color, dark-brown denims, soft loafers, and they went down to a self-serve continental-style breakfast.

Jim picked up two sweet rolls, orange juice, another coffee and led the way into the dining room where other Elderhostelers were already at breakfast.

"Good morning, Jim and Dodee," Rosario Emalda greeted them. She sat at a four-person table with a gray-haired woman and bald man with bifocals. "These are the Bakers from Greenville. Did you have a good sleep?"

He nodded. "Like I had died."

"How about you?" Dodee asked. "Did you get to your reading—"

"Yes, I did. I would have stayed around last night and been sociable if it hadn't been for that bumpkin pestering—oh-oh." She scrunched over to the side, close to the window. "Don't turn around. He just came in, oh no—" she glanced toward the ceiling "—he's seen us."

Amos Brown, still dressed in his plaid shirt, bib overalls, and ankle-high black shoes, strode straight to the table, eased past Jim, plopped into the vacant seat. He gave his spiked-out eyebrows a couple of wiggles. "Mornin' there, Roseio."

She sighed. "It's Rosario."

"Shore are pretty this mornin', Roseio."

Jim gave Dodee a nudge and led the way to a far corner table. He held the window chair for her and sat next to her so that they both faced the bridge with their backs to the dining room, working under the assumption that if he didn't see anyone, no one would see him, and if no one saw him, no one would join them.

Good in theory, not worth a damn in practice.

"Excuse me, are you Jim Dandy?"

He looked up into the hazel eyes of a man in his early forties and nodded.

"I'm Tom Pelican," the man said, brow wrinkling on his ruddy face. "Would you mind if I ask you a few questions? It was my brother you found on the beach yesterday."

"No," Dodee said, "of course not. Please sit down. I'm Dodee Swisher."

"Thank you." Tom Pelican unzipped a poplin jacket on an open-collared blue dress shirt, taking the seat opposite Jim. He smoothed down his reddish-brown hair and gave them a contagious smile. "You were together when you found...my brother, Leslie?"

She nodded. "We went for a walk and saw something in the surf. When it washed up on the beach we realized it was a person."

"You identified the body?" Jim asked.

The hazel eyes came back to him. "Not positively. I'm afraid we'll have to wait for dental records. I don't know how good a look you got, but— How good a look did you get?"

"Not much," he said, putting his hand on top of Dodee's, "except to see that there was no life left."

"Any idea what happened?" Dodee asked.

Tom Pelican ran a hand through his reddish-brown hair again and let out a sigh. "I don't know. It's all been a shock to me. The police think Leslie fell off a bridge and the tide took him out, but to do that he would have to have been in the middle of the bridge where no one's supposed to walk. And Leslie was a good swimmer, so…" He gave a half shake of his head and turned to the window. A moment later he turned back to them. "I guess you saw from the clothes that Leslie was a priest?"

"I could see he had on a clerical collar," Jim said, "but that's about it."

"Sergeant Atwater mentioned he was a Catholic priest?" Dodee asked.

Tom Pelican looked down at his hands and nodded.

Jim pushed his empty plate aside. "Did he do a lot of fishing? If he was on a bridge—"

"Some. A doctor who spends his summers down here took Leslie deep-sea fishing a few times, and some locals took him out on the bay, but I wouldn't say it was a favorite thing."

"Then why would he be on the bridge?" Dodee asked.

He gave another half shake of his head. "Wish I knew." The sad hazel eyes shifted to Jim and back. "But Leslie looked okay on the beach, I mean, not okay, but the clothes weren't ripped all apart, like a shark or a fish had gotten to him?"

Dodee looked at Jim.

He shrugged. "To tell you the truth, we didn't get that close. But from where we were standing, everything looked intact."

"Thank you." His lips spread in that contagious smile again, forcing Jim to smile with him, but it did nothing to light up his ruddy face. "You've relieved my mind a lot." He stood up and shook their hands. "I hope this doesn't ruin your vacation."

When he left, Jim returned to the buffet and refilled his coffee. He stared out at the bridge over the inlet on the way back. If Father Leslie Pelican had fallen off that, he wouldn't have had a problem even if he was a poor swimmer. "Did they say what bridge it was?" he asked, sitting next to her.

She turned and smiled at him.

"What?"

"I thought you said this was police business."

He nodded. "You're right. I was just wondering, because if it was that bridge, something is really fishy."

She shook her head. "That's not funny."

"Anyway, it couldn't have been that one if he was washed out to sea."

"He was not washed out to sea, sweetheart, *she,* whoever she was, was washed out to sea."

# SEVEN

WHEN THE ELDERHOSTEL class convened in the kitchen later that morning, Chef Andrea Davis took command.

"We'll be working with vegetables this morning, and I hope to introduce you to some of the imported vinegars and oils I've been using to give them a new twist."

Andrea Davis topped out at an even five feet, coffee-colored skin and body proportions most models would die for, but the fire burning in her dark eyes would cower Napoleon. She had on a white apron and a chef's toke starched brilliant white. She had set out various vegetables and condiments in small, stainless-steel containers.

"Who can tell me what vinegar is made from?"

"Easy," Amos Brown said, hooking his thumbs in his bib overalls, "apple cider."

The dark eyes leveled on him for a few long moments. "And...?"

"And," Amos said, wilting under the gaze, "apples?"

"And we make balsamic vinegar from?"

A weak smile spread on his russet face. "Balsamics?"

"Anyone else?"

Jim glanced around the room, but after watching Amos Brown go down in flames, no one else volunteered.

"What do you make vinegar from if you run out of apples and balsamics?" she asked, a warm smile splitting her face, showing even white teeth.

When no one answered, she opened up a canvas bag and started taking out bottles. "Blackberries, honey, black currants, oak-aged apples, and—'' she held up a bottle to Amos ''—apple balsamic. Balsamic vinegar is made from grapes, but they use the balsamic process here on apples to bring out a strong, sweet flavor. These are not your normal supermarket varieties. They've been blended and aged by brewmasters in European vinegar breweries, something that's alien to our American outlook. They're more expensive, but they're used sparingly with things you might not normally consider for a vinegar. For instance, we can use the apple balsamic's rich flavor and aroma to marinate fish, meat, fruits, and vegetables, to drizzle over blanched vegetables, and to sprinkle on blue cheese, pies and chocolate cakes. We'll be using some of these in our salads and vegetables today.''

She placed her hand on one of the containers she had before her.

''Anytime you want to prepare a recipe, you should first practice *mise en place.* Can anyone tell me what that means?''

Dodee half raised her hand. ''Get all your ingredients together before you start to cook.''

''Not bad. Not only get your ingredients together, but measured out and ready to go. We don't want to have diced onions and garlic popping in a hot pan and then find out we have to run to the store for potatoes or meat or whatever. Once we have everything measured out, we can start cooking and add each item as needed just like they do on the television cooking shows.''

She rubbed the palms of her hands together.

''Okay, the first thing we are going to make is a simple corn salad. We have our corn here—'' she rested her hand on one of the containers ''—whole kernels cooked and drained. We could actually use canned corn if we were pressed for time. We have diced garlic, bell pepper and a couple of Roma tomatoes, also diced, and four tablespoons of oak-aged apple vinegar from one of those vinegar breweries I told you about. I have Zatarain's Creole-style Seasoning here, but I could use Old Bay Seasoning as well. Finally, we have four tablespoons of pumpkinseed oil. By the way, this is not from local pumpkins, but from some grown in Austria."

Rosario raised her hand. "Why not from American pumpkins?"

"Because our pumpkins have a hard dry shell and they produce no oil. When Columbus returned from America, one of the things they took back to Europe was pumpkin. Over the years pumpkins have been planted throughout Europe and a species evolved in the highlands of Austria that have soft shells and produce oil. Again, it's a bit expensive because it takes one pumpkin to produce one ounce of oil, but it's become one of the new gourmet tastes in the U.S. that's been around for some time in Europe."

Chef Davis pulled out a mixing bowl and set it on the table.

"Okay, we have our ingredients all measured out and now we're ready for delicate preparation steps. Pay close attention to how this is done."

She dumped the corn into the mixing bowl, followed by the garlic, diced bell pepper and Roma tomatoes, oak-aged apple vinegar and finally the pumpkinseed oil.

"That's step number one."

She picked up a large stainless-steel mixing spoon and worked all the ingredients together.

"This is step number two. Step number three is to let it sit for an hour, going through step number two a few more times, then we serve it or refrigerate it." She smiled. "Everybody got that?"

She showed them how to make vinaigrettes using the pumpkinseed oil and the various vinegars, and then conducted a taste test for the class to vote on.

Jim found each had a hint of what they were made from: honey, blackberries, two wine varieties, a tart black currant that reminded him of cranberries and an apple vinegar with a slight bite, reminiscent of oak-aged whiskey or brandy.

When Chef Davis deemed enough time had passed for the corn salad to have steeped, she ladled it out in little dishes.

"Okay," she said, "we'll take a half an hour for a taste test and potty break—just don't get the two confused."

Jim passed a dish to Dodee and took one himself.

"What do you think?" she asked a few spoonfuls later.

"Good. Has a tiny after-bite to it, and a bit of lingering heat."

She showed him a business card; Helco Ltd., Austrias-Finest@worldnet.att.net, 800-348-5766. "I asked her where I can get the pumpkinseed oil and the vinegars." She tucked the card away, then touched his arm and motioned to the windows that opened onto the docks. Striding toward his boat at the end of the pier was the large figure of Cornelius Jansen.

"And...?" he asked.

"He invited us to come look over his boat."

"Didn't we do that last night?"

"Last night it was dark and we didn't go on board."

"And...?"

Her big blues leveled on him. "And I want to ask him about fishing from that bridge."

"Ah, now we are getting to it. Leave the job to the police, Dodee. Besides, the class will be starting soon."

"It will only take a few minutes, and we can get back a little bit late."

"I don't think so. Not with Chef Andrea Napoleon Davis commanding the kitchen."

"You're right. You stay here and I'll go talk to him."

She started for the door, but he grabbed her hand, stared at her for a moment, then sighed. "All right. But you're going to take the flack if we're not on time."

# EIGHT

THE AIR WAS still chilly, but the midmorning sun, lolling around a cloudless sky, hinted at warmer times before the day was done. They retraced their steps to the end of the pier where the white, forty-foot-plus boat rode easy on the water.

"Hello the *Commandment,*" Jim called out, "anyone aboard?"

"Be right there," came a high-pitched voice.

Dodee turned to Jim. "You know all these nautical terms."

He grinned. "Been around boats before. A longtime friend of mine is a marine policeman in Maryland."

Cornelius Jansen's face, framed by a square jaw and a red crewcut, appeared in the door of the cabin. "Well, there you are."

"You said we could visit your boat," Dodee said. "Is this a bad time?"

"Not at all, young lady." He held up a cup in his big hand. "Just fixing myself some coffee." He came out on deck and pulled on a mooring line, bringing the boat close to the pier. "Come aboard and I'll fix you one."

Jim stepped onto the deck and then helped Dodee.

She looked up at the tall flying bridge. "You don't fish from up there?"

"Oh, my, no," Corney said. "My first mate perches up there and keeps a lookout for schools of fish." He pointed to the steering console. "We also have a depth-finder that will pick up fish if we pass over them. And over here—" he tapped his foot over a stainless-steel pipe embedded at the aft end of the deck "—we fit a fishing chair for when we catch the big ones. We have fishing lines angled out on either side and off the transom, that's the back of the boat, and when something hits, those on charter take turns strapped in the chair."

Her brow wrinkled. "Strapped in?"

"Strapped in is right. When something big strikes we don't want our guests pulled overboard." He grinned. "Especially if they haven't paid all their charter money."

"Could a fish actually pull someone over?"

"You better believe it. People who are models of caution suddenly go crazy when they get caught up in the frenzy of fighting a big fish, and do stupid things." He patted the sheath attached to his belt, clasp securing his Buck knife. "Always need a blade handy to cut a line if somebody gets tangled up."

He invited them down into the cabin, that contained a small galley, a bunk on either side doubling as chairs for a table in between, and a plastic Madonna standing guard on a shelf beside an interior steering station. Corney Jansen stowed some clothes in an underneath locker. "Just been doing some housecleaning. Sit down, sit down. Can I pour you folks a cup of coffee?"

"No thanks," Dodee said.

Jim sat beside her and pointed to the plastic Madonna. "Are you Catholic or is that just for protection out on the ocean?"

"Right on both counts." He sipped from his cup. "Outside I have a little plaque saying, 'Oh Lord, your ocean is so big and my boat is so small.' Beetles are bugs if I don't think about that when I'm caught out in a nor'easter."

Beetles are bugs?

"Then you must have known Father Pelican," Dodee said.

The lips turned down in Corney's square face. "Knew of him, not him. We have different beliefs."

"He wasn't a Catholic priest?"

"Oh, sure, I guess. But I'm a Latin Mass Catholic, go to a church inland about thirty miles, where Mass is still said in the original way to maintain the mystery."

"I didn't know they still said Mass in Latin," Jim said.

"A few places have permission to do so. The great thing about Latin is, no matter where you go in the world, it's always the same."

Jim nodded.

Ah, the joy of not understanding it at home so you can also not understand it overseas.

Dodee pointed to Corney with her thumb and forefinger. "But you know Father Pelican fell off a bridge?"

Jim jerked his thumb aft. "The bridge here?"

Corney's lips turned down again as he shook his head. "No, not here. Over at Oregon Inlet that connects the sound to the sea. Tide rips through there when it's running. The local paper said that he was probably swept out with it. Surprised to hear the body came ashore."

"Catch many fish from that bridge?" Jim asked.

"I wouldn't know."

"And with the tide running? If it was strong enough to wash someone out to sea—oh, and they said for that to happen he would have had to have fallen from the middle of the bridge."

"Who said that?"

"The police, I think. And Tom Pelican told us."

Corney shook his head. "You people move fast."

"But if it was strong enough to wash someone out to sea, wouldn't it be too strong to catch fish?"

"I guess."

"But why else would he be on the bridge?" Dodee asked.

Corney shrugged. "I didn't know the man, so how would I know what he was doing there? Someone down island might know. Pelican lived on Hatteras, but even if they did, they wouldn't talk to outsiders about it."

Jim stood and looked at his watch. "Well, we'd better get back to class."

"Thanks for showing us your boat," Dodee said.

Corney smiled. "My pleasure. Think about chartering it. Take you out to blue water and land you in a mess of fish."

They started back up the dock and Dodee linked both her arms around one of Jim's. "How would you like to take a drive?"

"Let me guess. Down island to Hatteras? Even if we went, you heard what Corney said. They're not going to talk to strangers."

"We'll make something up so they'll want to talk to us."

"Like what? We're a couple of busybodies trying to find out what happened to Father Pelican?"

"And why he might want to disappear."

He shook his head. "I don't want to know."

"And who was it who washed up on the beach?"

"We're already late for class."

"And if the good priest wanted to fake his death, why use a woman's body?"

He faltered a step on that. "Yeah, that's something that makes absolutely no sense."

She held out her hand as if testing for rain. "It's a nice day for a drive—"

"Dodee, we came here for—"

"Stop off someplace and have something to eat—"

"We're supposed to be in class—"

"My treat for lunch."

"Are you trying to bribe—"

"Besides, if we walk in class late, we could face the ire of Chef Davis."

"That's true."

"Do you have your car keys with you?"

"I do."

# NINE

JIM SLOWED DOWN and stopped the Lincoln on top of the bridge over Oregon Inlet. The sun picked up highlights of the crashing surf off to the east and glistened on the calmer water of Pamlico Sound off to the west. A faded-yellow Oldsmobile sat in a small parking area on the Sound side at the bottom of the bridge, but the only way to hoof it from there to the top was to tightrope an eighteen-inch curb hugging the inside of the concrete side rail.

"What do you think?" Dodee asked.

He checked the rearview mirror for traffic—there was none—then looked down the long curb and shook his head.

"A crazy place to fish. He would have had to creep all the way out here, no room to cast without stepping into the road, and it's so high that even if he caught something it would slip the hook before he could get it to the rail."

Dodee pointed to the right of the Oldsmobile, past a line of scrub bushes, to where a man stood on the marshy shore, holding a pole. "Let's go look from down there."

"You want a lot for buying me lunch," he said, driving down and turning into the lot. "I might require further services in kind."

They parked near the Oldsmobile, not only faded-yellow, but salt-eaten as well, and got out. They lumbered through head-high bush until the midday sun invited them to peel off their jackets, hanging them over their backs with the arms tied around their necks, but when they broke out on the other side, a fresh breeze off the chilled water of the Sound sent them snuggling back into them again. The man on the grassy beach turned a weather-beaten face in their direction, inspecting them from behind a pair of aviator sunglasses shaded by the bill of a Coor's beer cap, then returned to his fishing.

Dodee pointed to a catwalk, which couldn't be seen from the road, built along the side of the bridge from each shore to a quarter of the way out. "What are they for?"

"Fishing, I guess. But I see what Tom Pelican was talking about now. The water under them looks too shallow to catch a man up. You'd have to go out to the middle of the bridge for that. Not a good place for fishing, but not a bad place for dumping a body if you wanted it washed out to sea."

Dodee's big blues came up to him. "Why would you say that?"

"Look." He swept his arm out to take in the Sound. "All of the water drains out of here. If the tide is running—"

"No, what made you think of dumping a body?"

He glanced back to see the old man recasting his line.

"Because, lady," he said, lowering his voice, "if you're right about the gender of the body on the beach, it sure in hell ain't Father Pelican. And it if ain't Father Pelican, someone had to dump it from somewhere."

She moved close to him, getting out of the wind. "Let's assume for a minute he was fishing from the bridge. What would he be fishing for?"

Jim glanced up at the arc of the bridge for a moment, then turned and walked out to the old man. "Catching anything?"

Dark sunglasses, Coor's beer cap, and a three-day gray stubble turned to him for a long moment, then the man shook his head.

"You live around here?"

A barely perceptible nod.

Jim pointed back to the bridge. "You know of a reason someone would want to fish from the middle of that thing?"

The old man followed Jim's finger, then shook his head again and turned back to his line.

Jim nodded. "I mean, what could you even catch from up there?"

"A cold."

Jim smiled. "That's what I was thinking."

But the old man just stared at his pole, gently flexing it, saying nothing in return.

"Well, nice talking to you."

He returned to Dodee.

"What did he say?"

"The best you could catch from up there was a cold."

"What else did he have to say?"

"Nothing. I guess Corney is right about the people here being closemouthed."

"I know what else you could catch from up there."

"Pneumonia?"

"Drugs."

He blinked at her.

"Think about it, sweetheart. If he has a heavy pole and line, a boat comes sneaking in and hooks drugs onto his line, he yanks it up, shoves it in the car, and he's ready to go."

"Have to reel it in and out a bunch of times to make it worthwhile. Why not just bring the boat up here and drop it off on land?"

"You said it yourself, it's too shallow."

He looked into the water, the overhead sun clearly showing the bottom, turned back to the bridge, then scanned the flat horizon. "One thing for sure, from up there you'd be able to see in all directions."

She held out a hand. "See. Perfect setup. If the Coast Guard or the police come along, the drug boat heads back out to sea and all you have is a man fishing." She pointed at him with her thumb and forefinger. "Not only a man, but a priest."

"What about the body of the woman?"

"Someone must have found out about the drugs so the priest went to his backup plan. Dress the body in his clothes to fake his death, then disappear. Maybe he's not even a real priest.''

He stared into her eyes for a moment, then shook his head. ''Doesn't work. It's not going to take a genius to figure out the woman wasn't the Catholic priest. And if it was washed out to sea, why care who it was or how it was dressed or even if it existed? In fact, why even go through all the trouble of dumping a body off the bridge? Just leave your fishing pole against the rail, your identification in the car, and skip out of town. No body to wash up on shore to clutter things up.'' He motioned toward the parking lot. ''C'mon. Let's go eat lunch.''

''So, what do you think?'' she asked as they trudged through the brush and past the salt-eaten Oldsmobile.

''I think we ought to let the police do their job.''

# TEN

JIM PULLED OUT of the parking lot and headed south on the deserted Route 12, cutting through empty sand dunes.

Dodee turned to him. "But suppose someone found out about the drugs, like the church secretary, and he has to bump her off."

"Bump her off? You sound like—"

"All right, kills her. Then to create an alibi, he dresses her up in his clothes, drives her someplace where she can be seen, then dumps her over the bridge, never expecting her to be washed ashore."

He passed a sign warning Soft Sand, Do Not Leave Road.

She leaned forward and looked at him. "You're not answering me, sweetheart."

"I didn't hear a question, lady."

She sat back and folded her arms.

Houses started popping up, deserted in this off-season, first on the seaward side, standing tall on stilts, two and three stories high, then on the Sound side among brush and live oak trees swept low by constant sea winds.

Dodee looked at her watch. "You know what we ought to do? See if we can find the parish house."

He glanced at her.

She swung her knees toward him. "We have time before lunch. Let's—"

"And why would we want to go to the parish house?"

"Just to get a feel for the place. Find out what we can about the priest. See if any women are missing."

"And how are we going to do that? I'm not breaking in, Dodee—"

"Why would you think I'd ask you to break in?"

"Because you have before."

"I just want to look it over. Maybe knock on the door. There's bound to be people around taking care of church business."

"Look it over and knock on the door. That's it?"

She palmed-up both hands.

"Because if it's anything more, I'm leaving you there."

He cut left into the parking lot of Pamlico Station, a two-story building containing seaside shops, most open this Saturday morning in spite of the off season, and in a furniture store called Exotic Cargo got directions to the parish house.

They headed south again and passed a Dairy Queen on the right. He made a mental note of it for future exploration and exploitation, yeah buddy.

Finally, down around Buxton where the ground was higher, he turned off on a winding, packed-sand road, trailed it past clapboard cottages squatting among live oaks, until they came upon a weathered-gray cottage with barn siding, down at the end. Two trees at opposite corners shaded the tin roof from the bright sun. A small stoop led up to a door, which accessed a screened-in side porch; a bench swing hung from chains, and two Adirondack chairs faced a small bright-green marsh and the sparkling water of Pamlico Sound. The mailbox had Father Leslie Pelican stenciled on it and two Reserved signs were attached to pilings in a deserted patch of packed-sand parking.

Jim got out, peeled off his jacket, breathed in the sea air, and followed Dodee up the stoop. The door knocker was in the form of an anchor and she gave it a couple of raps, scaring away some nearby yellow finches singing in the live oaks.

"What are you going to say if someone comes?" he whispered.

"My friend Jim Dandy would like to talk to you."

He stared down into her big blues.

She batted her eyelashes and smiled.

After a few minutes, Jim reached up and banged the knocker three more times, loud enough to wake the dead. Aside from a gentle breeze riffling through the marsh grass and the chirping of birds, it was dead silent.

"No one's home," he said.

"Um." She moved to the corner and looked into the screened-in side porch.

"No, Dodee, don't even think it."

She turned back to him, arched her eyebrows, then stared out to the street.

He followed her gaze to see a well-seasoned woman walking toward them in an ankle-length print dress and a big white bonnet that shaded no-nonsense lips and suspicious eyes.

"You folks need help?"

Dodee turned to him, but he casually put his hand over his mouth and stared back at her.

"We were looking for Father Pelican," she said at last.

"Ain't we all," the woman said. "Father Pelican's been missing for a week. Everyone's been praying he'll show, but so far..." She shrugged.

"So you know him?" Dodee asked.

"I'm his housekeeper, though why he needed a housekeeper I'll never know. He kept everything as neat as a pin, he did, everything in its place, unlike my husband, who places everything where it falls." She cocked her head and squinted an eye. "Can you tell me why you're looking for Father Pelican?"

Dodee glanced at Jim.

He smiled behind his hand and stared at her.

"We're doing research for a book on the Outer Banks and we wanted to know about the churches out here, how many members they have, things like that."

"Then you'll want to talk to Mage Blackstone. She's the

parish secretary. You just missed her, but I can draw you a map to her house."

She reached above the sill for a key, unlocked the door, and led the way into a large combination living room-dining room-kitchen. A couch and easy chairs with comfort sags, and a desk beneath the porch window occupied the living room portion. A round table with sturdy chairs tucked under filled out the dining room. A microwave oven held a prominent spot on a shipshape counter in the kitchen.

The woman was right, everything neat as a pin, with a hint of Lysol in the air. Sheer curtains looked as if they had been freshly washed and down a hallway he could see a clean dresser top in what looked like a bedroom, and off that what looked like the door to a second bedroom. If anything bordered on clutter it was a gaggle of framed pictures on the walls and end tables. And three more on the desk: two older people standing beside a 1940s Studebaker, probably the priest's parents; two men at a graduation ceremony; and a third picture, three figures beside a huge fish at a dock weigh-in, lay flat and unframed on a large blotter. Jim reached for his reading glasses, then thought better of it—talk about Dodee being nosey—and turned instead to the pictures on the wall: group photos at a picnic; people standing outside a small church; and, hanging on a side panel leading into the kitchen, two more big fish weigh-ins in a column of photographs, one above the other.

The housekeeper tore a piece of paper from a pad and handed it to Dodee.

"This is Mage's place. Tell her Katie sent you. Sure she'll be of some help to you, and it'll be a help to her to get her mind off Father's disappearance."

They came back out into the sunshine, scattering sparrows dusting themselves in the road.

"Good luck with your book," Katie said.

They got in the car and headed back down the winding, packed-sand lane.

"Well," he said, grinning at her, "at least we know the

secretary hasn't been bumped off.'' He avoided a rut in the road. ''And where did you come up with that business about writing a book?''

''I had to think of something. You weren't giving me any help.''

''It's not my business.''

''Maybe now we can find out if Father Pelican was tapping into the till.'' She waved the map Katie had given them. ''In our book research we need to know how much the church was taking in.''

''You're telling me you want to go see her?''

''Why not?''

''Why not? Because you were going to take me to lunch is why not.''

''We'll just ask a few questions and go. We can look for a restaurant along the way.''

He pulled to a stop when the packed-sand road met the highway. ''Speaking of way, which?''

''Way which? Oh, which way?'' She looked at the map, turned it around, and held out her right hand.

He turned the Lincoln south and picked up speed.

Oh yeah, this was gonna be good.

# ELEVEN

MAGE BLACKSTONE lived a block off Route 12 in a light-green double-wide on a bare, sandy lot. Cement blocks propped it three feet off the ground and a six-foot-wide weathered porch led to the entrance. A clay pot on either side of the front door showed the stubs of last year's flowers.

While Dodee rang the bell, Jim gazed down at a faded red pickup parked next to his Lincoln, then refocused on a restaurant across the highway, a large sign overhead with a picture of a fish and named The Flip-Flop Flounder.

"All right, there's a place we can have lunch."

She glanced toward it and rang the bell again.

Jim waited a few moments, then took his fist and pounded on the door. "She's not home."

"Or she's dead."

He blinked at her. "Where did you come up with that one?"

"Suppose she was in on the priest's disappearance? But now the body has been found and the priest has to cover his tracks, so he bumps off the secretary."

Jim rolled his eyes and started for the car. "I'm going to lunch. Want me to pick you up here afterward?"

"Well, think about it," she said, following him.

"I have thought about it." He opened the door for her. "With a week's head start and the secretary still here, it's not likely they're in cahoots."

She slipped into the seat. "Who said he left?"

He shut the door, climbed in his side, swung by the pickup and headed for the restaurant.

She pointed her thumb and forefinger at him. "Remember Tom Pelican at breakfast this morning? Suppose he was making that stuff up about his brother? Suppose he was snooping around about the body in the surf to find out how much we knew? In fact, suppose Tom Pelican is really Leslie Pelican pretending to be his brother?"

He pulled across the highway and parked in front of The Flip-Flop Flounder.

"Suppose, Dodee, we have lunch."

They stepped into a large room with walls of weathered gray boards, looking as if they had been bleached on the beach for a million years, fish trophies tacked to them in various places. All the tables, covered with plastic red-and-white-checkered tablecloths, sat empty, but the bar on the right was occupied by three grizzled and well-aged men. They looked like seafarers just off the boat. Two women, both on the plus side of plump, one with her hair in curlers under a bandanna, also sat at the bar. The conversation died as they entered. Jim led Dodee to a table by a picture window overlooking the highway and parking lot.

A trim woman came from behind the bar and placed menus before them. "How are you folks doing?"

"Fine," Dodee answered, with a smile.

"Are we past the lunch hour?" Jim asked, motioning to the empty tables.

"Still off-season. Picks up at dinner. You folks stayin' on the island?"

"In Manteo," Dodee said, "at the Tranquil House Inn."

"Nice place there," called one of the grizzled men at the bar, a Peterbilt cap on his head.

The waitress nodded. "Yes, that's real nice. What can I get you to drink?"

Dodee ordered iced tea and Jim a Sam Adams.

"Down here fishing?" the Bandanna Woman asked from across the room.

"We're down here on an Elderhostel," Jim answered.

"Good thing you're not here for the fishing," Bandanna Woman said, swinging back to the bar. "It ain't been good."

Jim stared into Dodee's eyes and lowered his voice. "I'd say we fished up more than our share yesterday."

"Just think about it," Dodee said. "A man shows up this morning and says he's the dead priest's brother."

He rolled his eyes. She hadn't missed a beat from the secretary's porch to the car to the restaurant.

"How do we know he's not the priest himself trying to find out what we know about the body?"

"Fishin' will pick up now the weather's changed," Peterbilt's voice drifted over from the bar.

"Oh, yeah," Jim whispered, "and because he suspects we know about the body, he bumps off his secretary?"

Her eyebrows shot up. "Yes. He can't leave any loose ends."

"What'd he say they was on?" Peterbilt asked at the bar.

"A Elderhostel," Bandanna Woman answered. "Where you learn stuff and go places. S'posed to be a lot of fun."

Jim leaned on the table. "Only one thing, Dodee. The police sure in hell know it's a woman by now, so what was the brother trying to find out from us? And besides, dumping a body in the drink and faking your death would hardly warrant killing your secretary."

Her eyebrows shot up again and her mouth opened, but before she could say anything, the waitress was back with their drinks.

"Folks decided on lunch?"

Jim pointed to the menu. "What's in a Rooburger?"

"Kangaroo and beef. Our cook used to work at Down Under when it was out on the beach, an Australian-type restaurant, and he brought the Rooburger with him. It comes with garlic fries."

"Okay, I'll try one."

"What's in a Mariner Salad?" Dodee asked.

"Whatever's fresh caught. Today we have lumps of sea trout, scallops and some shrimp."

"I'll try that, with vinegar and—do you have olive oil?"

"Uh-huh. We also have rice vinegar if you'd like to try that."

"Oh, that sounds nice."

Dodee's eyes swung back to him after the woman left, but he beat her to it.

"I know, I know. You're going to ask, 'How do we know the woman was dead when she was dumped in the drink?'"

She palmed-up a hand on the table. "Well?"

He took a sip of beer and gazed out the window. A white car was parked next to the faded red pickup now, and a man stood at Mage Blackstone's door.

Jim pointed the Sam Adams bottle toward the double-wide. "First you thought the priest skipped because he was dipping into the till, then he was a drug contact, and now you think he murdered the secretary because she knew about it."

"Who knows more about what goes on in a church than the secretary? Maybe the dead woman had an affair with the priest, and maybe then she was trying to blackmail him. Or maybe—" her eyebrows rose again "—maybe he needed the secretary's help to dispose of the body."

"And maybe the moon is really made of green cheese."

She shook her head and looked away.

Jim took another pull on his beer and turned back to Mage Blackstone's double-wide. The porch was deserted as the white car swung around the pickup, slipped behind a house and reappeared as it stopped at the highway, then crossed it to pull up next to his Lincoln. A stretched-rubber band of a man with a leathery face climbed the restaurant's stairs.

"Here we are," the waitress said, setting down his Roo-burger with garlic fries and Dodee's Mariner Salad. "Anything else for you folks?"

The front door flew open and Rubber-band Man called out to those at the bar.

"Anybody know what happened to Mage Blackstone?"

# TWELVE

"MAGE AIN'T HOME," Peterbilt answered from the bar.

"Went up to Manteo," the waitress said, circling behind the bar.

Jim grinned at Dodee and took a bite out of his Rooburger.

"Her truck's there," Rubber-band Man said.

"Daughter picked her up," Bandanna Woman said. "Taking her shopping."

So much for the secretary-being-murdered theory.

"Just wondering if we have any more news about Father Pelican?" Rubber-band Man asked, still standing in the door.

Dodee's eyes popped open on that.

"Only that a body washed up on the shore with his wallet," the waitress said.

"Oh, boy," Rubber-band Man said, "that doesn't sound good."

Peterbilt swung around in his chair. "I keep praying it's not him."

Jim took another bite out of the Rooburger.

"Place ain't never gonna be the same around here without him," Rubber-band Man said. "Had a faith that could move mountains, I'll swear. I really miss him, really, really miss him." He looked at his watch. "Well, gotta go. Hear anything, let me know."

The door closed and Jim stared into Dodee's big blues. "So what do you think of that?"

She put a finger to her lips and nodded at the bar.

"I'm gonna miss him, too," the waitress said. "Never met a priest I related to more."

"Me, too," Bandanna Woman said. "Whenever I went to him with a problem, he listened. You know, really listened. He didn't offer solutions and I didn't want any. Just wanted someone to listen, you know. Even enjoyed going to him for confession, if you can believe that."

Peterbilt tapped his glass on the bar.

The waitress filled it from the tap. "They came to him from all over for confession. Even some of those stiff-necked Latin Massers from up at Saint Infidel's."

"I guess they're too embarrassed for the priest up there to hear their sins."

"Or too afraid." She set the glass in front of Peterbilt. "He'd come in here sometimes, for a coffee-to-go after his morning run, clothes all sweaty, and he'd light up the place with his smile."

Dodee pointed to him. "Remember Tom Pelican's smile?"

"You're reaching for straws."

"See, I can't understand that," Peterbilt said, "given that he was out in the middle of the bridge, which I can't understand to begin with—"

"He was out there," Bandanna Woman said. "Jeremy Opie saw him."

"But given that, if he was in such great shape, why couldn't he have swum ashore? That's what I find suspicious."

Dodee nodded, as if she were at the bar and taking part in the conversation.

"You're blatantly eavesdropping," Jim whispered.

"Shh."

"Maybe Jeremy made a mistake," Peterbilt said.

Dodee nodded again.

"Besides," Peterbilt continued, "I sometimes wonder if Opie's fishing line is always in the water."

"Now don't go there," the waitress said. "He's a nice old man."

"Jeremy didn't make a mistake," Bandanna Woman said. "He not only saw him, he talked to him."

Peterbilt held out his hands. "Then why didn't he call for help when Father went over?"

"Because he'd moved around the point and never thought about it again until he headed back for bait."

"Sounds fishy to me."

"Me, too," Dodee mouthed.

"You about finished?" Jim asked, pointing to her torn-up salad.

She pushed her plate aside. "What do you think now?"

"I think we already missed this afternoon's class."

"No, about Pelican being a strong swimmer. Doesn't that sound like he waited until no one could see him, then dumped the body over the side?"

"But why dump a woman's body?"

"And he comes back this morning pretending to be his brother to find out what we know?"

The waitress came over and collected the plates. "Will there be anything else?"

Jim shook his head. "I heard you talking about the missing priest. We met his brother this morning."

"Uh-huh. I'll get your check."

He turned to Dodee and palmed-up his hands.

"That doesn't tell us anything," she said. "'Uh-huh.' She didn't say she knew he had a brother."

He took a breath and let it out.

She came back and placed the check on the table. "I'll take that when you're ready."

"I'm ready," he said and pulled out his wallet. "About the brother, did they look alike?"

The waitress stared out the window for a moment. "Not in stature, Tom is a lot taller, but when they were together you could see the resemblance, especially in the smile."

He smiled and paid the bill, leaving her a generous tip.

"So now," he said when they were in the car, "how does that stack up—"

"Okay, sweetheart, so Tom Pelican is not Father Pelican. I erred in my thinking there, I will grant you that. But you are obviously missing something of importance here."

He started the engine and turned to her.

She smiled. "And I'm not telling if you can't figure it out yourself."

He backed out and headed north. "The secretary is not dead as you thought."

"Oh," she swung around in her seat, "let's go see if she's returned."

"She hasn't. I could see the house from where I sat."

"I still think we should talk to her." She sat back in her seat. "Anyway, that's not it."

He tapped a finger on the steering wheel. "The priest was well liked it seems, from all the conversation a certain Ms. Nosy-body eavesdropped on."

She tilted her head back and looked down her nose at him.

"But that's not it?"

She shook her head.

He chewed on the inside of his lip. "Let's see, the priest was not only seen on the bridge, but that guy—what was his name—"

She snapped her fingers. "Jeremy…Jeremy Opie! We should go talk to him."

"He not only saw him on the bridge, but talked to him, so there was no mistaking—"

"We should go talk to him."

"But they said Jeremy Opie didn't always have his line in the water, so you can take what he says with a grain of salt."

"We should go—"

"And he didn't see the priest go over the side, so anything could have happened. Any of this what you think I'm missing?"

"We should go talk to Jeremy Opie."

"No. We've stuck our nose in it too much already. Besides, I have something else in mind."

"Taking a nap."

"No." He turned down his lips and nodded. "Although that's not a bad idea. See, I can play this game, too."

"Love in the afternoon?"

"That's also not a bad idea, but—"

"If you're not thinking of sex or sleep, sweetheart, that only leaves food—"

"Bingo. Did you notice we didn't have dessert? You might have thought that was an oversight on my part, but my superior mental acumen had already fitted the clues together to zero-in on A, the memory of passing a Dairy Queen on the way down here, and B, the knowledge that they served Blizzards which, C, far outstrip anything you could have bought back at the restau— Ah, sonofabitch." He slapped the steering wheel and shook his head. "Now I know."

"What?"

"*You* were supposed to buy *me* lunch."

She grinned and batted her eyelashes at him.

# THIRTEEN

THEY SAT OUT on a deck in front of the Dairy Queen, in the afternoon sun, eating their Blizzards, ice cream whipped up with nibblies—Heath bar pieces for Jim, blueberries for Dodee—so thick the standard for DQ employees was to stick in a spoon and hand it to customers upside down.

"You're addicted to these things, aren't you?" Dodee asked. "I saw how your eyes glazed when you introduced them to me in New Mexico."

He took a spoonful and let it ease down his throat, savoring the sweet taste of the ice cream mixed with crumbled Heath bar. "Not addicted." He took another spoonful. "But I must admit, if they had one back home in Prince Frederick I'd end up a butterball."

Dodee finished hers, a small compared to his large, and leaned back in the chair, face up to the sun. "You know what I think?"

"I think you owe me one lunch."

"I think we ought to go back and talk to the secretary."

"Nope. When I finish this we're heading to the shack."

"There's something we're missing about the priest, and if we talked to the secretary we could piece it together."

"Let the police piece it together. We already missed one cooking class, I don't want to miss another. Besides, I feel a nap coming on."

He finished his Blizzard and they headed north. Dodee curled up and conked out on the seat beside him as they reached a lonely stretch of sand dunes masking the seashore on one side and the Sound on the other. Rimski-Korsakov's "Scheherazade" played on the tape deck. Cruise control took care of the speed limit. All he had to do was concentrate on staying between the lines where the only thing that broke the monotony was an occasional Soft Sand, Do Not Leave Road sign.

He could use a cup of coffee.

But then the blast of a car horn snapped him wide-awake.

He glanced in the rearview mirror and caught a quick glimpse of a truck swerving into the passing lane.

Another blast of the horn.

The truck beside him now.

Then it cut into his lane.

He jammed on his brakes, but the truck slammed into him, crunch of metal against metal, counterpointed by Dodee's screams, and the big Lincoln went airborne. Off the road with the dunes coming up fast. He tried to hold the wheels straight, to keep them from catching in the soft sand and flipping them over, but even before he could think about it, the front end slammed down and dug in. The back end rose up, hung for a moment, then slammed back down. The seat belts hadn't broken. The air bags hadn't deployed. The engine still idled, but they were dead in the water. More likely, dead in the sand. And lucky not just plain dead.

Dodee put a shaky hand on his arm. "You okay, sweetheart?"

"I could use a bathroom."

"What happened?"

He looked down the road to glimpse the truck as it raced around a bend and out of sight. "We were sideswiped."

He put his shoulder against the car door and shoved. It gave with a crunch and he climbed out. Yep, dead in the sand fit the description; the car was in up to the frame. Someone had folded, spindled and mutilated the whole side of the car, faded red streaks slashed in the blue paint.

"Turn off the key, Dodee, we ain't goin' anywhere on our own."

She did and climbed out on the passenger side. "You didn't fall asleep?"

"Hell, no. This truck came zooming up out of nowhere, went to pass me, then cut into me." He looked down the road again. "Wonder if he even knew he hit us." He yanked his wallet out of his back pocket. "Got your cell phone?"

She stuck her head back in the car and came out with it. Jim dialed AAA for a tow truck and asked them to report the accident to the police as well. He placed the phone back in her still shaking hand, and wrapped his arms around her.

"We're okay now. Tow truck's on its way. Nothing to worry about."

She wrapped her arms around his waist and they clung to each other.

"You okay?" he asked.

"Un-huh," came her voice from somewhere down near his armpit. "But being jolted out of a sound sleep like that was pure terror."

"It was no fun being wide-awake either."

He peeked at the road in both directions; nothing in sight and all he heard was a slight breeze playing through the beach grass, the odd call of a bird, and the rumble of the sea behind the barrier dune.

Dodee came out from his chest and he kissed her, a warm, innocent kiss, a love kiss as opposed to the deep-down-and-dirty kind. "All right?"

She nodded, smiled and held out her hand to show him it was steady.

He nodded toward the sound of the surf. "We're gonna be here awhile. Wanna take a look at the beach?"

They took off their shoes and socks and climbed hand in hand up to the top of the dune.

A squadron of pelicans flew in formation over the water with hardly a wing beat as waves rolled in from the end of eternity to crash on shore, not with the anger of the day before, but still strong enough to bubble and bounce and foam around the wooden corpse of a ship three-quarters buried in the sand.

Dodee pointed to it. "It's a wonder souvenir hunters haven't carted that away by now."

"For one thing, it's illegal. The whole seacoast here is federally protected. For another, these wrecks are continually being uncovered and reburied by storms so what you see today is not always what you get tomorrow. They call this the graveyard of ships because the Diamond Shoals reach miles out to sea and trap the unwary."

She leaned into his side. "It's a lot better than what we found yesterday. This is peaceful."

He sniffed the salt air and watched sandpipers beachcombing at the waterline and nodded, except— He turned back to his car for a moment, and then stared out to the divide between sand and sky.

Except had the accident really been an accident?

And the streaks along his blue car were of faded red.

# FOURTEEN

THE TOW TRUCK DRIVER in a yellow Island Convenience Texaco cap attached a line to Jim's Lincoln as a gray, state police car pulled up. Sergeant Atwater unfolded his six-foot-three frame from the driver's seat. He tugged his wide-brimmed hat halfway down his brow, turned to them, and did a double-take.

"Aren't you the ones who found the body on the beach?"

Jim nodded.

"Anything new on that?" Dodee asked. "Did you find out who it was?"

"Wait a minute." Atwater walked up to them. "I'm here investigating— I thought I was here investigating an accident."

Jim motioned to the car. "We were on our way back up to Manteo when a truck sideswiped us, shoving us off the road. We're lucky we didn't flip over."

Atwater inspected the side of the car. "Red truck?"

"My guess," Jim said. "I was concentrating on the road in front of me when it roared out of nowhere, slammed into the side of me, and the next thing I knew we were flying off the road."

Atwater studied the side of the car some more, rubbing the inch-long scar on his right cheek with his thumb. "Definitely red, truck, car or flying saucer." He pulled out an accident report and glanced over at them. "Just kidding about the flying saucer."

The tow truck driver slowly cranked the Lincoln out of

the sand, unhooked the cable, and looked under the car. "Seems to be okay," he said, climbing to his feet. "Want to drive it or want me to tow—"

"Let me try it," Jim said.

He pulled open the door, which gave way with a crunch, and he climbed in. The car started right up. He drove it two hundred feet down the road, shoved it into reverse, and backed up.

"Seems to be drivable. Think I'll just take it."

He signed the AAA form for the driver, and the report for Atwater. "I'm surprised to see a sergeant answering an accident call."

"Just happened to be in the area on another investigation."

Dodee wrapped both arms around one of Jim's. "You were going to tell us about the identity of the body from yesterday."

"I was?" He looked at her, and then at Jim. "Mind telling me what you two were doing down here on the island?"

"Sightseeing," Dodee said, giving the man a big smile.

Atwater squinted. "I can check."

"Well," Jim said, holding out a hand and letting it flop. "Dodee did want to see where the priest lived. Afterward, we had lunch."

The dark eyes shifted between them. "Don't fool around in police business." He ripped off Jim's copy of the accident report and handed it to him. "Okay, might as well tell me what you found out."

"He was well liked. We stopped off for lunch in The Flip-Flop Flounder and everyone said they missed him."

"You asked about Father Pelican?"

"No," Dodee said, "we just overheard them talking. They thought that even if he fell off the bridge he should have been able to swim to shore." She gave Atwater a smile and flashed her big blues. "Do you think there was foul play?"

He closed his eyes and shook his head. "Stop playing detective. Did it occur to either of you that this collision might not have been an accident? Go back to your hotel and let us do the worrying."

"You got it," Jim said.

He dragged Dodee to the car and they headed up the road.

"How does it drive?"

He turned down his lips. "Seems to be okay. Except it looks like hell."

The late-afternoon sun lent a golden sheen to the Sound as they drove over the bridge at Oregon Inlet and played with the horizon when they got back to the Tranquil Inn. They hurried to their room, washed up and came down to dinner. Jim led Dodee to the corner table again, overlooking the bridge, and held the chair for her.

"You like sitting here?" she asked.

"We're out of the mainstream. With a little bit of luck, we'll be alone."

No such luck.

"There you two are," Rosario Emalda said. The platinum-blond woman wore a free-flowing pale-green dress covered with sea shells, crabs and scallops. "We missed you at class this afternoon." She took the chair opposite Dodee and set a handbag with a Marc Jacobs label on the place setting beside her. "We learned to make crème brûlée that was to die for." Her eyebrows rose. "So where were you two this afternoon? Did you have a good time?"

Jim looked at Dodee.

"We took the afternoon off and went sightseeing down on Hatteras Island," she said, turning to Jim. "I had a good time."

"Me, too." He faced Rosario. "Except Dodee was supposed to buy me lunch and somehow I ended up paying for it."

Rosario gave a little finger wave to someone, smiled and moved her handbag to the floor.

"Hello there, Roseio," Amos Brown said, still dressed in his bib overalls and plaid shirt. "Hello, folks. Didn't see you at class this afternoon."

"They were off sightseeing," Rosario said.

"You missed a great dessert, cream brulie."

A waitress came and served them fanned, char-grilled duck breast with a black mission fig and dried cherry spiked bordelaise sauce, accompanied by roasted garlic mashed potatoes and baby greens tossed with almonds in orange vinaigrette.

Amos rubbed his russet nose and wriggled his spiked-out eyebrows. "Whoee, would you look at this? Would... you...look...at...this, I say. Ain't had such good victuals placed before me since my old Aunt Emma made coon pie."

Jim stared at the man.

Was this a put-on, or was Amos really what-you-see-is-what-you-get?

But he had no doubt about one thing Amos said. The victuals were indeed good, to die for, savory, melt-in-your-mouth, exquisite cuisine—and whatever other cliché you could think of would still not do it justice.

"Mm-mm," Amos said. "The eatin' here just keeps getting better and better." He ogled the woman next to him. "Of course, Roseio, the company is really what makes it."

A spot of crimson appeared in Rosario's cheeks as she looked across to Jim and Dodee. "Tomorrow morning we're going to make eggs Benedict for our own breakfast, Chef Davis says. I think that should be fun."

"Fun?" Jim cut off a piece of his duck. "She seemed to me to be a no-nonsense lady."

"Yes, but she is fun, too." Rosario patted her lips with her napkin. "We learned a bit of gossip about that Mr. Cornelius Jansen, from last night."

"I liked his fish appetizers."

"Yes, but he was primitive, don't you think, compared to Angela, Chef Davis."

"What's the gossip?" Dodee asked.

"His wife ran away," Amos said.

"Don't tell my story, nasty man," Rosario said, patting

him on the hand. "It's a bit more complicated than that. She sold their house and cleaned out the bank account, and ran away with a younger man."

"An eighteen-year-old kid," Amos said.

"And they were never heard from again. All they left Cornelius Jansen was his boat and now he has to live on it."

"Where did you hear this?" Dodee asked.

"The woman at the front desk. The one with the auburn hair and bright smile. She went to grade school with them."

When dinner was over, Amos, gnawing every last duck bone and scraping his plate clean, smacked his lips. "Yes, ma'am, that were good eatin'." He turned to the woman next to him. "How about it, Roseio, we goin' dancing?"

The woman glanced toward the ceiling. "I'm not going anywhere with you unless you learn to pronounce my name. It is Ros*ario*."

"Right you are. How about you folks? Wanna come along and make it a foursome?"

Jim glanced at Dodee, who shook her head. "I think we've had enough running around for one day."

Rosario gathered up her handbag, gave them a finger wave, and followed Amos Brown in his bib overalls and clodhopper shoes.

"What do you make of that?" Jim said.

"I don't know."

He sipped his coffee and watched a car cross the bridge, its light pushing back a black velvet night. Then the wide body of Cornelius Jansen suddenly obstructed his view.

He sat down in the chair vacated by Rosario, a smile on his square-jawed face.

"Heard you folks went down island today," he said in his falsetto voice.

# FIFTEEN

"DOWN ISLAND?"

Corney nodded. "Hatteras."

"Jim wanted to look at the lighthouse," Dodee said.

"Heard you stopped off at the rectory," Corney said.

Jim stared into the big man's brown eyes. "How did you hear that?"

Corney folded his large hands on the table, turned one side of his lips down and shrugged. "Birds have wings."

Jim blinked.

Birds have wings? What the hell did that mean?

"So, you find out anything more about Father Pelican?"

"Only what we overheard while eating lunch." Jim took another sip of coffee. "He was well liked and everyone hoped that the body washed up on shore wasn't his."

Jansen nodded. "I guess it's hard to tell, being in the water that long. The clothes were ripped off, I guess."

Dodee shook her head. "No, but they—"

"They were waterlogged," Jim said, placing his hand on hers.

"The sheriff thought it was strange the body floated up where it did," she said. "What do you think?"

Corney turned down both ends of his lips this time. "Fickle current can sometimes fool you."

"It should have been washed out to sea?"

Corney shrugged.

"I mean, probably?"

"Yeah, probably, I guess you could say that."

Jim drained his cup. "No one could figure out why he was on the bridge. Was he a big fisherman?"

"I didn't know the man. Knew of him, but not him."

Dodee leaned her elbows on the table. "I'm so sorry to hear about your wife."

That popped Jansen's eyes open. "Wow. You two have learned a lot of local gossip in a short time."

"I don't mean to pry—"

"Then don't."

Jim turned to her. Where the hell was she going with this?

She looked at him and then back to Jansen. "I was just thinking that maybe she didn't run away."

That also popped Jansen's eyes open.

"Suppose instead she was murdered and the killer threw her body off the bridge?"

"Is this supposed to make me feel better?"

"I'm sorry, I was just thinking, overthinking as Jim says. I'm just wondering how it's connected with Father Pelican."

Jim studied her big blues. "How do you figure that?"

"I don't know, unless it had to do with what we heard at lunch. People came from all over to go to confession with Father Pelican." She nodded, looking from one to the other. "How about this? What if the man she was supposed to run away with killed her instead, and threw her body off the bridge. Then he confesses it to Father Pelican, but afterward gets to thinking the priest will go to the cops—"

"A priest can't reveal that," Jim said.

"—and so he kills Father Pelican and throws his body off the same bridge, only this time the body washes up on shore."

Jim shook his head. "You're forgetting some things here, lady. First, Pelican was seen fishing from the bridge—"

"That's right." Jansen slapped his hand on the table. "And you're forgetting that, if Harry Sneed did throw Sarah Jane, my wife—ex-wife—in the water, she would have washed up on the shore at Waikiki, because the last I heard from them was a postcard from Hawaii, saying they were having a wonderful time and wished I was there. It wasn't enough for her to clean me out, oh no, she had to rub my face in it. And he probably put her up to it.''

''I'm sorry.''

''You should be.''

''Even without the postcard from Hawaii,'' Jim said, ''why would Pelican go out on the bridge? So the guy could kill him?''

''The guy could have asked the priest to meet him for some reason.''

''Yeah, and cows can chew their cud,'' Jansen said.

''If he was meeting someone,'' Jim said, ''it would be in his appointment book.''

Dodee's eyebrows arched. ''Right, or if not an appointment book, his secretary should know.''

''I'd bet on an appointment book. Seeing how he kept everything neat as a pin, I'm betting he had an appointment book.''

''You know what I think?'' Jansen stood up. ''I think you two snoops are making mountains out of the Rockies.'' He pointed at them, jabbing his finger. ''You ought to stay out of snooping in other people's business.'' He spun and marched out the side door into the dark.

Dodee's brow wrinkled. ''I think we upset him.''

''No, lady, you upset him. Brought up all that stuff about his wife. What were you thinking?'' She opened her mouth, but he held up his hand. ''Besides, bottom line, unless Pelican had a sex change while he was bobbing about in the briny, it wasn't his body.''

''No, but I thought it might be Corney's wife.''

He blinked. ''Then what about the postcard from Hawaii?''

''I didn't know about that then, only what Rosario said. I guess I got carried away.''

''Even if it was Corney's wife, why dress her up in Pelican's clothes?'' He turned to her. ''You're sure the body was that of a woman?''

"Positive."

"Because no one else has mentioned it yet."

"But a lot of people keep asking about the condition of the body. Like they're trying to find out if we know what they know, what maybe everyone knows, but doesn't want to say."

He pushed his coffee cup aside and stood up. "Well, sooner or later the police autopsy will prove the body is not Pelican's. Then the big search for him will be on. In the meantime, let's keep our mouths shut. Remember what Sergeant Atwater said about us being run off the road? Maybe someone out there *is* trying to shut us up."

# SIXTEEN

JIM AND DODEE, joined by the rest of the Elderhostel crew, gathered early the following morning in the kitchen of the 1587 Restaurant to receive their marching orders from the five-foot culinary Napoleon, Chef Andrea Davis.

"The secret of making eggs Benedict is everything."

She stood at attention, as if she were modeling her crisp white apron and the starched toke on her head.

"Screw up one process and you're better off with an Egg McMuffin, which, by the way, is a bumpkin cousin to the sophisticated Eggs Benedict."

Her dark, fierce eyes scanned the Elderhostel circle.

"So don't screw it up."

Then a big smile brightened up her face.

"Once again we go through *Mise en place,* getting all your ingredients together and measured out before we start."

She reached out and touched plates, dishes and pans as she mentioned the items contained in each: sugar-cured Canadian bacon that she had sliced into quarter-inch-thick rounds; English muffin halves, split gently with a fork rather then a knife; sticks of butter at room temperature; two tablespoons of white wine; eggs already shelled and placed in individual glass cups, some with the yolks separated from the whites; cayenne pepper in a saucer; a salt shaker; a pepper grinder; a lemon cut in half; and a large dish greased with butter. A bowl of large strawberries capped and sliced in half, and a warm pan of asparagus were set to one side. In one of two double boilers on the stove, water barely simmering, she had some Hollandaise made before they had arrived.

"I wanted to have this ready for when we start dishing it out, but we'll make up a small batch now so you can see how it's done." She pointed to the second double boiler. "Here I've melted twelve tablespoons of butter on low heat, scooping off and discarding the foam so it's almost clarified."

She squeezed out a tablespoon of lemon juice, added it to the white wine and brought it to a low boil. "This is a sauvignon blanc from New Zealand's Cloudy Bay vineyard, an excellent wine, and I use it because now—" she gave them all a smile "—I'll have some left over for myself."

She plopped three egg yolks into a blender, turned it on low, and added the wine and lemon juice. Then, with the blender still on low, she gently poured in a slow stream of the melted butter, threw in a couple of pinches of salt and cayenne pepper, made sure it was thoroughly combined, then added it to the double boiler.

"So much for our Hollandaise sauce. We could have added a few drops of Worcestershire sauce if we were so inclined."

Then she put volunteers to work, some to lightly toast the muffins and spread the cut side with a generous dollop of butter, and others to quick-fry the Canadian bacon until it was just brown, while she added heat to a large pan of water.

"One way to know how much water to use is to place your eggs in the pot and cover them with about an inch of water. Take out the eggs, measure the depth of water, then drain and add fresh water."

She brought it to the edge of boiling, reduced the heat slightly, then started slipping in individual eggs from the glass bowls, using a slotted spoon to gently bunch the egg whites into a ball around the yolks and keep them from sticking to the pan.

"The ideal is to have the whites completely cooked, but soft yolks. Takes about three minutes."

She spooned out the poached eggs with the slotted spoon, beginning from the first to last, and placed them to drain in the buttered dish. She repeated the process with the rest of the eggs, then started plating those already done. First came the English muffin butter side up, then a slice of sugar-cured Canadian bacon lightly browned, a carefully placed poached egg, and three generous tablespoons of Hollandaise sauce.

"As an option," Chef Davis said, as she ran the pepper grinder over them, "you can garnish them with fresh black truffles, but at eighty dollars an ounce, when you can get them, it can be a big option. And if I were serving this at an elegant brunch, I would serve it with champagne or an excellent pinot noire." She added three strawberry halves and four asparagus to the plate and held it up. "Who's first?"

Everybody wanted to be first. Jim held back toward the end of the line and was rewarded when Chef Andrea Davis saw there was more than enough to go around and started doubling the men's portions.

He carried his plate to the corner table and held the window seat for Dodee, this time facing the marina with the boats riding easy in the morning sun. If people were determined to join him no matter what, he might as well enjoy the view.

Rosario arrived right behind Dodee, taking the chair opposite him. "Isn't Chef Davis wonderful?"

Jim cut his egg yolk just enough to make it flow. "I'll tell you after I taste it." He forked up a mouthful of the rich mixture of eggs and the buttery sauce that came with a slight tang of lemon, five million calories bursting upon his taste buds, along with the sugar-cured Canadian bacon and lightly toasted muffin, and nodded. If taste was the criterion for a wonderful chef—and what else was there?—then Andrea Davis fit the bill. In spades.

"I've had such a good time being here," Rosario said as she swung around in her chair and waved. "Amos, over here. Amos, here."

The man looked unsure of where to go for a moment, then headed toward them.

Rosario moved over to the window seat to make room. "You sit right here," she said, patting the chair seat when he arrived.

He was still dressed in bib overalls and checkered shirt, face grizzled and eyes bleary. He gave Dodee and Jim a limp wave. "Hello, folks."

"You feel okay?" Jim asked.

"Oh, yes, he does," Rosario said, stuffing Eggs Benedict into her mouth. "We had such a nice time last night, tell them Amos."

He stared at his eggs. "We had such a nice time last night."

Rosario motioned toward the window. "And look at this bright morning. Two more classes and our Elderhostel will be over. You two leaving today?"

Jim shook his head. "We're spending the night."

"We're going to my daughter's summer place," Rosario said. "She has this big house on the beach. You two are welcome to spend the night if you like."

Jim put his hand on Dodee's. "Thank you, but we're already paid up here and we need to get an early start in the morning. Real early."

Amos nodded. "I should be heading back myself, Roseio."

"Now don't you even think of it," Rosario said, and looked across at Dodee. "We have this big bedroom with a view of the ocean." She giggled at Amos. "What a wonderful way to wake up in the morning."

Amos gave them a wan smile, picked up his fork, and took a small bite of eggs Benedict.

After breakfast, Jim went out and looked over his blue Lincoln. He bought the car after his wife died, trying to give a lift to his life, except as a replacement for Penny, on a scale of one to ten, it had been a minus eight million. Now, with the side crumpled in, it looked like another minus eight million.

Dodee came up and put an arm around his waist. "I didn't realize there was so much damage."

"It's mostly cosmetic."

"So what's this about getting an early start tomorrow?"

He smirked at her. "Fast thinking. I don't want to spend our last day with a lot of other people around."

"Strange you should say that."

He folded his arms and stared at her.

She batted her eyelashes back at him. "How would you like me to buy you a Blizzard?"

"Depends. There's a Dairy Queen across the bridge in Nags Head."

"I was thinking of the one on Hatteras where we went yesterday."

He grimaced. "Let me get this straight. We're going to drive straight down to the Dairy Queen, have our Blizzards, and drive right back?"

Her brow wrinkled. "I was thinking of the comment you made last night, about an appointment book—"

"See, I knew you were going there. The answer is no, Dodee. Absolutely not. One side of my car is already crumpled. Are you trying to even it up?"

She batted her eyelashes at him again. "I'll buy you two Blizzards, one on the way down and one on the way back."

# SEVENTEEN

HE DROVE SOUTH over the Oregon Inlet bridge as the sun turned the crashing surf into foaming champagne and glazed the calm water of the Sound, then sped down the lonely highway and past the spot where the Lincoln went airborne.

He had to be out of his freaking mind to be going down here again. He took a deep breath of sea air and let it out. "I want to go on record that I'm against this."

"Against what?"

"Against talking to the secretary."

"So noted, sweetheart."

"So noted? A lot of good that will be if Atwater catches us butting into police business."

The same houses he had seen yesterday started popping up again, standing tall on stilts, two and three stories high. He passed Pamlico Station where they had stopped for directions and slowed down as dwellings bunched together into a community.

"Stop!" Dodee shouted.

He jammed on the brakes and screeched to a halt.

"What?"

"Back there, turn right."

"Sonofabitch, Dodee." He glanced in the rearview mirror. "If someone had been behind us, we'd have been creamed."

"I'm sorry, sweetheart. I just saw that name on the mailbox and reacted."

He put the car in reverse and backed up to the street. "What name on what mailbox?"

"Jeremy Opie. We should turn right and get off the highway."

He glanced into the rearview mirror again to see a clear road behind him, but he took the right anyway, onto a rutted, sandy road, bright in the clear sunlight. "And Jeremy Opie is...?"

"Remember from The Flip-Flop Flounder? They said he talked to Father Pelican on the bridge before he disappeared."

He took another deep breath and let it out through puffed out cheeks. "And I want to go on record that I'm against this as well."

"Don't you want to know why the priest was on the bridge?"

"It's Sunday. Guy's probably at church."

He followed the lane to a faded yellow, salt-eaten Oldsmobile. Beside it stood a tinroofed, board-and-batten cottage on six-foot-high pilings, built on a little hook of land with a view back across a strip of water to the island. A whirligig in the form of a duck with rotating wings sat on a post with Jeremy Opie's name in black store-bought letters. Jim shoved open his crumpled door with a crunch and at the sound a man came out from behind the pilings with a fishing reel in one hand, a rag in the other.

Jim looked into a pair of aviator sunglasses under a Coor's beer cap, the same weather-beaten face, now shaven, he had seen by the bridge the day before.

"Hi," he said, "you Jeremy Opie?"

The man pointed to the whirligig as if to say "Read the sign, stupid."

"I'm James Dandy and this is Dodee Swisher."

The man nodded.

Jim nodded back.

Not going to get a whole lot of information here.

Dodee gave Opie one of her big smiles. "We heard you talked to Father Pelican up on the bridge the last day anyone saw him."

Opie shrugged.

"You must think we're snoops, and I guess we are." She gave him another smile.

He shrugged again.

"Well, we were the ones who found the body on the beach and were just wondering about it."

Opie nodded again.

Jim rolled his eyes.

The man at the restaurant had it right. Opie didn't have his line in the water.

"Thank you for your time," he said and started for the car.

Dodee held her ground. "I feel so sorry for Father Pelican." She crossed her arms and shook her head. "It was terrible finding him washed up all alone like that."

Oh, yeah, like it would be different if there were two or three others to keep him company?

"I just can't figure why he was out on the bridge."

Jeremy Opie nodded.

Jim opened the car door.

"I can't figure that out either, missus." Opie placed the reel on the porch steps and wiped his hands with the rag. "I been trying and trying to figure that out. He said he was fishing, but any fool knows you ain't gonna get any fish that high up, with the tide running or not."

"Did anyone come by while he was there?"

"Not that I seed." He took off his Coor's cap and scratched a mostly bald head. "But I didn't see when he went over, neither. Was hopin' he didn't, you know? Like maybe someone did come by and he got in a car and drove off like. But you found his body?"

Dodee nodded.

"Terrible thing to happen to such a good man. Yes'm, the good die too young. He be sorely missed, yes he will."

Jim tried to see through the dark glasses. "Did she, did he, Father Pelican, fish a lot?"

Opie's lips turned down and one shoulder came up.

"About middlin'. Went out with me a few times in my boat, but he can never stay out long, even with the fish running. And sometimes we go fishin' up by the bridge where you saw me."

"His brother said he went out deep-sea fishing."

"A time or two." Opie pointed across the strip of water toward the big houses on stilts. "A doctor fella over there comes down from up north and spends summers here. He's always goin' out on one of them charter boats. Sometimes Father goes with him, but I don't think he had his heart in it."

"Did you go to his church?" Dodee asked.

"Yes'm. Now that's where his heart was. Lookin' out for people and the church. That was his life. We ain't gonna find the likes o' him again. No ma'am."

# EIGHTEEN

THEY DROVE BACK over the rutty road and south on the highway again until he turned in at the Dairy Queen.

Dodee looked at him. "You're going to eat ice cream this early in the morning?"

"Not only am I going to eat it, you're going to pay for it."

"I don't know if I want any now."

He shoved opened his crumpled door. "You don't have to, just bring your wallet." He strolled into the building and ordered a large blueberry Blizzard.

"This lady will pay for it," he said to the woman behind the counter. He pulled a couple of napkins from a holder and blinked as he spotted a familiar face. "Tom Pelican?"

The midforties man looked up from adding sugar to a foam cup of coffee, the hazel eyes in his ruddy face registering no recognition.

"Yesterday morning? At the Tranquil Inn?"

The hazel eyes shifted to Dodee and back. "Of course, you're the ones who found...who found the body."

"I'm James Dandy and my girlfriend, Dodee Swisher."

"Of course, of course, it just took me by surprise seeing you here."

Dodee motioned to Jim. "My friend had to stop to get an ice cream fix, even at this time of day."

"Hey, I ordered blueberry so you could consider it part of my breakfast."

She shook her head and turned back to Tom Pelican. "You down here sorting out your brother's things?"

He ran a hand through his reddish-brown hair. "Trying to make sense of it." He motioned to the chairs out front. "You in a hurry?"

They walked outside and sat in the sun.

Jim slipped on his sunglasses. "How are you holding up?"

"Okay, I guess." Tom took the lid off his coffee and sipped. "I had no idea it would hit me so hard."

Jim took a spoonful of Blizzard and let the burst of blueberry and ice cream slide down his throat.

"Taste good?" Dodee asked.

"Food for the gods."

"Let me have a taste, sweetheart."

"No, go get your own."

"All I want is a taste—"

"No, I know you. You'll end up eating half of it." He turned to the ruddy-faced man. "From the way everyone talks, they loved Father Pelican."

Tom nodded. "Me, too." The hazel eyes leveled on him. "Everyone?"

"We had lunch yesterday at The Flip-Flop Flounder and overheard some people talking."

"And you're back today? May I ask why? Not just for ice cream."

Jim pulled the end of the long plastic spoon from his mouth and pointed it at Dodee. "Because this lady insists on butting into police business."

Her eyes bore into him before softening and turning to Tom Pelican. "We just came down to see where your brother lived, and maybe talk to his secretary." The big blues shifted back to Jim. "I can't believe you won't let me have a taste."

He gave her a big, phony grin, took another spoonful of Blizzard, and looked back at Tom. "Then last night we got to wondering if your brother could have been on the bridge for some other reason besides fishing."

"Like what?"

He shrugged. "Like I don't know."

Dodee leaned forward in her chair. "But we thought there might be something in his appointment book."

"Did he have an appointment book?" Jim asked.

The hazel eyes blinked a couple of times and he nodded. "Yes, he did."

"Have you looked through it?"

"I don't even know where it is." He sipped some more coffee as he stared into space. "But it must be at the house." The eyes shifted to them. "What do you think might be in there?"

Dodee turned up the palms of her hands. "Maybe he was meeting someone."

Tom nodded, thinking about that, then his eyebrows rose. "I'm going to the rectory and check it out. Want to come?"

Jim held up his spoon and shrugged. "Well—"

"Yes, we'd be glad to," Dodee said and turned to Jim. "For the last time. Are you going to let me have a taste—"

"No way."

"Then I'm getting a small one of my own. And if I can't finish it, I'll give it to a dog before I let you have any." She stood and turned to Tom. "Mind waiting a few minutes? Can I buy you one?"

He chuckled and shook his head.

She hurried inside and Tom put the lid back on his cup. "You say you talked to Leslie's secretary?"

"No, we never saw her." He finished his Blizzard and dropped the cup in a trash can. "We went to her house, but no one was home. That's how we ended up at The Flip-Flop Flounder, across the highway."

Tom pointed a remote at a late-model aqua Buick, which unlocked with a little beep. "Maybe we should also see her."

Dodee came out and they climbed into the Buick. Tom pulled onto the highway and they headed south.

Jim swung around to Dodee in the back seat as she scrunched down her Blizzard. "I'll finish that if you can't."

She raised one finger to indicate that was a fat chance.

He grinned and swung back.

They turned off toward the Sound on the same winding, packed-sand road he and Dodee had traveled the day before. Live oaks shaded cottages nestled among them, while in the clearings butterflies flittered over yellow dandelions.

Only one black thought crept in to darken the idyllic scene.

If Tom Pelican was involved in his brother's disappearance, he and Dodee might just have stepped into the spider's parlor.

# NINETEEN

THEY PULLED UP to the weathered-gray parish house. Tom Pelican turned off the ignition, stared at the two-bedroom cottage for a moment, then heaved a body-racking sigh.

"We had some wonderful times here." He pointed to the swing and Adirondack chairs on the screened-in side porch. "Leslie and I solved a lot of the world's problems sitting here of an evening with a beer or two to keep us company." He heaved another sigh and climbed out of the car.

Jim followed, smelling brackish water off the marsh, and held the door for Dodee.

She handed her paper cup to Jim. "Don't say a word."

He looked down at the unfinished Blizzard and smiled. "Never look a gift horse in any of its orifices."

They climbed the porch and Tom reached into his pants pocket. "I have a key here somewhere."

"Up on the sill," Dodee said.

He turned to her, brows knitted.

She shrugged. "The housekeeper got it from up there."

"She drew us a map to the secretary's place," Jim said. He spooned up some ice cream and turned toward the woman's house. "I'm surprised she hasn't come over."

"Probably at church." Tom found the key, opened the door, and led them in.

Tom headed toward the back bedroom. "Think I remember seeing it on the night table."

Jim dropped the empty Blizzard cup in a trash can beside

the desk, then noticed two drawers were partially opened and the papers jumbled inside.

"I think someone's been here."

That stopped Tom in his tracks, the hazel eyes turning to him.

He pointed to the drawers. "I don't know, but everything is so tidy about the place, I'd think the desk would be also."

"Maybe he had been looking for something," Dodee said.

Tom rushed back, pulled the drawers fully open and shook his head. "If you knew Leslie, you'd know that wasn't so."

"Anything missing?" she asked.

Jim glanced around. "I'd call the police." He came back to Tom. "There might be some fingerprints we'd mess up by rummaging around. You have a cell phone?"

"Good thinking. In the car, but I'd like to have more to go on before I call."

Dodee pointed to a corner panel of wall leading into the kitchen. "Looks like there are a couple of pictures missing."

In a vertical row of what had been five pictures, two off-color squares on the wallpaper testified to their absence.

Tom headed for the door. "That's good enough for me."

Jim turned back to the desk, put on his reading glasses, and studied the two framed pictures he had seen the day before. The first could be Leslie's young parents standing beside the open door of a late 1940s Studebaker. In the second, Tom Pelican stood next to a shorter man in a Roman collar, obviously Leslie from the family resemblance, while other priests milled about in the background.

But yesterday there had been a third picture.

He scanned the desk.

Unframed and lying flat.

He raised his head and stared out past the porch to marsh grass bending in a breeze, and searched for the memory. Three figures standing next to a trussed-up fish as big as they, the best he could come up with, but he had not worn his glasses and none of the details came through.

He strode across the room to the corner panel with the off-color squares and examined the remaining photographs: two men fishing off a beach; another one of Leslie and another man holding up three fish; and in the third he and Jeremy Opie fishing on the spit of land by the bridge.

So were the missing ones also fishing pictures?

"You know," he said, wheeling to see Dodee carrying on her own examination of photographs plastered across the living room wall, "this could be perfectly innocent."

She stared at him.

"Maybe the housekeeper or the secretary took the pictures as remembrances."

Her big blues remained fixed and unblinking as something boiled and bubbled behind them.

"What?"

She headed toward the back of the house. "I want to look in the bedrooms."

"Don't touch anything," he called after her, then turned to the photographs she had been studying.

Church picnics and bazaars, most with Father Leslie Pelican in their midst, one of Tom and Leslie, in a Roman collar, outside a small church, and another of a young Tom Pelican in a Little League uniform standing with his parents. On an end table he found an older Tom and his parents at a high school graduation.

He looked up at the sound of footsteps crossing the porch and saw a white-faced Tom Pelican standing in the doorway.

"Mage Blackstone's been killed in a hit-and-run."

Dodee hurried in from the bedroom. "The parish secretary?"

The hazel eyes stared at her and he nodded. "Mage Blackstone." He turned to Jim. "She was killed in a hit-and-run this morning. Sergeant Atwater is down here investigating it." He motioned toward the road. "He's on his way over." He swung back to Dodee. "Find anything back there?"

She shrugged. "I don't know. Nothing out of place that I could tell."

"You didn't go through the drawers or anything, like, touch anything?"

"I kept my hands behind my back."

"Because that's what Atwater said, not to let anyone touch anything." He chewed on his lip a minute. "You see an appointment book back there?"

"Not that I know of."

"Let's look again."

They made a hands-off search of the two-bedroom house and as they prowled over the large combination living room-dining room-kitchen, Atwater arrived. The six-foot-three sergeant ducked his head as he came through the door and did a double-take at seeing Jim and Dodee.

"You two get around."

"Anything on the hit-and-run driver?" Tom asked.

"Not yet." He made a motion to take in the cabin. "You sure there's been a break-in?"

"Not positive, but pretty sure."

Jim pointed to the wall. "Some pictures are missing that were here yesterday, but maybe the housekeeper took them."

Atwater glanced at photographs spread across the room. "Been here a couple of times for lunch. Well, Father invited my wife and I got to tag along." He pinched his lips as he took it all in. "Should have paid more attention." Then he cocked his head at Jim. "You were here yesterday?"

"Remember when we were run off the road? I told you we were down here."

"The housekeeper brought us in," Dodee said. "She drew us a map to get to Mage—" She held out a hand and let it drop.

Tom walked up to the desk. "These drawers have been rifled through. Leslie wouldn't have left them like that."

"Don't touch anything. I have another car on the way. We'll seal off the place and get a crime lab in." He turned to Jim. "Speaking of cars, where's yours?"

"We ran into Tom at the Dairy Queen and rode here together."

"You can account for your time this morning?"

"Except for the time it took to drive down from Manteo."

"Sweetheart," Dodee said, looking at Atwater, "we stopped off at Jeremy Opie's."

The sergeant's mouth dropped open and he turned back to Jim.

He shrugged. "I forgot about that."

"Like I say, you get around. What were you doing at Opie's?"

"Just talking about Father Pelican being out on the bridge."

Dodee put an arm around Jim's. "Have they found out anything about the body on the beach?"

Atwater's jaw set and he turned to Tom. "I'm afraid I have more bad news, not that I'm sure you haven't been expecting it. The dental records matched." He grimaced and shook his head. "It was Father Pelican on the beach."

# TWENTY

ATWATER DROVE them back to the Dairy Queen. He got out and inspected the blue Lincoln, all the way around, and finally nodded, obviously convinced it hadn't been involved in a hit-and-run.

"Okay. I want you to go back to your hotel and stay there. You understand?" The dark brown eyes shifted between them. "No side trips to talk to anyone. Straight back and stay at the Tranquil House Inn until I get there. Soon as I can break away I'll be by with more questions."

Jim nodded.

That didn't sound good.

But it was nothing compared to the bombshell Atwater had already dropped, that the body on the beach had been Leslie Pelican.

They piled into the Lincoln and rolled north.

"Forgive me, Dodee, but I have to ask one more time—"

"Yes, I am absolutely positive it was a female body on the beach."

He drove on in silence for a few miles.

"Whatever's going on, the conspiracy is wide enough to include Atwater. So where does that leave us?"

"The missing photos," she said, turning to him a few miles later, "could they have been family pictures?"

"If I remember right, and I didn't have my glasses on, they were of a large fish hanging from something and people standing around it."

"Mmm."

"What do you mean, 'mmm'? You think some family pictures are missing?"

She shrugged. "Not pictures missing, but what was missing from the pictures. The only photographs containing Leslie Pelican were after he was ordained. Like he didn't exist before then."

He glanced at her. "What are you saying?"

"Is it possible Father Pelican could have been a woman?"

"Catholic priests are only men."

Dodee arched her eyebrows and palmed-up a hand.

"You're saying she hid the fact that she was a woman?"

She repeated the gesture. "It would be one reason there are no young Leslie Pelican pictures, because they would have shown her as a young girl."

He stared at the road as Pamlico Station rushed by.

The problem with that was, if Dodee was right, Leslie would have had to maintain the cover-up for the last five, six, or more years.

He checked the rearview mirror, making sure a red truck wasn't creeping up on him, and turned to her.

"That begs the question, why?"

Her brow wrinkled. "Because she really wanted to be a priest?" Then she swung her knees onto the seat to face him. "Remember what they said at The Flip-Flop Flounder? They thought Father Pelican was the best priest they ever had. Someone who really listened. Someone who had a faith that could move mountains. And didn't Atwater say his wife thought Father Pelican could walk on water?"

"Considering what happened, I think we can rule that out. And if she had that much faith, how could she be living a lie?"

"It's not a lie if no one asks. At ordination do they ask if you're a man?"

"I have no idea, lady."

He checked the rearview mirror again, empty road behind now, empty road in front with the bridge over Oregon Inlet coming up.

"You know, when you stop to think about it logically, what's the only hang-up the Catholic Church has about women priests?"

He glanced over to see he had her full attention.

"I mean, we've had women governors, senators, prime ministers and presidents. Plumbers, architects, astronauts, whatever. So what they're really saying is, when you think it through logically—" he shrugged "—any woman can become a Catholic priest provided she first goes through a sex-change operation."

"And sucks out half her brains, sweetheart."

"Yeah, right."

He motioned to the bridge as they started to cross it. "That still doesn't tell us what he, or she, was doing out here."

"Meeting someone?"

"Doesn't make sense." He topped the rise, with Nags Head and Kitty Hawk and the shoreline spread out before them, basking in the midday sun. "If you're going to meet someone, why out here? So they can dump you over the side?"

When they made it back to the Tranquil House Inn, they were pushing the lunch hour, and Jim was torn between heading for the bathroom or the dining room.

"C'mon," he said, the dining room winning out, "if we hurry we can make it."

"I still owe you a lunch, sweetheart."

"But this one is paid for."

They rushed inside to see the waiters starting to clear away a buffet. Most of the others, with the Elderhostel now officially over, were already checking out with the auburn-haired desk clerk. He moved along the buffet line, loading his plate with chunks of pork tenderloin Havana, scallion mashed potatoes, and roasted vegetable risotto.

Their favorite corner was occupied, so he led the way to a window table off the lobby, held her chair, then leaned over and whispered into her ear. "Do they have a bathroom down here?"

"To the right, before the entrance."

"Agh." He sat down. "I'll wait and go up to the room."

At least with everyone scurrying to hit the road, Rosario Emalda leading a hangdog Amos Brown out the front door, they'd have a peaceful lunch together.

Peace didn't last long.

A large shadow fell across their table as Cornelius Jansen plopped in the seat opposite Jim. A smile slid across his square-jawed face as he ran a hand through his crewcut. "Haven't seen you two this morning," he said.

"We've been out riding around."

"Down island again, huh? What did you find out this time?"

Jim forked in some pork tenderloin Havana and shook his head. "We just stopped for a Blizzard at a Dairy Queen."

"Um." He stared out the window at the water for a moment and came back. "You're staying over tonight, right? Thought you might want to charter the *Commandment* for the afternoon. We'll go out to the Gulf Stream and dip in a couple of lines."

Dodee turned to Jim. "Want to go? You're the fisherman."

He shrugged. "Don't know that I want to go fishing today."

"Give you a special price," Jansen said. "In fact, if I don't land you in a spot where you catch a big fish, I'll give you your money back. What else you got to do now that Father Pelican's body has been identified?"

"For one thing," Jim said, feeling his stomach muscles tighten up, "right now I have to make a quick trip up to my room." He stood and turned to Dodee. "If they have dessert, I want some."

"Suppose they have more than one?"

"I'll take two."

He headed across the lobby, returned the smile of the auburn-haired woman at the front desk, and glanced at the column of charter boat pictures as he turned to the stairs, then stopped, came back and put on his reading glasses.

He found Father Pelican in one, standing next to a man he didn't recognize, and a man-size fish he didn't recognize, but standing on the other side, with the transom of the *Commandment* in the background, was Cornelius Jansen.

Jansen claimed he had never known Father Pelican.

Then how come they were in the picture together?

He looked back to the table to see Jansen staring right at him, then he turned and hurried up the stairs.

# TWENTY-ONE

WHEN HE CAME BACK down and turned the corner, they were gone. He looked over to the auburn-haired clerk behind the front desk.

"You didn't happen to see where my girlfriend went, did you?"

"The lady with Corney Jansen?" The woman gave him a bright smile. "He said she was chartering his boat as a gift for you and you are to meet 'em onboard. Know where it is?"

He glanced back to the photographs on the wall. One missing now. "Do you have a piece of paper?"

She passed him a notepad.

"I'm going to leave a message for Sergeant Atwater of the state police. He's supposed to come by here."

"Want me to tell him you went out with Corney?"

He looked up to her. "You know him?"

"Corney? Known him since grade school."

"His wife ran out on him with a younger man?"

"That's the story. But no one's seen hide nor hair of them since."

"Corney said he got a postcard from Hawaii."

"From Sarah Jane?" She shook her head. "I didn't approve of everything Sarah Jane did, but she was my best friend since kindergarten. We told each other everything. If Sarah Jane had sent only one postcard to only one person, it would have been to me."

He turned to the windows.

First he had to get Dodee off the boat.

Jansen wouldn't be stupid enough to try anything, not when the big man learned he had left a note for Atwater with the desk clerk, but he still wanted her off the boat.

He scribbled down about the missing pictures, on the wall and at the parish house, and that Jansen had Dodee on board. He folded the note and gave it to clerk. "Sergeant Atwater of the state police. Make sure he gets this."

"You going out with Corney?"

"Not if I can help it."

He hurried down the boardwalk and out onto the pier to where the *Commandment* rode on her water marks. Jansen looked up from the aft deck and smiled.

"Hi, Jim," he said. "Come on aboard."

"Where's Dodee?"

"Down in the cabin. Let me give you a hand."

Jim hopped aboard and strode to the cabin. "Dodee, we have to get—"

The word was right there.

Off.

Have to get off.

But a burst of pain in the back of his head obliterated the path from mind to mouth, and the word just hung there, in the ether, then faded away, along with everything else.

WHEN EVERYTHING popped back in, all jumbled together, he was being manhandled onto a pitching deck, bright sunlight and fresh salt air mixed with a trace of gasoline exhaust.

Dodee was slumped on a booth seat beside a table, across the cockpit from the steering station. She turned her white face up to him. "Are you all right?"

"Course he's alright," came Jansen's squeaky voice as he dumped Jim on the seat beside her. "If he survived being run off the road, a little bump on the head ain't gonna hurt him."

Jim squeezed his eyes, then opened them wide, trying to bring the world back into focus, the guttural sound of idling engines, the whistle of a breeze across the deck, the cry of a lone gull looking for a handout off the transom. Fishing lines hung out sideways like thin wings, and off in the distance more charter boats bobbed about on the choppy ocean, but land was nowhere in sight.

And, oh yes, his hands were tied behind his back.

"Where are we?"

"Out in the Gulf Stream." Jansen motioned to the other charter boats. "Had to put out the lines or someone would be wondering what we were doing here."

And double oh-yes, he had never gotten the chance to tell Jansen about Atwater.

"You know, I left word for the police."

Jansen grinned. "Nice try."

"I'm not kidding. And I left word with the desk clerk."

"All the better. Now everyone knows we're out here on a charter."

"I don't understand why you're doing this," Dodee said.

"Because Corney never received a postcard from his wife in Hawaii."

"See—" the big man jerked around and stuck his face into Jim's "—that's why you're out here. You insisted on snooping into things that don't concern you."

"Big deal," Dodee said, "so she didn't send you a post-card. Nothing wrong with that."

"Nothing wrong if he didn't dump her body off the bridge." He stared back into Jansen's blazing eyes. "What about the priest—"

"She was no priest." Jansen straightened up and scanned the horizon. "That was the problem. Found tampons in a rest room after she was the only one to use it." He turned around to Jim. "Only I found it out too late. Sarah Jane took me for every cent. Both of them. I couldn't get my money back, but I'd be damned if I'd let them spend it." He squinted at Dodee. "So I dumped them from the bridge, just like you said last night."

"I'm not kidding about the police," Jim said.

"And yes, I confessed it to Father Pelican, just like you said. But she was no priest and so I knew she was going to tell the police, just like you said."

Jim half-closed his eyes against the bright sun. "Sergeant Atwater of the state police."

"But see, she had something to hide herself. So I told her to meet me on the bridge or I'd expose her. I made sure she was seen, just like you said, then I hit her on the head and dumped her in the water. Same spot, same tide running like with Sarah Jane, but no-oo, she has to wash up on the beach."

"I'm not kidding," Jim said again. "I told the desk clerk and left her a note for the police about the missing pictures—"

"See—" Jansen shook his finger at him "—that's what got you out here. I was able to get the appointment book, thank you very much for that, but I couldn't be sure what the secretary knew. Felt bad about her. But I forgot about the picture in the lobby until I saw you looking at it."

The boat lurched under the force of a wave and Jim had to brace his feet on the deck to keep from falling, then the automatic pilot brought them back on course.

Jansen unsnapped the sheath at his side and pulled out his Buck knife. "Sorry about this folks, but I have no chum." He tested the blade with his thumb and replaced the knife in the sheath. "So I'm going to have to chum you up a little bit for the fish. I can't take a chance of having you pop up somewhere." He opened a cubby in the bulkhead and took out his filleting knife. "This is razor sharp. You won't feel a thing."

"I'm not kidding about Atwater. You won't be able to get away with this."

Jansen stared at him a moment, then shrugged. "I have a shot at it. Your girlfriend gets caught up the hysteria of fighting a big fish—" he gave a half shake of his head "—happens all the time, and she falls overboard. You jump in to save her. By the time I bring the boat around, both of you are out of sight. I call the other boats to come help, but unfortunately, you never resurface. See? As for you telling the police, well, maybe that's true and maybe not, but either way, without you to confirm it, will a jury convict a local boy without more evidence? And even if they do lump everything all together, they can only hang me once."

A fishing reel screamed and one of the outrigger rods bent as something hit the line.

"Judas priest."

Jansen rushed to the side of the boat and looked over the water. "Yeah, they're watching us, probably wondering why no one is playing the fish." He turned and stared at Jim for a moment, making up his mind about something. "Judas priest!" He jammed the knife into the table. "Can't take the chance."

He pulled on a pair of leather gloves, grabbed the pole and walked it around to the fishing chair. Then he took up the fight, working the pole and the reel.

Jim leaned over to Dodee. "Sit still."

He stood and sat on the table, but another wave swatted the boat and he had to brace himself against the lurching deck before the automatic pilot corrected their course. He maneuvered his rear end around the table until he felt the knife between his hands, then started rubbing his bindings against the blade.

He watched Jansen, fighting the fish in a frenzy to get it aboard, and whispered over his shoulder. "How am I doing?"

"Come on, you bugger," Jansen shouted.

"I can't see," Dodee said. "Your hands are in the way."

He went at the blade again, pulling his hands apart to keep tension on the rope, then jerked around at the scream of the fishing reel as Jansen lost the line.

"You think you're gonna win?" Jansen shouted once more, stopping the reel and fighting the rod upright until veins popped out against the muscles in his neck and arms. "You think you're gonna win?"

Jim worked the rope against the knife, caught up in a frenzy of his own, as he kept an eye on Jansen.

"You ain't gonna win." The big man pulled back on the rod again, and again after reeling in more line, and again. "You ain't gonna win," he yelled as he pulled back on the rod yet one more time, "I'm gonna win."

Jim felt a sense of exasperation. He had no way of knowing if he was cutting one clean groove in the rope or just raking it like a rasp.

"Gotcha, you bugger. Gotcha now."

Jansen suddenly swung around in the chair and Jim froze.

The brown eyes focused on him for a moment, then moved on to stare at a steel gaff hooked to the side of the boat. The big man peeked over the transom, then back to the gaff, as if measuring the distance in his mind. Then he lowered the rod, reeling the line in tight, and fought the fish until he brought the pole upright again, muscles straining in his arms and neck. He glanced back to the gaff one more time, then heaved out of the chair, double-wrapped the line around his gloved hand, dropped the pole, and started across the deck. But the line yanked taut and flicked him around, swinging him from side to side like an excited dog tugging on a leash. He battled back with both hands, one over the other, and towed the line after him, planting one foot after another across the cockpit, and reached for the gaff. Then suddenly the line slackened, sending him crashing into the gunwale. He stared at the loose line, tugged on it a couple of times, then turned to Jim and shrugged.

"After all that the bugger threw the hook."

But the line snapped taut, jolting Jansen across the deck and slamming him against the transom. He jiggled his caught hand, trying to shed the glove as he reached for his Buck knife with the other. The line slackened again. He jumped to his feet and unsnapped the knife, but just as quick the line cracked again, hurling the big man into the transom, and over the side.

"Corney!" Jim shouted and stumbled across the deck.

Jansen hung there, one hand in a death grip around the steel railing, the other trying to shake the line that stretched him out between sunshine and blue water.

The squared-jawed face came up to him; wild brown eyes glared into his. "A knife. Get me a knife."

"Hold on. My hands are tied—"

A wave slapped into the side of the boat and heaved it sideways. Jim staggered under the impact, took a couple of quick steps, and regained his footing.

The fishing reel screamed as the line paid out.

Jim spun around to see Jansen plunge under the surface, clear as glass, an invisible force dragging him down, his free hand undulating behind, like he was waving goodbye; the reel shrieked as Jansen spiraled deeper into the blue, growing smaller, fading into an indigo darkness, until only a speck remained.

Then the line parted.

The reel fell silent.

And Cornelius Jansen slipped from the light.

# TWENTY-TWO

JIM STOOD at the rail with his arms around Dodee, staring into the night.

It had only taken a few minutes working against the knife blade to cut through his bindings, a few more to free Dodee, and a few more to get Atwater on her cell phone. The sergeant ordered him to stay put—oh, yeah, like maybe he'd go out for a walk on the water—and to keep the details of everything confidential until he talked to them. Then a charter boat, responding to a call from Atwater, had pulled alongside and the *Angel Face*'s first mate, a lithe young woman who could easily have been the inspiration for the boat's name, had come aboard to navigate the *Commandment* home through the tricky waters of Oregon Inlet.

A question nagged at Jim as he peered into the darkness, cold and hungry and worn-out.

Why hadn't Corney cut the line instead of reaching for the gaff? Would the other boats have known it? Or had he been caught up in the frenzy of the fight?

He shook his head.

For that matter, suppose he had kept sawing away with the knife instead of remaining still when Corney had reached for the gaff. Would he have been able to free himself in time to help Corney? Or would Corney have taken him down into the deep?

The image of the man fading into the indigo waters sent a shiver through him that had nothing to do with the cold.

They rounded a point of land and the well-lit dock in Manteo came into view. He made out the six-foot-three figure of Atwater and the shorter Tom Pelican standing beside him.

They pulled into the pier, tied up, and Jim thanked the *Angel Face*'s first mate. He helped Dodee ashore, followed her, and fought the urge to bend down and kiss the ground.

Atwater ushered them into the Tranquil Inn's 1587 Restaurant, to the same table, it turned out, where Cornelius Jansen had joined them for lunch half a day and a lifetime ago.

Tom took a window seat opposite Dodee and Atwater sat across from Jim.

A waitress came up to the table and Atwater waved her away.

"No, wait a minute," Jim said. "I'm freezing. Can we have some coffee?" He turned to Dodee, who nodded, and to the two men across the table, who also nodded. "Four coffees."

When she left, Atwater stared at them. "You didn't mention any of the details of the case?"

Dodee shook her head. "We only said that Corney got tangled in the line and was pulled overboard."

"Okay." Atwater nodded. "Now, how about telling us what really happened?"

"Well," Dodee said, then hesitated, glancing at Jim. She continued when he nodded, "Corney killed his wife and her lover. Then he confessed it to Father Pelican, and then killed her when he thought she would tell the police."

The two men looked at one another.

Jim leaned on the table. "Corney found out your sister was a woman and not a priest."

Tom sucked in a deep breath and let it out. "That's not exactly true."

"That she's not your sister—"

"That she wasn't a priest."

That shut down the conversation.

"But she was a woman."

"Oh, yeah," Atwater said, grimacing. "It was a shocker to find that out myself."

Tom placed his hands flat on the table.

"Leslie always wanted to be a priest, ever since she was a little. Didn't do any good to tell her a girl couldn't become a priest. She went into the Air Force for four years out of high school and I thought that was the end of it. Then when she got out, she went to school to study theology, but I didn't know it was in a seminary until she invited me to her ordination."

They fell silent as the waitress returned with their coffee.

"She started it as a lark," Tom said, "and prayed she would be found out, but after the first year she just went with it, trusting in the Holy Spirit to guide her. She had a faith like that, a faith that could move mountains. Always did. 'The Spirit never told me no, Tom,' she said to me, 'and no one asked me to pass a physical.' It helped that she was small breasted and athletic."

He raised one shoulder and let it drop.

"I've never seen her happier than the day she celebrated her first Eucharist."

Jim opened his hand. "But wasn't that living a lie?"

Dodee swung around to him. "I don't think so."

He blinked at the steadiness of her gaze.

Tom pushed his untouched coffee aside.

"Leslie's intention was to answer her call to the priesthood, not to lie. 'If we only have meat,' she would say, 'do you feed it to the starving on Good Friday, a day of abstinence, or let them go hungry? Which is the greater good?' When she got posted down here in an out-of-the-way place, she felt it was the Holy Spirit guiding her. Her hope was to serve here with joy and love without anyone ever finding out. She was a good priest."

Atwater nodded. "I can vouch for that. My wife thought he—she—could walk on water."

Jim sipped on his coffee and ignored the temptation to make the obvious remark. "What happens now?"

Tom turned to Atwater, who set his cup down. "Depends. The only ones who know her true story are sitting at this table. If the truth comes out you can bet we'll have reporters running all over the place.''

Tom leaned forward in his seat. ''The Church would rock with that, and maybe it would be a good thing. What I'm thinking of is the community here, those who put their trust in Leslie's priesthood, all the marriages, baptisms and funerals. If they thought Leslie was just playing with them, what would happen to their faith?''

Jim looked from one to the other. ''You're asking us to keep it quiet?''

''Yes.'' Dodee nodded. ''We can do that.''

''Wait a minute. What about Corney murdering his wife? And your sister? And the hit-and-run, you know he also did that?''

''Corney's dead.'' Atwater pushed his bowl aside. ''Can't punish him any more by calling him a murderer. As for Sarah Jane, she has no living relatives, and no one's been able to trace where her boyfriend came from. As for Mage Blackstone, well, Mage also thought Leslie walked on water. I know what her vote would be if it were a choice between exposing Father Pelican or Cornelius Jansen. If we call it an unsolved accident it leaves a lot of good behind.''

''And as for Leslie,'' Tom said, ''she fell off the bridge, a terrible tragedy, but there it is.''

Dodee nodded. ''We can keep it quiet.''

Suddenly, Jim felt all eyes on him. He finished off his coffee and placed his cup on the saucer.

''Sweetheart?'' Dodee asked.

He stared into her big blues. ''I've been telling you all along it's not our business.'' He turned to the two men on the other side of the table. ''It belongs to your community and your church. And if this lady here—'' he took Dodee's hand ''—what's your name again? If she thinks she can forget it, who am I to say what happened here in—where are we again?''

Later that night they curled up together in bed, her head resting on his arm, a leg and an arm draped around his body.

"If we never speak about it again, sweetheart, it's something unspoken we can share silently, can't we?"

"Ha. You? Never speak about anything again?"

That got him a poke in the ribs.

"Okay, okay, what are you, the wrath of God?" He leaned down and gave her a feather-kiss on the lips. "It's something unspoken we can share in silence. From this moment on, right?"

She pretended she was snoring, and a few minutes later, stopped pretending.

He stared up at the ceiling, shadows rippling from light reflected off the water, and thought back on Leslie Pelican, a person he had only known through photographs and the words of those she served.

The lady must have had a lot of determination to hide her identity and sex in her desire to become a priest.

What did it say in the Bible?

If you had the faith of a mustard seed, you could order the mountain to go throw itself into the ocean and it would do so.

Then, good for Leslie Pelican.

Her faith had saved her.

And moved the mountain.

MYSTERY
WORLDWIDE LIBRARY®
TM